Vi

"Breathtaking blend [illegible] anormal. I wished I lived in the world Singh has created. This is a keeper!" —*USA Today* bestselling author Gena Showalter

"This author just moved to the top of my auto-buy list."
—*All About Romance*

"Brace yourselves because the second installment of the Psy-Changeling series will set all your senses ablaze and leave your fingers singed with each turn of the page. *Visions of Heat* is that intense!" —*Romance Junkies*

"*Visions of Heat* is penned with an intensity that only Nalini Singh can give to a story . . . If you're a paranormal reader, this is one book that you have to read!"
—*Romance Reader at Heart*

"The phenomenal sequel to the equally phenomenal *Slave to Sensation* . . . Nalini Singh proves without a shadow of a doubt that she is an absolute master at world-building with this gem! . . . Don't miss out on this series as it is a definite keeper!" —*CK²S Kwips and Kritiques*

"A page-turning sexy read that fans of paranormal romance are sure to devour . . . I highly recommend *Visions of Heat* to one and all, especially if you love a great story, exciting characters, and a new world to explore! . . . This is one book that is sure to find it's way onto your keeper shelf!"
—*The Romance Readers Connection*

"A fantastic paranormal romance series! Singh puts her own unique spin on psychics and shape-shifters." —*Fresh Fiction*

"In a genre filled with talent, Singh really stands out. Book two of her original and complex series has all the necessary ingredients for an outstanding story. She breathes life into her characters, filling them with passion and strength. This is one of the best paranormal series out there!" —*Romantic Times*

continued . . .

Praise for

Slave to Sensation

"I LOVE this book! It's a must read for all of my fans. Nalini Singh is a major new talent."

—*New York Times* bestselling author Christine Feehan

"An electrifying collision of logic and emotion . . . An incredible world where fire and ice mix to create an unforgettable sensual eruption. *Slave to Sensation* is a volcanic start to a new series that'll leave you craving more." —*Romance Junkies*

"AWESOME! . . . A purely mesmerizing book that surely stands out among the other paranormal books out there. *Slave to Sensation* is captivating from beginning to end. It's a must read for any paranormal fan!" —*Romance Reader at Heart*

"Superb science fiction romance . . . Readers will enjoy Nalini Singh's excellent futuristic thriller and demand more tales from this fascinating realm." —*Midwest Book Review*

"You won't want to miss *Slave to Sensation*, the tremendous first book in the new Psy series by Nalini Singh . . . I highly recommend this book and suggest you make room for it on your keeper shelf." —*Romance Reviews Today*

"A sensual romance set in an alternate-reality America with just a bit of mystery to keep readers flipping pages. Character-driven and well-written, it's not easy to put down at bedtime; it kept me reading well into the night." —*Fresh Fiction*

"A fresh, intriguing, and thought-provoking mythology and a very appealing cast of characters . . . I look forward to the next installment from this talented writer." —*BookLoons*

"A must even for those uninitiated in the paranormal genre. The story ends much too quickly, and the author's magical writing conjures up sensual images and intense emotions that linger long after the last word is read." —*Romantic Times*

Berkley Sensation Titles by Nalini Singh

SLAVE TO SENSATION
VISIONS OF HEAT
CARESSED BY ICE
MINE TO POSSESS

Mine to Possess

NALINI SINGH

BERKLEY SENSATION, NEW YORK

THE BERKLEY PUBLISHING GROUP
Published by the Penguin Group
Penguin Group (USA) Inc.
375 Hudson Street, New York, New York 10014, USA
Penguin Group (Canada), 90 Eglinton Avenue East, Suite 700, Toronto, Ontario M4P 2Y3, Canada
(a division of Pearson Penguin Canada Inc.)
Penguin Books Ltd., 80 Strand, London WC2R 0RL, England
Penguin Group Ireland, 25 St. Stephen's Green, Dublin 2, Ireland (a division of Penguin Books Ltd.)
Penguin Group (Australia), 250 Camberwell Road, Camberwell, Victoria 3124, Australia
(a division of Pearson Australia Group Pty. Ltd.)
Penguin Books India Pvt. Ltd., 11 Community Centre, Panchsheel Park, New Delhi—110 017, India
Penguin Group (NZ), 67 Apollo Drive, Rosedale, North Shore 0632, New Zealand
(a division of Pearson New Zealand Ltd.)
Penguin Books (South Africa) (Pty.) Ltd., 24 Sturdee Avenue, Rosebank, Johannesburg 2196, South Africa

Penguin Books Ltd., Registered Offices: 80 Strand, London WC2R 0RL, England

MINE TO POSSESS

A Berkley Sensation Book / published by arrangement with the author

PRINTING HISTORY
Berkley Sensation mass-market edition / February 2008

Cover art by Phil Heffernan.
Cover design by George Long.
Hand lettering by Ron Zinn.
Interior text design by Stacy Irwin.

For information, address: The Berkley Publishing Group,
a division of Penguin Group (USA) Inc.,
375 Hudson Street, New York, New York 10014.

ISBN: 978-0-425-22016-0

BERKLEY® SENSATION
Berkley Sensation Books are published by The Berkley Publishing Group,
a division of Penguin Group (USA) Inc.,
375 Hudson Street, New York, New York 10014.

PRINTED IN THE UNITED STATES OF AMERICA

10 9 8 7 6 5 4 3 2 1

For my dad, Vijay, for all that you do,
but most of all, for the laughter.
With love.

THE FORGOTTEN

When the Psy Council proposed, in the year 1969, to instigate the Silence Protocol, a protocol that would wipe all emotion from the Psy, they were faced with a seemingly insurmountable problem—a lack of racial uniformity.

Unlike the cold, isolated Psy of today, the Psy then were an integral and entangled part of the fabric of the world. They dreamed, they cried, and they loved. Sometimes, as was only natural, those they loved came from a race other than their own.

Psy mated with changelings, married humans, bore children of mixed blood. Predictably, these racially impure Psy were among the most virulent opponents of the Silence Protocol. They understood what drove their brethren to denounce emotion—the fear of vicious insanity, of losing their children to the madness sweeping through their ranks in an inexorable tide—but they also understood that in embracing Silence, they would lose everything and everyone they loved. Forever.

By the year 1973, the two factions were at an impasse. Negotiations ensued, but neither side was willing to compromise and the Psy broke in two. The majority chose to remain in the PsyNet and give their minds to the emotionless chill of absolute Silence.

The fate of the minority, some with mixed blood themselves, others with human and changeling mates, is not so clear. Most believe they were eliminated by Council assassins. Silence was too important—the Psy race's last hope—to chance disruption by a rebellious few.

There is also a rumor that the rebels died in a mass suicide. The final theory states that those long-ago rebels were the first patients of involuntary "rehabilitation" at the newly christened Center, their minds wiped, their personalities destroyed. Since the Center's methods were experimental back then, any surviving patients would have come out in a vegetative state.

Now, as spring dawns over a hundred years later, in the year 2080, there is only one consensus: the rebels were neutralized in the most final way.

The Psy Council does not allow dissent.

CHAPTER 1

Talin McKade told herself that twenty-eight-year-old women—especially twenty-eight-year-old women who had seen and survived what she had—did not fear anything as simple as walking across the road and into a bar to pick up a man.

Except, of course, this was no ordinary man. And a bar was the last place she'd expected to find Clay, given what she had learned about him in the two weeks since she'd first tracked him down. It didn't bode well that it had taken her that long to screw up the courage to come to him. But she had had to be sure.

What she had discovered was that the Clay she'd known, the tall, angry, powerful *boy*, had become some kind of high-ranking enforcer for the dominant leopard pack in San Francisco. DarkRiver was extremely well respected, so Clay's position spoke of trust and loyalty. The last word stabbed a blade deep into her heart.

Clay had always been loyal to her. Even when she didn't deserve it. Swallowing, she shoved away the memories, knowing she couldn't allow them to distract her. The old Clay was gone. This Clay . . . she didn't know him. All she knew was that he hadn't had any run-ins with the law after being released from the juvenile facility where he had been incarcerated at the age of fourteen—for the brutal slaying of one Orrin Henderson.

Talin's hands clamped down on the steering wheel with white-knuckled force. She could feel blood rising to flood her cheeks as her heart thudded in remembered fear. Parts of Orrin, soft and wet *things* that should have never been exposed to the air, flecking her as she cowered in the corner while Clay—

No!

She couldn't think about that, couldn't go there. It was enough that the nightmare images—full of the thick, cloying smell of raw meat gone bad—haunted her sleep night after night. She would not surrender her daytime hours, too.

Flashing blue and white lights caught her attention as another Enforcement vehicle pulled into the bar's small front parking lot. That made two armored vehicles and four very well-armed cops, but though they had all gotten out, none of the four made any move to enter the bar. Unsure what was going on, she stayed inside her Jeep, parked in the secondary lot on the other side of the wide street.

Sweat trickled down her spine at the sight of the cop cars. Her brain had learned young to associate their presence with violence. Every instinct in her urged her to get the hell out. But she had to wait, to see. If Clay hadn't changed, if he had grown worse . . . Uncurling one hand from the wheel, she fisted it against a stomach filled with roiling, twisting despair. He was her last hope.

The bar door flew open at that second, making her heart jump. Two bodies came flying out. To her surprise, the cops simply got out of the way before folding their arms and leveling disapproving frowns at the ejected pair. The two dazed young men staggered to their feet . . . only to go down again when two more boys landed on top of them.

They were teenagers—eighteen or nineteen, from the looks of it. All were obviously drunk as hell. While the four lay there, probably moaning and wishing for death, another male walked out on his own two feet. He was older and even from this distance, she could feel his fury as he picked up two of the boys and threw them into the open bed of a parked truck, his pure blond hair waving in the early evening breeze.

He said something to the cops that made them relax. One

laughed. Having gotten rid of the first two, the blond man grabbed the other two boys by the scruffs of their necks and began to drag them back to the truck, uncaring of the gravel that had to be sandpapering skin off the exposed parts of their bodies.

Talin winced.

Those unfortunate—and likely misbehaving—boys would feel the bruises and cuts tomorrow, along with sore heads. Then the door banged open again and she forgot everything and everyone but the man framed by the light inside the bar. He had one boy slung over his shoulder and was dragging another in the same way the blond had.

"Clay." It was a whisper that came out on a dark rush of need, anger, and fear. He'd grown taller, was close to six four. And his body—he had more than fulfilled the promise of raw power that had always been in him. Over that muscular frame, his skin shone a rich, luscious brown with an undertone of gold.

Isla's blood, Talin thought, the exotic beauty of Clay's Egyptian mother vivid in her mind even after all these years. Isla's skin had been smooth black coffee, her eyes bitter chocolate, but she had only contributed half of Clay's genes.

Talin couldn't see Clay's own eyes from this distance, but she knew they were a striking green, the eyes of a jungle cat—an unmistakable legacy from his changeling father. Set off by his skin and pitch-black hair, those eyes had dominated the face of the boy he had been. She had a feeling they still did but in a far different way.

His every move screamed tough male confidence. He didn't even seem to feel the weight of the two boys as he threw them into the pile already in the back of the truck. She imagined the flex of muscle, of power, and shivered . . . in absolute, unquenchable fear.

Logic, intellect, sense, it all broke under the unadulterated flow of memory. Blood and flesh, screams that wouldn't end, the wet, sucking sounds of death. And she knew she couldn't do this. Because if Clay had scared her as a child, he terrified her now.

Shoving a hand into her mouth, she bit back a cry.

That was when he froze, his head jerking up.

* * *

Dumping Cory and Jason into the truck, Clay was about to turn to say something to Dorian when he caught an almost-sound on the breeze. His beast went hunting-still, then pounced out with the incredibly fine senses of a leopard, while the man scanned the area with his eyes.

He knew that sound, that female voice. *It was that of a dead woman.* He didn't care. He had accepted his madness a long time ago. So now he looked, looked and searched.

For Tally.

There were too many cars in the lot across the wide road, too many places where Talin's ghost could hide. Good thing he knew how to hunt. He'd taken one step in that direction when Dorian slapped him on the back and stepped into his line of sight. "Ready to hit the road?"

Clay felt a growl building in his throat and the reaction was irrational enough to snap some sanity into his mind. "Cops?" He shifted to regain his view of the opposing lot. "They gonna give us trouble?"

Dorian shook his head, blond hair gleaming in the glow of the streetlights that had begun flicking on as built-in sensors detected the fading light. "They'll cede authority since it's only changeling kids involved. They don't have any right to interfere with internal pack stuff anyway."

"Who called them?"

"Not Joe." He named the bar owner—a fellow member of DarkRiver. "He called *us*, so it must've been someone else they messed with. Hell, I'm glad Kit and Cory have worked their little pissing contest out, but I never thought they'd become best-fucking-friends and drive us all insane."

"If we weren't having these problems with the Psy Council trying to hurt the pack," Clay said, "I wouldn't mind dumping them in jail for the night."

Dorian grunted in assent. "Joe'll send through a bill. He knows the pack will cover the damage."

"And take it out of these six's hides." Clay thumped Cory back down when the drunk and confused kid tried to rise. "They'll be working off their debt till they graduate."

Dorian grinned. "I seem to recall raising some hell myself in this bar and getting my ass kicked by you."

Clay scowled at the younger sentinel, though his attention never left the parking area across the road. Nothing moved over there except the dust, but he knew that, sometimes, prey hid in plain sight. Playing statue was one way to fool a predator. But Clay was no mindless beast—he was an experienced and blooded DarkRiver sentinel. "You were worse than this lot. Fucking tried to take me out with your ninja shit."

Dorian said something in response, but Clay missed it as a small Jeep peeled rapidly out of the lot that held his attention. "Kids are yours!" With that, he took off after his escaping quarry on foot.

If he had been human, the chase would've been a stupid act. Even for a leopard changeling, it made little sense. He was fast, but not fast enough to keep up with that vehicle if the driver floored it. As she—definitely *she*—now did.

Instead of swearing in defeat, Clay bared his teeth in a ruthless grin, knowing something the driver didn't, something that turned his pursuit from stupid to sensible. The leopard might react on instinct, but the human side of Clay's mind was functioning just fine. As the driver would be discovering right about . . . now!

The Jeep screeched to a halt, probably avoiding the rubble blocking the road by bare centimeters. The landslide had occurred only forty-five minutes ago. Usually DarkRiver would have already taken care of it, but because another small landslide had occurred in almost the exact same spot two days ago, this one had been left until it—and the affected slope—could be assessed by experts. If she'd been inside the bar, she'd have heard the announcement and known to take a detour.

But she hadn't been in the bar. She'd been hiding outside.

By the time he reached the spot, the driver was trying to back out. But she kept stalling, her panic causing her to overload the computronics that controlled the vehicle. He could smell the sharp, clean bite of her fear, but it was the oddly familiar yet indefinably *wrong* scent under the fear mask that had him determined to see her face.

Breathing hard but not truly winded, he came to a stop in the middle of the road behind her, daring her to run him over.

Because he wasn't letting her get away. He didn't know who the hell she was, but she smelled disturbingly like Tally and he wanted to know why.

Five minutes later, the driver stopped trying to restart the car. Dust settled, revealing the vehicle's rental plates. The birds started singing again. Still he waited . . . until, at last, the door slid open and back. A slender leg covered in dark blue denim and a black ankle-length boot touched the ground.

His beast went preternaturally quiet as a hand emerged to close over the door and slide it even farther back. Freckled skin, the barest hint of a tan. A small female form unfolding itself out of the Jeep. Even fully out, she stood with her back to him for several long minutes. He didn't do anything to force her to turn, didn't make any aggressive sounds. Instead, he took the chance to drink in the sight of her.

She was unquestionably small, but not fragile, not easily breakable. There was strength in the straight line of her spine, but also a softness that promised a cushion for a hard male body. The woman had curves. Lush, sweet, curves. Her butt filled out the seat of her jeans perfectly, arousing the deeply sexual instincts of both man and cat. He wanted to bite, to shape, to pet.

Clenching his fists, he stayed in place and forced his gaze upward. It would, he thought, be easy to lift her up by the waist so he could kiss her without getting a crick in his neck. *And he planned to kiss this woman who smelled like Talin.* His beast kept growling that she was his and, right this second, he wasn't feeling civilized enough to argue. That would come later, after he had discovered the truth about this ghost. Until then, he would drown in the rush of wild sexuality, in the familiar-yet-not scent of her.

Even her hair was that same unusual shade as Talin's—a deep, tawny gold streaked with chocolate brown. A mane, he'd always called it. Akin to the incredible variations of color in a leopard's fur, something that outsiders often missed. To a fellow leopard, however, those variations were as obvious as spotlights. As was this woman's hair. Beautiful. Thick. *Unique.*

"Talin," he said softly, surrendering completely to the madness.

Her spine stiffened, but at last, she turned.

And the entire world stopped breathing.

CHAPTER 2

"Hello, Clay."

Air rushed back into his body with the force of a body blow. A roar built in his throat, but he didn't release it, violently aware of the acrid fear scent coming off her in waves.

Son of a bitch! Tally was scared of him. She might as well have taken a knife to his heart. "Come here, Tally."

She rubbed her hands on her thighs, shook her head. "I came to talk to you, that's all."

"This is your way of talking to me? By taking off?" He told himself to shut it, to not snarl at her. This was the first conversation they had had in *two decades*. But it felt as if they had spoken yesterday, it was so natural, so effortless. Except for her fear. "Were you going to stop the car anytime soon?"

She swallowed. "I was planning to talk to you at the bar."

The leopard had had enough. Moving with the preternatural speed of his kind, he was an inch from her before she could draw in the breath to scream. "You're supposed to be dead." He let her see the rage inside of him, rage that had had twenty long years to ferment. Ferment and spread until it infused every vein in his body. "They lied to me."

"Yes, I know . . . I knew."

He froze in sheer disbelief. "You what?" All this time while he'd been tracking a ghost, he'd been absolutely certain that he had been lied to, and without Talin's knowledge. It had destroyed him that she was out there thinking he'd broken his promise to return to her. Never once had he considered that she might have been a willing participant.

Eyes the color of storm clouds met his. "I asked them to tell you I was killed in a car crash."

The knife twisted so deep, it carved a hole in his soul. "Why?"

"You wouldn't let me be, Clay," she whispered, torment a vicious beast in those big gray eyes ringed by a thin band of amber. "I was with a good family, trying to live a normal life"—her lips twisted—"or as normal as I knew how to live. But I couldn't relax. I could feel you hunting me the second you left juvie. Twelve years old and I didn't dare close my eyes in case you found me in my dreams!"

The leopard who lived inside of him bared its teeth in a growl. "You were mine to protect!"

"No!" She fisted her hands, rejection writ in every tense line of her body. "I was never yours!"

Beast and man both staggered under the vicious blow of her repudiation. Most people thought he was too much like the ice-cold Psy, that he didn't feel. At that moment, he wished that were the truth. The last time he'd hurt this badly—as if his soul was being lacerated by a thousand stinging whips—had been the day he'd gotten out of juvenile hall. His first act had been to call Social Services.

"I'm sorry, Clay. Talin died three months ago."

"What?" His mind a blank, his future dreams wiped out by a wall of black. "No."

"It was a car crash."

"No!"

It had driven him to his knees, torn him to pieces from the inside out. But the depth of that hurt, the cutting, tearing pain, was nothing to this rejection. Yet in spite of the blood she'd drawn, he still wanted to—no, needed to—touch her. However, when he raised a hand, she flinched.

She couldn't have done anything designed to cause more harm to his protective animal heart. He fought the pain as he always did—by shutting away the softness and letting the rage out to roam. These days, he rarely stopped being angry. But today, the hurt refused to die. It clawed through him, threatening to make him bleed.

"I *never* hurt you," he grit out between clenched teeth.

"I can't forget the blood, Clay." Her voice shook. "I can't forget."

Neither could he. "I saw your death certificate." After the first shock had passed, he'd known it for a lie. But . . . "I need to know that you're real, that you're alive."

This time, when he raised his hand to her cheek, she didn't flinch. But neither did she lean into his touch as she'd always done as a child. Her skin was delicate, honey-colored. Freckles danced across the bridge of her nose and along her cheekbones. "You haven't been staying out of the sun."

She gave him a startled look followed by a shy smile that hit him like a kick to the gut. "Never was much good at that."

At least she hadn't changed in that respect. But so much about her *had* changed. His Tally had come running into his arms every day for five of the happiest years of his life, looking to him as her protector and friend. Now, she pushed at his hand until he dropped it, the silent reiteration of her rejection searing a cold burn across his soul. It made his voice harsh when he said, "If you hate me so much, why did you find me?" Why couldn't she have left him his memories—of a girl who had seen in him only goodness?

Those memories were all he'd had left in his fight to stay in the light. He had always carried darkness inside his heart but now it beckoned every waking minute, whispering silvery promises of the peace to be found in not feeling, not hurting. Even the powerful bonds of Pack were no longer strong enough to hold him, not when the lure of violence beat at him night and day, hour after hour, second after excruciating second.

Talin's eyes widened. "I don't hate you. I could never hate you."

"Answer the question, Talin." He wouldn't call her Tally again. She wasn't his Tally, the sole human being who had ever loved his misbegotten soul before he'd been dragged into DarkRiver. This was Talin, a stranger. "You want something."

Her cheeks blazed with fire. "I need help."

He could never turn her away, no matter what. But he listened impassively, his tenderness for her threatening to twist into something that wanted to strike out and hurt. If he betrayed the depth of his fury, if he sent her running again, it might just push him over the final deadly edge.

"I need someone dangerous enough to take on a monster."

"So you came to a natural-born killer."

She flinched again, then snapped her spine straight. "I came to the strongest person I've ever known."

He snorted. "You wanted to talk. So talk."

She looked out past his shoulder. "Could we do it somewhere more private? People might drive up here."

"I don't take strangers to my lair." Clay was pissed and when he got pissed, he got mean.

Talin tipped up her chin in a gesture of bravado that sent flickers of memory arcing through his mind. "Fine. We can go to my apartment in San Francisco."

"Like hell." He occasionally worked in DarkRiver's business HQ near Chinatown, but that HQ was built for cats. It didn't hem him in. "I spent four years in a cage." That didn't count the fourteen he'd passed in the small boxlike apartments he and his mother had called home. "I don't do well inside walls."

Naked pain crawled over her features, turning the stormy gray of her eyes close to black and eclipsing the ring of amber fire. "I'm sorry, Clay. You went to prison because of me."

"Don't flatter yourself. You didn't make me rip out your foster father's guts or tear off his face."

She pressed a hand to her stomach. *"Don't."*

"Why not?" he pushed, a caustic mix of anger and possessiveness overwhelming his fiercely protective instincts where Tally was concerned. Again, he reminded himself that this woman wasn't his Tally, wasn't the girl he'd have split his veins to keep safe. "I killed Orrin while you were in the room. We can't ignore it like it never happened."

"We don't have to talk about it."

"You used to have more spine."

Color flooded her cheeks again, bright against the fading daylight. But she took a step forward, anger vibrating through her frame. "That was before I had a man's blood spray across my face, before my head filled with his screams and a leopard's roars."

A predatory changeling could hunt in complete quiet—in either human or animal form—but he had felt such rage that day that the animal in him had risen totally to the surface. For those blood-soaked minutes, he'd been a human insane, a leopard on two feet. They had had to shoot an overdose of animal tranqs into him to pull him off Orrin Henderson's mutilated body.

The last thing he'd seen as he lay on the floor, his face pressed into still-warm blood, was Tally curled up in a corner, face flecked with blood and other things, pink and fleshy . . . and gray, lumps of gray. Her eyes had looked through him, her freckles stark dots against the chalk white skin visible between all that red. Some of the blood had been her own. Most had been Orrin's.

"You used to have more freckles on your cheeks," he commented, caught in the memory. It wasn't horrifying to him. He was animal enough not to care about anyone outside of his pack, especially not those who dared harm his packmates. Back then, Tally and Isla had been the sole members of his pack. He'd always known he would kill to protect either of them.

"Don't change the subject."

"I'm not. Your face was the final thing I saw on the outside." He brushed a finger over those freckles of hers. "They must've faded or moved as you grew up."

"No, they didn't," she snapped, and—for the first time—sounded exactly like the girl he'd known. "They've multiplied, spread. Damn things."

"You own them now," he said, amused as always by her antipathy toward those tiny spots of pigment. "They're yours."

"Since the creams don't make them disappear and I don't want to have laser surgery, I guess they are."

He almost relaxed, caught in the echoes of a past long gone. Oh, the power Talin had over him. *She could make him crawl.* The realization of his continued weakness for a woman who found the violent heart of him repulsive, turned his next words razor sharp. "Give me your key."

She took a wary step back. "It's stalled. I can—"

"Give me the fucking key or find another fool to help you."

"You didn't used to be like this." Big, haunted eyes, soft lips pressed together as if to withhold emotion. "Clay?"

He held out his hand. After a taut second, she put the flat computronic key on his palm. Most cars were keyed to the owner's print, but for that very reason, rental places gave out a preprogrammed key instead of spending half an hour coding in each new customer. It saved time, but it also let thieves steal the vehicles. Idiots. "Get in."

He stalked around the Jeep without another word and took the driver's seat. By the time she stopped sulking and jumped in, he had the vehicle running. He gave her only enough time to belt up before reversing, turning, and heading back the way she'd come.

The bar was on the outskirts of Napa, close to the massive forests that edged the area, forests that were a part of DarkRiver's territory. He headed toward the cool privacy of those trees, doing his best to ignore the spicy feminine scent of the woman who sat so close. Intriguing as that scent was, there was still something off about it, and it confused the leopard. But right then, he wasn't in any mood to analyze his reaction. He was running on pure adrenaline.

"Where are we going?" she asked ten minutes later as he drove them off-road and into the shadows of the huge firs that dominated the area. "Clay?"

He growled low in this throat, too damn pissed with her to care about being polite.

Talin felt the hairs on the back of her neck rise in primitive warning. Clay had always been less than civilized. Even trapped in the claustrophobic confines of the apartment complex where they had met, his animal fury contained beneath a veneer of quiet intensity, he had walked like a predator on the hunt. No one had ever dared bully Clay, not boys twice his age, not the aggressive gang-bangers who lived to terrorize, not even the ex-cons.

But that was then—his current behavior was something else. "Stop trying to scare me."

He actually snapped his teeth at her, making her jump in her seat. "I don't have to try. You're scared shitless anyway. I can smell your fear and it's a fucking insult."

She'd forgotten that aspect of his changeling abilities. For more than twenty years, she had lived among humans and nonpredatory changelings, deliberately increasing the space between her and Clay. But what had it gotten her? Here she was, right back at the start . . . having lost everything that ever mattered. "You said that the first time we met."

He had been this big, tall, dangerous boy and she'd been more than terrified of him. All her short life, people had hurt her, and he had seemed like exactly the kind of person who would. So she had kept her distance. But that day when she'd seen him fall and break his leg in the backyard of their complex—a junkyard, not a park—she hadn't been able to leave him to suffer alone.

So frightened that her teeth had threatened to chatter, she had walked out into the living room and to the phone. Orrin had been on the couch, passed out. Somehow, she'd managed to make a forbidden call outside—to the paramedics. Then, unlocking the door, she had run down to sit with Clay until help came. He hadn't been happy. Nine years to her precocious and fully verbal three, he'd been a creature of pure danger.

"You snarled at me to get lost and said you liked to crunch little girl bones." It was a trick of hers, this memory. She could remember everything from the moment of birth and sometimes before. It was how she'd learned to talk before others, to read before she could talk. "You said I smelled like soft, juicy, delicious prey."

"You still do."

The comment made her bristle in spite of her wariness. "Clay, stop it. You're being adolescent." He was also succeeding in ramping up her fear—did he even realize how intimidating he was? Big, incredibly strong, and so damn angry it almost felt like a blow when he turned his eyes on her.

"Why? I might as well get some fun out of this visit. Tormenting you will do."

She wondered if she'd made a mistake. The Clay she had known, he'd been wild, but he'd been on the side of the angels. She wasn't so sure about this man. He looked like pure predator, without honor or soul. But her too soft heart told her to keep pushing, that there was more to him than this incandescent rage. "You belong to the DarkRiver pack."

No answer.

"Was that your father's pack?" Isla had been human. It was from his father that Clay had gained his shape-shifting abilities.

"All I know about my father is that he was a cat. Isla never told me anything else."

"I thought, maybe—"

"What? That she'd changed her mind, become sane on her deathbed?" His laugh was bitter. "She was probably mated to a cat and he died. I'm guessing she was fragile to begin with. Losing her mate broke her completely."

"But I thought you didn't know if they'd been married."

"Mated, not married. Hell of a difference." He turned down a pitch-black path, the fading evening light blocked out by the canopy. "I knew shit-all about my own race back then. Unless doctors intervene—and even then it's a crapshoot—leopard changelings aren't fertile except when mated or in a long-term stable relationship. No accidental pregnancies, no quickie marriages."

"Oh." She bit her lower lip. "DarkRiver taught you about being a leopard?"

He threw her a sidelong glance and it was nothing friendly. "Why the sudden need for conversation? Just spit out what you want. Sooner you do, sooner you can disappear back into the hole where you've been living for twenty damn years."

"You know what? I'm no longer sure I came to the right man," she snapped back, reckless in the face of his aggressiveness.

The air inside the car filled with a sense of incipient threat. "Why? Because I'm not as easy to handle as you remember? Your pet leopard."

She burst out laughing, her stomach hurting with the force of it. "Clay, if anyone followed anyone, it was me tagging along after you. I didn't dare order you around."

"Load of shit," he muttered, but she thought she heard a softening in his tone. "You fucking made me attend tea parties."

She remembered his threat before the first one: *Tell anyone and I'll eat you and use your bones as toothpicks.*

She should've been scared, but Clay hadn't had the "badness" in him. And even after a bare three years on the planet, she'd known too much about the badness, could pick out which grown-ups had it. Clay hadn't. So, wide-eyed, she'd sat with him and they had had their tea party. "You were my best friend then," she said in a quiet plea. "Can't you be my friend now?"

"No." The flatness of his response shook her. "We're here."

She looked out of the windscreen to find them in a small clearing. "Where?"

"You wanted privacy. This is private." Extinguishing the lights and engine, he stepped out.

Having no choice, she followed suit, stopping in the middle of the clearing as he went to lean against a tree trunk on the other side, facing her. His eyes had gone night-glow, shocking a gasp out of her. Dangerous, he was definitely dangerous. But he was beautiful, too—in the same way as his wild brethren.

Lethal. Untouchable.

"Why did you bring me here?"

"It's in DarkRiver territory. It's safe."

She folded her arms around herself. Though the early spring air was chilly, that wasn't what made her search for comfort. It was the cold distance Clay had put between them, telling her what he thought of her without words.

It hurt.

And she knew she'd brought it on herself. But she couldn't pretend. What she'd seen Clay do had traumatized her eight-year-old mind into silence for close to a year. "You were brutal," she found herself saying instead of asking for what she wanted, the reason she'd fought the vicious truths of the past and tracked him down. She needed him to understand, to forgive her betrayal.

"You were my one point of safety, the one person I trusted to never lose himself in anger and hurt me," she persisted in the face of his silence. "Yet you ended up being more violent than anyone else. How could I help but wonder if the violence wouldn't be directed at me one day, huh, Clay?"

His growl raised every hair on her body.

CHAPTER 3

***Run!* her mind** screamed.

Talin didn't run. She was through with running. But her heart was a drumbeat in her throat.

"You always knew what I was," Clay said, tone full of a bone-deep fury. "You chose not to think about it, chose to pretend I was what you wanted me to be."

"No." She refused to back down. "You *were* different before." Before he'd discovered what Orrin had done. Before he'd killed to keep her safe. "You were—"

"You're making up fairy tales." The harshest of rejoinders. "The only thing different about me was that I treated you like a kid. You're not a kid anymore."

And he wasn't going to sheathe his claws, she thought. "I don't care what you say. We're still friends."

"No, we're not. Not when you're quaking in your boots at the sight of me. My friends don't look at me and see a monster."

She couldn't say anything to that. She did fear him, maybe more than she feared anyone else on this planet. Clay had almost destroyed her once, was the sole person who could do that even now. "I'm sorry." Sorry that her weakness had made him a murderer, sorry that she wasn't strong enough to get past what she'd seen in that blood-soaked room. Sorry that she'd come here.

No.

She wasn't sorry about finding him. "I missed you." Every single day without him, she had missed him. Now, he was a shadow in the darkness. All she could see clearly were those cat eyes of his. Then she sensed him move and realized he'd crossed his arms. Closing her out.

"This isn't going to work," she whispered, conscious of something very fragile breaking inside of her. "It's my fault, I know." If she had come to him at eighteen, he might have been angry at what she'd done, but he would have forgiven her, would have understood her need to grow strong enough to deal with him. But she had waited too long and now he wasn't hers anymore. "I should go back."

"Tell me what you want, then I'll decide." The roughness of his voice stroked over her in a disturbingly intimate caress.

She shivered. "Don't give me orders." It was out before she could censor herself. As a child, she had learned to keep her opinions to herself. It was far safer. But half an hour with Clay—a Clay who was almost all stranger—and she was already falling into the old patterns between them. He was the one person who'd gotten mad if she *had* kept her mouth shut, rather than the other way around. Maybe, she thought, a bright spark of hope igniting, maybe he hadn't changed in that way. "I'm not a dog to be brought to heel."

A small silence, followed by the sound of clothes shifting over skin. "Still got a smart mouth on you."

The tightness in her chest eased. If Clay had told her to shut up . . . "Can I ask you some questions?"

"Auditioning me for your job? Sorry, Talin, I hold the power here."

The emotional taunt hurt more than any physical blow. They had always been equals—friends. "I want to know you again."

"All you need to know is that I'm even more deadly than I used to be." He moved far enough out of the shadows that she could see the unwelcoming planes of his face. "I'm the one who should be asking the questions—tell me, where did you go after they took me away?"

His words opened another floodgate of memory. A groggy Clay being hauled to his feet by black-garbed Enforcement officers, his hands locked behind his back with extra-strength cuffs. He hadn't resisted, had been unable to do so because of the drugs they had shot into him.

But his eyes had refused to close, had never left her own.

Green.

That was the color that drenched her memories of that day. Not the rich red of blood but the hot flame of incandescent green. Clay's eyes. She'd whimpered when they'd taken him away but his eyes had told her to be strong, that he'd return for her. And he had.

It was Talin who had dishonored their silent bargain, Talin who had been too broken to dare dance with a leopard. That failure haunted her every day of her life. "There was media attention after Orrin's death," she said, forcing herself past the sharp blade of loss. "I wasn't aware of it at the time, but I went back and researched it."

"They wanted to put me down. Like an animal."

"Yes." She dropped her arms and fisted her hands, unable to bear the thought of a world without Clay. "But the Child Protection Agency intervened. They were forced to after someone leaked the truth about Orrin . . . and what he'd been doing to me." Bile flooded her mouth but she fought it with strength nurtured by a sojourn through hell itself.

She couldn't erase the past, her eidetic memory a nightmare, but she had taught herself to think past the darkness. "It became a minor political issue and the authorities charged you with a lesser offense, put you in juvie until you turned eighteen."

"I was there. I know what happened to me," he said, sardonic. "I asked about you."

"I'm trying to tell you!" She squared her shoulders in the face of his dominating masculinity. "Stop pushing."

"Hell, I have all night. Take your time. I'm here for your convenience."

"Sarcasm doesn't suit you." He was too raw, too earthy, too of the wild.

"You don't know me."

No, she accepted with another starburst of pain, she didn't.

She had given up all rights to him the day she'd let him believe that she'd been crushed to death in a car wreck. "Because of the media attention," she continued, "lots of people came forward with offers to adopt me."

"I know—it was in the papers."

She nodded. "My old social worker was fired after the media discovered he'd spent most of his work hours gambling." With the very lives he had been entrusted to protect. "The new guy—Zeke—had a little girl my age. He went above and beyond, personally vetted all the applicants."

Clay was silent but his eyes had gone cat, perilous in the extreme. And she remembered—it was Zeke who had lied to him about her death.

She met the eyes of the leopard who stood opposite her, afraid, bewildered, stupidly *needy*. Sometimes, it felt as if she'd been born needing Clay. "He placed me with the Larkspur family, deep in rural Iowa." The space, the endless fields of green, the constant supply of food, it had been a severe shock to her system. "You'd like it at the Nest—that's what the Larkspurs call the farm. Plenty of space to run, to play."

It seemed to her that his stance became a fraction less aggressive. "They were good to you?"

She nodded, biting down hard on her tongue before she could give in and beg him to go back to the way things had been before the day everything shattered. Orrin had split her lip, broken her ribs, but it was seeing Clay being hauled out the door that had destroyed her. "I was damaged, Clay." No getting around that. "I was damaged even before Orrin died. That just pushed me over some edge in my own mind. But the Larkspurs took me in, didn't judge me, tried to make me a part of the family. I suddenly had two older brothers, one older sister, and one younger sister."

"Sounds like too much to handle."

"For a while, it was." Overwhelmed by the loud, laughing family, she had curled up in corners and hidden. "Then one day, I realized I'd been there for a year and no one had hurt me. By the time you were released, I was twelve and functioning fairly well." Nightmares only once or twice a week, acting out at school less and less.

"So you decided to leave me in the past." A bitter laugh. "Why the hell not?"

"No. It wasn't like that." She reached out to him, dropping her hand in midtouch when he withdrew even deeper into the darkness. "I just—" How could she possibly explain the tortured confusion that had driven her? She'd known she wasn't yet strong enough to stand up to Clay, to face the horrors of the past, but she had worried for him, too.

"I stole four years of your freedom. I was determined not to be a burden on you for the rest of your life." Barely twelve years old and she'd known he would give up everything to keep her safe. "I didn't want to force you into bondage, into caring for me because I was too weak to care for myself. You'd already spent most of your life doing that for Isla." That fact had twisted the relationship between mother and child, turned it into that of caretaker and patient. The thought of Clay putting her into the same category had made Talin distraught. It still did.

"Don't lie to me." It was a lethal warning. "You were scared so you ran."

"I'm telling the truth." She swallowed. "But yes, I was scared, too. You didn't see what I saw, Clay. That day in Orrin's bedroom, you turned into someone I didn't know, someone more vicious than anyone I'd ever known." She waited for him to say that he'd done it for her, but he didn't. Her guilt intensified. "Why don't you blame me? It would make this so much easier. Blame me, yell at me, God damn it!"

"For what, Talin? What did you do? Be my friend. That was your only crime." He remained unmoving, so much a part of the forest that she could hardly tell where he began and the night ended. "These Larkspurs—why aren't you going to them for help?"

"I brought darkness into that family. I can't bring evil."

"They're your pack, they would stand by you."

She was startled at his word usage. "My pack? No, I don't think they are. I—I was a visitor. I made myself a visitor, left the family at sixteen after getting a full board and study scholarship." Even their name, she had borrowed only until adulthood—long enough to blur the waters and dead-end any search Clay might have mounted. "I never let them in."

"Why not?"

"Do you let your pack touch your soul?" she asked, desperate to learn about his new life, his new world, years of hunger coalescing into this single moment.

"DarkRiver cats have a way of adopting you even if you don't particularly want to be adopted." It was a snarl. "If I bleed, they'll come to my aid. They would kill for me."

She shivered at the wild violence of his statement. But there was also a seduction in that kind of loyalty. It made her wonder about bonds of a far different sort. "Do you . . . do you have someone in your pack?"

He went very still. "I don't scent a mate on you."

"Me?" Her voice came out high, startled. "No. I— No."

He remained silent.

She coughed. "I don't want to get in the way of a relationship by involving you in my problems."

"Leave my relationships to me."

Her insides twisted. "Fine."

Clay waited. Juvie had been hell, but it had taught him to contain emotion, to hold his anger inside until it was needed—then use it like a weapon. The Psy scientists who had come to observe "captive animal behavior" had been his unwitting teachers.

At the time, he'd been the lone predatory changeling under long-term incarceration—changeling packs usually dealt with their own without Enforcement involvement. But not only had Clay not had a pack, he'd crossed a racial boundary in his crime. Orrin had been human.

Yet instead of subjecting him to hard study and learning things—things that could have given the Psy Council an edge in the cold war it was currently waging against the changelings—the Psy had treated him as a curiosity, an animal behind bars. It was the animal who had watched and learned. Now he watched as Talin shifted from foot to foot before folding her arms around herself again.

"I work with kids in San Francisco," she said without warning. "I've been doing it ever since I graduated. But not here. I was in New York until the start of this year."

"Is one of them in danger?" He felt the embers of his fury flare into life at the realization that she'd been in his territory for close to three months. All those times he had caught a hint of her scent in Chinatown or down by Fisherman's Wharf, only to find himself trailing a stranger; he'd thought it a sign he really had gone over the edge.

"Not like that." Dropping her arms, she looked at his eyes, which he'd allowed to go night-glow. "Clay, please. Stop doing the cat thing and come out so I can see your face."

"No." He wasn't ready to show her anything. "Did you know I was in the city?"

"Not at first. I had no way to track you after you got out of juvie." She kicked at the grass. "Then one day, a few weeks ago, I thought I saw you. Drove me crazy—I thought I was hallucinating, making up fantasies of what you would've looked like as an adult."

He didn't respond, despite the near-echo of his earlier thoughts.

She blew out a breath. "I swear—" The abrasive sound of teeth grinding against each other. "I went back to where I thought I'd seen you, realized it was the DarkRiver business HQ, and looked them up on the Internet. I still wasn't sure—there was no photo and you changed your last name to Bennett."

It had been a way to drop off the face of the world, to lose any simmering media attention. But over the years, it had become his name. "We'll talk about you tracking me later," he said, cold fire burning a hole in his gut. "First, tell me why you need my help."

"If you're trying to scare me, it's working. That doesn't mean I'm going to cut and run."

In that bravado-filled challenge, he caught another fleeting glimpse of the girl she'd been. The day they had met, she'd sat there beside him, wide-eyed and terrified to her tiny toes, but stubborn enough not to leave till the paramedics came. "Why not?" he said, shifting his anger into sarcasm. "You're real good at it."

She raised her face to the canopy and took a deep breath, as if trying to hold on to her temper. He wondered if she'd succeed. His Tally had always been very quiet . . . except with him. He alone had known that she was neither shy nor particularly calm. The girl had a temper like a stick of dynamite. Quick to heat, quick to blow over.

"Kids are disappearing, not only here but across the country," she now said, her anger red-hot, but no longer directed at him. "At first, they were labeled runaways, but I knew some of them. They weren't that kind." Her shoulders drew up. "Now I have proof I was right, and I wish every night that I didn't." Her voice broke.

"Talk to me." He didn't like seeing her in pain, never had, probably never would. This familiar stranger, this woman who saw him as a monster, was his one fucking fatal weakness and didn't that just suck?

"They found Mickey's body two weeks ago." A tear streaked down her cheek. She dashed it away with a furious swipe. "He was eleven years old, bright, so bright, could remember everything he'd ever read."

"Like you."

"Yeah. Except instead of being abandoned as a baby, he had the bad luck to live with a mother who always chose abusive men." She gave him a smile but it was nothing happy. "He was *mine*, Clay. I promised him safety and in return, he went to school every day." Tremors shook her frame, whitened her knuckles. "Someone beat him to death. Everything was broken. The bastards pulverized his face—like they were wiping him out!"

Anger shot through his bloodstream. He thought of the children in the pack, of what he'd do to anyone who dared harm them. "One of his mother's men?"

"I might have thought so, but Mickey was at a camp out of state when they took him. And it's not only him we lost." A breath that sounded as if her throat was lined with broken glass. "They found two more bodies this week. At least one more kid remains missing."

The leopard half of his soul—angry, hurt, and still in shock at her return—wanted to go to her. To hold her. Tactile contact, affection as a method of healing, was the way of changelings, something he'd been taught after being pulled into DarkRiver. But Talin was scared of him. She had told him that to his face, and the sharp knife of it was still buried in his heart. The man wasn't sure he wanted to chance another rejection. Keeping the animal's instincts in check, he finally stepped out of the shadows. "Do you want to be held, Talin?"

Her damp eyes widened at the blunt question, then she nodded in a little jerking motion. Something in him quieted, waiting. "Then come here."

A pause during which the entire forest seemed to freeze, the night creatures aware of the leopard's tense watchfulness.

"Oh, God, Clay." Suddenly her arms were wrapped around his back, her cheek pressed against the white cotton of his T-shirt.

Hardly daring to breathe, he closed his own arms around her feminine warmth, blindingly aware of every inch of her pressed into him, every spot of wetness soaking through his T-shirt.

She was so small, so damn soft, her humanity apparent in the delicacy of her skin, the lightness of her bones. The Psy might be fragile in comparison to changelings, but they had powers of the mind to compensate. Humans had the same fragility but none of the psychic abilities. A wave of protectiveness washed over him.

"Shh, Tally." He used the nickname because, at this moment, he knew her. She had always had a heart too big for her body, a heart that felt such pain for others while ignoring its own. "I'll find your lost one."

She shook her head against him. "It's too late. Three bodies already. Jonquil is probably dead, too."

"Then I'll find who did this to them and stop him."

She stilled against him. "I didn't come here to turn you into a killer again."

CHAPTER 4

"I *am a* killer," he said, unwilling to let her hide from this. "I'm a leopard changeling and in my world, killing to protect your pack is understood and accepted."

"I'm not part of your pack."

"No." So why was he going to help her? Especially after she'd made her opinion of him crystal clear. "No child deserves to die that way."

A small silence. "Thank you." She didn't let go. "You've become so strong."

"I was always strong compared to you." Now he could snap her in two without thinking. It was that difference in strength that had always kept him away from human females. The rare lovers he took were all changeling. He was who he was. And gentleness was not part of his nature. "Unless you've muscled up and it doesn't show on the surface?"

She laughed, a warm, intrinsically feminine sound. "I'm still a shrimp, but you—you've become a leopard."

He understood. She had known him as an angry boy trapped inside the claustrophobic walls of their apartment complex. The lack of clean air had stifled the leopard, wounded him on an elemental level. He hadn't even been able to shift without someone calling the cops to report a wild animal on the loose. Then there was Isla, unable to bear the sight of her son in leopard form.

"Are you happy with DarkRiver?" Talin asked now.

"They're my family, my friends." For Clay, that loyalty meant everything. They accepted him as he was, didn't give a shit that he preferred to roam alone more often than not, invited him into their homes without compunction.

"Who was the blond man with you?"

He stiffened. "Dorian's a sentinel, too." A pretty one according to most women.

"You two were being rough with those boys."

"They earned it. Got drunk and smashed up the bar."

"So you came to take them home." He could hear the smile in her voice. "You look after each other. Your pack, I mean."

"I'll be kicking their asses three ways to Sunday soon as they sober up. We're no Swiss Family Robinson." They couldn't afford to be, especially not now, with the Psy Council attempting to take down the only changeling groups—DarkRiver and SnowDancer—that had dared challenge its absolute rule.

Something made a rumbling sound.

"Hungry, Tally?"

She nodded, but remained plastered to him. "I was so nervous about meeting you, I didn't eat all day."

"If you don't want to piss me off," he snapped, "stop talking about how much I scare you."

"It won't change the truth." Talin knew she'd surprised him. His muscles bunched. Then he let out a low growl that rolled down her spine like a thousand tiny pinpricks.

"Stop flinching or I'll bite you and really give you something to worry about."

She blinked. "You wouldn't bite me." Would he?

"Try it and see."

Surrounded by all that powerful male muscle, feeling warm and safe, she decided not to push him. Not today. "Will you help me?"

Her answer was a hot breath at her ear. "Keep asking silly questions and see where it gets you."

She took that as a yes and, though her heart threatened to rip out of her chest, she remained stuck to him. And she prayed. Prayed that she could do this without betraying the one secret that would make Clay truly hate her.

Twenty minutes later, she found herself sitting in the same bar the young males had smashed up. "It doesn't look too bad." She nodded at the relatively undamaged walls.

"Manager knows how to build tough. Joe's a packmate."

"Oh." She went silent as a curvy blonde with a bad-tempered expression placed Talin's meal in front of her before turning to Clay.

"I hope Cory, Kit, Jase, and the rest of those drunken monkeys get the same punishment I did. Joe thinks it's hysterical to make me wear this frickin' getup." Her voice was a snarl as she waved at her pink baby-tee and black miniskirt. Teamed with knee-high boots, it turned her into a sexy stunner. But Talin had a feeling that any man stupid enough to put a move on this woman would soon find his arm broken into tiny little pieces.

Clay lifted his beer and took a long pull. "Should've thought of that before you punched out his real waitress, Rina. You're Opal as long as it takes for her nose to heal."

Rina stamped her foot. "There's nothing wrong with Opal's nose! I only tapped her!"

"You're a DarkRiver soldier. You don't get to throw your temper around."

Rina's scowl turned into a sensual pout. "Clay, please."

"Don't even think about it, kitty cat," he said, a spark of amusement in his eyes that hit Talin with the nausea-inducing strength of a punch to the solar plexus. "Where's my burger?"

Rina actually hissed, all flirtatiousness leaving her face and body. "You know what your problem is? You need to get laid!"

Talin tensed, waiting for the explosion of Clay's sleeping volcano of a temper, but all he did was put down his beer and crook a finger at the blonde. When the scowling woman leaned down, he whispered something in her ear that made her blush bright red. Rising back up, she went straight to the kitchen.

"What did you say to her?" Talin was shocked by the sharp claws of jealousy dragging their way through her body.

"Rina's young. She just needed a little gentling." His eyes watched her play with her food with disconcerting intensity. "Eat."

She couldn't, stomach churning with thoughts of how he had "gentled" the sensual young woman. But she took a bite in an effort to keep her mouth shut.

Clay's meal arrived seconds later, delivered by a still-blushing Rina. The young woman hesitated, then leaned down to peck him on the cheek before walking away, all feminine heat and long blonde hair.

Talin had to force herself to swallow the bite she'd taken. That kiss—it had been familiar, affectionate. It didn't fit with the image she'd formed of Clay over the past hour. "She's very pretty." Damn it! She stuffed the burger into her mouth.

Clay raised an eyebrow. "I don't fuck little girls."

She almost choked, had to take a long drink of water to get the food down her throat. "That's not what I meant."

"You always were a possessive little thing." He took a bite of his own burger and washed it down with beer. "So, who have you talked to about these kills?"

The abrupt change in subject threw her, but only for a moment. "Enforcement when Mickey disappeared. They didn't take it seriously." She put down her half-eaten burger.

"After the bodies were found?"

"They launched an investigation," she said. "One of the detectives—Max Shannon—he actually seems to care. He's the one who told me about the other disappearances around the country."

"But?"

"But I don't think it's anything as simple as a killer targeting runaways. This feels wrong, Clay."

"Still getting your feelings, huh?"

She shrugged, uncomfortable with the topic. "They're worth nothing. Just this feeling of 'wrongness.' Women's intuition. What good is that to anyone?"

She'd had the same feelings about Orrin, the man who had been supposed to be an exemplary foster father. She'd made the mistake of sharing those feelings with her old social worker and had gotten her face slapped.

You should count yourself lucky he and his wife are happy to take in a piece of trash like you. If it was me, I'd leave you to rot in the state orphanage.

As an adult, she knew that that social worker had been way out of line, a being who should have never been allowed near his charges. But as a child five weeks from her third birthday, she had believed him. She'd had nowhere else to go, no one to turn to. So she had learned to keep silent about her feelings . . . and everything that came after.

Having no desire to relive the terrors of the past, she focused her attention on the here and now, counting the beads of condensation rolling down the side of Clay's beer bottle. "You said you'd find him—the man who's doing this."

"Yes."

She looked up into the indescribable green of his eyes. Forests, she thought, she had always seen forests in Clay's eyes, a freedom that was his gift to her. "Why does everyone automatically assume only men can do bad things? Women can be as evil, as depraved."

"Delia's still in prison." His hand clenched around the bottle. "Not long after I got taken in, they found the bodies she and Orrin had buried in the junkyard. There was so much forensic evidence she'll be rotting in jail till the undertakers haul her away."

"I know." After being relocated to Larkspur's Nest, she had had constant nightmares in which Delia would come to drag her back to Orrin. He'd be sitting on the bed waiting for her, a rotting corpse with maggots crawling out of every possible orifice. Those dreams had lasted until Ma Larkspur had walked into the bathroom one night and found Talin cowering in the bath. The older woman had gone on the Internet right then and there and downloaded footage of Delia being bundled up into a prison van. Talin had watched that footage obsessively for a month. "They found home recordings of the murders, did you know?"

"My lawyer told me." He held her gaze, a cool, calm predator with a heart of turbulent fire. "Did they use those recordings to terrorize you?"

She shook her head. "That was their secret pleasure—I used to hear them watching the vids late at night." While she'd been locked up in her room. They had much preferred to put her in the special punishment closet, but had quickly worked out that her terror was all the greater if they let her run free and unpunished for a few weeks—never knowing when she'd be shoved back into that airless, lightless hole had been a whole different level of torture.

"No one's sure how many kids they murdered," she said, closing the lid on that bleak memory. "They were smart. They only took a couple of their foster kids. Rest were all runaways." The dam broke without warning. "You should have never gone to prison! You did the whole world a favor by getting rid of Orrin!"

Clay shrugged. "Judge White offered me a choice of juvie, with an attached anger management course and regular school hours, or a residential psych facility."

"Psych? Why?"

"He saw I had an anger problem and he was a good enough man to try and sort me out before I went completely off the rails." He finished off his beer. "I knew if they locked me up in a little white room, I'd go crazy. At least the juvenile facility where I did my time was out of the city and set up for boys. We had space to run, to get physical."

"But there were fences," she whispered.

His eyes sharpened. "You say that like you visited me."

She began to methodically destroy a piece of lettuce that had fallen from her burger. "Zeke got desperate when I still wouldn't talk long after Orrin's death. He thought if I saw you it might help."

"Tell me."

"We sat in the parking lot overlooking one of the exercise yards." She'd been close to nine by then. Mute, broken, lost. "He bribed an administrator to get you to come out somehow. You were dressed in gray sweatpants and a gray tee with the sleeves cut off. I watched you run circuits around the track."

Clay knew the exact date and time of her visit. His beast had gone crazy that day, desperate for the scent of her—so desperate he'd imagined he could smell it on the breeze. "I ran for hours."

"I know. I stayed there until you went back inside." She gave him a shaky smile. "I knew you had to hate the fences but there you were, surviving. I thought if you could do that for me, I could do the same . . . for you."

Clay's hands clenched into fists. Damn her. His anger was a whole lot easier to hang on to when she didn't remind him of the girl she'd been. "How did you do?" he asked, giving in to the compulsion to know everything about her.

She took a breath to answer but someone chose to boot up the jukebox at that second. Loud music crashed into the room. It was modulated so as not to damage keen changeling hearing, but it wasn't exactly conducive to talk.

He ran his debit card over the reader built into the table and rose. "Let's go."

Nodding, she took a quick sip of water, then followed, staying close to him. They met Dorian just outside. The blond sentinel was in the process of getting off his sleek black motorcycle. "That your rabbit?" Hanging up his helmet, he smiled at Talin and it was a charming smile with a hint of the feral. Clay had seen women throw themselves at Dorian after being on the receiving end of that smile. "She's kind of bite-sized for you. Why don't you give her to me?"

Clay waited to see what Talin would do, well aware the other sentinel was simply messing with her. According to Pack law, Talin was Clay's because she had come to him. Until and unless she wanted out—Clay's hands fisted again—no packmate would touch her.

"What do you say, little rabbit?"

"I'm sorry," Talin replied, sweet as honey. "I don't do pretty boys. In fact, I don't do boys at all."

Dorian choked on a laugh, then glanced at Clay's shocked face. "Well, shit. She's all yours, buddy."

Clay hustled Talin to her Jeep and pinned her to the passenger door with his hands on either side of her body. Her fear was a live thing between them, a slimy intruder that had no place being there. He fought to contain the leopard's corresponding rage and knew from the look in her eyes that he'd only been partially successful.

"You like girls?" he asked very, very quietly.

She shook her head, eyes big.

"I can still tell when you're lying and you weren't lying to Dorian."

"No, I wasn't." She bit her lower lip. "I was jerking his chain 'cause he was jerking mine. I said I don't like pretty boys."

The leopard was too wound up to see the logic. "What do you like?"

"Men."

Time stopped as he digested the knowledge in her eyes. "You've been with men." He felt as if she'd cut him off at the knees and he shouldn't have. Leopard changelings were sensual creatures—regular sexual contact was considered healthy and natural. He had never before judged a woman for who or how many others she'd been with.

"Yes." Her skin paled. "Lots of men. So many I can't remember their faces, much less their names. Too many for even my memory to handle."

Was she trying to hurt him on purpose? That she had the ability to do so enraged the leopard. Keeping that anger at bay only by dint of years of experience, he pushed off the car. "Why? You weren't like that."

"You knew me before puberty hit," she said, a tight bitterness to her tone. "Can we go now or would you like a blow-by-blow?"

"Get the hell in!"

Talin got in, conscious of a deep sense of self-loathing. She'd never intended for Clay to know the depths to which she had sunk, but it had been like someone else was controlling her mouth, as if some defiant part of her *wanted* him to know. Now he did. And whatever chance they had had, it was gone.

Talin couldn't blame him for his reaction. The counselor she had finally gone to for a short period after beginning her work for Shine, had assured her that her acting out as a teenager and as a young adult had been an understandable reaction, something often exhibited by victims of childhood abuse. The woman had classified it as a kind of self-harm, said there was no need for Talin to feel shame. But even after eight years of celibacy, except for—

No, she wouldn't think of those times. Her fists turned bloodless. It had been eight years since the final therapy session, eight years since she had begun to try to treat her body as something good, something worth holding precious, *eight years* . . . but Talin still wasn't sure she believed the counselor.

Maybe she was the slut Orrin had tried to make her. Maybe that defect was built into her genes. The clinic where she'd been abandoned as a baby had been a free one, utilized almost exclusively by prostitutes after all. Orrin had called her the daughter of a whore. Like mother, like daughter.

"Where's your apartment?"

Snapping upright at that cold question, she realized they had reached the outskirts of San Francisco. Lips dry, mouth full of cotton wool, she gave him directions to the small high-rise where Shine had leased her an apartment. "Thank you," she said when he parked on the street out front.

"Here." He threw her the key. A split second later, he had opened the door and was gone, a lethal shadow invisible against the rising fog. Eyes stinging, she shifted into the driver's seat and drove the Jeep down into the underground parking area.

Clay had been disgusted by her.

A sob caught in her throat as she sat in the dimly lit garage. Even when Clay had first discovered her grim childhood secret—only seconds before he'd killed Orrin—he had never looked at her with blame in his eyes. Instead, he had written her letters from juvie, telling her that she was still his Tally, still the best thing in his life. Those letters had gotten her through more years than Clay would ever know.

But now . . . now he blamed her for what she'd become. How could he not? He'd spent four years in a cage so she wouldn't have to live in a nightmare and what had she done? She'd spit on his gift, cheapened it to tawdriness. No wonder he hated her.

That she had been close to insane during those lost, tormented years didn't sound like a particularly good excuse.

Giving in, she pressed her head against the steering wheel and cried.

CHAPTER 5

Ashaya Aleine was an M-Psy with a Gradient rating of 9.9. The latter made her very unusual. Most Psy that powerful tended to make the 0.1 leap into cardinal status. There was no measuring cardinals. Some were more powerful than others but all had the same eyes—white stars on black velvet.

Distinctive. Memorable.

Ashaya was neither. Her eyes were an unremarkable blue gray, her hair a plain black. It was curly but once pinned into a severe knot, it became forgettable. Her dark brown skin, too, was nothing surprising among the genetically mixed population of the Psy. But Psy weren't the only ones she had to consider. For her plan to succeed, she had to learn to become invisible among the humans and changelings, a far harder task.

The clear panel of her computer screen flashed an incoming call. She answered it to find herself facing a woman with almond-shaped eyes and ruler-straight black hair. "Councilor Duncan. What can I do for you?"

Nikita Duncan put down what appeared to be an electronic pen. "I'd like a progress report. How far along are you?" Her face was a static wall, a testament to perfect Silence.

"Back at the start." She remained as unmoving as the

Councilor. "The saboteurs' attack on the previous lab destroyed the majority of my research." And her little twist in the programming of the prototype implants had taken care of those few that had been liberated from the lab without her consent.

"Nothing can be salvaged?"

"It may be possible," she admitted. "However, in my opinion, it would be more effective to start from the very beginning. There were errors in the earlier prototypes I was unable to pinpoint. If I restart with those errors in mind, I may be able to eradicate them."

"Of course." Nikita's dark eyes were unblinking. Like a snake's. It was an apt comparison, given that Nikita was reputed to possess the deadly ability to infect other minds with mental viruses—an excellent, untraceable way of getting rid of competitors. "When can the Council expect a full update?"

"I'll send one this week, but it will simply be a detailed reiteration of what I've already indicated."

"Understood. I'll wait for that report." Nikita clicked off.

Ashaya found nothing unusual in the Councilor's ready agreement. As the head M-Psy on the team dedicated to the implementation of Protocol I—also known as the Implant Protocol—Ashaya had complete autonomy over research and development.

Their goal was simple: to develop an implant that could be fitted into all Psy brains—but with a focus on infants—in order to create a totally unified society. In other words, a hive mind.

CHAPTER 6

By the time Talin made it up to her apartment, having no idea how long she'd spent in the Jeep, her eyes were swollen, likely bloodshot. Tasting salt on her lips, she pressed her palm against the scanner beside her door, waited for the lock to disengage, then pushed the door open. The lights came on automatically—she hated being in an enclosed space in the dark. Being outside in the dark didn't scare her. It was the sense of being shut in that got to her—and she didn't need a degree in psychology to figure out why.

Closing the door behind her, she took a step forward. And froze. At first, she couldn't comprehend what it was that she was seeing. Then it hit her in a stomach-churning rush, a kaleidoscope of color and destruction perfumed with the smell of death.

The intruders were gone, that much was obvious. But they had left their mark. She slid down the back of the door to collapse into a sitting position, unable to take her eyes off the message dripping down the opposite wall in a dark red that screamed with the iron-richness of blood.

Stop. Or you're next.

What a stupid message, she thought, childish in its snigger-ing simplicity. But it worked. The chill of a visceral fear crawled up her body until it closed around her throat, making her want to gag. Still she didn't blink, didn't look away.

How dare they? How *dare* they!

She didn't care about the intrusion or the mess. Those things meant little to a woman who had never allowed any place to be home. But to do what they had done with the photos of her kids?

The holo-image frames had been crushed into the carpet, but they hadn't stopped there. The hard copies had been shredded, the pieces stuck into the blood creeping down the wall. That desecration she couldn't forgive. It made her want to scream and cry and crawl forward to gather up the broken pieces.

But she wasn't a fool. Though anguish and a bone-deep anger roiled in her gut, she didn't attempt to rescue those small things that meant so much to her. That was what they wanted, the monster or monsters who had taken and murdered the chil-dren under her care. They wanted to shred her credibility, turn her into a crazy woman no one would believe.

Well, fuck them.

Reaching for her cell phone, she began to press the keys. Only at the last second did she realize she was punching in the code for Clay's office line. A different kind of nausea filled her mouth.

Taking several short breaths, loath to drag in the violated air of her apartment, she shook her head, cleared the screen, and pressed in a far more familiar code.

After leaving Talin, Clay made his way back to the bar and proceeded to get blind drunk. He was aware of Dorian coming to sit with him, aware of Rina throwing worried glances in his direction and of Joe coming by several times, but he ignored them all, determined to wipe out the image of Tally, *his Tally*, with other men.

"Enough." Dorian grabbed the bottle out of his hand.

Clay backhanded the other sentinel, retrieving the bottle at the same time.

"Jesus H. Christ." Dorian got up off the floor, rubbing at his jaw. "I am not letting you pass out here."

"Get lost." Clay had every intention of drinking himself into an unconscious stupor.

Dorian swore, then went quiet. "Well, thank bloody God. Maybe you can talk some sense into him."

Clay said nothing as Nathan settled into the other side of the booth. DarkRiver's most senior sentinel folded his arms and leaned back against the crimson leather-synth of the bench seat. "Give us a minute, Dorian. Get Rina to ice that bruise."

"Call me if you need a hand to drag him out of here."

Clay waited for Nate to light into him, but the other man simply watched him with those dark blue eyes that were always so damn calm.

"What?" he said, his tone flat. Other leopards might have growled or snapped, but Clay knew if he allowed his rage to surface tonight, it would end in blood.

"The one and only time I've ever seen you drunk," Nate replied, "was when I hauled your sorry ass out of that bar in New York."

Clay grunted, well aware that Nate had saved his life that night. Fresh out of juvie and having just been told that Talin was dead, he had been well on the road to self-annihilation. It was in that pain-fueled anger that he'd picked a fight with Nate. Over ten years older and a trained fighter, Nate had wiped the floor with him.

But instead of leaving him to the scavengers, the sentinel had dragged Clay back to his hotel room. Nathan's mate, Tamsyn, had taken one look at him and said, "Good Lord, I didn't think there were any big cats in New York!" That was the first time in his life that Clay had been in the company of fellow leopards.

"That time," Nate commented, "it was a girl. You'd lost your Talin."

"I should've never told you about her."

"You were young." Nate shrugged. "Rina said you were in here with a woman earlier."

"Rina has a big mouth."

Nate grinned. "Pack law. Being nosy about fellow packmates is required. So, you gonna tell me?"

"No."

"Fair enough." The other man rose to his feet. "When you've finished destroying yourself, you might recall Lucas and Sascha have a meeting with Nikita Duncan tomorrow. You're supposed to be watching our alpha pair's backs."

"Fuck!" Clay put down the bottle, the black haze of his anger clearing in a harsh burst of reality. Nikita Duncan was Sascha's mother, and a member of the powerful Psy Council. She was also a murderous bitch. "I'll be there."

"No." Nate's eyes grew cold. "You're compromised. I'll cover."

That got through to Clay as nothing else could have. His loyalty to DarkRiver was what kept him on the right side of the line. Take that away and he'd be a stone-cold killer. Especially now that Talin had cut his heart right out of him. "Point taken."

"You're still off tomorrow." Nate held out a hand. "Come on."

After a dangerous pause in which the leopard rose to crouching readiness, hungry for violence, Clay accepted the offer and let one of the few men he called friend haul him upright. The floor spun. "Shit. I'm drunk." He slung an arm around Nate's shoulders.

"You think, Sherlock?" Dorian appeared to prop up his other side. "Man, it must've cut you up that your girl only likes other girls."

"*What?*" Nate stumbled, threatening to take them all down.

Clay bared his teeth. "She likes *men*"—another surge of fury—"just not pretty *boys* like you."

Dorian began to scowl. "Smart-ass. Wait till the next time I see her."

Clay was about to reply when the hard alcohol caught up with him, his changeling body deciding it would be better if he slept off the drunk.

Max arrived with a crime scene team half an hour after Talin's call. By then, she'd taken the chance to wash away her tears, thinking clearly enough to buy bottles of cold water from the vending machine on the ground floor instead of going in and using her own sink.

"Did you touch anything?" Max asked after looking over the scene, his uptilted eyes and olive skin giving his face an exotic cast.

Clay's skin was darker than Max's, she found herself thinking even as she shook her head. "Nothing but the door and the bit of carpet around it."

"Good." He nodded at the crime scene techs.

Talin watched dispassionately as the white-garbed men and women walked in, their shoes enclosed in protective booties, their hair and clothing covered to minimize contamination. "They won't get anything. It might look like a teenage prank, but this was a slick operation."

Max walked her a small distance from the open doorway of her apartment. "You're probably right. But this is bad, Talin. One of my men is changeling—his nose tells him that that's definitely human blood."

She felt her fingers curl into claws. "It'll be from one of the children." The monsters were playing mind games, sickening, brutal, and without conscience.

Max didn't bother to dispute her claim. "What bothers me is that they know how hard you've been pushing the investigation."

"Enforcement is a sieve," she muttered.

"Yeah." An uncharacteristically bitter look clouded his expression. "If I hadn't been born with airtight mental shields, I'd probably have made captain by now."

She rubbed a hand over her face. "Psy spies can't read you?"

"No. But that doesn't make any difference here." He put his hands on his hips, below his trench coat. "Council plants are simply the most obvious. We've got others who think nothing of selling information for profit."

Dropping her hand, she shook her head. "Why stay in such a corrupt system?"

"Because we do more good than harm," he said, his dedication clear. "The Psy don't interfere in most investigations, especially not when it involves the other races."

"Maybe not," she agreed, "but they still treat humans as a lesser species. It makes me wonder why they let us live at all."

"Every society needs its worker bees." The dry sarcasm in

Max's words didn't negate their truth. "We do all the jobs they can't be bothered with. But we can't blame the Psy for the lack of support in this case. This is because of plain old human prejudice. People see the victims, their lifestyles, and make judgments."

"What use is Enforcement if it ignores those who need it most?" She knew Max didn't deserve her anger, but God, she was mad. "These are *children*, most of whom have no one else to speak for them."

Max's jaw locked tight. "I prefer the changeling way sometimes," he said, to her surprise. "You hit one of them, you get executed. End of story."

Her stomach twisted. "Who does the executions?"

"The high-level guys in the predatory packs."

High-level guys like Clay. Talin wasn't going to lie to herself—she wanted to kill these bastards, too—but the reminder of the brutality implicit in Clay's world made her break out in a cold sweat.

You always knew what I was. You chose not to think about it, chose to pretend I was what you wanted me to be.

She'd refuted his assessment but now wondered if he hadn't been right. Had she given lip service to accepting his leopard, while expecting him to be human—exactly as his mother had done? The realization fractured the already shaky foundation of her current emotional state. Shoving her hair off her face, she forcibly contained her confusion and focused on something she could understand. "When can I have my place back?"

Max shook his head. "You can't stay here, you know that. You need to be in protective custody."

"No." The last time she'd run, she'd lost all claim to the only man who had ever seen goodness in her.

"Talin, don't be stupid. If these people"—he jerked his head toward her apartment—"think you're getting too close, they won't stop with a warning."

"I know." She stared back at him. "I'll be fine. I know how to take care of myself." No more hiding. No more cowering in the corner while someone else fought for her.

Max threw up his hands, having learned his lesson after butting heads with her more than once. "At least find a safer place to stay. This apartment isn't secure enough to deter anyone determined to break in. Do you have somewhere to go?"

Clay. The answer hovered on the tip of her tongue, but she bit down hard before it could escape. The pain brought tears to her eyes but it did the job, cutting through the confusion to illuminate the stark truth—*Clay wasn't hers any longer, hadn't been for two long decades.* That admission was discordant music in her head, painful and sandpaper rough.

"Yes," she lied. "I have a friend who'll put me up." She had no friends, had spent a lifetime avoiding commitment. Even the Larkspurs hadn't been able to break through. The truth was, she trusted no one. Not even herself. Especially not herself.

Clay, her mind whispered again. *Call him. You trust him still.*

Not true, she argued. Yes, she had trusted the boy he'd been, but she didn't know the man he'd become. And he hated her, was right to hate her. When she thought of the way she'd treated her body, her soul, she hated herself.

"I'll have one of my officers drop you off."

She jerked at the sound of Max's voice. "No. I'll wait until you guys are done, pack up some gear, and go."

"It'll be daylight by then. If you're worried about a leak, don't be. The man I had in mind is changeling. Leakproof." He tapped his temple as if to remind her of the other race's superior natural shields. "More important, I trust him."

"I'm not leaving without my stuff." An excuse. It would buy her time, give her a chance to figure out where to go.

He sighed. "Fine. Park yourself out here until we're done and I'll give you a ride myself."

"Great." *Damn.*

Clay woke with the knowledge that he wasn't in his lair, his head clear. Changelings processed alcohol far quicker than humans and he had stopped drinking just short of hangover territory. Of course, his mouth felt like something small and furry had crawled in and died there, and his disgust at his own behavior was intense, but physically speaking, he was fine.

Tiny scrabbling sounds came from the floor beside the bed.

It was those sounds that had wakened him though it was still dark outside. Reaching down without looking, he caught one leopard cub by the scruff off his neck and hauled him onto the bed, catching the second as he tried to dart out. "You two are supposed to be in bed," he growled.

The two small leopards looked at each other, then rushed him. He held them off without too much trouble, amused. It was the last emotion he'd have thought he'd feel upon waking, but these two made anything else hard.

"Down," he said after a few minutes.

The cubs obeyed at once, well aware he was dominant to them. In fact, all of a sudden they appeared to be on their best behavior. Suspicious, he focused his hearing and caught the sound of Tamsyn, their mother, searching for them. "Sharp ears," he muttered, not bothering to get up when Tamsyn gave a soft knock.

"They're in here." His throat felt lined with grit.

She opened the door. "Oh, did they wake you?" As she came to pick them up, the cubs shifted into human form in a burst of flickering color. Naked, they scampered out of the room, laughing.

Tamsyn smiled and shook her head. "More energy than sense."

He grunted. "Time?"

"Five a.m." Sitting on the bed, she looked at him, her hair sliding over one shoulder. "You feeling okay?"

"A shower and I'll be fine." He deliberately ignored the real meaning of her question. Having been DarkRiver's healer from a very young age, Tamsyn had a disturbing way of getting under people's skins.

Now, she sighed. "You're exactly like my boys—no sense at all. I love you, you idiot. Talk to me."

He wasn't ready to talk to anyone about the ghost who had walked back into his life. "Leave it, Tammy."

She shook her head. "Lord, but you men drive me crazy. All testosterone and pride. Well, you know where I live. I'll go find you some fresh clothes." Leaning over, she brushed his hair off his face in a gentle move. "We're Pack, Clay. Remember that."

He waited until she left before shoving down the sheet and wandering into the bathroom. *Pack.* Yes, they were Pack, a healthy, functioning pack. He'd never known the like until Nate had dragged him into DarkRiver.

His mother, Isla, had deliberately chosen to live away from the leopard-controlled areas of the country, hiding her son among humans and nonpredatory changelings. The fact that they had never been tracked down told Clay that his father's—and by extension, Isla's—pack, had been, or was, nowhere near as strong or as healthy as DarkRiver. It hadn't protected, hadn't sheltered, and definitely hadn't healed.

When Nate had offered to sponsor Clay into DarkRiver, he'd accepted mostly because he didn't really care where he went. He'd figured he could take off if he didn't like it. He had discovered different within days. In DarkRiver, isolation wasn't an option. Loners were accepted, but they weren't forgotten. And if someone lost their way, the pack hauled them back in kicking and screaming.

Stepping out of the shower, he pulled on the clothes he'd heard Tamsyn bring in a few minutes ago. They were his own—because Tamsyn was their healer, they often came to her bleeding or worse, their clothes useless. It made sense to have spare clothing here. As he dressed, he could hear her and Nate talking downstairs, the low murmur of their voices interspersed with the higher-pitched tones of the twins.

A healthy pack. A healthy family. They were both lessons Clay had learned from DarkRiver. Why hadn't Talin learned the same from the family that had taken her in? She hadn't lied about them being good people. He would have picked up the signs of deception—increased heart rate, perspiration, the subtle shift in scent. Not all leopards had that skill but Clay had always been good at it, especially with Talin.

Lots of men.

She hadn't lied about that either. The thought of his Talin with others continued to stoke the dark fire inside of him, but at least he could think past it this morning. Going downstairs, he grabbed a cup of coffee and a bagel, then left before either Nate or Tamsyn could ask any awkward questions.

He had no time for delays. He was on a hunt.

No way in hell was Talin going to get away from him a second time.

CHAPTER 7

There was an Enforcement car outside her apartment. Clay's heart kicked violently in his chest.

He'd left her alone in the dark. Tally was scared of the dark.

Disgusted with himself, he was about to get out of his own vehicle and track her down when she walked out holding a small duffel bag. His relief was crushing, but hard on its heels came a jagged mix of anger and possessiveness laced with razor-sharp tenderness. How dare she put herself in danger? And how dare she not call him the second she knew something was wrong?

Instead of Clay, there was another man walking by her side, the small gold shield of an Enforcement detective clipped to his collar. As Clay watched from across the road, the detective put a hand on her lower back and urged her toward the vehicle Clay had already noted. She resisted but didn't break the touch. The detective dropped his hand, his face wearing a scowl that told Clay Talin was being stubborn.

That didn't mean the man wasn't one of her lovers.

The leopard growled and the sound threatened to travel up through Clay's human vocal cords to fill the air inside the car.

He almost didn't stop the sound from escaping, no matter that he knew full well he was behaving like an ass. He had no right to judge Talin. But that was the cool, logical, human side of his brain talking—where Talin was concerned, he was less human and more possessive, domineering cat.

Sliding back the door, he got out and strode across the street.

Talin's head snapped up the second his foot hit the ground, as if she'd felt the vibration. A chaotic mix of emotions swept across her face, waves of liquid flame: Relief. Surprise. Pain. That ever-present fear.

Her lips shaped his name as he reached her side and drew her to him with an arm around her neck. She flinched at the rough move. He ignored it. "What happened?" he asked the cop and it was a challenge.

The man looked to Talin. "Is this the friend you said you called?"

Talin nodded. "Yes."

Clay let the lie go. They'd discuss it later. "I'm Clay."

"Max." He held out a hand and as they shook, Clay saw the detective note everything about him, from his jeans to his sweatshirt to the fact that he needed a haircut. "You'll look after her," the man said as they broke contact.

Clay's anger quieted at that statement, turned assessing. "What do I need to protect her from?" It looked like Max was the only remaining cop, so whatever had happened, either it had been minor or it had happened long enough ago for the forensics people to have come and gone. Which meant Talin should have called him hours ago.

His protective fury grew anew as Max laid out the bare facts. "Unless someone's just getting their kicks terrorizing her, Talin's doing more damage than she thinks."

"I need to know what you've got, so I can make sure the bastards don't come anywhere near her." Clay could feel her heart beating as wildly as a panicked bird's. But he didn't release her and she didn't fight to be let go. The leopard calmed.

Max paused. "Officially, I can't give you anything. But you're one of Lucas's top men, aren't you?"

Clay wasn't surprised the cop had made him. DarkRiver was a power in San Francisco and it was Enforcement's job to know that. Mostly because they were Psy stooges, but sometimes for other reasons—like making sure justice was done despite Psy interference.

He made a mental note to ask his contacts about Max, but his instincts said the man stood on the right side of the line. "Yes. I'm with DarkRiver."

The detective nodded, as if reaching a decision. "Then we need to have an unofficial chat after I finish up today. Any-place safe from prying eyes and ears?"

"Joe's Bar." Isolated near the edge of DarkRiver territory and frequented exclusively by cats, wolves, and their invited guests, it was close to airtight. "You know where it is?" At Max's nod, he said, "Leave the recorder at home."

"Funny that. I have a reputation for losing my recorder." A deadpan statement. "I'll see you around eight. Talin—you need me, you call."

"She won't be needing you." Clay felt his arm tighten, sensed her panic, but couldn't control the primitive animal im-pulse. "We'll see you at the bar."

Talin waited until Max had driven away before tugging at Clay's arm. "Let me go."

He leaned down until his lips brushed her ear. "I told you to stop flinching." And then he bit her. A slow, painless nip but there were definitely teeth involved.

Shocked, she couldn't speak for almost a minute, during which he hustled her across the road and into his large all-terrain vehicle. Its street name was the Tank, though it was far sleeker and faster than the outmoded war vehicle.

She finally found her voice after he dumped her bag in back and slid into the driver's seat. "You bit me!"

He threw her a scowling look. "I gave you plenty of warn-ing. Put on your belt."

She was already doing it—out of habit, not because of his order. "You can't go around biting people!"

He maneuvered the car out into the street. It didn't surprise her in the least when he stuck to the manual controls, despite the fact that they were on a road embedded with the computronic chips that allowed automatic navigation. But he did engage the hover-drive, retracting the wheels so they skimmed soundlessly over the fog-shrouded streets.

"Clay?" she said when he seemed to be ignoring her.

"How did they get into your apartment?"

The shift in topic didn't surprise her in the least, not when she knew how protective he was. "I don't know. The building's about average in terms of security, but I put in a top-of-the-line system on my door." Even then, she rarely slept all the way through the night.

"Only on the door?"

"Yes. Why— Oh, the windows. I figured being on the eighth floor was enough."

"Not against Psy telekinetics."

"Psy?" She laughed. "Far as I know, teleporting is a major ability. I can't see the Psy wasting that kind of a resource on terrorizing an ordinary human."

"Hardly ordinary," he muttered. "But there are other ways to enter through a window. Any changeling with climbing abilities, or wings, could have done it."

She hadn't considered that and now it appeared a glaring oversight. "The blood hadn't stopped dripping when I arrived." Shivering, she hugged her arms around herself.

"Was it warm?"

"What?"

"The blood."

She almost threw up. "What the hell kind of question is that?"

"If they used fresh—"

"Stop!" she interrupted. "Stop the car!"

He came to a rocking halt.

Sliding back the door, she leaned out and retched. Since the only thing she'd eaten over the past twenty-four hours was that burger with Clay, there was nothing much to throw up. But her stomach didn't know that. It cramped for what felt like hours, flooding her mouth with the ugly taste of bile and tearing her insides apart.

When it stopped at last, she found Clay by her side, one hand in her hair, the other holding a bottle of water. "Drink."

With her throat feeling like someone had taken a hacksaw

to it, there was no way she was going to refuse. The water proved ice-cold. "Where?" she rasped.

He understood. "Iced bottles. All of us carry them—changeling soldiers burn a lot of energy. The water's infused with minerals and other stuff."

She nodded and took another delicious gulp. "Tastes good."

He tugged back her head with the hand he had in her hair. "What the hell was that about?"

She couldn't bring herself to tell him the complete truth but she forced herself to tell one. Her deadly little secret didn't need to be revealed. Not yet. Perhaps not ever. "I told you, I hate violence," she reminded him. "You went too far with that talk of warm blood."

His hand clenched in her hair before he released it, a penetrating expression on his face. "You had no trouble with discussing the dead boys."

She clutched at her stomach. "It's psychological." She stood her ground, knowing if she gave even an inch, Clay would walk straight over her. "Can we go? There's . . ." She nodded at the people peering out the windows of a nearby apartment building.

He ignored her request. "Why didn't the Larkspurs take you to someone who could've helped you get a handle on these things?"

"They did." She swung her legs back into the car and, closing her eyes, leaned her head against the seat. "I'm too screwed up to fix."

The passenger door slid shut and a second later, she felt Clay get back into the driver's seat. "That's a load of crap," he said once he had them moving again. "You never were good at handling blood. You almost passed out that time I cut my knee on a fence."

Her gorge rose at even that harmless memory. Taking another drink, she focused on the piercing sparks of light exploding behind her eyelids. "I got worse. After."

Silence.

Then, "After me or after *him*?"

"Does it matter?" She realized she'd drained the water bottle.

"I guess not. You're still as fucked up."

It hurt. "Yeah."

He swore. "Jesus, Talin. Where's your spine?"

That made her eyes snap open. "You're insulting me to get me to react? What the hell kind of a bedside manner is that?" Outraged, she chucked the empty bottle into the pristine backseat. "I almost threw up my guts and you—"

"When did you become such a scared little mouse?" His tone was hard, his eyes trained on the road.

"Trauma, Clay! I was traumatized. It had an effect."

"So was I," he said, merciless. "I didn't deal by sticking my head in the sand."

She knew immediately that he wasn't talking about the killing. "You saved me."

His laughter was harsh. "Years too late."

"No." She had to reach him, had to make him see. "Orrin never tried to choke me before." He'd wanted to watch the life leave her eyes, just like he'd done with those other girls he'd buried.

"He abused you, Talin. Hurt you, touched you, made you suffer through things no little girl should have to endure. So what if he saved the brutal murder for your eighth birthday! I fucking should have stopped him long before that!"

"I never told you," she cried. "And you were a child, too."

"I should have known. I'm a cat—I could smell him on you."

"He was my foster parent. I remember you telling me you could smell their parents on all the kids."

He didn't respond. She stared at the dark stubble along his jaw, at the ebony silk of his hair. He was so close and yet she didn't dare touch him. "Clay?" Talk to me, please, she wanted to beg. He had always spoken to her, even if he didn't to anyone else.

His fingers clenched on the steering wheel. "Tell me about your life with the Larkspurs."

Relieved, she took a deep, shuddering breath. "They're farmers, all of them. Well, Dixie isn't, but she's a farmer's wife. Already has two babies. It's what she wanted."

"You like Dixie."

"Yes." She smiled. "She's the baby of the family and so sweet, so gentle. She used to follow me around and hug me every day, as if— I like Dixie."

"The others?"

"Tanner and Sam run various parts of the farm. It's a huge operation. Samara—Sam's twin and older by a minute—organizes the business end of things. Ma and Pa Larkspur supervise everyone."

"They sound like a happy family." His eyes were cat bright when he glanced at her. "So why are you still stuck in that room, watching me tear Orrin apart?"

She should've known it wouldn't be that easy to escape the past. "I tried to get better. I pretended I was. But I never did and I don't know why." Though after her recent slew of medical tests, she could guess at some of it. "Where are you taking me?"

"Somewhere safe."

She watched the city retreat behind them. "Where?" she insisted.

"My lair."

Her heart stopped. "I thought you didn't take strangers there."

"I'm making an exception."

It almost made her want to smile. Except . . . "Don't. These people who are after me, they're probably the ones taking the kids. They could follow and hurt you and your pack."

He laughed and it was a deep masculine sound she felt in the innermost core of her body, a place no one had ever touched. "We're not some minor pack you can blink and miss. DarkRiver controls San Francisco and the surrounding areas. We're also allied to the wolves. No one enters our forests without our knowledge."

"These people are smart."

"Are you saying we animals aren't?"

"Don't pull that racial crap on me," she said, scowling. "Or I'll tell you what I really think of big cats who like to growl and bite."

Clay felt his lips curve despite himself. "Meow."

To his surprise, a sound that was almost a giggle escaped Talin's lips. "Idiot."

And that suddenly, she was his Tally again. Sweet, funny, and strong. So damn strong. The only human being who had ever stood up to him and won. "What happened to you, Tally?"

The laughter seeped out of the air. "I broke."

Talin noticed the flowers the second she entered the low-level aerie Clay called his lair. Outwardly, it appeared nothing more than a forgotten tree house lost in the spreading branches of a heavily leafed tree. Inside, it proved wide and clean, with a retractable ladder that led up into a second level invisible from the outside.

"There's a third level, too." His voice gave away nothing. "I built it so it could be isolated from the ground at a second's notice. You'll sleep up there."

"Oh." She couldn't get her mind off the beautiful, *feminine* flower arrangement. "Nice flowers."

It seemed to her that his expression softened a fraction when he looked that way. "From Faith. She said I needed color in this place."

Talin's fingernails dug into her palms as he named the woman who had been allowed to meddle in his lair—in the lair of a man she'd known as a boy who rarely let anyone close. Even now, flowers aside, the stark masculinity of the place was undeniable. Everything was in shades of earth, with only occasional splashes of forest green and white, from the rug on the floor to the large, flat cushions that seemed to function as Clay's version of sofas. It made sense, she thought. His leopard probably much preferred to curl up on the cushions.

The image of him in cat form made her fingers tingle in sensory memory. "You have visitors often?"

"No."

So, this Faith was special. Folding her arms, she watched him as he pulled down the ladder, stepped on the first rung, and threw her bag up to the second level. When he stepped back down, his expression was one of grim determination. "Now, tell me the truth."

Her stomach was suddenly full of a thousand butterflies. "The truth?"

His eyes turned so dark, they were close to black. "At first I thought it was because you'd grown up, but that's not it."

She swallowed. "What?" *He couldn't know. How could he know?*

"Your scent." He closed the distance between them, a graceful, dangerous predator with a mind like a blade. Tempered. Honed. "You smell wrong, Talin."

"How can I smell wrong?" Dread morphed into honest confusion. "I smell like me."

He moved around her to her back. She stood her ground, though irrational fear struck again. Memories of blood and—

"Ouch!" She tugged her hair out of his grasp. "What do you think you're doing?"

"Snapping you out of panic."

Her answer stuck in her throat as she felt the heat of his breath whisper along the curve of her neck. He was no longer touching any part of her, but she couldn't move. Her body remembered his. He'd been the only one who had touched her in affection before the Larkspurs. But her adoptive family occupied a far different space in her heart than Clay. He was a deep, intrinsic part of her, a part she both feared and craved.

"You smell of woman, of fear, of *you*, but there's an ugliness below the surface, a badness."

Her soul curled into a tight self-protective ball. "I revolt you."

"No, it's not that kind of badness. It's just wrong, shouldn't be there." He put his hands on her hips. They were big. Heavy. "Scared, Tally?"

She fought her shiver. "You know I am." Her body might remember his warmth and protectiveness, but it also remembered his capacity for the most bloody violence.

His fingers pressed down a fraction before he released her. She waited for him to face her again. When he did, she found herself looking into eyes no longer the dark green of man but the paler gold-green of leopard.

Unprepared for the shift, she took a stumbling step backward. Her palms hit the wall.

"Why the wrongness in your scent, Talin?"

"I don't know."

"Try again."

She was about to repeat her answer when she realized it would be a lie. Her mouth snapped shut. "As long as you can live with it, what does it matter?"

"Tell me."

He was a barricade in front of her, an impenetrable mass of stubborn male muscle. Instead of increasing her fear, the display of unvarnished dominance made her anger spike. "No," she said. "Stop being a bully."

His face reflected surprise. "Wrong answer." He came closer.

She went to duck out of the way but he'd already moved to trap her against the wall, his hands palms down on either side of her body. She felt her heart rate speed up, her own palms start to sweat. "Intimidation is hardly going to make me more inclined to tell you."

He leaned down until his face filled her vision. A long, still pause. "Boo."

She jumped at the husky whisper and hated herself for it. "Not nice."

"According to you, I'm a rampaging monster."

"No, I never—" She shook her head. "I can't help what my mind feels, Clay."

"Why?"

"Why not?" she snapped. "It's my coping mechanism. Deal with it."

"It's nothing but a pile of shit." He pressed even closer, the heat of him an almost physical caress. "And baby, if you're coping, then I'm Mother Teresa. Now, what the fuck is wrong with you?"

"I'm sick!" she yelled. "Dying! There, happy now?"

CHAPTER 8

Clay went so motionless she couldn't even hear him breathe. Her frustrated anger disappeared, to be replaced by a sense of slow horror. She hadn't meant to tell him, didn't want him motivated by pity. "Just forget it. It has no bearing on anything."

He growled at her again and this time it was for real, a low rumbling sound that made her clutch at the wall, even as something long buried inside of her stirred in wary interest. "Stop it," she said, pushing at his chest. It was like trying to shift a steel wall. He was hard, warm . . . beautiful. "Clay."

"Forget it?" His voice wasn't quite human. *"Forget it?"*

She wanted to stroke him, had some mad idea it would calm him. Dropping her hands, she pressed her palms back against the wall. "There's nothing you can do," she stated in the face of his aggression. "Remember when I used to get sick as a kid?"

Black clouds rolled across his face. "I remember."

"Not that kind of sick," she said quickly, knowing he was recalling the secrets she'd kept in a childish effort to protect him from her shame. "I used to faint, and sometimes I'd have odd patches of lost memory, when usually I remember everything?"

He nodded. "But you always remembered those things in a few days' time."

"I never grew out of that." She was referring to the diagnosis of the harried doctor who had performed her mandatory childhood health checks. "It's gotten worse year by year. When I lose consciousness, I stay that way for longer periods. The memories sometimes don't come back at all."

His eyes went even more impossibly cat. "Who told you you were dying?"

"Three different specialists." She had gone to them four months ago, after losing most of a day to a fugue state. Things had only gone downhill from there. So much so that, after she found Jonquil, she planned to resign from her position at Shine. "They all agreed my brain's not working properly. It's almost as if I have something eating away at my cells."

"You see an M-Psy?"

She shook her head.

"Why not? They're no humanitarians, but M-Psy can diagnose things far more accurately than normal doctors."

"I didn't want to—they rub me the wrong way." Her skin began to creep with dread every time she came near an M-Psy. "The other doctors were certain the Psy probably wouldn't be able to help anyway."

"We'll see."

She didn't bother to argue—she could almost feel her brain dying, step by excruciating step. It wasn't something anyone could stop. "Our first focus has to be on finding Jon," she said. On that one point, she would not compromise. "I can wait."

The skin along his jawline strained white over bone. "How long before you go critical?"

"It's hard to predict." Not technically a lie. The doctors' estimates had ranged from six to eight months. None of the three had differed in their actual diagnosis: *Unknown neural malignancy with potential to cause extensive cell death. Risk of eventual fatal infarction—one hundred percent.* "Even if I knew the date of my death to the day, Jon comes first." Not even Clay could sway her from that goal.

He pushed off the wall, temper evident in every rigid line of his body. "Go set yourself up on the third floor."

She stayed in place. "Do I look like a dog? 'Go set yourself up on the third floor,' " she mimicked, dangerously aware she was provoking the leopard.

"You look like an exhausted, idiotic woman," he snapped. "Would you rather I yell at you for the next hour like I want to?"

"Why would you yell?"

"You should've come to me years ago." He turned from her, hands fisted, and she knew they were no longer talking about the disease eating at her from the inside out. "I might have been able to forgive the girl for running."

But he couldn't forgive the woman. "And the men?" she asked, knowing she was ringing a death knell over any hope of a renewed friendship between them. "Can you forgive me that?"

He was silent. The most crystal clear of answers. But in place of sadness, all she felt was a blinding fury. It was the last thing she would have expected—what right did she have to be angry with him? But she was. So damn *angry* that she left the room, afraid of what she might say.

CHAPTER 9

His name was Jonquil Duchslaya but most of his friends called him Jon. Talin sometimes called him Johnny D. But the last time he'd messed up and gotten busted, she'd pulled him out and then she'd called him Jonquil Alexi Duchslaya.

"One more time and we're through." Her eyes had been black ice as they stood outside the justice office. "I won't pay your shoplifting fine and I sure as hell won't turn up as a character witness and convince the judge to give you probation instead of jail time."

He'd flashed her a smile, certain she was just blowing off some steam. "Aw, come on—"

"Shut it." She'd never before used that tone on him. Shocked, he'd obeyed. "Three chances, Jonquil, that's all I give. That's all I have to give. I don't have time to waste on lazy thieves—"

"Hey!"

"—who can't be bothered to respect my rules," she had finished, sounding nothing like the gentle, encouraging Talin he had come to know. "Once more and we're done. You can start collecting jailhouse tattoos."

He'd flinched at the pitiless reminder of what had become of the rest of his family. Every single member, male and female, had ended up behind bars. Now they were all dead. "You're supposed to be nice to us. That's your job." She worked for some big-deal nicey-nice foundation.

"No. My job is to be your friend." Her eyes had blazed with an emotion he'd never before felt directed at him. "I'm not your nanny or nursemaid. I made sure you had a safe place to stay and study. I made sure you were out of reach of your old gang. I've done my job. It's up to you now."

"I don't have to take this shit," he'd said. "I can take care of myself." He had been on the streets for years before she walked into his life.

"I love you, Johnny D. I want you to make it."

Embarrassed at how her words had made him feel, he'd smirked. "So that's it. You want a piece of young meat. What the hell—you're not bad for an old piece of ass."

"I love you," she'd repeated in that strong, gentle voice of hers. "You're one of mine. I will fight for you. But you have to fight, too."

It had almost broken him. "I don't need or want your love! So you can shove it."

That was the last time he'd seen Talin. *They* had taken him a week after he had run away from the home Talin had found for him. He didn't even know why he'd done it. That foster family had been nice to him. No one had tried to steal his stuff, no one had tried to touch him, and no one had used him as a punching bag. But full of stupid pride, he'd run.

Now he lay in this lightless cage, able to hear the screams of other children. They hadn't come for him yet, but they would. And it didn't matter what he'd told himself over the endless hours of captivity, he knew he'd scream.

He was fourteen years old and he'd told the only person who had ever loved him that he didn't want or need her. A tear streaked down the angular barely man planes of his face. "Please, Talin," he whispered. "Please find me."

CHAPTER 10

Talin woke from an inadvertent nap with a jerk, her heart beating triple time. After almost exploding at Clay in inexplicable rage, she had headed upstairs to put down her stuff, then collapsed on the bed to try to get her emotions under some sort of control. She couldn't remember anything after that.

Afraid the disease had struck again, she glanced at the clock. To her relief, she'd only been out ten minutes at most. A nap, that's all it had been. Getting up, she staggered to the bathroom and threw some cold water on her face.

The eyes that looked back at her from the mirror above the sink were haunted, bruised. She wished she had the magical power to wipe away all the badness, all the evil in the world, and make everything right. A stupid wish. But that didn't mean she couldn't hope. Her resolve firmed. As of today, she would act with the absolute and total belief that Jonquil was still alive. "I'm going to bring you home, Johnny D. Hold on for me."

Decision made, she got moving, aware if she delayed too long, Clay would come searching. And though that violent surge of anger at him had passed, her emotions were a turbulent stew where he was concerned. Nevertheless, fifteen minutes later, she had put away her things, taken a shower, and brushed her wet hair back into a ponytail while admiring the leafy morning view from the balcony of her third-floor aerie.

It was time.

Wiping her hands on her jeans, she went to open the trapdoor. Her eye fell on the large bed as she passed and she bent to smooth out the marks she'd made on it during her nap. Her fingers lingered—she might be human, with senses far less acute than Clay's, but she could smell the earthy masculinity of his scent in this room, in this bed. It was frighteningly easy to imagine the muscular strength of him sprawled over the white sheets, arrogant and assured of his right to dominate that intimate territory.

The image caused an odd, melting sensation in the pit of her stomach. She blinked, shock rooting her to the spot. This slow curl of need in her body, it was something wholly new. Her previous sexual partners had been . . . nothing. Faceless, nameless bodies. None had touched her emotions, much less given her pleasure.

When she'd admitted her senseless promiscuity to her long-ago counselor, she had expected censure, but the other woman had simply nodded. "You're punishing yourself," she'd said. "Punishment is meant to hurt. And it does hurt, doesn't it?"

The counselor had been right and though Talin had been unable to trust her enough to create a long-term relationship, the woman had helped her find her way out of that morass of pain. She had never felt as alone or as cold as she did—or had done—during sex. At no time had she ever experienced anything like this dark lick of heat inside of her.

Her face flushed, mortification temporarily wiping away everything else. She was aware of her breasts swelling, her blood rushing to places it didn't normally caress with such primal heat. "No." She couldn't be falling victim to lust. Not for Clay.

He was repulsed by her.

The reminder threw ice water over her incipient feelings. She was glad. Thinking of Clay in that way scared her. Despite their years apart, despite how angry he was with her—and even despite her own inexplicable rage at him—she thought of him as her friend, the only friend she trusted without reservation.

She didn't want to destroy that precious relationship. And sex destroyed everything and everyone once it got in the way.

She was willing to admit that her view of sex might be skewed, distorted by what had been done to her during childhood. But one truth was indisputable: lust never lasted. Then it was, "Adios and hope I never see you again." The rare relationships that survived were those like the Larkspurs had—warm, stable, friendly, without the overwhelming rush of lust. But that wasn't a viable option for her and Clay.

He was too intense, too deeply passionate. The woman who took him on would have to be fearless, with enough strength of will to withstand his autocratic nature and enough heart to love him no matter how dark his dreams. Her hands clenched so tight, she felt her nails cut into skin. The idea of Clay with another woman—

Biting off a curse, she pulled up the trapdoor and headed down.

Clay was on the second level, in the small kitchenette to the left. "Eat." He thrust a plate of food at her and pulled out a chair at the nearby table.

A second ago, she would've sworn her stomach was too twisted up to eat. But now, it rumbled. She took the seat. "Thanks." He had made her toast and eggs. Simple enough. Except for the muffin that accompanied it. Her appetite dulled. "Faith?" She picked up the offending piece of baking, barely able to stop herself from crushing it to a pulp.

He put down his own plate and grabbed a seat opposite her. "Tamsyn," he said, eyes cat-sharp. "She sneaks in here and leaves things in the cooler."

She couldn't stand the suspense. Stupid muffin. "Who is she?"

"Nathan's mate."

That cut off her simmering jealousy midstep. "And Faith?"

His lips curved a little and she suddenly felt very warm. "Careful, Tally. Your claws are showing."

"I'm human," she retorted, knowing she shouldn't be so happy at the sign of a thaw in his earlier mood, but she was. "The best I can do is grow my nails." She stared at her stubby nails. "And I'm not exactly good at that." He'd wait forever if he thought she would ask about Faith again. She shoved some eggs into her mouth.

Clay had already finished his toast and now took a sip of coffee. "Faith is Vaughn's mate," he said, looking at her over his cup. "Coffee?"

She let him pour her a cup, feeling silly. "Nathan and Vaughn are your friends?"

"Yes. So are Faith and Tammy."

It shook her. The Clay she'd known had been her only friend, and she had been his. But now he was part of a pack and she was an outsider. "I'm glad for you," she whispered, even as an ugly possessiveness bared its teeth inside of her. "It must be nice."

His response was a grunt. "Eat."

She ate, cleaning her plate far quicker than she would have believed possible when she first came downstairs. The muffin proved delicious. "Tamsyn's a good cook."

"How about you?"

Surprised by the question, she answered honestly. "Weird, but I like cooking. I used to do it with Pa Larkspur."

"*Pa* Larkspur?"

She smiled. "Don't be so chauvinistic. He's the best cook in the county. His baskets bring in more money than any others at the picnic auctions."

"Jesus. Baskets? Picnic? Just how country is the Nest?"

"Very." His horrified expression made her laugh. "Clay, you live in a tree. I don't think you should throw stones."

"I guess the corn would provide some cover when grown," he muttered. "Nowhere to climb or create a lair though. Not unless you build a house." He almost shuddered.

She'd never thought about the farm from a predator's point of view. "Well, yeah. But there is one thing you might like."

He raised an eyebrow.

"There are caves." She had spent a lot of time in them as a teenager, pushing away the love the Larkspurs tried to give her. She had never talked back, never created trouble at home. She'd simply disappeared to where they couldn't find her and she couldn't hurt them. "They're deep enough underground that it doesn't affect the farming operation, but the area's riddled with them."

A gleam of interest lit the dark green of his eyes. "They ever been mapped?"

"I didn't find any records when I researched them for a school project," she said, "but there have to be maps."

He laid his arm on the table. "Why?"

"Because"—she leaned forward—"I'm certain the caves are man-made. They're almost like proper tunnels in places."

Interest turned to intrigue, the forest green getting brighter. "Your town have a big changeling presence?"

Catching his line of thought, she shook her head. "A small horse clan, and an owl one—predatory but not particularly dominant. They always used to vote me in as captain when they split us into teams for gym class." And she was no superathlete.

"You're a strong personality," he said, surprising her. "Most nonpredatories would automatically see you as dominant, and as for predatory changelings, they decide according to the individual. Your owl schoolmates must've figured you were tougher than them."

"Huh." But it made sense. The owls had been scholars from a nice family, while she had been very hard-case. "Anyway, the horses and owls can't have dug the caves. They hate being shut in."

"That's it?"

"Yep."

"No snakes?"

She almost spewed coffee all over the table. "There are snake changelings?"

"Why wouldn't there be?" He refilled her cup. "They're rare, but they exist."

"You think a bunch of snakes created those caves?" She shivered, recalling all those times she'd been alone in them.

"*Changeling* snakes, Talin." A reprimand. "No more or less animal than I am."

She bit her lower lip, feeling about five years old. But this was Clay, so she admitted the truth. "I can't help it. Leopards are dangerous, beautiful. Snakes are creepy."

"I think the snake changelings would disagree." He leaned back in his chair, a predator at ease in his territory.

She felt his foot touch the rung of her chair, knew it to be a possessive act. But she was having too much fun to call him on it. "Are they as human?" She scrunched up her nose at his scowl. "You know what I mean. When you walk, it's with this feline grace. What do they take from their animal?"

His lips curved again, full, tempting. "Calling me graceful, Tally?"

"I'll call you vain in a minute." But he *was* graceful, lethally so.

Both his feet touched her chair now. "Snakes are very . . . other. They tend to scare people on a visceral level, even when in human form. But that makes them no less human."

"No," she agreed, thinking of how the world judged her children.

"A long time ago, I saw one after she shifted. She had black-diamond scales that shimmered like an oil slick does in the rain—full of rainbows."

The image was startlingly beautiful. "If they were there, under the farm," she asked, "why would they leave?"

"A hundred things—maybe the colony disbanded or they decided to migrate elsewhere." He shrugged. "Now, tell me about the dead children."

That quickly, their little interlude was over. No more talk about mysterious changeling snakes and the quaint beauty of corn-farming country. But his feet remained on the rung of her chair. Taking strength from that, she began at the beginning. "I left the Larkspurs at age sixteen to enroll in a scholarship program at NYU." Somewhat to her shock, she had proven very bright once given a chance, so much so that she'd graduated the purgatory of high school two years ahead of schedule.

Clay sat with such feline stillness, she couldn't even see him breathe. "You never gave the Larkspurs a shot, did you?"

"No." The simplest and most painful of truths. "The scholarship was one provided by the Shine Foundation." She looked up to see if he recognized the name.

"Human backed," he said. "Financed by donations from a number of wealthy philanthropists."

"Its aim," she picked up, "is to support bright but underprivileged children who might never otherwise have a chance to shine. That's what the brochure says and I guess they really follow it. All the kids I look after are disadvantaged in some way."

"What did you study?"

She folded her arms. "Child psych and social work."

"You hated the social workers."

"Ironic, huh?" She made a rueful face. "I thought I might be able to do a better job. But I never got into the system. I graduated at twenty-one, and was offered a position in the foundation's street program."

He didn't push her to get to the point, and for that, she was grateful. She had to approach the horror obliquely, wasn't sure she could survive full-frontal exposure. "We help get kids off the street and into school or training. Devraj—the director—makes sure there's no corruption, no favoritism."

"Sounds very worthy." Open cynicism.

Her hackles rose. "It is! The foundation does so much, helps so many." He had no right to mock them. "I work with the eleven-to-sixteen age group."

"Tough crowd."

"Tell me about it." So proud, so unwilling to accept the helping hand she offered. "I get all sorts. Runaways, nice but poor kids, gang members who want out."

"What's your success rate?"

"About seventy percent." The other thirty, the lost ones, they broke her heart, but she kept going. She couldn't afford not to or the ones she *could* help would suffer.

"You said Mickey was yours."

She gave a jerky nod. "So was Diana. She was found this week, around the same time as Iain. He belonged to one of my colleagues in San Francisco. Thirteen and already able to speak seven languages—can you imagine what he might've become?"

"Three Shine kids? Interesting coincidence."

"Not really. The killers and the foundation work in the same pool—marginalized and vulnerable children."

He nodded. "True."

"And the other seven Max told me about were scattered across the country. None were Shine scholars."

"So there's no specific connection to San Francisco. Why come here?"

"To set up Jonquil. He's fourteen, ex-gang. This was a new start." Her voice broke.

Getting up, Clay walked around the table and tugged her to her feet. The simple contact destroyed her center of gravity even as it gave her courage. "Clay."

"What happened to force you to come to me?"

The turbulence of his renewed anger was a wall between them. "I finally confirmed you really were here two weeks ago but—" *No,* she thought. Enough. Clay deserved absolute honesty, even if that meant she had to rip open every painful scar. "Jon disappeared." And all she'd been able to think was that she needed Clay, the same thought she'd had a thousand times before. Except this time, he had been within reach.

He curved his hand around the side of her neck. "Why are you sure the killers have him? One of your feelings, Tally?"

A knot in her throat at the way he understood her without words. Nobody else ever had. "Yeah." Instead of fighting the blatant possessiveness of his touch, she found herself leaning into it, soaking up the heated strength of him. "We had a fight before he ran away. I lost my temper, Clay." She'd just had another small sign of her medical degeneration, had been so scared she'd run out of time to help that bright, hurt boy. "I took out my frustration on him."

"Teenagers are good at getting on your last nerve." Pragmatic. Oddly comforting. "So he was pissed at you?"

"Yes, but my gut says he would've contacted me by now if he had been able to—even if was to flip me off. He was no angel, but he was mine." The things that boy had survived, the things he had done and still come out sane, it humbled her.

Clay's hand tightened on her neck, warm, solid . . . suddenly dangerous. "When did this boy disappear?"

She didn't move, though her mind wanted to panic at her vulnerability to this predator. "Four to seven days ago," she said, trying to focus. "I traced him after the foster family reported him missing and had fairly reliable sightings for the next three days, then nothing. It's like he vanished into thin air."

Clay's head lifted without warning. "We've got visitors."

An odd kind of fear clamped over her chest and she could feel her heartbeat accelerate. "Your pack?" People who mattered to him, but wouldn't necessarily like her. Probably wouldn't.

"Yes." Clay released her. "Wait here. And, Tally, try not to hyperventilate." He was gone through the trapdoor in the blink of an eye, moving with inhuman speed—because, of course, he wasn't human. He was changeling. He'd heard her racing heartbeat, smelled the sweat beading along her spine. Sometimes, she thought, being human sucked.

Unable to sit still, she cleared the table and was about to wipe it down when Clay called for her. Taking a deep breath and feeling very vulnerable, she went down, not looking up until she was standing beside Clay. As it was, she didn't know which of the two strangers shocked her more.

CHAPTER 11

Even at rest, leaning against the wall, the male—tall, dark, startlingly handsome—exuded a sense of lethal danger. Once you added in the savage clawlike markings on the right side of his face, well, it made her want to take a wary step back and hide behind Clay. Except she had a feeling that her long-ago playmate posed far more of a threat to her than this watchful stranger with eyes a paler shade of green than Clay's.

Still shaky, she turned her attention to the woman who stood in the loose circle formed by the male's arms. Black hair in a braid, skin a deep honey, and eyes of midnight with pinpricks of white. "You're Psy." Not just any Psy. A cardinal. Those eyes . . .

"I'm Sascha." Her expression was guarded. She turned slightly. "My mate, Lucas."

She recognized both names. Lucas Hunter was DarkRiver's alpha, Sascha Duncan the daughter of Councilor Nikita Duncan. Talin had heard reports of Sascha's defection from the Psy, but hadn't credited them. "Nice to meet you," she said at last, very aware that neither Sascha nor Lucas had made any overtures of friendliness.

Clay shifted to lay his hand against her spine. She went

stiff without meaning to and knew everyone had noticed. But he didn't drop his hand, and for that, she was grateful. It was obvious his packmates didn't approve of her. Usually she would've shrugged off their reaction, but this time it mattered. Because these people were important to Clay.

"Talin's been told she's sick," he said to Sascha. "Can you check her out?"

Sascha's eyes widened. It disconcerted Talin to see such open emotion on the face of a Psy, but not as much as when Sascha spoke and she heard the warmth and affection in it. "Clay, I'm not an M-Psy. I'm not sure—"

"Try."

Lucas raised an eyebrow. "She gets mean when you give her orders." Though his tone was amused, his eyes never moved off Talin.

She leaned more heavily into Clay's hand.

"Please."

Talin was still trying to swallow her shock at the word that had come out of Clay's mouth when Sascha stepped out of her mate's embrace. "Out. Both of you," she said, imperious and clearly sure of her power. "I need to be alone with Talin."

Lucas dropped a kiss in the curve of his mate's neck, the action speaking of an intimacy that ran deep and true. Talin wondered what Clay's lips would feel like against her own neck. She swallowed, inner muscles clenching. That was when Lucas raised his head, breaking the spell. "Come on," he said to Clay. "I have to talk to you about something anyway."

Clay scowled down at Talin before leaving. "Cooperate."

"I take it you didn't agree to let a strange Psy poke and prod at you?" Sascha's tone was wry, but Talin didn't drop her guard. This woman had no loyalty to her.

"No."

"Would you like to tell me what he's worried about?"

Since Clay already knew, she saw no harm in sharing the information. "An unknown disease is messing things up, maybe killing off cells, in my brain. I've had the diagnosis, such as it is, confirmed three times over."

The cardinal's face grew pensive. "Will you allow me to see if I can help?"

"He trusts you." Another flood of jealousy. It made her feel small, petty, but she couldn't stop it—she had never been rational where Clay was concerned. "You're Pack."

Sascha sensed Talin's ambivalence, understood it. "Yes." Clay was a leopard who chose the shadows even in the tight circle of the sentinels, but when it came down to it, they were tied together by a bond of deep, unflinching loyalty. "Yes," she repeated.

The curvy brunette across from her bowed her head in a wary nod. "All right."

But try as she might, Sascha found she could do less than nothing. "You have a shield."

"What?" Talin frowned. "But I'm human."

"True." The lack of anything beyond the most basic shields was what made humans the weakest of the three races. That in mind, Sascha tried another push. "But not only do you have shields," she said after being violently rebuffed, "they're airtight."

"I have no idea why that would be."

Sascha raised her hand. "If you don't mind . . ." The other woman didn't pull away when Sascha went to touch her cheek. Often with changelings, contact made all the difference. But not with Talin. Breaking the connection, Sascha stepped back, her instincts telling her Talin didn't like people too close. Yet it appeared she had already given Clay skin privileges. Intriguing.

"I'm no expert on human mental processes," she said, "but your shields are, without a doubt, unusual. For some reason, your mind has learned to protect itself." Her heart tripped a beat as her own words penetrated. She *had* heard of these kinds of shields before. They had been noted in an addendum to an old *Psy-Med Journal* article.

Conclusion: Low incidence in human population. No genetic components.

The latter finding was probably why the Council hadn't gone about eliminating the bearers of such shields. That and the fact that regardless of what the Psy did or didn't do, these particular shields would always occur in a certain percentage of the human population. "The shields," she continued, keeping her tone very gentle, "are so strong, you must've begun constructing them during childhood."

"Why—" Talin froze.

Sascha could no more ignore the waves of emotion coming off her than she could stop breathing. Being an E-Psy meant she had the capacity to sense and neutralize hurtful emotion. It also meant she couldn't just stand by when someone was in that much pain. Now she gathered up Talin's self-hatred, revulsion, and anger—such incredible anger—in her psychic arms and absorbed it inside of herself. She had the gift to turn those destructive emotions harmless, but it hurt.

A few seconds later, Talin gave her a startled look. "What are you?" Not an accusation but the kind of innocent question a child might ask.

It surprised Sascha, given what she suspected this woman had endured. "An empath." She explained what that meant. "I'm sorry if I intruded—I forget to ask sometimes." The gift was too powerful, too instinctive.

"What a pure gift." Talin's face filled with something close to wonder. "Does that mean you'll never be evil?"

"I'm as vulnerable to negative emotions as anyone," Sascha admitted, "but the empathy won't let them fester inside me."

"Like I have?" Talin's gaze was direct. "You don't like me very much, do you?"

Sascha felt a moment's disorientation at the blunt clarity of that question. A sense of shame followed—after everything she had learned in the past year, it was criminal that she'd automatically equated human with weak. Talin was nothing if not strong. "It's not a case of disliking you. I don't know you—how can I judge you?"

"But?" Talin pushed, holding her body in a way that reminded Sascha of the vulnerable pride of the young males in the pack. However, Talin was no child—her emotions were too aged, too flavored with time.

"Clay is one of mine." Even Sascha was surprised at the depth of protectiveness in her tone, an echo of what she so often heard in Lucas's voice when he spoke of Pack. "He's been choosing to walk alone more and more, and it worries me. I was hoping his growing friendship with Faith would change things, bring him back to us."

Talin swallowed, at once resentful of Sascha's right to care about Clay and almost violently glad that he had friends who loved him with such fierce determination. "But now I'm pulling him under."

"Clay leads, rarely follows." The cardinal's words were light, her eyes solemn. "But whatever you are to him, whatever demons you waken, they're already blackening his emotions."

Talin wanted to defend herself but knew Sascha was right—the things she brought with her were the very things Clay had left in the past. "I'm sorry."

"No, you're not." Sascha's gaze was piercing.

Talin felt her jaw tighten. "Don't spy on my emotions."

"I don't have to." The other woman tilted her head a fraction to the side. "You should see the way you watch him. Such hunger, Talin."

Color threatened to fill her cheeks. "Whatever is between us is our business. You have no right to interfere."

Instead of being furious, Sascha smiled, a smile filled with withheld laughter. "Pack is One. Pack is family. Interference is a fact of life. Get used to it."

Talin's anger flatlined into a column of pure guilt. "I really am sorry," she said, shoulders slumping. "I should have stayed away." Clay had made it. She hadn't. End of story. "I had no right to come back into his life."

"Maybe, maybe not," was the enigmatic response. "But, Talin, those shields of yours? They're the kinds of shields traumatized children develop."

Talin took a physical step back from that gentle, so gentle, voice. It was a voice that made her want to cry and scream and *trust*. "Don't try to manipulate me."

"I'm not." There was only truth in those eerie night-sky eyes. "I'm a mind-healer. If you ever decide you deserve to be forgiven for whatever it is you think you've done, I'll be there for you."

"It's no use," she said, tone flat. "I'm dying." Time ran faster with every second.

The cardinal shook her head in quiet reproof. "Some

wounds should be healed, no matter how much time has passed or how much time is left."

Talin stared at the floor, barely able to see through the swirling darkness of memory, pain, and a savage need that threatened to destroy her world. "After," she whispered, not knowing why she made even that concession. "After." After they found Jon. "Maybe."

Clay followed Lucas enough of a distance that the women had privacy, but the lair remained in their line of sight. "Thanks for coming so quickly." He'd made the call after sending Talin upstairs when they had first arrived home.

"You would've done the same." Lucas took a seat on the forest floor, bracing his back against a nearby tree trunk.

Clay took the same position forty-five degrees to the left, a position that allowed him to watch the lair as they talked. But neither of them said anything for several minutes. Leaves rustled, smaller animals went about their business, the sky hung a heavy gray crisscrossed with forest green.

"She's the one," Lucas said into the whispering quiet.

"You see the future now? You going to tell me she's my one true love next?" Flippant words but they cut like shards of glass.

Lucas snorted. "No. I meant she's the one you said Faith reminded you of back when you two first met. I'm right, aren't I?"

Clay had snarled at Faith that day, almost gotten into a fight with Vaughn because of it. "Yeah. There's not much resemblance aside from the height." Faith was a redhead to Talin's brunette, Psy to her human. "But they're both stubborn and—" He shook his head. "They're nothing alike. Maybe I just wanted to see what I saw."

"Maybe," Lucas agreed. "You've been hung up on this Talin for a long time. Thing like that can drive a man a little crazy."

Clay had never spoken to Lucas about Talin. He stayed silent now, too.

Lucas stretched out one leg, braced his arm on the one that remained bent at the knee. "I don't know her, but I know you. And I know when a man's got demons chasing him."

Clay waited.

"The pack women like you, actively seek you out. I don't know why the hell they bother." He grinned. "It's not as if you're pretty like Dorian."

Clay growled but his mood lightened. Ribbing Dorian about his surfer-dude looks was a familiar pastime. "What's your point?"

"That you've never been in a single stable partnership."

"Luc, you're a fucking gossip."

A bark of laughter. "I'd be a bad alpha if I missed the fact that one of my best men, one of my sentinels, had never gone possessive over a female, not even a little bit."

"You never did either until Sascha."

"Exactly." Lucas's tone hid nothing of what he felt for his mate. "You were all over Talin."

"What's between us isn't anything simple." Too much history, too much pain, too many secrets. *Zeke got desperate when I still wouldn't talk . . .* He bet Zeke had never figured out the real truth of why Tally had stopped talking. Clay knew. And it tore him apart all over again. "She fucking turns me inside out."

"Women who matter have a way of doing that." Lucas scowled. "We sound like a couple of women, talking about feelings. I think Sascha's having a bad influence on me."

"You started it." But the discussion had given him the time he needed to wipe away the crap clogging up his mind. "She's asked my help on something." He laid out the facts about the disappearances. "I'll need time off my regular duties." He didn't ask permission because that wasn't how their pack worked. Lucas had chosen his sentinels because of their strength. They were all perfectly capable of running the show if things went wrong.

It said something about Luc that not one of those other dominant cats had ever challenged his rule. Clay had never even considered it—he was too used to walking alone, and an alpha was the physical and emotional center of his pack. "You want me to talk to Cian about the roster?"

"I'll organize it," Lucas offered. "Kit can do some of the easy stuff—it'll be good for his training." He was referring to the tall, auburn-haired juvenile who held the scent of a future alpha. "I'd pair him up with Rina, but he might see having his big sister around as a sign that we don't trust him."

Clay thought about it for a while. "If you switch my watch routes so the experienced soldiers do the outlying territory, Cian can run with Kit, show him the ropes." The older man was both strong and patient. "He'd still be a sentinel if he hadn't decided he preferred being a trainer and advisor."

Lucas made a sound of agreement. "Should work. Kit knows Cian's the one who trained me, so there can't be any cries of babying him." Another silence as they listened to the rhythms of the forest, their animal halves content. "Your Talin, she's human. Fragile."

And Clay, despite his control—control great enough that it was all most people ever saw—was brutally physical, even for a changeling. "I won't hurt her."

"She thinks you will."

It didn't surprise him that Lucas had picked up on Talin's skittishness. "I'm no Prince Charming. She knows that better than most." Twenty years apart had done nothing to diminish the blood-soaked bond between them, warped though it might have become. "She'll get over it." No other option was acceptable.

"Our animals starve without touch, Clay." Lucas's tone was a reminder of the consequences of such starvation. "It's not healthy for you to be in a relationship with a woman who isn't willing to give it to you. Ask Vaughn if you want to know how badly that kind of thing can screw up a man."

"You and Vaughn both courted Psy," he said. "At least Tally doesn't try to hide her emotions." She might make him furious but there was no doubt in his mind that her feelings for him were just as strong. "So back off."

"Good point." Lucas shrugged. "Your woman, your call."

Yes, Tally was his. His to protect. His to possess. Of that the leopard was as certain now as it had been the day they'd first met. That didn't blind him to the second vicious truth—that she had run from him and into the arms of other men.

She was his. But Clay wasn't sure he could ever forgive her.

* * *

Talin looked at Clay over the top of her coffee. Though they were in Joe's Bar again, Clay, too, had stuck to coffee as they waited for Max to arrive.

"How long have you known Max?" he asked.

The question was like all the ones he'd asked since Sascha and Lucas's departure from his lair earlier that day. Crisp, unemotional, to the point. That hadn't changed even when he'd ferried her around the city—in an untraceable vehicle—after she had told him she needed to check in with some other Shine children.

Since she had been steadily decreasing her workload in preparation for giving notice, none of those children were actually under her direct care. Jon had been the final one she'd had to place into a stable situation. The San Francisco Shine Guardian was Rangi, but due to a major family emergency back home in New Zealand, he'd had to leave his charges, and the hunt for the childrens' killer, in her hands. She'd told Clay all that as he'd driven her around, but his responses had been monosyllabic—when he'd replied at all. The cool distance was easier on her nerves than that smoldering temper of his, but she felt shut out.

If she had been an unselfish woman, she would have left it. Clay would take her eventual demise far better if he hated her. But Talin discovered she wasn't that good a person. She was horribly selfish when it came to Clay. "What's put a burr up your butt?" she said instead of answering his question.

Those beautiful forest-in-shadow eyes fixed on her with a predator's unblinking stare. "Be careful, Talin. You don't want to wake this sleeping leopard."

"Maybe I do." She pushed aside her coffee cup, adrenaline spiking through her bloodstream. "Maybe I want to see the real Clay."

His laughter was derisive. "You saw him, remember? The sight of claws and blood made you run."

"I was a child," she said, unwilling to be silenced this time. "I was eight years old and I had my foster father's brains splattered across my face. And that was after what he'd already done to me. *Excuse me* if the whole thing left a few scars."

He blinked and it was a lazy, quintessentially feline move. "Where did you find your spine all of a sudden?"

"You make me so mad!" She blew out a frustrated breath. "I wish I did have claws. I'd use them to scratch out your eyes." Never in all these years had she been as close to violence as she was now.

Clay got up.

Her heart stuttered.

With a dark smile that said he knew exactly what she was feeling, he came around and got into her side of the booth, trapping her between the wall and the muscular stone of his body. "Keep talking." It was a dare.

Fear threatened to swamp her, especially when he moved one hand behind her and closed his fingers over her nape. "Lost your voice, Tally?"

The taunt snapped through the vicious haze of memory. Putting her hand on his thigh, she dug down with her nails. Her intent had been to teach him not to goad her. Except that his muscles proved about as pliable as rock. "Shit."

"Such language." He crowded her even more, big, dangerous, and more than a little pissed with her. "But keep petting my thigh and maybe I'll let you use your little human claws on other parts of my anatomy."

Red filled her cheeks as she snatched her hand from the heavy warmth of him. "Stop it." His fingers tightened on her nape and it was such a possessive, territorial act, the feminine independence in her rebelled. "You don't want me. I'm used goods, *remember*?"

CHAPTER 12

Clay's entire body stilled and to her shock, his eyes shifted to cat right in front of her. Feral. Wild. Inhuman. As they had been that day in Orrin's bedroom. Memories of slaughter—vivid, *perfect*—crashed into her mind and suddenly she was that shell-shocked girl again, terrified her best friend would turn on her, use his claws and teeth to tear her to pieces. "C-Clay." She hated that involuntary catch in her voice. "Clay."

He released her without warning. "Don't worry, little bird. Fucking a woman who sees me as a monster isn't on my top ten things to do list." Harsh words, an even harsher tone. "You want me to act human"—a pitiless renunciation, a reminder of what his mother had demanded from him—"don't try to change the status quo of this relationship. You came to me because you needed my help. I'm helping you because, hell, you were a kid I knew once. That's it."

Talin knew she'd failed a very important test. Only hours ago, that knowledge would've turned her silent, made her cry internal tears. Now, a latent fury awoke in her. "Not fair," she whispered. "Maybe I'm not what you wanted me to be, maybe I made some mistakes, but who went and made you God? You have no right to judge me. My Clay, the boy who was my best friend, never would have."

"Yo!"

Whatever Clay might have said was lost as Max called out from his position by the door. Or that was what she thought until Clay leaned close, his breath hot against her ear. "We'll discuss this later. When we're alone."

That was when she realized she very definitely had succeeded in waking the sleeping leopard. And, bravado aside, she had no idea how to deal with him.

"Nice place." Max shook Clay's hand, then slid into the opposite side of the booth. "Guess I'd have been quietly rebuffed at the door if I hadn't been cleared by you?"

"There would've been nothing quiet about it."

Max grinned despite the fatigue lining his face. "My kind of joint."

A slender young male with the suggestion of future muscle about him stopped by the table and put a beer in front of Max. Though his face with its full lips and exotic Mediterranean bone structure was striking, it was his blue and black shiner that held center stage. His color faded when he met Clay's eyes. "How deep in the shit am I?"

Talin suddenly recognized that cap of black hair. He was one of the teenagers who had been hauled out of the bar two nights ago.

"We'll talk later." Clay dismissed the boy, who winced but left without further ado.

"Isn't he already being punished by being made to serve here?" she asked, ignoring the part of her that warned it might be better to stay below Clay's radar after the way she had provoked him—it'd be a cold day in hell before she let him intimidate her into silence.

"I'm Nico's trainer."

That just confused her, but Max nodded. "There's punishment and then there's getting reamed by your superior." Shrugging off his coat, he took a long drink of the dark gold liquid in front of him. "Shit, that feels good. Only thing better would be to fall into bed for the next twenty-four hours."

"Max followed the case from New York," Talin told the leopard beside her.

"How did you swing the authorization?" Clay's tone held a possessive darkness that she knew was meant for her alone.

Max leaned back against the faux leather of the seat, smile wry. "I have friends. Good people. But you already know that—you checked me out."

"Had to be sure."

"Fair enough."

"Any Psy interference in your investigation?" Clay's thigh shifted to press against hers and she had to bite back a gasp. Every time he moved, it reminded her of his strength, his predatory nature. But more than that, the contact tugged at hot, tight things in her, creating a hunger that threatened to destroy the already brittle equilibrium of their new relationship.

"No." Max's voice broke into her wandering thoughts. "They usually don't bother unless it involves a loss or gain for their race." He took another swig of his beer. "But someone is covertly monitoring my progress."

"How do you know?" Talin asked, fighting her body's reaction to the rough masculinity of the man who sat crowding her as if he had every right to invade her space.

"I put in some advanced security software on my files and they show unauthorized access. I keep the real files elsewhere so no harm done."

"Your boss?" Clay asked.

"No. He has authorized access." The detective finished his beer and put the bottle down on a coaster advertising the warm seas of Vanuatu. "To be honest, no one has much interest in this case on the surface. But the hacking was done by an expert. I wouldn't have picked it up without the software."

"Who supplied the software?"

Max's eyes gleamed. "Funny that. It was the Shine Foundation."

"What!" The word escaped at high volume. Face coloring, Talin lowered her tone—though oddly, none of the other patrons had turned. "When?"

"About eight months ago." Max shoved up his sleeves. "They're the reason I got this investigation. They made some calls and I was assigned."

Clay shot her a sardonic look. "Maybe Shine's not the saintly outfit you think it is."

"They haven't done anything wrong," she retorted, though Max's revelation disturbed her enough to blunt her razor-sharp awareness of Clay's aggressive mood. "Did they ask you for something in return?"

"To keep them informed." Max shrugged. "But I do that with all victims' families, and for Mickey, Iain, Diana, and Jon, they're it. I don't give them anything extra."

That made her feel a little better. "The things you're going to tell us tonight . . ."

"Classified." He looked around the busy bar. "Lots of sharp changeling ears here."

Clay shook his head. "No one can eavesdrop. Speakers built into the booth are sending out a low-frequency hum designed to disrupt sound. It can come in but not get out."

"Impressive." Max raised an eyebrow. "Can you actually hear the frequency?"

Talin was curious about that, too. As a child, Clay's abilities had delighted her. More than once, he had turned into a leopard simply because she'd wanted to stroke him—which now that she thought about it, had exhibited an incredible amount of amused indulgence on his part. She wondered if she'd ever get to stroke him again. That quickly, the slumbering need in her belly fired to brilliant life, sexual but also deeply, intensely emotional. She didn't care how selfish it was—she wanted her Clay back.

"No," Clay answered. "The frequency is pitched below our hearing but it works. That's why no one turned when you yelled." That last was directed at her.

"I was surprised." She caught the smoldering embers in his gaze—he hadn't forgotten her earlier provocation and, crazy as it was, she was glad. Being subject to that brooding temper of his was far better than being ignored.

Looking away, but with his arm now rubbing against hers, he nodded at Max. "Talin's apartment. Anything?"

"Blood was— I'm sorry, Talin. It was Mickey's."

Even as Talin's stomach threatened to revolt, Clay's hand closed over her thigh. He squeezed hard enough to disrupt her nausea, drawing her attention to the heated power of his presence instead. Adoring him a little more, she put her hand on his. His skin burned hotter than hers, warming the cold in her bones.

"Go on," he said to Max. "Tally can handle it."

Max looked at her, gaze bruised by the cruelty he'd witnessed. "He right? This is going to be bad."

Her hand clenched on Clay's. Not making a sound, he broke the contact, raised his arm, and placed it around her shoulders. Such a simple act, but one she'd never allowed any other man. It had felt too much like a cage . . . and none of those others had been capable of breaking her neck with a single violent move. But at this moment, the memory of the safety she'd always found in Clay's arms trumped that of tearing flesh and a monster's shrill screams. She drew his scent deep into her blood, into her very cells. "I'm ready."

Max didn't ask again. "There wasn't much else at your apartment. What evidence we have comes from the kids themselves." He paused, rubbed a hand over his face before continuing. "The apparent pattern until Diana and Iain was a murder every three weeks."

"You don't think it's the actual pattern?" Clay asked.

"I'm not sure we have all the victims," Max said. "Finding Mickey, Iain, and Diana so close together—within two weeks of each other—tends to support that theory."

"Any geographical pattern?" Clay asked with a predator's sharp intelligence, his deep voice a rumble that vibrated in her bones, at once comforting and a warning that he was something other, something as lethal as he was beautiful.

"No," Max answered. "I'm only in San Francisco because it's the last known body dump. Diana was taken from New York but found here with Iain. She was the last of your New York charges, right, Talin?"

"After they got Mickey, yeah." Oh, God, it hurt to think of her kids broken and bloodied. "Officially, Di didn't need a Guardian anymore, not once she'd been accepted into the boarding school." But she had still called to chat every so often, had still been Talin's. "She loved being on the track team." Talin curled a hand against the hard strength of Clay's abdomen, mind filled with the sound of Diana's laughter. Clay didn't say anything but shifted his hold so that his thumb stroked over the sensitive skin of her neck.

"Four Shine kids if you count Jon," he murmured. "I'm not buying the 'fishing in the same pool' argument, Tally."

Her loyalty to Shine made her want to protest, but she tried for logic. "But there were seven others, all unconnected," she reminded him.

"That's what I have to tell you," Max said.

Horror uncurled slow and insidious in the pit of her stomach. If Shine was evil, then what did that make her? Had she been leading the children she loved to their deaths?

Max reached for the bowl of peanuts on one side of the table. "You mind?" At the shake of their heads, he started picking out nuts and placing them on the tabletop. "We have fifteen confirmed fatalities."

"Fifteen?" Her hand spasmed, gripped Clay's T-shirt. "So many?"

"I'm guessing there are more." Having counted out fifteen peanuts, he pushed the bowl aside and put the saltshaker in the middle of the table. "I only found these fifteen because I went digging. Most times kids like this disappear, no one reports them missing. By the time they're found, it's often too late to see soft-tissue damage."

"Soft-tissue, that's your link?" Clay asked what Talin couldn't force herself to.

"Yeah," Max answered, "but one step at a time. This"—he picked up a nut—"is the first confirmed victim. Harish, age eight. Died a year ago—so this has been going on longer than we initially thought. The forensic team found the card of a Shine Foundation Guardian hidden in his shoe. The Guardian confirmed he'd approached the boy two days before the abduction." Max put the peanut about five centimeters from the saltshaker.

Talin's sense of horror multiplied a thousand times over.

"Second confirmed victim: Miu Li, age thirteen, died eleven months ago. She was a walk-in at Shine's Oklahoma facility. Did some tests, was entered into the tracking system, and disappeared." That peanut, he put closer to the saltshaker. "Victim number three: Hana Takuya, age fourteen, in her first year of an accelerated course funded by the Japan-Korea War Widows Trust. Its major donor is Shine.

"Victims four and five, Depe Lacroix, age ten, and Zoe Charles, age fourteen, threw me because they seemed to have no connection to Shine. Until," he said, mouth a grim line, "I traced their families and found they both had younger siblings who had been tapped by the foundation. Seems logical that Shine must've approached the older kids, too, and been rebuffed."

It continued like that until Max had connected all fifteen victims to Shine.

"My God." Her mind refused to believe. "But Shine is good . . . they help kids. They helped me." She rarely trusted, but she had given them a sliver of it.

"They might still be good," Clay said, to her surprise. "You have to have considered the idea of a mole in the foundation."

Max nodded. "Either that or Shine is a slick front for some very bad things. But I doubt that. If you're out to hunt kids, there are cheaper ways of doing it than by setting up a multimillion-dollar foundation. Whatever the truth, it's our best lead."

"You can't attack head-on." Talin leaned forward, desperate. "If they think you're getting too close, they might kill Jon." Hope, she thought, *hope*. Johnny D was still alive.

"I know." Max tapped the saltshaker. "That's where you were supposed to come in. You have a legitimate 'in' at Shine. I was going to ask you to go in, be my eyes and ears."

"But now she's been warned off, it's too dangerous." Clay slid his arm down to rest around her waist, his hand curving over her hip in a blatantly territorial gesture. "There's no question of her going in."

She bristled. "Hold on. You don't get to dictate—"

"He's right," Max interrupted. "If it is a mole and not a case of the entire organization being dirty, that mole has to be pretty high up. The bastard clearly has access to preliminary contact reports from around the country. He or she will either make sure you don't see anything useful or shut you up for good."

"Men," she muttered, agreeing with them but loath to show it, given Clay's arrogant pronouncement. "Okay, even if I don't go in, we need information from the inside somehow."

"Anybody you trust there?" Max asked.

"Dev—Devraj Santos," she said without hesitation. Clay's hand tightened on her hip. She retaliated with a scowl. "He's a good guy."

"He's also the director." Max's face was grim.

"No. He'll help us." She turned to Clay. "You know what I mean. Tell him."

After a taut second, he nodded. "Talin's instincts about people are pure gold."

His support warmed her even as she realized he was calling her Talin again. They had only been together a day and already she knew that meant trouble. A strange exhilaration in her gut, she returned her attention to Max. "That's not everything, is it?"

Max nodded. "First thing—absolutely no one but me, the medical examiner, and a couple of detectives I trust—knows this. The bodies were all missing some organs."

It was too much. Her heart felt frozen in her chest.

"Which organs?" Clay's hand stroked over her hip, jerking her out of her shell-shocked state and firmly back into the present. "Could we be talking black market?"

Talin saw where he was going. While the world had come a long away in the field of artificial and cloned organs, certain parts of the human body continued to defy medical science's efforts to create perfect replicas. Added to that, a small subsection of society preferred donor organs over cloned ones. "Did they take the heart or eyes?" It was impossible not to remember those eyes filled with laughter and hope.

Max nodded. "But I think those removals were a front for the real goal, red herrings to divert our attention in exactly this direction."

"I don't understand." Talin frowned. "Hearts are the most expensive and difficult to clone and eyes follow close behind."

Clay suddenly went predator-still. "There's one other very complicated organ you haven't yet mentioned."

Talin watched the men's eyes lock, felt the murky truth pass between them. But her mind refused to make the connection. "What?" she asked, frustrated.

"The brain, Talin." Max's tone was full of quiet grief. "All the victims found early enough to perform a soft tissue analysis were missing their brains."

Clay sensed Talin's shock, her driving pain. It threatened to tear the heart right out of him. "How good was the surgery?" he asked, holding her tighter.

"Top of the line. This is an organized operation, not some lone whack job, especially if you factor in the geographical spread of the victims, the schedule of body dumps, and the lack of evidence—the kids had literally no trace on their bodies but for a single fiber."

"It help narrow things down?"

"Not to a specific location, but the material is used in high-tech surgical labs." Max shoved a hand through his hair. "The victims were taken to some kind of medical facility, and I'm betting it was the same one in all cases, which means they were transported across state lines without raising any alarms. Smacks of organization."

"Were they tortured?" Talin's voice was raw, as if she'd been screaming silently.

Clay's leopard flexed its claws, disliking the scent of her anguish. "Come on, Tally. You don't need to know that."

"Yes, I do." She swallowed and when she looked up, he saw that her eyes were dull gray, that exotic ring of fire muted to pale bronze. "It might tell us why these particular kids were taken, the deviance driving the killers. If we know, we can narrow down the list of other children who might be at risk."

"What the hell. I'll send you everything I've got." Max pushed aside the peanuts he'd spread on the table, his fist clenched. "You know these kids, the way they think—you might pick up something I've missed."

"What about the search for Jon?" It broke her heart, but Di, Mickey, and the others were already dead. Their justice could wait. "He has to come first."

Clay brushed his lips over her hair. "Leave Jon to me." It was a promise. "I don't particularly want you looking at Max's files, seeing what was done to the victims," he admitted, tone rough, "but you need to go through them. It might help us locate the boy."

She didn't even trust Max to fight for Jon, but it was frighteningly easy to fall into her old rhythms with Clay. "Okay." He would never allow harm to come to a child.

"That'll leave me free to follow up the Shine connection." Max rubbed at his eyes. "I just pray to God they don't grab any more kids before we figure this out."

Talin felt her stomach knot at the thought. "Thank you for sharing all this, Max."

"Why did you?" Clay's eyes were watchful, his hold on her so proprietary it made her feminine instincts spark in warning. "It's confidential information."

"I researched this town before I came in." Max might've been human but he held Clay's gaze with solid confidence. "Aside from the obvious Psy presence, DarkRiver and SnowDancer control San Francisco. And"—his tone shifted, became sharper—"the jury's recently gone out on whether the Psy really do continue to have more influence than the cats and wolves."

CHAPTER 13

Talin's mouth went dry. The Psy made certain they were the sole power in any major metropolitan city, were ruthless in eliminating opponents. But if Max was right, then she'd begged the aid not of a friend, but of a man with a powerful network of influential connections. It shook her. What if Clay thought she'd only come to him because of his link to DarkRiver?

"You always intended to ask us to get involved," Clay responded, his fingers stroking over her hip. She would've objected except she had a feeling that it was an unconscious act. And disturbing as it was to her senses, she liked it.

"I wanted to meet one of the senior pack members first. Changelings help their own—I wasn't sure you'd bother with lost human children." Max's tone was blunt.

"Still doesn't answer the original question."

"I need backup." Max's mouth twisted. "Like I said, Enforcement doesn't see this case as a priority."

Talin felt her anger spike but kept her silence. None of this was Max's fault.

"You're saying you're on your own on this?" Clay asked, sliding his hand up and down in a caress that threatened to make her shiver. She shifted but it only made him pull her closer, the heat of his body both a warning and a seductive kind of comfort.

"I have some friends in this city who'll step in if necessary," Max answered, "but yeah. The M.E.s usually get excited about unusual murders, and with the organ removals, these would qualify, but all I got this time were by-the-numbers reports. There's pressure coming from somewhere, but hell if I know where. Especially if Shine is clean." He tapped the side of his beer bottle.

"And," he continued, "whatever marked these children's brains as different, well, we don't have it to work with. I've been able to get hold of some medical scans taken prior to death—usually as part of a Shine eval. Maybe you'll spot something the M.E.s didn't. Won't be hard. I'm not sure they even looked." A cynical smile. "Enforcement, the great protectors."

"I don't have medical training." Frustrated, she clenched her hand against Clay's T-shirt again, gripping the soft material in her fist.

"I know someone." Clay fingers stilled before he cupped his hand boldly over her hip and squeezed. Stomach tight with awareness, she released his T-shirt but remained tucked against him, needing him more than she feared whatever it was that was growing between them. "You have any issue with me sharing the files?"

"I asked for your help. I have to trust you." Max's face took on a thoughtful cast. "You know the one thing I've always admired about the Psy?"

Startled by the sudden change in the direction of the conversation, Talin asked, "What?"

"They might be a race of ice-cold bastards, but they don't abuse their kids. I've never heard of any sexual or physical abuse within a Psy household. Leave it to us animal races to sink that low."

"Don't be impressed." Clay's voice vibrated with withheld fury. "They begin their abuse at birth. Psy aren't born emotionless, they're conditioned into it. Their children have no choice but to obey—refusal gets you rehabilitated."

Max frowned. "Rehab?"

"The process wipes memory, destroys mental capacity, basically turns them into walking vegetables."

"Christ." Max shook his head. "But even with that, I'm not convinced they didn't make the better choice. Their children aren't the ones being beaten to death."

Talin was still wrestling with what Max had told them when they reached Clay's lair late that night. He pushed something on the Tank's dash. "I've unarmed the lair's defenses. Get your butt inside before you start snoring right here."

"I'm not the one who snores," she muttered, walking away from the vehicle and into the lair.

Darkness, complete darkness.

"Lights." Her breath began to come in panicked bursts. "Full power."

Nothing.

Strangling fear threatened to close around her throat as she scrabbled at the wall, trying to find the computronics panel. She was sure she'd seen it earlier today. God, she had to find it. The dark, it was closing around her. Suffoca—

"Talin, breathe."

She spun around, gasped at the sight of him. His eyes were night-glow, an eerie green-silver that was completely cat. "You can see in the dark!"

"Of course I can." He said it like it was the most normal thing in the world. "Panel's five inches to your left. Middle pad."

She tried to pretend calm as she found it, then pressed the central pad. Light poured out from a ceiling fixture. "You don't have voice activation."

He grunted. "Does this look like a palace?" A pause. "I'll get one of the techs to put it in tomorrow."

"No, you don't have—"

"I said I'll get it done." His tone told her he was just itching for a fight.

She decided for grace instead. "Thank you."

A dark scowl as he began to unbutton his shirt.

Her barely steady heartbeat took another jagged leap. "What are you doing?"

"Not attacking you." He turned to throw the shirt on one of the large cushions that acted as his sofas. "I'm going for a run. I prefer that my clothes not disintegrate when I shift."

"Oh." She couldn't take her eyes off the shifting muscles of his back. Clay had always been strong, but now . . . now he could break her like a twig. And yet even as she thought that, she couldn't get past his beauty. Her fingertips tingled, her thighs clenched. She wanted to reach out and trace that tattoo high on his left shoulder, wanted to taste—

"Scat." His hands went to the snap of his jeans.

She jumped, heart racing for a completely new reason. "We need to talk."

"You need to sleep." He stalked toward her, revealing a chest thick with muscle. Dark curls of hair stroked over that luscious, glowing skin, arrowing down in a viscerally male fashion. "Get upstairs." His jaw was tight, his eyes anger bright.

Her jaw dropped. "You're still mad at me. God, you're stubborn!"

"I'm a hell of a lot more than mad." Turning, he kicked off his shoes and began to undo his jeans. "I'm through talking. Leave unless you want a peep show."

She could feel her cheeks flaming. "I don't like you very much right this second."

"Good. The feeling's mutual." He went as if to push down the jeans.

She ran to the ladder, able to feel his mocking gaze on her back. A huge part of her wanted to watch him shift, to experience the stunning sparkle of color and light as his form changed, then the wild intoxication of being face-to-face with a leopard. But another part of her was frustrated enough to scream. It was clear that the Clay she'd known hadn't changed in at least one crucial respect. He had seldom exploded in open fury, but man, could he *brood*!

"What if someone comes?" she asked, once she was safe on the second level.

"No one will." His tone dared her to question him.

"But what if—"

"Pull up the trapdoor on the third level and activate the internal security trap. The panel's hidden by the trapdoor. That will keep the bogeyman from you."

Her eyes narrowed. "Fine. Good night." No response. "I hope a bear eats you."

A growl drifted upstairs.

Smiling, satisfied, she made her way to the third level. The panel was exactly where he'd said it would be. She opened it and had a look. Her eyes widened. This was serious security. Once activated, this entire section of the aerie would be surrounded by lasers. Anyone attempting to cross that barrier without the access code would get one warning. If they didn't retreat, they'd find themselves cut up into neat little cubes of flesh and blood.

Gruesome.

But it made her feel safe.

Fast and powerful in his leopard form, Clay wanted to run forever, but he stayed close to home. This was his range and he knew every shift of air, every animal resident, every scent. He'd be home before anyone ever reached Talin.

Right now, *he* was the real threat.

The leopard let out a short, sullen roar. The forest creatures froze. But he wasn't hunting tonight, too angry at Talin. She'd let him touch her at the bar, but he'd felt the tension in her body—as if she were bracing herself for violence. That wariness was a constant insult and it infuriated him. While that anger was on a leash right now, it threatened to break free and turn to a rage that might make him the very monster she accused him of being.

The danger was very real . . . because he wasn't like the others in his pack.

It wasn't his half-human blood. There were other half-bloods in DarkRiver. No, it was the fact that he'd grown up in surroundings incredibly wounding to a predator's soul. All those years of being trapped inside the stifling walls of apartment buildings had taken their toll. The animal wanted *out*, wanted control. But ironically, he could act human better than anyone in the pack, his leopard disguised by a veneer of silent calm.

It had made Isla cry to see the leopard in him and because he had loved his mother despite her flaws, he'd buried the leopard, crippling himself in the process. Changelings weren't human and they weren't animal. They were both. They *needed* to be both. To be one but not the other, it was a kind of amputation. Yet he had pretended to be fully human for most of his childhood.

However, in the past decade, his leopard half had made up for lost time. He could still pretend to be human, but blood hunger and animal wildness raced through his bloodstream every second of every day. Like the predator it was, the leopard didn't see anything wrong in the cold logic of survival of the fittest. It was willing and able to kill without compunction. And Clay didn't particularly want it to leave.

That was the real danger.

Lucas had never said it. Neither had Nate. But both men had to know that though it was Vaughn who was the more outwardly animal, it was Clay who was the most near to going rogue . . . to never becoming human again.

Shaking his head in an angry growl, he clambered up a tree with the lethal grace of his kind and stretched out on a high branch, from which he could glimpse the light in Talin's bedroom. If he turned rogue, he'd lose the right to touch her. To go rogue was to give in to the animal so unconditionally as to forget his humanity. But though a rogue's mind held nothing of the person it had once been, some spark of knowledge remained. When a rogue attacked, it inevitably went after those who had once been Pack.

Clay had been fighting his beast for years. At fourteen, when he'd violently repudiated the inhuman control that had been forced onto him by Isla's fragile mind, it had changed him. He had learned what he was, what he could do, learned the taste of blood and fear. Learned that part of him liked it. Exulted in it.

Being locked up for four years had only enraged the animal further. The day he'd walked out of the juvenile facility, he'd gone on a bloody hunt. He had taken down three deer and it was through blind luck that they had been true animals, not changelings. Back then, lost and unaware of the meaning of his heritage, he hadn't known how to distinguish between the two. More to the point, he'd been too blinded by eighteen years of stifled blood hunger to care.

Over time, he'd become better at controlling that hunger. The fact that he was a DarkRiver sentinel spoke to that control. But it was inside of him, a pulsing need. He knew that Tally was his greatest vulnerability, the trigger that could push him over the edge. What he felt for her—protectiveness, rage, affection—it was all tangled up in a caustic stew. Each time she flinched, he came one step closer to going rogue. But today she had leaned into him and that had had an even more unpredictable effect.

Extreme, blinding, *violent* sexual attraction.

He'd been drawn to her as a man is drawn to a woman from the instant she'd walked back into his life, but with her small act of trust, that attraction had ratcheted up into a craving that scratched at his gut, made his cock hard with the need to claim, to brand. But he knew Tally. She had been sexually betrayed by the very people supposed to protect her. For her, trust and sex were incompatible. If he pushed her in that direction, it might equal *her* last straw.

Then there were the other men. So many she couldn't remember their names.

He roared again, the sound vicious.

Why? Why had Tally sold herself so cheap?

Lost in the coils of sleep, Talin frowned, turned, then settled back down. A few minutes later, she did it again. And again.

Fear twisted the sleeping peacefulness of her face, shuddered over her body, locked around her throat. Gasping for air, she sat straight up. She didn't scream. She never screamed. Never had. Not even as a child.

For five long minutes, she sat there, adrenaline pumping, as she examined every corner of her well-lit room. Only when she was satisfied that no one had opened the trapdoor, that no one had entered while she'd been sleeping, did she get out of bed and pull on a cardigan over her sweatpants and tank top combo.

Walking into the bathroom off the room, she threw some water on her face, then tucked her hair behind her ears before walking back out. The bedside clock told her it was four a.m.

The hour of nightmares. The time of night a terrified child's bedroom door had creaked open for so many years.

Shaking her head to clear the vile memories, she went to the security panel and turned off the lasers. She wanted a cup of hot chocolate. Maybe the Larkspurs hadn't been able to banish her demons, maybe she hadn't let them love her like they had wanted to, but they had helped her sometimes. Ma Larkspur had been a light sleeper—even with Talin's quiet creeping about, she'd noticed. Those nights they had spent sitting in the kitchen drinking hot chocolate were some of the best memories of Talin's life after Clay. Before, he had been the only good thing, the only wonderful thing, in her life.

Pulling open the trapdoor, she glanced down. Clay had left on a light, but she couldn't see him from where she was. She made her way down on silent feet. Once she reached the bottom, she scanned the room. There were a couple of cushions on the other side, below the window, but the room was otherwise empty. She realized Clay must have bunked downstairs. She frowned. The cushions on the first level were huge but he was a big man. It couldn't be comfortable sleeping on those. Maybe he had a collapsible mattress.

Her curiosity almost made her open the second trapdoor but she stopped herself. Turning up the light from soft to superbright, she headed to the kitchen alcove and began to search for the ingredients. She found milk and sugar but no chocolate.

"Idiot," she muttered under her breath. Clay had never liked sweets. For his eleventh birthday, Isla had given him a box of knockoff Godiva chocolates. He'd given the whole lot to Talin. She'd made herself sick gorging on them. And loved every minute of it.

She stared at the milk, thinking about simply having a warm glass of it. But she wanted hot chocolate! Tears pricked her eyes. Stupid. Stupid. But the emotional reaction kept gaining speed. She was in a house she didn't know, with a Clay who was almost all stranger, someone had crushed her cherished photographs and splashed blood on her walls, and her kids were dying. All she'd wanted was a moment's respite.

Something moved below, snapping her out of her bout of self-pity.

She rubbed at her eyes and waited, back against the counter, as Clay climbed up. His hair was tousled and he didn't look in a particularly good temper. He'd pulled on his jeans before heading up, but the top buttons were undone, the denim perched perilously low on his hips. That was another confusing thing—this sudden sexual attraction to Clay.

Intellectually, she could understand it. He was a prime example of beautiful male. Women probably begged to be allowed to crawl all over him. Add in that brooding sexuality and it was no wonder her body reacted. But . . . this was Clay. Her friend. Well, when he wasn't furious with her. She fisted her hands, dreadfully aware that if he yelled at her right now, she might just burst into tears. "Sorry if I woke you."

He thrust a hand through his hair and yawned, the act full of a lazy feline grace that held her spellbound. "You walk like a cat. I was already awake."

"Oh." She bit her lower lip when it threatened to tremble. "You don't have any chocolate."

"Christ, you never grew out of that sweet tooth?"

She shook her head, still feeling a little fragile.

He closed the distance between them with three long strides. "Move."

Eyes wide, she shifted to the side as he leaned up and opened a high cupboard she hadn't been able to reach. Her eye fell on his right biceps, on the tattoo there—three slashing lines, they reminded her of the markings on Lucas Hunter's face. "When did you get inked?"

A grunt was his only response. Curious, she peered at his back to check out the tattoo she'd glimpsed earlier. There it was, on the back of his left shoulder, an exquisitely detailed leopard curled up in sleep. Animal and human in one, she thought, understanding his need to acknowledge the leopard as he had never been allowed to do as a child. "I like the cat," she said, watching him close the first cupboard and open the one beside it. "Who did it?"

"A guy I knew from juvie—turned into a hotshot artist," he muttered. "Where the hell did I put it?"

Hopes rising, she stood on tiptoe beside him, trying to peek inside. "Chocolate?"

He reached deep into the space. "Chocolate." Pulling out his hand, he put a bar of luscious dark chocolate in her palm.

She could've kissed him, growly face and all. "Do you like chocolate now?"

"Hell, no. I can't stand the stuff." He closed the cupboard and leaned his hip against the counter. "Sascha, however, has a love affair with it. She gave it to me." He sounded puzzled.

"Maybe because she likes you?" Talin suggested, setting the milk to warm on the small heating unit she guessed was powered by an eco-generator. Everything in Clay's house seemed to have been designed with the forest's delicate ecology in mind. "She wanted to make you happy and probably figured that everyone likes chocolate."

"I guess." He yawned again but didn't move from where he stood only two feet from her, all dark masculine beauty. "You do this a lot?"

"Most every night," she admitted. "I don't sleep much."

"I'll need to get more chocolate, then."

"No." She looked up from peeling open the bar. "I can't stay here."

His eyes gleamed. "Why not? Afraid I'll bite you?"

"You already did," she reminded him with a scowl.

"You survived." He sounded very much like a cat at that moment.

"You know why I can't stay. We keep setting each other off. It's not exactly a peaceful environment."

"When did you get so hung up on peace?" He nodded at the milk. "Put in the chocolate."

"What? Oh." She broke off several chunks and dropped them in. "This kind makes good hot chocolate. Some of the others end up tasting weird."

Reaching into a drawer in front of him, he gave her a wooden spoon. She began to stir, inhaling the rich scent into her lungs with a sigh. "Heaven."

When Clay didn't say anything, she looked at him. He was watching her with a stare that was frankly assessing . . . and very sensual. Her heart kicked and she broke the searing eye contact, tucking her hair back when it twisted out from behind her ear. "Don't."

A hint of steel entered his languid pose, as if with her rejection, she'd pushed one of his damn male buttons. "Why not?"

The arrogance in his question put her back up. "Because!"

"You're a clearly sexual female. I'm a male. You want me. I want you. What's the problem?"

Her hand trembled as she turned off the heating unit. "Who says I want you?" She pointed the dripping spoon at him.

He winced as a drop of hot chocolate hit his chest but didn't move. "I can smell arousal, Talin. You get hot every time you see me half-naked."

The erotic need that flared through her body was mortifying. Perhaps that explained the stupidity of her next words. "Maybe I get that way for every half-naked man."

He stilled, becoming so very motionless that she felt like some tiny forest creature in front of a beast of prey. "So you'll have no problem spreading your legs for me, will you?"

CHAPTER 14

Putting the spoon very carefully on the counter, Talin picked up a mug from the stand. "Go away."

Clay had expected anger. This calm distance left him flat-footed. She sounded so focused, so controlled, she might as well have been Psy. "Talin, look at me."

She picked the pot up off the stove and poured her drink into the mug. He waited until she'd put the hot object safely into the sink before grabbing her wrist. Her skin was damp, cold. "Talin?"

"What?" She looked at him, face serene in a way he'd never before seen. Tally had too much energy, too much emotion, to ever be that *quiet.*

His beast sniffed at her, found something terribly wrong. "Talin, who am I?"

"Clay," she said, but didn't tug at his hand, didn't display any of the reactions he'd already come to expect from her. Her calm was eerie, unnatural. "Can I go now?"

He frowned at the childlike question. Her tone had shifted, as had her rhythm. She sounded like a six-year-old version of herself. "Tally, sweetheart, are you in there?"

"'Course I am, silly." She smiled and it was that sweet,

innocent Tally smile. The one she had stopped smiling a very long time ago. "I want my hot chocolate."

"Go sit on those cushions. I'll bring it to you."

She followed his gaze to the other end of the room. "Is this your clubhouse?"

"Yeah." Cold fear squeezed his heart. "Go on, baby."

Smiling with absolute trust, she went to a cushion and sat, one of her legs tucked under her. He picked up her drink and took it to her. She accepted it with a smile. "Yum. Did ya learn to make hot choccie, Clay?"

His rational mind noted that her enunciation and syntax were also regressing, but all he could see was the look in her eyes. He'd seen that look before, those eyes. This was Tally as she had been over twenty years ago. Raw terror made the leopard pace in bewildered circles inside his mind.

"You made it, Tally," he said, gathering every ounce of tenderness he possessed in an effort to be gentle for her. "Don't you remember?"

She frowned at him. "No, silly! Not allowed—" Her eyes glazed over. She took a sip of hot chocolate, then . . . nothing. She didn't move. If he hadn't been able to see her breathing, he wouldn't have known she was alive.

"Tally?" He touched her cheek. No response. Desperate, the leopard starting to panic, he cupped her face. "Tally, wake up!" The last word was a growl.

She blinked. Then again, as if it took great effort. Her hands started to shake. Grabbing the mug before she dropped it, he put it to the side. "Tally, damn it, you come back to me right this second."

Lines appeared on her brow. "Don't . . . give . . . me orders." She shook her head, reminding him of a kitten shaking off wet. "Clay?"

"I'm here." He wanted to hold her but was terrified of her reaction. "I'm right here."

Her eyes were scared when she looked at him. "How did I get here? I was at the counter." Panic edged her words, jagged shards that bit into his skin.

"Something happened." He shifted position, sitting down in front of her with his legs bent at the knees, effectively bracketing her curled-up body.

"An episode?" She reached up as if to push back her hair, stopped, curled her hand into a fist, and pressed it to her stomach. "What did I do?"

"Do you remember what we were talking about?"

A pause, then a red flush high on her cheeks. "We didn't—" Her tone was reedy.

"No!" he said immediately. "No, baby. It's only been two or three minutes at most. Look, your chocolate is still hot." He pushed the mug into her hands, needing to do something to get that anguished look off her face.

She closed her fingers around it, sighing in relief. "Sometimes I do things when I'm—" Her face scarred over with the most cruel pain. "Sometimes I wake up in strange rooms. Then I have to go to the clinics and make sure my vaccinations are all up-to-date, and the doctors look at me like I'm a whore." The last word was a broken whisper.

Protective fury clawed at his vocal chords. He fought back the roar by focusing on Tally. "You're safe here. From that kind of abuse at least." Her hurt, lost look was tearing his heart to pieces, the leopard shuddering in pain as the man fought to find the tenderness she needed. "Tell me you know that, baby."

A jerky nod. "I just get so scared because I wake up and there's this black gap where my memory should be. Please—tell me what I did so I don't have to imagine."

"Nothing so bad. You talked like a kid."

That seemed to startle her. "What?"

"You sounded like you were six-years-old."

"Something bad happened that year." Her voice dropped, became a whisper.

He swallowed the leopard's scream of rage—if Tally could live through it, then he could damn well hear it. Because no matter what she said, he'd failed her then. "Have you had this kind of regression before?"

She shook her head. "Not that I know of. One of the specialists had me wear a tracker when the episodes started getting bad. Most of the time—" She swallowed and drank some of her chocolate. "It's sexual. Most of the time it's sexual. Not always sex but acting out. Acting different. Dressing different."

His claws pushed out slowly through his skin. He had to force them to retract. "Is that why all those men?"

Her face was sad. "Don't try and make me innocent again. I'm not. I never was."

"You were a child then. You weren't responsible."

"But I was responsible for my adult actions. And I did sleep around. You can't erase that!" she cried. "These episodes have only gotten so bad in the last year and a half. The doctors call them dissociative states. There are lots of psychological words to describe what just happened but most people recognize it as a fugue."

He knew less than nothing on this subject, felt as if he were scrambling in the dark. Making it worse was that mixed in with his need to protect was this agonizing, vicious fury. God, but he was mad at her, at how she'd mistreated herself. Didn't she know that no one—not even she—had the right to hurt what was his? And Talin was his, had been since that day twenty-five years ago when she'd first dared tangle with a wounded leopard. "Tell me about these fugues," he grit out. "Tell me so I understand."

"I don't know if I do." She gave him the mug to put aside.

He stopped himself from crushing it by the thinnest of margins. "Start with what you do know."

"Okay." She took a steadying breath. "A person in a fugue is on autopilot, that's how the doctors explained it to me. They can walk, talk, even do complex things like drive, but with no conscious control."

He wanted to hold her so bad it hurt, but he kept his distance. "What brings one on?"

She shrugged. "No one really knows definitively. For some people it's a brain imbalance—hormonal, biological, a tumor. For others, it seems related to stress."

"Which is it in your case?"

"I don't know. But the more the disease progresses, the worse they are, so it's probably biological."

"We were fighting pretty hard, Tally." He was disgusted at how he'd stoked the sexual heat between them when he had *known* it would be too much for her. But the second she had ordered him to back off, the leopard had taken over, furious and so damn possessive he couldn't fight it. He was getting too close to the edge, becoming dangerous. So fucking dangerous. "Enough to stress anyone out."

"Yes." She swallowed, took another deep breath. "The doctors said it might even be a mix of things. The biological problems making me more vulnerable to the psychological—my brain is already compromised so it takes less pressure to effect a fugue."

It was an effort to remain logical. "Were you able to isolate any triggers when you wore the trackers?"

"Not really." She drew up her knees and rested her chin on them, looking strangely childlike. It was unsettling after the regression he'd witnessed only minutes ago. "Sometimes it's nothing. Or it feels like nothing. I once fugued in the middle of a jet-train with people all around. I went shopping like normal, then sat in Central Park for an hour."

"That's all?"

"Yeah. Weird, huh?" She shook her head. "I wish all the episodes were like that. But I guess you know they're not. Once I woke up in a bar in Harlem about to get into a taxi with two strangers."

The red glazing his vision was starting to burn, but he knew that if he walked away from her tonight, he'd break something very fragile. "Go on."

"Beds, sometimes I wake up in beds. Beside men I don't know." Tears trailed down her face. "I hate it! I hate myself! But I can't stop it!"

"Shh." He ran a hand over her hair, shaking with the need to hurt what had hurt her. But this disease, it mocked him, hiding in the body of this woman he would never so much as bruise.

"Sometimes the blackouts last for half a day. The longest one I'm aware of was sixteen hours." She was crying in earnest now, deep, hiccuping sobs that made him bleed on the inside.

"Come here, Tally." He tried to gentle his voice but that wasn't who he was. It came out rough, almost a growl. "Come on, baby."

She scooted a little bit closer. Carefully, he closed the gap between her body and his bent knees, one hand stroking over her hair, the other clenched into a fist so tight, he was bleeding from cuts in his palm as his claws broke through to bite into skin.

Ever since joining DarkRiver, he'd been taught to take care of the pack, to protect. He'd taken to the task like a natural, funneling all his anger and rage into something that made him feel like a better man. His packmates might find him a loner, but not one would hesitate to come to him for help. But tonight he could do nothing for the one person who mattered most to him. In spite of how badly they clashed, or how angry he was with her, she was his to protect. "Baby, I need to help you."

"Don't," she whispered, "don't treat me like a patient." *Like Isla.*

He heard the words she would never say. "You give me far too much lip to be a patient. You're Tally." His to fight with, his to keep safe. "Do you want me to call Sascha?" He wasn't too proud to ask the pack for help, not if it would lessen Tally's pain. "She's good at this kind of stuff."

Talin bit her lower lip again, a lip already swollen from previous bites. He wanted to kiss the hurt, lick his tongue over it. The leopard couldn't understand why he didn't.

"I want to say no," Talin replied even as he fought the internal battle. "I don't know her. She's a stranger and . . . well, I'm not sure what she feels about me."

Knowing she would hate platitudes, he gave her the truth. "I didn't smell any hint of dislike on her, and I'm damn good at picking up scents."

"That doesn't mean she likes me." Talin took a deep breath and sat up straighter. "I don't think anyone in your pack will ever like me. Look what I do to you." Her hand brushed over his fist. "You're bleeding."

He released the fist and flexed his fingers, soaking in the heat of her touch. "It's not the first time and it won't be the last. Don't worry about it."

"Your pack worries about you," she insisted. "I'm hardly bringing flowers and butterflies into your life."

He gave her a tight smile. "I'm not sure I'd know what to do with those things anyway." Giving in to the needs of the leopard, he cupped her cheek with his good hand. "I am who I am. They know that. If they worry, it's because of things you can't control."

Her hand rose to lie over his, soft, fragile. "But part of who you are is because of me and what you did for me."

"That goes both ways—part of who you are is because of what I did." *And what he had failed to do.* He sat unmoving as her hand clenched on his, as her eyes darkened, that fine ring of bronze almost cat-bright against the gray.

"Do you think we can ever get past that?"

He shrugged, his leopard gaining strength as a fiercely sexual hunger uncurled inside of him, fostered by the delicacy of her touch, the soft warmth of her scent. The leopard needed to mark her, to convince itself she was okay. "Who says we have to?"

She frowned. "It's like a white elephant between us, Clay."

"No." He moved his hand from her cheek to the side of her neck, closed. Careful, he told himself, be careful of your strength. "That would imply we aren't aware of it. Which is definitely not true."

Her frown turned into a scowl. "Are you saying you're sick of talking about it?"

"Talking never solves anything." He could feel her pulse, thudding hard, out of time. A panicked beat? Or something else? He was sure it was the latter—she wasn't scared of him right this second. "I have no idea why women seem to like doing it so much."

"It's a good thing I make you talk—left alone you'd forget how to speak," Talin said, trying to tease. "I'll talk to your Sascha, too." She was no use to anyone if her mind kept crashing out of control. "But not now." Not when she was at such a huge disadvantage. The cardinal Psy was so composed, so elegantly beautiful, that Talin felt like a drab sparrow in comparison.

Clay's eyes were on her lips and suddenly she remembered what had started this whole thing. Her palms dampened. "I told you not to look at me that way."

He blinked, but it was the slow, lazy blink of a predator very sure of his prey. "Why does it bother you so much?"

"Because even as you touch me, you're hating me." She saw the truth in the rich, sensual green of his eyes. "Admit it—you hate me for what I did."

"Why?" A stark demand, his hand remaining clasped

around the side of her neck. "Why did you give away what you should have protected?"

The question caused an emotional rock to lodge in her throat. "Will you let me go?"

His answer was to stroke his thumb over her skin.

"Clay." When his eyes focused on her this time, she sucked in a breath. The cat was clearly in charge. Irrational fear spiked, but she refused to buckle under again. "Intimidation never worked with me."

He growled low in his throat. "Answer the fucking question."

"I did it so I'd feel something," she snapped, wanting to growl back at him. "I went through life feeling nothing. I couldn't love the Larkspurs, I couldn't make friends, I couldn't do anything but pretend!"

"And did you?" His hand tightened on her neck.

Cold sweat broke out over her body but she stayed. "No. I've never felt as dead as I did when I was in those beds. I went into my mind like I used to do as a child—so I wouldn't be present while my body was used."

His eyes shifted back to human, as if she'd caught him by surprise. "Then why keep doing it?"

"Because I thought that that was all I was good for." A blunt response and the utter truth. "I was messed up, Clay. What Orrin did to me—it twisted me up on the inside. I couldn't get past all that poison he put into my head. I kept hearing his voice telling me that I was nothing but a whore."

"I'm glad I killed him," Clay said, his tone so quiet it was a blade. "I only wish I'd been more patient. I should've ripped off his dick first, made him eat it."

Her gorge rose but she was so damn tired of running, of disappointing Clay. Maybe she was weak, broken, *human*, but she was no coward. Not anymore. Making a small move, she put her hand on his knee. He seemed to come back to her at the contact.

"Let it go," she whispered, eyes tracing over the harsh masculine lines of his face. "Don't let him poison you, too. I've finally broken free."

"Have you?"

"I haven't chosen to share a man's bed in eight years.

That's why the fugues hurt so much," she admitted. The time for lies had passed. "I know I'm worth more now. The therapist I went to for a while helped me see that. But it was the kids at Shine who really saved me—they're the reason I decided I couldn't keep going as I had been."

He watched her, a cool, dangerous predator with rage coating him in a seemingly impenetrable shield.

"So many of them come from the same place we did or worse, and they keep going, keep fighting. How could I possibly think to help them, lead them, if I wasn't strong enough to do the same?" She swallowed. "They have courage and heart and they're *mine*. I can't let any more of them die, Clay. I can't."

"I told you—I'll find this boy, Jon, for you."

"I know you will." Her trust in him was rooted not only in childhood memory but in her growing knowledge of the man he'd become. Strong. Protective. Beautiful. And more than a little wild. "I trust you." A confession that took more courage than she knew she had.

Flames in the depths of his eyes. "You going back to bed?"

"No." She tensed, wondering where this was leading. She might not be changeling, but she knew how to read desire in a man's eyes.

As if he'd heard her unspoken fear, he rose to his feet, held out his hand. "Come on, then. I'll show you some of my forest. I need to get out of here."

Her heart smiled, that defiant hope spreading across her soul in an unstoppable inferno. "I'd like that."

CHAPTER 15

Ashaya looked at the holographic map projected above her desk. It showed the location of her lab in relation to nearby towns and farms. "You're sure the lab won't be discovered?" she asked the man on the other side of the transparent wall of light particles.

Councilor Ming LeBon nodded. "You're surrounded by acres of cornfields, with only a single, apparently unused, access road. From above, the lab looks like a crumbling farmhouse."

"Forgive me if my confidence doesn't mirror yours." She terminated the projection. "You assured me the previous lab was secure. The saboteurs had no trouble getting in, detonating their bombs, and destroying the original prototype. Not to mention the targeted psychic strike that killed several of my top scientists."

"That was an unfortunate mistake on my part," Ming admitted with the emotionless confidence of a man so deadly, most people spoke his name in a whisper. Psy might not feel emotions, Ashaya thought, but even those of her clinical race valued their lives.

"That mistake," Ming continued, "will not be repeated."

His eyes were those of a cardinal but unique in that Ming's had less white stars than most. Liquid black filled his eyes, broken only by one or two pinpricks of light.

The uniqueness of his eyes wasn't a well-known fact—most people had no idea of Ming LeBon's physical appearance. He was a true shadow in the PsyNet. Ashaya was well aware that the sole reason he'd allowed her to see him was because he knew the Council had her totally under their control.

It might have made a human or changeling angry to be so manipulated. Ashaya wasn't human or changeling. She didn't feel fear, anger, any negative emotion. But that didn't mean she agreed with the Councilor. "Explain the security features to me," she said.

"Your job is on the inside. My officers will take care of security."

"With respect, I disagree." If she backed down now, it was all over. "I need to know the options in case of emergency—you have no way to accurately factor in the variables I'd be working with to stabilize safe transport of the prototypes. A fire would require a different response than an earthquake."

Ming watched her, unblinking. His presence filled the room, though he wasn't a large man. The word that came to mind was compact. Compact and sleek, like the assassin he'd been before he became Council. "You're suddenly very interested in security."

"Self-preservation." She didn't look away. "The attack on the previous lab taught me that I am the sole person who can be trusted with my own safety."

"Are you sure you're not considering an escape?"

Ashaya hadn't made it this far in the cold machinery of the Psy world by being easily shaken. "You don't believe that to be a true threat—you've assured my compliance."

"True. And unless you've broken Silence, you aren't a woman prone to making foolish, *emotional* mistakes."

She knew the emphasis had been very deliberate. "I assure you, my conditioning is intact." Even more so than the day she had officially graduated from the Protocol. She felt nothing. There was ice where the emotional heart might have been in a human or changeling woman. "I've made my decisions and I intend to stick by them."

He nodded once, the light catching on the pure white of his hair. She had heard that he'd been born with that hair, that skin. The lack of pigmentation in his body probably accounted for his eyes, but Ming was not an albino in the true sense of the word. No, he straddled an odd line between colorless and too much color. His hair and skin were white but the left side of his face bore a spreading birthmark the color of fresh blood.

"My physical imperfection intrigues you," he said in that oddly accented voice that made it impossible to pin down his origins.

"From a purely scientific standpoint." A true statement. "Why haven't you had it corrected? It would be a simple procedure." Though Psy cared little for looks, serious imperfections were not acceptable. She knew that truth far too well. The single exception was for those born with high-Gradient powers of the mind. However, that dispensation only went so far. The Psy had no chronically ill children, no unfortunate victims of spontaneous mutations. Which made her wonder why Ming chose to flaunt his genetic flaws.

"It is about power," he answered, though she had expected silence. "The difference between what people perceive and reality."

Was that a threat? "I see."

"No, you don't." His tone didn't change. "But what I see is that you continue to argue against Protocol I."

"I've never hidden my views." The idea of drowning all individuality and turning many into one, a one controlled by a privileged few, was nothing she wanted to support. "I made my stance clear when I was asked to head this project."

"You were always the best M-Psy for the job."

So the Council had made sure she couldn't say no. "An interesting paradox, but it proves my point—escape is not an issue."

"No."

Ming's confidence was justified. After all, the Council held Keenan as insurance against her continued cooperation.

They held her son.

CHAPTER 16

Talin was still glowing with the wonder of the night hours she'd spent with Clay when he told her to get in the Tank. "Where are we going?" she asked, putting away the last of the breakfast dishes. "I have to go through these files." Max had kept his promise. The Enforcement data had come through an hour ago.

"To see someone with medical training. They can look over the autopsy reports for you." He began to gather up the hard copies she'd printed out.

"You're right." She picked up the rest of her stuff. "That way, I can concentrate on finding the commonalities between the children." It would help, she told herself. She wasn't just spinning her wheels while Jon was being hurt. "Clay, I'm scared."

"Don't be. We'll find him." With that, he led her outside and to the vehicle, putting the files in the backseat. He was all business, no sign remaining of the man who'd shown her the magic of a moonlight-dappled clearing where a herd of deer slept, his voice a warm whisper against her ear. "Tamsyn's the pack healer, but she's got a medical degree as well."

She nodded, treading lightly. The forest run aside, last night had left them both with emotional bruises.

Clay shot her a sharp glance once they were on their way. "Stop biting your tongue, Talin. It doesn't suit you."

So she was back to Talin in the light of day? "I was trying to be considerate."

"Like I said, it doesn't suit you." He navigated the vehicle down a different forest track from the one they had used to arrive at his lair. "How're you feeling?"

"I thought you didn't like to talk about feelings."

He bared his teeth at her.

She smiled, happy now that she'd gotten under his skin. "I'm fine. I tend to bounce back pretty fast after an episode." It had been either that or give up on life. And though she might not have cherished her body as she should have, she cherished the life Clay had fought to give her. If he hadn't killed Orrin, the other man would have used her in the most brutal fashion, then buried her in the same graveyard as his other "brides."

"Talin?"

She came back from the memories with a shiver. "Sorry, woolgathering. Thank you for taking me out last night. It really helped." She'd never known there was so much life in the night, so much beauty.

"That's not what you were thinking about before. It was the junkyard, wasn't it?"

She didn't have to ask how he knew. "It's our nightmare, isn't it?" No one else could hope to understand. "After they found the bodies, I used to think about how we played there. On top of their graves."

"Yeah." His voice was matter-of-fact. "But you brought something good into that junkyard. Maybe they felt it. Maybe it helped them rest in peace."

It was the last thing she would have expected him to say. "I never thought of it that way. Do you really think that?"

"Why not?"

Yes, she thought, why not? "Did they ever identify all the bodies?" Pa Larkspur had banned her from following the case after she began to get obsessive about it. He'd been right—much longer and she would have fallen back into the abyss.

"Yes." Clay's hands tightened on the wheel. "They were all DNA-banked at birth."

"I'm glad. I visited two of their graves," she confessed.

"So did I." His tone hardened. "After I was told you were dead."

The tension between them went from bearable to cutting. "I thought we'd gone past that." Had last night meant nothing to him? "How many times do you want me to apologize?" Her guilt was crushing.

"I don't want apologies. I never did." He swung out onto a relatively clear track. That wasn't saying much—trees stood tall and thick on either side, blocking them in a tunnel of dark green. "I want an explanation."

"I told you," she said between gritted teeth. "I wasn't in a good place. I needed some space. You're so bossy, you take over everything and I needed to be my own person."

He threw her another look. "There might be some truth in that, but it's not everything. Why, Tally? Why tell me you were dead?"

"Clay—"

"Why?"

"I don't want to—"

"Why?"

"Because you left me!" she screamed, driven to the brink. "You left me!"

Clay brought the Tank to a rocking halt, his brain stunned into silence.

"You promised you'd be there for me always," she whispered, hugging herself. "Then you left." She shook her head and swallowed. "I know you had no choice. You were arrested. But it didn't matter. You were the only person I ever trusted, do you know that, Clay? The only one. Then you were gone and I was alone with strangers again. I was so *mad* at you!"

All this time, he had believed she hated him for killing Orrin the way he had, hated the violence of what he was. "I let you down," he said, accepting her charge.

"Don't," she whispered. "Don't be so nice. It makes me feel even worse."

" 'Nice' is not a word that applies to me." He let the leopard color his voice. "So you were angry as hell with me—why not just tell me to get lost? Why go so far?"

"Don't ask me that." She looked out the window.

He reached across and clasped his hand on the back of her neck. "Look at me."

"No."

"Tally, now is not the time to piss me off."

"You can take your orders and shov—"

Biting back a growl, he shifted across the bench seat to block her in the corner, his free arm braced palm down beside her head. "Would you like to repeat what you just said?"

Big Tally-colored eyes looked up at him. No one else had eyes like hers. Out in the sunlight, the rings of amber almost seemed to disappear but here in the dark of the forest, they glowed hot.

"I was insulting you," she said, echoes of the girl he'd known sparking in those fire and dawn eyes. "And doing it rather well if I made you lose control."

He could smell her fear, but she hadn't budged. "Why fear me? You know I would never put a bruise on your body." He paused, decided to trust the strength of will in that small body, and *pushed*. "Well, I might in one situation."

"What?" She blinked. "You'd never hurt me."

"I didn't say I would. I said I might bruise you." He leaned in and nipped at that soft, luscious mouth of hers, drawing back before she could do more than suck in a shocked breath. "I might bite during sex." No rejection in her scent. His gut unclenched. It had been a risk, founded on their fragile new bond of trust and his leopard's clawing need.

"I am not having sex with you." Her voice was breathy. "Nuh-uh. Not ever."

"Why not?" He wanted to bite her again. "What's wrong with me?"

"I don't like dark men."

That halted him for a second. Until he picked up the deceit in the air. "Lying is a sin, Tally darling." His leopard relaxed, soothed by the realization of her susceptibility to him.

"You're conceited, pushy, and you scowl too much."

He tightened his hand on her nape, just a little. Then he bent his head and licked the full curve of her lower lip. She shivered and pushed at his chest. "No licking. Definitely no licking."

"Why not?" He was almost sure he saw flames racing in the ring of amber around her irises. "I'm a cat. I like licking—all sorts of places."

Her cheeks blazed. "You don't want me that way."

"What way?

"Sexually." It seemed as if she had to force the words out. "You hate me for what I did with those other men, remember?"

Both man and cat continued to wrestle with the sharp edge of jealous rage, but . . . "How can I hate you after what you told me last night? I'm learning to deal."

Her mouth dropped open, then snapped shut. "Yeah, right."

"Hey." He leaned closer, until all he could scent was her. "I'm trying. You could be a bit more encouraging."

"Why?" Her lips pressed down into a harsh line. "So you can play at being the all-forgiving leopard and I can abase myself at your feet? Don't tell me you're a virgin!"

"I've about had it with you," he threatened, such a feeling of life shooting through him that he was drunk on it. Fighting with Tally was more fun than doing anything else with any other woman. "It has nothing to do with the sex."

"Uh-huh."

"You *hurt* yourself, Tally. You fucking did to yourself what—" He bit off his words, refusing to bring Orrin back from the grave. "That's what makes me really mad. And yeah, maybe I'm too possessive with you, but fuck that. You were ready to claw out Faith's eyes over some flowers."

She sat silent, mutinous.

"I figure we're even in the forgiveness stakes."

A narrow-eyed glance. "How's that?"

"I'll try to handle you being with other men that way, and you try to forgive me for not saving you from Orrin all those years ago when he hurt you."

Silence in the car. So deep. So painful.

"How did you know?" she whispered, such naked vulnerability on her face that his leopard shuddered under the blow. "I didn't even know until you said it."

"Because I can't forgive myself either." He kissed her and it was soft, a whisper. "I'm sorry, Tally. I'm sorry."

Talin's heart broke into a thousand pieces. With a jerk, she wrapped her arms around the big body of this man she adored beyond reason. Her fingers dug into his back and she buried her face against his chest, able to hear the powerful beat of his heart under her ear. "I never blamed you," she whispered. "Not consciously."

He leaned back against the seat, taking her with him until she was almost on his lap. "You have every right to blame me."

"No, Clay. We were children."

"Speak the truth now, baby. Only I and the forest will hear you."

She didn't answer for long minutes, letting the hush of the trees settle around them. So many years, she'd kept that knot of anger and pain inside of her, letting it fester, sharing it with no one. And all that time she'd been telling herself that she was doing fine, that she'd make it. But how could she?

"I called your name," she whispered, ripping open a wound so painful, it had never before seen the light of day. "When it started, I didn't have anyone to cry out for. But the first time it happened after we met, I called your name."

Clay's arms squeezed, threatening to cut off her breath but she didn't complain.

"Maybe I blamed you," she admitted, bleeding inside, knowing how much her words had to cut him. "But it wasn't anything so simple. You were the most important thing in my life. I wanted to protect you, too. That's why I never told you the truth." So many layers, so many hurts. "And you blame me for my silence."

"Not for what happened, Tally. Never that."

But she knew he did blame her for stripping from him his chance to help her. "I would still make the same choice." This moment, this instant, it was about honesty. "Orrin would have killed you if I'd told and you'd come after him. You were too young when we met." Nine years old and mostly skin and bone, as if he couldn't eat enough to keep up with his growing body. Not to say he hadn't been tough—but Orrin had been a killer.

"I'm a leopard," he said. "Our women are everything to us. I would rather die than have you hurt. Don't ever try to protect me again."

"I can't promise that." He was her life. It was that simple.

"You're the female." His teeth grazed her ear. "You have to be submissive."

She was tempted to use her teeth on him in retaliation. "Does that ever work?"

"It worked when you were five."

That made her laugh and though it hurt, it was also good—with her acceptance of the truth, a truth that was a child's, not a woman's, she had unlocked the shackles binding her to the past. But even as she laughed, she wondered and worried about the impact of her words on Clay. He was protective and loyal to a fault. He also had a temper that could simmer for hours, days, sometimes weeks, before snapping. If that temper turned inward . . . No!

She set her jaw. She would not let that happen to her beautiful, wonderful Clay. Let this damn disease try to kill her. She would not let it win, not until she'd brought the light back into Clay's eyes.

CHAPTER 17

Safely alone in the car with Clay, it had been easy to make a promise to help him. Now that Talin was in the presence of his packmates, she wondered at her arrogance. He was clearly a much loved and respected member of DarkRiver. What had made her think he had any need of her interference?

Then he glanced at her from where he stood with Nathan and her panic calmed. No matter how much he belonged to these leopards, he belonged to her first.

"I've never seen him look at a woman that way."

Startled, she turned to face the tall brunette who had walked up to stand beside her. Clay had introduced her as Tamsyn, the pack healer. Nathan was her mate. "You don't have to say that," she began, leaning back against the kitchen counter.

"Don't worry." The other woman shook her head. "I might be a healer, but I'm no soft touch. Just ask Kit and Cory." She nodded out the window—at the two teenagers who appeared to be running herd on her twins. "They want chocolate chip cookies, they babysit." She grinned.

Talin found herself smiling in turn. "Excellent trade."

"I thought so." Tamsyn's eyes were warm, an unusual color closer to caramel than true brown. "And what I said earlier, I wasn't doing it to be nice. If you'd been a threat to Clay, I'd have kicked you out of DarkRiver land myself."

"You could've tried." No one was going to separate her from Clay.

"Atta girl." Tamsyn's grin widened. "Sascha said you had spine. She likes you."

Talin didn't drop her guard, though the abandoned child in her melted at the small sign of acceptance from Clay's new family. "Do *you*? You don't think I'm not good enough for him?"

"Hmm, well, now, maybe you're not."

It wasn't what Talin had wanted to hear, though she knew it to be the truth.

"But," the healer continued, "Sascha wasn't particularly good for Lucas when they started out, either. There were some damn heated discussions about him falling for a Psy."

Talin kept getting thrown by these leopards. "Really?"

A nod. "In the end, it doesn't make a difference what anyone else thinks. DarkRiver men make up their own minds." The healer's expression grew pensive. "But that doesn't mean I won't poke my nose into it. You should know that—we're crazy protective of our own."

The back door swung open with a bang and one of the teenagers stuck his head inside. "Juice?" His tone was plaintive.

Tamsyn waved a finger as she went to the cooler. "Your debts are adding up, Cory."

"You totally fleeced us on the cookies—Julian and Roman are like demons on crack. Do they ever stop?"

Talin was taken aback by the boy's smile—a bright slash of unvarnished affection. The teenagers she knew never smiled with such absolute and utter trust.

Walking over, Tamsyn put a jug of something cold and almost colorless in his hand, reaching out to muss up his hair at the same time. "You were exactly the same."

"Aw, come on, Tammy. Don't tell baby stories about me in front of a pretty girl."

Talin was about to turn around and look for that girl when she realized he was looking at her. The cocky charm on his face made not smiling impossible. Just like with Jon. Her smile dulled.

"She's way too old for you." Clay's voice was relaxed as he came to stand beside her. "Go play with girls your own age."

Cory took the glasses Tamsyn was holding out. "Hah! I *told* Kit you were hot for her!" A gleeful look on his face, he backed out the door and jogged to the others.

Feeling her face flush at the boy's estimation of Clay's feelings, she didn't know what to say or where to look. As long as he'd thought of her as a . . . a slut, she forced herself to think, it had been easy to not examine her own reactions too deeply. Why torment herself with things she couldn't have?

But after the devastating honesty of those minutes in the car, she'd started to wonder if maybe there was hope. He'd been direct in expressing his desire to kiss her, but this confusing need aside, what did *she* want? She felt no fear when she lay with a man. Worse, there was an absence of emotion. But with Clay . . . so many feelings, chaos inside her mind, her heart.

Would she feel if he touched her? What if she didn't? Her mind chilled. No way in hell she was letting the ugly isolation of sex taint their new relationship. If they slept together and it made her go to the cold place inside herself, she wouldn't be able to bear it. And Clay would know. It would wound him. She couldn't do that to him.

No, Clay had to remain her friend. Nonsexual. Safe. Forever.

"Hey." His hand touched her lower back, making her jump.

Turning quickly, she faced him. "We should show Tamsyn the autopsy reports while the kids are outside and we can talk without interruption."

Those forest-in-shadow eyes sharpened. "That's what I just said."

"Oh."

"What's going on in that head of yours? Your scent's not right."

It disconcerted her to be in the presence of people who could taste her sweat, her fear, her absolute terror at the thought of messing up this relationship. "It's not right anyway, remember?" If nothing else, she thought with bitter humor, the insidious disease eating away at her mind was good as an excuse.

Frown lines marred his forehead. "This is different."

"The reports."

"I already gave them to her." He nodded at the huge kitchen table behind her.

She turned to find Tamsyn leafing through the pages. Nate stood close by, gripping the back of her chair. "Tammy's not seeing anything obvious," he said, looking up, "but it might help if Talin went over the reports with her."

"Sure. At least I'll be able to split the injuries up into new and old." It would rip her to pieces but she needed to do this—for Jon, perhaps for other lost children they didn't yet know about.

"While you do that," Clay told her, eyes disturbingly intent on her expression, "we're going to see if we can pick up Jon's trail. We'll start from where you lost the scent."

Having already given him the location, she nodded. "Thank you." It was all she could trust herself to say without betraying the turbulence threatening to take her under. After a pregnant pause, she walked to the table and sat down facing Tamsyn.

The healer tilted her head to kiss her mate good-bye and Talin looked away, ashamed to be in the presence of something so beautiful. She had once been loved, she knew that. Clay had loved her. And look what she'd done.

Then a big male hand was touching the back of her head and she was looking up, startled. The kiss he brushed over her lips caught her breath, blew her confusion to shreds. His skin was a little rough, his mouth pure demand . . . and his kiss so right it hurt. He was out the door a second later. She raised trembling fingers to her lips, more than a little afraid of the strength of the feelings he'd aroused.

"You want to talk about it?" Tamsyn's voice was gentle but it broke the spell.

She dropped her hand, wanting to hide away the memory where no one could steal it from her. "Talk about what?"

The healer shook her head. "When you're ready, I'll be here. Now, tell me about this boy."

Talin looked at the file Tamsyn had spread out in the middle of the table. It was Mickey's. Rage hit her in a violent rush and she had to close her eyes for long seconds to compose herself. When she opened them, she found Tamsyn putting a cup of hot chocolate in front of her.

Grateful, she wrapped her hands around the mug as the other woman retook her seat. "Do you always take care of people?"

"It's part of me," was the simple answer. "Would you like more time?"

"No." If the kidnappers stuck true to form, Jon had very little left. "Can you translate the medical jargon?"

"Yes."

For the next five minutes, she listened as Tammy described Mickey's wounds. To her surprise, the beating appeared to have taken place postmortem. "Possibly to hide something else," Tamsyn said. "But if so, they went overboard."

Talin's gut burned at the reminder of the way Mickey's face had been turned to pulp. "Do you think he was killed as a result of the organ removals?"

"Likely." Anger lined the healer's face. "I wish I could tell you he didn't suffer, but what I can tell you is that his death was probably painless. He would've been anesthetized for the procedure, if only to keep him from moving. This beautiful boy went to sleep and never woke up."

Talin didn't cry. She had no right. Not when the monster or monsters who had done this continued to roam free. "The organ removal process?"

"Even the beating couldn't hide the marks of high-level surgery," Tamsyn said immediately. "We could be looking at black market organ sales."

"Max thinks that's a red herring."

Tamsyn's eyebrows rose. "Max?"

"The detective in charge," she explained.

"Oh, right. For a second there you startled me. Clay doesn't share well."

The pit of anger and horror in her stomach threatened to turn to ice. No, Clay didn't share well. And no matter how hard she tried to forget, deep inside, a part of her kept waiting for him to leave her again. But none of that was important at this moment. "Clay and Max think it's about the brain."

Tamsyn picked up the photos of Mickey's brutalized face and body. "Hmm. You know, something's not quite right with these images—I can't put my finger on what . . . The Enforcement pathologists looked at this?"

"They didn't spend much time on it. Just street trash, you know."

Tamsyn's eyes were suddenly pure leopard, a reminder that under that warm human skin lay the heart of a predator. "I'd like to get my claws on anyone who describes these children as street trash."

"So would I." She flexed her fingers. "I might not have claws, but I can use a knife."

Tamsyn's eyes flashed to human in a heartbeat. "You sound very sure."

"One of my adoptive brothers—Tanner—he taught me to use knives when I developed and he thought men were looking at me funny."

"Brothers." The single word held a wealth of affection.

Talin had never really considered how much that act of Tanner's had meant to her, but now she smiled. "Do you have any?"

"No need. I had the whole damn pack watching over me." She put the photos down, then stood. "I need to think." To Talin's surprise, she went to the counter and began pulling out ingredients for some type of baking. "I think better this way," she said, noticing Talin's expression. "The whole Earth Mother routine works for me."

Though it was said in a self-deprecating tone, it was clear Tammy was deeply content with who she was. Talin ached for that kind of peace, that kind of self-acceptance. "I like cooking, too," she found herself saying, when she didn't usually share anything. "I used to do it with my adoptive father."

"Do you want to help?" Tamsyn's eyes brightened. "I'd love a cooking buddy. And if you do the cookies, I can finish up a batch of muffins. I figure Kit and Cory deserve something extra."

Talin hesitated. "I have to work on why these particular children might have been targeted."

"You can do that as well on your feet, stirring"—she brought a bar of dark chocolate to her nose, breathed in the scent—"or chopping chocolate."

"You fight dirty." Pushing back her chair, Talin walked

over. Yes, she could think about the kids even as she did this. It was not thinking about the kids that was the problem. They were ghosts in her mind day and night, whispering at her, pleading with her.

We'll get the bastards, she promised them, subconsciously including Clay in her vow. *And we'll come for you, Johnny D. Just hold on a little while longer.*

CHAPTER 18

Jonquil could hear the sounds of their shoes in the corridor. His hearing had always been good. Better than good. It had saved his life more than once, helped him avoid getting the crap kicked out of him even more times. But today, he knew danger approached and he had nowhere to run.

You have every right to be proud. Stand up straight.

Talin's voice was a whip in his head. She'd said that to him the day he'd been nominated for some dumb city medal. All he'd done was pull a scared little kid out of a building going up in flames. The small burns he'd sustained hadn't even hurt much. But they had wanted to give him an award. He'd been planning to sneak out of the whole deal—like his posse would care that he had a medal—but then Talin had come along, bullied him into a stupid-ass suit, and brushed his hair.

That was when she had told him to stop slouching and be proud. Damn if he hadn't walked onto that stage and taken that worthless bit of tin from the frickin' mayor. Stupid. Except that he'd never thrown the medal away, hiding it in his stash of important stuff. He hoped his stash was still where he'd left it when he got out of this hellhole. And he would get out—he had to apologize to Talin.

The footsteps were getting closer. Closer. They stopped in front of his door.

Fear coated the back of his throat, but he pushed himself upright, back straight, head held high. They could hurt him, but he wouldn't let them break him.

The door slid open to reveal two figures. For a second, before his eyes adjusted to the light, he thought they were painted white. Then he separated out the elements that made up the whole. Their hands were gloved, their faces covered with white surgical masks, and they wore white scrubs like he'd seen at a clinic once.

The only points of color came from their skin, eyes, and hair. The tall one on the left had dark skin, sort of like the color of really thick toffee, the kind that made your teeth stick together. It was all sort of glowing and rich and would have been pretty if he hadn't known that she was there to hurt him. Her eyes were a freaky, pale bluish gray—like a wolf's, he thought—her hair so dark brown it was almost black. He decided to name her Blue.

The one on the right had deep blonde hair, hazel eyes, and the kind of golden skin he'd seen on some rich tanned babes, but never on a woman who looked like she sprayed her hands with antiseptic after shaking, she was that *clean*.

"This way." It was the Blonde who spoke, but as Jon walked out without argument—no use in fighting before he knew the lay of the land—he was certain it was Blue who was in charge. That woman had hips, serious shoulda-been-hot curves, but there was something off about the way she walked, the way she watched him.

In fact, there was something weird about both of them. Before they'd started walking, he'd looked straight into their faces and could have sworn that there was nothing looking back at him. Those eyes. Dead eyes. That's what they were. They reminded him of the eyes he'd seen on some of the street girls, the ones that weren't quite there anymore.

But that made no sense. These women were dressed like scientists, not street pros.

Then they turned a corner and he heard the screams. "Jesus," he whispered. "That's a little girl."

No answer.

"What kind of monsters are you?" He'd meant to play this cool but fuck it, there was some stuff you didn't do, not if you were human.

Blue glanced at him over her shoulder and he realized she wasn't human, not by a long shot. "We're the kind of monsters responsible for your nightmares." Then she opened a door. "Come inside."

CHAPTER 19

Clay nodded to the shopkeeper and jogged back to where Nate stood waiting by a lamppost. "Tally did a good job. That guy confirms he saw Jon. He remembers the kid."

"Who wouldn't?" Nate looked down at the holo-slide Talin had salvaged from her apartment. It bore a jagged crack down one side but was otherwise undamaged. "He's even prettier than Dorian."

It was true. The boy was male without question, but he was also good-looking enough to be on a catwalk. "Boy like that on the street—" Gut tight, he shoved a hand through his hair. "We could be looking in the wrong direction."

"Yeah, I thought so, too, so I checked up on the gang tat." Nate tapped at the spiderweb pattern on the boy's neck, half-hidden by long white-blond hair. "The Crawlers aren't some toy gang. If the kid survived in there, he's got brains and balls. I can see him taking up a career as a bank robber but not as a pro selling his body."

The angry disgust Clay felt was reflected in Nate's face. To DarkRiver, children were everything. They would fight to the death to protect the cubs, but neither man was a romantic. As Clay knew from brutal experience, changelings, too, sometimes fell short. So did humans. Ironically, as Max had said, it was the cold, merciless Psy who appeared to take the best care of their children—aside from the forcible imposition of Silence. There were no Psy street kids, no Psy orphans, no Psy child prostitutes.

Clay looked down the street, at the teenagers he could see hanging out on the corner, all smirks and punk bravado when they should've been in school. "Never thought I'd say this, but the Psy are good at one thing."

"Yeah," Nate agreed, even as the teens gave them wary glances and began to disperse. "We never see their kids fucking around like this. But we never see anything the Council doesn't want us to see. Maybe they simply erase their mistakes."

"You're probably right. Hell, they called Sascha a mistake." And despite the fact that he preferred to keep his distance from Sascha and her too-perceptive gift, Clay knew she was something good, something worth bringing into this world.

"Yep." Nate blew out a harsh breath. "Look, I'll put out the word that we're looking for Jon. We've built up a good network with the businesspeople around here."

Clay nodded. The human and nonpredatory changeling shopkeepers helped DarkRiver in return for the pack's protection against gangs. Over time, as DarkRiver had cleaned house to the extent that no major criminal networks operated in their territory, that relationship had evolved into one driven less by necessity and more by shared interests. "While you do that, I'm going Down Below."

Nate made a face. "That place gives me the creeps. Have fun."

Down Below was literally that. After a short delay caused by taking care of a persistent annoyance, Clay found a backstreet alley, lifted open an antiquated manhole cover, and dropped into the narrow passage that would lead him down into the shattered remains of the unused subway tunnels. A hundred and twenty years ago these tunnels, and the trains that utilized them, had been the height of technology. Then had come the seismic events of the late twentieth century, which in turn had led to innovation in safer methods of transportation. The city's sleek, clear skyways had long since eclipsed the subways.

Coughing against the dirt, he pulled the manhole cover closed behind himself. It was a good thing he had the night vision of a cat because it was pitch-black down here. Tally would hate it, he thought. His leopard wasn't too pleased, either.

As he made his way down and into the tunnels, he could hear the whispers of the Rats. They were scurrying away, leaving their leader to deal with the predator who had invaded their home. Clay knew he was in no danger of being attacked—DarkRiver kept an eye on the denizens of Down Below and, for the most part, the Rats were nothing more than human misfits who had made a ragtag pack of their own. The name—Rats—was a misnomer. Only three of the Down Below residents were actually changeling.

Now, one of those three stepped out of the darkness. "You don't have permission to pass this way. Leave." A flash of razor-sharp canines.

"Cut the theatrics, Teijan." Clay folded his arms and leaned against the tunnel wall.

"Clay?" Teijan stepped closer. "I didn't recognize you—your scent's got human all over it."

Rats had a superior sense of smell, so Clay didn't doubt Teijan's assessment. But it was a surprise. For a man to be branded that deep with a woman's scent, it generally required a sexual relationship. But then again, he and Tally had belonged to each other since childhood. The leopard wasn't fussed—it liked the idea of having her so close. "How's your domain?"

Teijan's near-black eyes darted away and back, an act that would have denoted deceit Above. In the tunnels it was a far more nuanced action. "Don't you mean, 'How's the domain I keep on Lucas's sufferance?' "

Clay shrugged. "Your status is transitory because you choose not to swear full allegiance to DarkRiver." The world of predatory changelings was an unforgiving one. There were allies and enemies. Lines of gray were few and far between.

Teijan shifted his body in jerky movements reminiscent of his animal form. "You know why we're hesitating—if we give full allegiance to DarkRiver, we become linked to the wolves through your blood bond with them. And both DarkRiver and SnowDancer have a way of pinning bit fat targets on their backs."

"We don't use nonpredatories or humans as cannon fodder," Clay responded, sensing a change in Teijan's previous stance.

"Rats aren't exactly nonpredatory." He bared his teeth.

"But you're not strong enough to control San Francisco, even if you had a whole colony." A simple fact dictated by the physical attributes of their different beasts and the natural food chain. "We're locking this city down, Teijan. You have another four weeks to make your decision. Ally with us or leave."

Before the devastating attack orchestrated by the Psy Council on another one of DarkRiver's allies—a deer herd—the Rats had been too weak to bother with. Now they were a possible strength and a current weakness—the tunnels needed to be watched in case this cold war with the Psy escalated into a very real one. But unless the Rats swore allegiance, their word couldn't be trusted.

"We ruled here before DarkRiver," Teijan snapped.

"No, you cowered Below while Psy walked Above," Clay returned, pitiless. "You're no match for us." A human might have read his words as a humiliation but changelings understood dominance.

"If," Teijan now ventured, "we were to swear allegiance, we'd have to come to your aid if called? And to the wolves'?"

"Yes. We'd come to yours in turn."

A pause. "A cat will protect a mouse?"

Clay grinned. "Unless the mouse tries to bite the cat." Betrayal would not be tolerated.

The other changeling's eyes gleamed. "Then perhaps, I should talk to Lucas."

"I'll tell him." Reaching into his pocket, he pulled out a copy of Jonquil's picture. "Right now, I need a favor. Show this photo around to your folks—ask if anyone saw anything."

Teijan took it in an inhuman burst of movement. "A favor? Not an order?"

"A favor." Clay pushed off the wall. "One predator to another."

A sharp smile, full of teeth. That was the problem with the Rats—they lived too much Down Below, forgetting their humanity. It was why there were only three of their kind left in the city. The others had been hunted down after going rogue.

Last year, Clay recalled, Dahlia had succeeded in killing seven residents of Down Below before Teijan had tracked down and slit his former lover's throat. It was a chilling reminder of the road Clay had almost taken. *Almost.* Now he had Tally's kiss and no way in hell was he giving that up. He smiled, wondering what she'd made of their parting this morning. He could still taste her on his lips—a hint of coffee, spice, and pure female heat.

"I'll ask," Teijan finally said. "You swear that if we ally ourselves with you, our home is safe?"

"Hell, Teijan, these tunnels are shot with cracks—but we won't do anything to push you out." The alliance would establish hierarchy once and for all, allowing coexistence. Without that agreement, once the grace period ran out, the Rats were dead. No arguments. No second chances. A harsh law, but it kept peace in the volatile world of predatory changelings.

The only reason the Rats weren't already dead was that Lucas had better control over the blood hunger of his beast than most alphas and he thought decades in advance—ten years ago, when DarkRiver had first begun flexing its muscle, he'd seen potential in the odd dwellers of Down Below.

"The tunnels are sound." Teijan's pride was in his voice. "We keep them repaired."

"Then you'll be fine. We don't want to move in."

A pause, then, "Something's happening. We're everywhere under the city—basements, garages, tunnels, house foundations—and there are times when we hear whispers we shouldn't be hearing."

Like Clay had thought—Lucas was fucking smart. "Any details?"

"An assassination. Psy target," he added when Clay went leopard-still. "Definitely one of them. Someone high up. I can't tell you who's planning the hit but things are shakier with that cold-blooded lot than it looks like from the outside."

"Anything we need to worry about?" The information Teijan had already provided was critical. If the Psy were getting closer to implosion, DarkRiver and SnowDancer both needed to know, to prepare, because like it or not, the psychic race occupied a vital spot in the world's ecosystem. "You get names?"

"They mentioned an Anthony Kyriakus," he threw out. "Never heard of him. Must be one of them."

Clay snapped to attention. "You're sure?" Anthony was Faith's father and the possible leader of a quiet revolution against the Psy Council. Aside from Faith and Vaughn, only the sentinels and DarkRiver's alpha pair knew that deadly secret.

"Yes. But I don't know if he was the target." His eyes flicked to the photo in his hand. "There's something about this boy—he's different. I'll see what I can find out." He was gone in a dark flash.

Retracing his steps, Clay pulled himself out of the manhole before using his cell phone to make a call to Vaughn. "Tell Faith to warn her father."

"I have a feeling even if he is the target, it's Anthony who'll come out alive," Vaughn drawled. "He's a tough son of a bitch."

"If you see him, try and get a feel for the general weather in the PsyNet."

"Last time we spoke, he said the storm winds are building. This other rebel—the Ghost—he's done some serious damage in the past few months." The sound of metal against stone, as if Vaughn was continuing to sculpt as they talked. "So what's this I hear about you?"

"What?"

"You've shacked up with a woman?"

Clay scowled. "None of your damn business."

"Tell that to Faith—she's got a thing for you." Sheer amusement in the jaguar's tone. "She thinks you need a protector. I told her you need one about as much as a pit bull needs one."

"Thanks." He meant that. Talin, regardless of what she said, was damn possessive where he was concerned. She would *not* react well to another woman's interference.

Ending the call, Clay made his way to DarkRiver's business HQ, located in a medium-sized office building near Chinatown. Lucas was meant to be there today—he had a meeting with the heads of a human corporation. Clay, as construction supervisor on the project, had originally been scheduled to attend.

Ria, Lucas's executive assistant, was working at her desk when Clay entered the outer part of Lucas's office.

"He free?"

She smiled. "The meeting wrapped up a few minutes ago."

"Thanks." He entered after a quick knock, knowing Lucas would have already caught his scent.

The other man was sitting on one of the black leather-synth sofas he kept for clients. "Grab a seat while I finish this sandwich."

Clay collapsed into the opposing seat but couldn't relax, his mind on Talin and what it would do to her if they didn't find this boy in time.

"Here." Lucas threw him an apple.

Catching it by reflex, he bit into it. "It's like this kid disappeared into thin air." Clay was one of the most patient hunters in the pack, but today, he felt dangerously on edge.

"What have you got so far?" Sandwich finished, Lucas picked up a bottle of water.

Clay laid out the facts, then glanced toward the doorway. "Nate's here."

There was a perfunctory knock before the other sentinel walked in. His eyes lit up at the sight of food. "I'm starving. Couldn't find anything I liked out there."

"That's because you're used to Tammy's cooking." Lucas pushed the plate of sandwiches in his direction.

"I've got something to tell you about the Rats, too." Clay repeated what Teijan had said, polishing off his apple in the process.

"What's your take?" Lucas asked.

"I say he's serious." He grabbed a couple of crackers. "He hinted at this the last time we spoke but I told him we wouldn't agree to anything but a full pact." A pact, not a true alliance, because the Rats weren't equal to DarkRiver in power. That agreement, DarkRiver had only with SnowDancer. A pact was an acknowledgment of the weaker group's submissive status and a promise by the stronger party to provide aid if necessary.

"He has to come to me." Lucas picked up a bottle of water and set it in front of Nate, lobbing another in Clay's direction. "I go Down Below, it's a concession. Send Barker to deliver the message."

"I'll handle that," Nate said around the cracker he'd bitten into. "This works, we get a built-in spy network. And to think

I argued with you about the Rats when we first took control of the city."

Lucas shrugged. "Calculated gamble. It could've turned out badly if the Psy had ever figured out they were down there, but they didn't. So now we take advantage. Let's have a meeting tonight, decide this. My place."

"Make it Nate's," Clay said. "I can't leave Talin alone." And she wasn't yet trusted enough to be shown the location of their alpha pair's lair. The only reason he'd taken her to Tammy's house was because it was already well known by a number of parties. That was why it was guarded round the clock by a rotation of soldiers most visitors never saw.

"Fine with me," Nate said. "Kids are heading to see their grandparents tonight anyway."

"Talin can't attend the meeting." Lucas met Clay's eyes. "You okay with that?"

"Yeah," he said, but the leopard flexed its claws in disagreement. The protective animal heart of him wanted her accepted unconditionally by the pack—an impossible task. Now, more than ever, DarkRiver had to be careful who it trusted with its secrets. Because not only were the Psy watching, so were changeling and human spies. "She can stay in one of the upstairs bedrooms while we meet downstairs."

"All right." Lucas glanced at Nate. "So, what did you find out about this kid?"

"Boy's a smart troublemaker, but he kept his nose clean until a recent shoplifting charge." Amusement danced in his eyes. "Tried to steal some fancy women's perfume."

Clay snapped off a curse. "For Tally. Idiot kid. He should've known she'd be on to him in a second, even if he wasn't caught."

"Yeah well, what kid thinks straight when he has a crush?" Nate shot Clay a sharp glance. "I know a few men who don't do a lot of thinking either."

Clay refused to be baited. "Nothing's sending up red flags, but then it wouldn't if this is an organized group."

"There is one thing," Nate said. "Everyone I spoke to mentioned that the boy had a beautiful voice. One man said he felt half hypnotized by it."

"That tells us nothing." Lucas frowned.

The leopard in Clay caught a hint of something important but he couldn't pin it down. "It's a factor to add into the mix," he said, getting up to leave. "By the way, Luc, can you ask one of the soldiers to pick up a package for me?"

The alpha raised an eyebrow. "Sure. Any special instructions?"

Clay gave him the details. "Don't damage it." Not yet.

Clay had to force himself not to drag Tally to him the second he and Nate returned to the house. His beast wanted to bite, to taste, to draw her lush Tally scent into his lungs. He satisfied himself with taking the seat beside hers and putting an arm along the back of her chair. "We heard Jon had a good voice," he said, tracing her features with his eyes. "What about the other kids?"

Her gaze clashed with his and he saw her read the depth of his hunger. "Mickey couldn't even do karaoke," she said, cheeks flushing as she bit down on her lower lip. He gripped the back of her chair to keep from taking over the task.

"There goes that theory." Nate collapsed into a chair beside his mate.

Tamsyn kissed him in affectionate welcome. "Talin's done profiles on the kids, but I haven't had much luck—there's something in the autopsy photos. I just can't figure out what."

Clay was about to look down at those photos when his attention was caught by the lists Talin had made, the attributes she'd noted beside Mickey's and Diana's names. The one for Iain was almost as detailed. It listed everything from their heights to known hobbies. Excitement fired in his blood, the cutting bite of a hunt begun.

"What do you see?" Talin leaned into him, her body a soft, luscious weight.

He was suddenly one second away from taking her and damn the consequences.

CHAPTER 20

Clamping down on the savage possessiveness that threatened to derail the new trust between them, he focused on the pages in front of him. "Mickey couldn't sing but it says here that he was a mathematical prodigy. Aren't music and math connected?"

"I think so." She frowned. "But look at Iain's profile—he was a genius at languages."

Clay uncurled his fingers from the back of her chair and stroked his fingers over the skin bared by her sleeveless top, giving in to the starving edge of his need. "Do you have info like this—stuff not in Max's files—on the kids you didn't know personally?" Under his fingertips, she was smooth, resilient, strokable.

"I've been calling around all day," she said, not breaking the contact. "Don't worry, I kept it real low key. A lot of these kids still have open case files at the branches where they connected with Shine, so I pretended to be some office lackey checking data. Sometimes, I called their last known school instead." She dug through her papers.

"Okay, one girl was a brilliant painter. Another had off-the-scale design skills." Talin was very aware of Clay's fingers training up her arm and shoulder to brush her nape. After so many hours without him, she was acutely sensitive to his nearness. More than that, she needed his touch. It anchored her even as it shattered her defenses.

"What else?" His voice was a rumble.

She scrambled to reorder her thoughts. "Diana was a phenomenal runner. Art, sport, math—their strengths are all over the place, no link." It was impossible to hide her disappointment.

Clay's hand closed around her nape and she had the feeling that he wasn't even conscious of the territorial act. "What about the others?"

"My records are incomplete, but I know two more were top athletes," she said, confused by her own reaction to his hold. She was at once wary of what it implied, and hungry for more of the same. "This boy aced every MCAT test that—"

"What?" Tamsyn interrupted. "That's a very specific test. It's used to rank med school applicants."

Talin was so surprised, she almost forgot the dark heat of Clay's possessive touch. Almost. "It's given to all the prospective Shine kids, along with a lot of other tests. To figure out what they're good at."

"But it's so hard." Tamsyn shook her head. "The only people who ace it are M-Psy, and that's understandable because a lot of them can see inside the body."

"This boy was human." Of that Talin had no doubt. "That's the one thing about Shine I'm not comfortable with. They won't widen their mandate to help changelings."

"Gifted human children," Clay said, tone quiet. "That's the link."

Tammy's gaze sharpened. "What about you, Talin? What was your gift?"

"Me?" She shrugged. "Nothing too special. I have an eidetic memory." Except for when the disease ate holes in it, but she didn't want to think about that. It was hard enough to focus with her body rejecting the dictates of her mind, her skin tight with an unnerving depth of sensual hunger. She didn't want to feel desire for Clay. It panicked her to think of their friendship changing in such an irreversible way. "I never forget anything."

Releasing her nape, Clay reached up and tugged at her

ponytail. When she shot him a startled glance, he said, "That is special, Tally. How many other people can say that?"

She still felt it like a kick to the heart each time he unbent enough to use her childhood nickname. She had never allowed anyone else the right. "But if you're right," she said, mind clearing in a thundering wave of horror, "that means it's Shine that's recruiting gifted kids. They're the ones separating out these children from the general population, making them targets."

Disliking the shocked pain he could sense within her, Clay hugged her against his side. He'd braced himself for her flinch, but she came without a fight. It was all he could do not to pull her into his lap. "I know you think it's a mole," he murmured, "but is there even a small chance it could be the foundation as a whole?"

"No." She shook her head, as if thrusting off her shock. "No, they care. All the Guardians—that's my title—are ex-Shine kids. We're the kind of people who'll tear the world apart to find our charges. Iain's Guardian, Rangi, is dealing with a huge family crisis right now, but he contacts me twice every day for updates.

"Most of the other kids that were taken, they didn't have assigned Guardians yet, or believe me, you'd have a whole pack screaming for answers. If Shine wanted easy prey, they wouldn't have chosen people like us to watch over the children."

The leopard appreciated her fierce dedication to those under her care. But that only went so far—soon as they found Jon, she was going to see a hundred specialists if that was what it took. She couldn't die. End of story. His eyes narrowed. "Three of your kids got taken, Tally. Why, if they're looking for those who won't be missed?"

"You're right." Her hand trembled. "Jon's easy to explain—he never agreed to an official Guardian. I just sort of bullied him into cleaning up his act." Clay could see how it tore into her that in trying to give Jon a better life, she might have put him in harm's way. He decided he'd kiss the sass back into her when they were alone. "On the official records, I'm listed as his street contact, nothing more."

He nodded. "Mickey and Diana?"

Talin's chest rose as she took a deep breath. "Mickey, he was mine on the records. I don't know why he was targeted."

She wanted to touch Clay for comfort, curled her hand into a fist to stop from doing so, though she did lean deeper into his embrace. "Di, I'm almost sure was at the wrong place at the wrong time. Easy prey."

"That implies a certain lack of control," Nate broke in. "Everything else points to clockwork precision."

Clay frowned. "Could be the structure's breaking down."

"Or," Tamsyn suggested, "they've become overconfident. They could have started taking the specific children they want instead of waiting for a safe target."

"Maybe," Nate agreed, eyes intent. "Bottom line—you need to get Shine to give up the reason they single out children who might be termed gifted."

"Not all of them are," she pointed out.

Clay stroked his hand up and down her arm, a comforting act but also a disturbing one. "Maybe not, but there are enough that we need to know why."

"I'm not anywhere high enough in the organization. Dev knows me but—" She broke off as something beeped. "What's— Oh, crap." She dug through her pants pocket to retrieve a small silver phone. "The kids I'm watching over for Rangi have this number." Flicking it open, she held it to her ear. "It's Talin."

So close, Clay had no trouble catching the response. His entire body went on alert. A second later, Talin's hand reached out to clutch at his. "Tonight?" She looked at him, eyes huge with shock.

He nodded.

"Yes, okay. What time?" A pause. "All right. I'll talk to you then." She closed the phone. "Whoa, that was weird."

Clay tangled his fingers more firmly with hers as his cat batted the tone of what he'd heard in the air, considered the taste of it.

"I didn't catch the name," Tamsyn said. "Who was that?"

Talin stared. "You heard everything from the other side of the table?"

"Sorry." The healer winced. "Bad manners, but in my defense, human-level speech is pretty loud for us."

"I guess I need to invest in an earpiece." Her tone was intrigued rather than offended.

Clay wondered if she realized she was already thinking in the long term. Something very tight in him unfurled a fraction.

"The name," Nate prodded, when she remained silent.

"Clay." She looked to him, mischief in her eyes. His Tally had bounced back as she always did. But he still intended to pet her afterward. Being able to get past the pain of losing those under her care didn't mean it had stopped hurting. "You want to do the honors?"

He scowled at her for the way she was teasing the others. She grinned, unrepentant. "It was Devraj Santos," he said, his cat delighting in the small bit of fun. It would've surprised his packmates—he wasn't known for indulging in the kind of play that was second nature to them. But Talin had always made *not* playing impossible. He hadn't known how much he missed that aspect of their old relationship until this instant.

"Weird doesn't describe it," Nate muttered. "We talk about him and he calls. You sure he's not an F-Psy?"

Talin laughed. "No, he's very much human—I've heard he's got such a temper, he can't keep a secretary." She rubbed the pad of her thumb along Clay's where their hands lay intertwined. "The meeting's for nine at a restaurant about an hour from here."

Need a raw ache in his throat, Clay looked at Nate. "If we push the pack meeting to six, I can leave with Talin around eight."

"I'll make the calls." Nate stood. "Tammy, how about a hand?" His tone held an intimacy that was so deep and true, it needed no words to communicate itself.

Talin swallowed the lump in her throat and waited until the other couple had gone upstairs before turning. "Clay, you heard Dev say I should come alone."

He nodded, changing their handclasp so he could stroke his thumb along her palm.

Her cheeks colored. "Then, can I borrow your truck?"

"No." Soft, she was so soft.

Lines formed on her forehead. "Why not?" She tugged at her hand.

He refused to let go. "Dev knows very well I'm going to be with you."

"And you know this because you're a foreseer, too?" She smirked.

He wanted to kiss that smirk right off her lips. So he did. She gave a startled little whimper and then a curious stillness stole over her. He didn't push, didn't force, but neither did he back off. She could've done so by making a single move to the side but she didn't. So he kissed her, nibbled at that deliciously tempting lower lip, then licked his tongue over the small injury.

"I said no licking," she whispered into his mouth, her free hand closing over his shoulder.

He squeezed the one he held. "Don't you like it?"

"That's never really been a consideration with me," she said, sounding far too practical for a woman with kiss-wet lips. "To like, I'd have to be involved."

He wanted to bite at her for daring to tell him he might be nothing more than a faceless fuck, the urge so primitive, so animal, it stripped his emotions bare. "We already are involved." He waited for her to disagree—he'd kiss the lie right out of her.

"Yes." She returned his stare, unflinching. "You make my body respond."

He almost smiled. He knew Talin, understood the depth of her scars. Her body would've stayed dead to him if she hadn't already bonded with him on an emotional level—as a smart, independent adult female. Their past bond had survived everything, but it was based on the memories of the children they had been. But this, this was something that required the cooperation of the woman she'd become. And it required patience on his part. Exquisite, gut-wrenching patience.

Releasing his hold on her hand, he reached out to rub a thumb over her mouth. It was one of his favorite parts of her body. "You didn't answer my question."

"W-what?"

He liked that little hitch in her voice, that fracture in her composure. His Tally was tough, but she was beginning to trust him again. It was a trust he'd damn well earn this time. Memories of how he'd let her down the first time threatened to darken his mood but he fought them off. This moment was about a sweet, sexy, simple kiss. He let his eyes brush over the plump curves of her mouth again. "I asked if you didn't like the licking."

She sucked in a shaky breath, her breasts rising in silent invitation. "Does it matter?"

"Hell, yeah." He moved one arm to grip the back of her chair, while closing his other over the seduction of her hip. "Because if you don't like it, I'll have to learn some new tricks. I like doing it, have plans to lick my way across every freckle on your body."

Her skin flushed hot, her eyes brightening with a startled flash of touch hunger. "When did you get so verbal?"

He smiled, slow, pleased. "I talk when I have something to say. Stop avoiding the question."

"Fine." Jerking forward, she flicked her tongue along *his* lower lip.

One hot, wet, stroke and his cock so was damn hard it felt like it was made out of granite. "You like it." Body heavy with need, he began to lean toward her.

"On the mouth," she said, just before their lips touched.

He blinked. "The body?"

"Well, most parts of the body would probably be okay," she answered, her mouth brushing his. "But not *there*."

Surprised by her shyness with him—no matter their years apart, they had never been strangers—he ran his lips along her jaw and nuzzled gently into her neck. Her hand rose from his shoulder to push into his hair. It was tempting to take his other hand off the back of her chair and stroke it down to her breasts, but he kept it where it was, his grip white-knuckled. *Slow*. This had to be a seduction not of the body alone but of the mind, too. He'd lost Tally once. Damn if she was ever leaving him again.

"Why not?" he whispered against her neck, flicking out his tongue to taste the lush femininity of her skin.

She jerked but then, to his shock, nipped at his ear with sharp little human teeth. He'd never before had to worry about spilling in his jeans. "I haven't forgotten the question." But he had realized that Tally was going to drive him insane in bed. God, he couldn't wait.

"It's just so . . . well, the whole thing seems very embarrassing and undignified."

It was the last thing he'd expected to hear. The leopard wasn't quite sure how to react. "Well, now," he said after getting his voice back, "that's a challenge if ever I heard one."

Her hand clenched in his hair. "I didn't mean it to be." She sounded very young and very honest.

Unexpectedly, he felt the same way. "How about you let me? Once?" Right then, he could've been a teenager trying to talk his date into the backseat. But only if that date had been Tally—he'd never flirted this way with any other. Neither had she. He knew that in his gut.

"*Clay.*" Her face was hot against his cheek, the tendons of her neck stretched taut. "We aren't going there. I told you."

He began to kiss his way up her neck. "Just once," he said, pressing a kiss below the curve of her ear and drinking in her responsive shiver. "You can even set a time limit."

"Stop it." But she made no effort to halt him as he nibbled his way along her jaw and back up to her mouth. "We aren't going to sleep together."

"Fine, we can do it with you on the kitchen table," he murmured, drowning in the rapid beat of her pulse. It echoed the thunder of his own. "Or maybe on the cushions with you on your hands and knees. I like that one."

She moaned and the kiss this time was open and hot and wet. When they broke apart, her eyes were huge, her lips bruised. "No."

He gave in to the leopard's urge to bare his teeth. "Why not? We're good together." And she sure as hell wasn't going to be touching any other men. A growl built up in his throat.

"You're my friend." She scowled. "Sex will mess that up."

He looked at that stubborn mouth, those expressive eyes, and suddenly understood what she couldn't say. Sex had ruined her childhood, scarred her so badly that she'd used it as a weapon to hurt herself. For her it was nothing good, nothing that could be allowed into this relationship.

Because, he understood at last, *this relationship was important.*

His beast calmed. It wasn't the calm of surrender but that of a predator sizing up his prey. "I'm a healthy adult male," he began.

"And you have needs." All softness leaked out of her face. "Spare me the lecture—if I don't give it to you, you'll get it from somewhere else. Do I have it right?"

CHAPTER 21

Clay decided it would be impolitic to laugh. If she'd been a leopard, she'd have been showing him her claws about now. "Not quite."

"What, there's been a new development?" she snorted. "Men are all the same."

"As a healthy adult changeling male," he continued, ignoring her glare, "touch is part of my life. I won't turn into a raving lunatic if I don't get it—living without a pack for so many years taught me how to go without the kind of touch most of DarkRiver takes for granted."

She continued to watch him, eyes narrowed.

"But," he said, "it's important to me." He was known as a loner but that had never meant exclusion. Not in DarkRiver. "Same as when I was a kid."

She folded her arms. "You just said you got used to not having it so much when you were young."

"No, I said I got used to living without the kind of touch the pack takes for granted," he corrected. "I had another kind of touch to keep me sane. I had you."

"I have no idea what you're talking about," she said, arms falling to her sides.

But he could see she did remember. All those times when she'd crawled into his lap, neither of them saying a word as he held her and they watched the sun set over the broken edges of the city. All those hugs she'd given him without guile. All those days she'd held his hand as he led her safely through the junkyard.

"That was friendship." Her eyes filled with memory. "You were my best friend."

"I still am." He always had been, in spite of what he might've said in anger.

"So, why . . . ?"

"Is that all you want? That we be friends?"

A hesitation, then she nodded. "Friends." Talin needed this relationship to be something pure, unsullied by lust and the evil it spawned.

"And if I need the touch of a friend from you, will you give it to me?"

Wary of the cat's nature, she looked into his face. "Friends don't kiss."

"Actually, a small kiss given to a packmate is considered normal," he told her, "but I won't ask that of you if it makes you uncomfortable. I'm asking about the things you did before."

The hugs, the friendly contact, without expectation, without the dark stain of sex. "Yes." She smiled and wrapped her arms around him. "Yes."

His own came around her. "Good."

Her smile threatened to crack her face. This would work. Without desire to sully up the waters, maybe they could forget the mistakes they had both made and go back to the innocence of what had once been between them.

Clay hoped to God he knew what he was doing. Sitting there on the carpet in Nate and Tamsyn's living room, his legs sprawled out in front of him, it was all he could do not to groan aloud in frustration. A few hours ago, Tally had agreed to a friend's touch. What if she never took the step into accepting a lover's? And he would try to become her lover, of that he was certain.

By leopard logic, he was her friend, therefore any touch of his was a friend's touch. That bit of feline reasoning gave him space to play with her and slowly, oh-so-slowly, convince her that sex between them didn't have to mean the loss of everything good. What he refused to consider was that he might fail in that endeavor.

"Sorry I'm late," Mercy's voice broke into his thoughts.

With her arrival, all the sentinels—Clay, Vaughn, Nate, Dorian, and Mercy—were there. Lucas sat on the floor opposite Clay, Sascha curled up on the sofa behind him. Vaughn's mate, Faith, usually attended, too, but had decided to sit upstairs with Tamsyn and Tally today. Clay was a little worried about that. Then again, he thought with a burst of possessive pride, Tally was more than capable of looking after herself.

"Okay," Lucas said, "this is about the Rats." He laid out the facts. "Do we accept their offer and give them free run of the tunnels?"

"Would they be reporting back to us?" Mercy asked from her armchair.

Lucas nodded. "The pact equals a formal acceptance of our rule."

"Big decision," Nate said, "letting another predator, even a weak one, in on our patch."

"They get aggressive, the pact's nullified." Lucas's face was icily practical. "They'll be dead within hours."

"Strategically," Vaughn said, "their range is one of our most vulnerable spots—our beasts don't like it down there. If the Psy learn enough about us to take advantage of that, they could do a hell of a lot of damage." He turned. "Clay?"

"I agree." Oddly enough, despite the aggressive lure of his beast, this was what he brought to the sentinels—a perspective shaped by his humanity. It was less because of his genetic inheritance than the fourteen years he'd spent pretending to be fully human. That human side could look beyond the leopard's territorial instincts. "Teijan's solid—that's why it took him so long to decide. He won't break the deal if we don't." There was a streak of honor in the rat that might've surprised those who judged him on the nature of his beast.

Dorian began to play his ever-present pocketknife in

and over his fingers, the absent movements smooth as white lightning. "I've dealt with Teijan—trading info. His people aren't the best fighters, but they're excellent spies. Human members included."

Lucas raised an eyebrow. "Takes one to know one?"

Dorian's grin was quicksilver. "Something like that."

"At our initial meeting to discuss a formal pact, they struck me as honest though wary," Sascha said, speaking for the first time. "Teijan won't give his loyalty lightly, but I don't think he'd betray an alliance either. There's something very proud about him."

"That a professional opinion?" Dorian asked. "Did you read him, Sascha darling?"

Sascha scowled at the blond sentinel. "That would be unethical. My instincts say he's trustworthy."

Dorian shrugged. "Your instincts are those of an empath."

Clay agreed. Sascha might not have done a conscious reading, but she had to have picked up something that had led her to make that statement. "Maybe you need to have another meeting with Teijan and his people."

"I'm not reading them." Sascha's scowl grew deeper.

Lucas reached up to tug at the end of her plait. "Damn ethics."

"I'll go to the meeting," she said, slapping away his hand but with a smile edging her lips, "and I'll let you know what I think, but it'll be my *opinion*, nothing else."

"Jeez, Lucas," Dorian muttered, "I thought you said you were corrupting her."

Sascha threw a cushion at him. Laughing, Lucas caught Dorian's return volley. "Stop teasing my mate. She's in a temperamental woman mood."

Mercy's low growl filled the air.

Dorian snorted. "You're just mad because you drew the short straw."

"Why do I have to be the liaison with the wolves?" Mercy demanded. "Riley is such a damn stick in the mud, I want to—" She clawed her hands and made feral sounds.

"I'll lend you a knife," Dorian drawled. "That way, you won't get your girly nails dirty."

Mercy tackled him in a pounce that Dorian fielded with expert grace. He still failed to keep her from pinning him to the ground—because he was laughing too hard.

Clay looked around at his grinning packmates and knew Tally belonged in this circle. She was his now. No one and nothing—not her fears, not that damn disease—was going to keep her from him.

Talin had thought of Sascha as a tough sell, but Lucas's mate had nothing on Faith. While the small, curvy redhead had the same night-sky eyes as Sascha, the similarity ended there. Faith's smile was rare, an indefinable darkness to her that Talin recognized—because she held echoes of the same thing inside herself.

"So, you knew Clay in childhood?" Faith asked as they sat in the large rumpus room upstairs. "He's never mentioned you."

Talin felt a stab of hurt followed by irritation. Who was this woman to question her about Clay? "Unsurprising, really. We were very young the last time we saw each other." But he had walked in her soul every day of her life.

"I knew about you," Tamsyn said from where she sat in an armchair between Faith and Talin. She was knitting something using a green wool that reminded Talin of Clay's eyes. " 'My Tally,' that's what he called you."

"You knew?" Faith frowned, the expression so subtle it was as if she hadn't yet learned to share her emotions without shields. "Of course, you've known him much longer."

Tamsyn continued to knit as she talked. "Yes. But he's become good friends with you very quickly. You must have some kind of magic."

The jealousy that hit Talin was a vicious creature, tearing and ripping and violent. "I guess he must've developed a thing for helpless women." The bitchy comment was out before she could stop it.

Tamsyn's knitting needles paused, then resumed. Faith raised an eyebrow. "What makes you think I'm helpless?" Her smile was ice.

Talin wasn't backing off, not after the cracks Faith had taken at her. "You look like a touch would bruise you." The other woman's skin was a creamy gold with not a freckle in sight. "The word that comes to mind is fragile."

Tamsyn laughed. "Sorry, ignore me. You two go on."

Talin glanced between the DarkRiver women, felt a flush creep up her neck. "Clearly I'm missing something." The sense of exclusion hurt all the more because she'd thought Tamsyn liked her.

"I'm sorry, Talin." There was no laughter in Tamsyn's gentle voice. "I was only thinking of what Clay would say if he heard you two."

Talin kept her attention on Faith. "What are you, a telekinetic or something?" she asked, very aware of being outside the closed circle of Clay's new family.

Faith's eyes were intent, eerie in their focus. "I see the future."

"You're an F-Psy?" A being so rare that Talin didn't know anyone who had ever actually met one. "A cardinal F-Psy?"

"Yes. Believe me when I tell you—the things I see, they're not for the weak."

"I take back the crack about you being fragile then," she said. "But friend or not, you have no right to get between me and Clay." She might be a puny, powerless human, but just let anyone, even a cardinal, try to keep her from Clay.

"You and Clay. So there is a relationship?"

"Yes." With that single word, Talin felt a fundamental shift inside of herself. "If you have something to say about that, say it to my face instead of dancing around it."

Tamsyn's needles stopped completely, but Faith didn't flinch. "I see the future. Sometimes, I see things about people who matter to me."

That destroyed Talin's anger as nothing else could have done. "What?" she whispered. "What do I do to Clay?"

"I don't know." Faith's response was quiet, her voice so crystal clear it reminded Talin of Jon's. "But what I do know is that the future hasn't yet changed."

"What does that mean?" She wanted to shake the foreseer, make her stop talking in riddles.

"It means that whatever you are, you're not yet the woman who'll stop him from crossing the final line . . . from losing his humanity."

CHAPTER 22

Max turned to block the attack an instant too late.

They fell on him in a sadistic swarm, kicking and punching. They didn't yell, didn't scream, and their utter silence was a threat in itself. He fought back, but there were too many. After a while, his world narrowed down to a repetitive chorus.

The thud of flesh on flesh, the rasp of skin against the asphalt, heavy, pained breaths. A trickle of warm blood down his face.

The sound of a gun being fired. Then . . . nothing.

CHAPTER 23

Clay took one look at Talin's face when she came downstairs into the kitchen and knew she'd gone head to head with Faith. She stopped with a good foot of space between them. Scowling, he closed the distance and took her stiff, cold hand. When she tried to pull it away, he had to remind himself to act civilized. "I thought we were friends."

That made her press her lips tight, but she stopped fighting him.

"Are you going to tell me what happened?" Silence. "Fine. I'll ask Faith."

Her eyes narrowed. "Are you in love with her?"

Where the hell did women get ideas like this? "She's Vaughn's mate."

"So?"

"So, what?" Clay shoved a hand through his hair. "Meddling in each other's business is what packmates do. I don't like it much, but you learn to live with it."

"She thinks she has rights over you."

Now *this* was interesting. "Your possessive side is showing again, Tally."

"Stop it." She tugged at her hand.

He refused to let go. "She does have rights over me," he said. "Just like I have rights over Sascha or Tamsyn. It's about looking after your own. They're Pack."

"And I'm not."

"Not yet." Wanting to possess her until his scent was a permanent marker on her skin, he pulled her toward the door. "Come on, we need to get to this meeting on time."

They were there in plenty of time as it turned out. Entering the restaurant, Clay let Talin talk. She'd been quiet on the ride over and he knew her well enough to know she was working things through in her own head. That could be dangerous, but he was playing for keeps and he wasn't going to lie to her. Distract while he persuaded, but never lie.

"We're here to meet someone," she told the maître d'.

The rigid man looked first at Talin's jeans and the thin V-necked sweater she'd pulled on over her top, before moving to Clay in his jeans and white T-shirt. "I believe you have the wrong establishment," he suggested, his nose so high, it was a wonder he was able to see them over it. "The nearest bar is two blocks over."

Clay waited to see what Talin would do. He could almost see the steam coming out her ears. "Where's the nearest unemployment office?" Saccharine sweet and oh-so-innocent. God, she turned him on when she got all pissy like that.

"I'm sure I wouldn't know." A sniff.

"You will pretty soon if this is the way you treat your guests." Her voice turned to steel. "I could be anyone."

The man smirked. "Your clothes give you away, my dear. If you're going to play in grounds above your station, I suggest you get a better costume. And," he sneered, "a more refined companion."

That last made Tally narrow her eyes. "Why, you stiff-necked prick. My *companion* is worth a thousand of an arrogant snob like you."

Clay was enjoying this but no one insulted Talin in front of him. "Hey, Tally."

She glanced over her shoulder. "What?" Her tone was close to a snarl.

"You think I should show him how refined I can be?" A quick flash of lengthening canines, eyes cat-green.

The maître d's face went white behind her.

Clay barely held back his laughter.

Talin smacked his arm. "Behave, you're not helping." She returned her attention to the maître d'. "Now, where were we— Are you all right? You look very pale."

"I'm, uh, fine." His fear an astringent irritant to Clay's senses, the maître d' ran his finger along the screen of his little computer tablet. "Who did you say you were meeting?"

"Mr. Devraj Santos."

The man's voice was reedy when he spoke. "Mr. Santos booked one of our private dining rooms. If you'll follow me."

Clay put his hand on Talin's lower back as they climbed the stairs behind the other man. "I don't think he likes me," he whispered in her ear.

"I thought I told you to behave," she hissed. "Why did he react like that?"

"Because"—he pressed a kiss to her jaw, sensing her amused mood—"he figured out that I was a big, bad pussycat."

Halting, she glared at him but it was without heat. "This is a leopard town—they should be used to you. What do you guys do to people who cross you?"

"We don't eat them . . . well, not often," he teased. "But a reputation is a handy thing." The reality was that people were starting to realize the cats controlled several major parts of the city. "We have massive clout." However, since DarkRiver was a disciplined unit, not a band of thugs, they didn't, as a rule, go around flaunting that power.

On the other hand, an occasional reminder by one of the senior pack members—as he'd given tonight—ensured no one got complacent. That happened, other predators would start trying to move in, human, changeling, and Psy. "They know we can make life difficult."

"Like the mafia?" Reaching out, she fixed his hair, tone affectionate.

He preened under the attention. "Hey, we don't ask for protection money." And they didn't pursue petty vengeance, but the maître d' didn't know that. "Plus, cement shoes are so last century."

"You're terrible," she whispered, and started climbing again. "You scared that poor man half to death."

"He deserved it." He squeezed her hip with his hand, wondering if she really was against biting—'cause he was dying to test his teeth against the sweet temptation of her butt. "No one except me gets to be mean to you."

She rolled her eyes, but he saw her fighting a smile. "Ditto, kitty cat." That smile peeked out at his scowl. "It was kind of funny, but I'll deny that if you ever call me on it."

When they cleared the steps, it was to find the maître d' standing in front of an open door midway down the hall. "If you would like to wait inside," he said, careful to keep his distance from Clay, "I'll show Mr. Santos up as soon as he arrives."

"Thank you," Talin said.

Clay paused long enough to give the other man the cool smile of a predator on the hunt before Talin dragged him inside and shut the door. "Enough."

Liking the fact that she was comfortable enough to give him orders, he searched the room for a secondary exit. The window was high but more than big enough. He could climb out with Talin on his back. Satisfied, he walked back to where she stood against the door.

"Most people don't react as badly as that guy," he said, bracing his arms palms down on either side of her head. He left enough room that she didn't feel trapped, but still, his leopard purred when she remained in place. "He must be one of those humans who thinks of us as animals. Probably waiting for me to order live venison."

"Don't take that high-and-mighty tone." She poked a finger into his chest. "Unless you don't know of any changelings who think of humans as prey."

He winced. "You're right. Some of the predatory species tend to lump humans in the same group as cattle and deer." Prey, kept safe only because even in animal form, a changeling's mind was half man.

"What do you think?" she asked, tone arch.

"I think I don't want to feel the sharp edge of your tongue." Pushing off the door, he walked to the western side of the square table and pulled out a chair. It was a position that would allow him to keep an eye on both exits. "A seat, my lady."

She wandered over, looked him up and down. "Funny, you look like Clay."

He jerked up his chin in a silent question.

"You're being charming."

If she knew the control it was taking to keep the brutal possessiveness of his nature from taking over, she would've been terrified. His hands clenched on the back of the chair as she sat, the high tail of her hair brushing over his fingers. Though he knew she didn't consciously realize it, her acceptance of the seat—of allowing him behind her—was an act of primal trust, baring as it did the vulnerable nape of her neck.

He wanted to lean down and press a kiss to that creamy skin. Tally didn't have freckles there. "Don't worry," he assured her, intrigued by his discovery. "I'll be back to surly and uncommunicative soon enough."

"Idiot." She laughed as he took a seat beside her, on the side closest to the door. No one would be able to get to her without going through him. He was about to give in to temptation and reach out to play with a strand of her hair when he heard footsteps. Rising, he went to the door and opened it.

A tall man—dark hair, dark eyes, possible weapon in a shoulder holster—exited the staircase behind the maître d'. Clay heard him dismiss the restaurant employee and head directly to the door. "You must be Clay Bennett." Reaching him, the man extended his hand.

"And you must be the SOB who tried to pin a tail on me this morning."

He heard Talin gasp but ignored it, his attention on Santos's reaction as their hands dropped away from each other. The man was smooth, he'd give him that. Not a flicker of surprise marred his expression. "You sound very sure."

"He sang like a canary." Clay had taken care of the tail before going Down Below.

"Ah." Santos raised an eyebrow. "That explains the lack of a communiqué from him. Is he still alive?"

"For now." Clay moved back, allowing the other man to enter but blocking his access to Talin.

Santos closed the door behind himself. "Talin, you're looking well."

"Uh-huh."

Clay was pleased to see Talin's skeptical expression as she eyed her boss's elegantly cut suit. The man looked like a corporate shark, but Clay's animal saw him as something far more interesting—a predator clothed in human skin.

Giving them a meaningless smile, Santos took a seat. "Perhaps we should order first?"

Clay returned to his chair. "We've already eaten, but coffee might be good."

Talin picked up the menu pad and input selections for both of them. "I'll have coffee, too. Maybe a slice of cake."

"You'll excuse me if I eat. I've had a rather hectic day." Santos made his selections and sent them through as Talin sent hers. "I've just come from a private hospital."

"One of the kids?" Talin's concern colored the air.

"I'm afraid Max is no longer in play."

Clay tensed at the tone of his voice. "What happened?"

"He was attacked." Santos's eyes went flat, deadly. "Beaten into unconsciousness."

Talin sucked in a horrified gasp. "Is he—"

"He has several broken bones and some cranial swelling but he's alive, thanks to an interruption by a group of civic-minded individuals." The Shine director passed over a card. "That's the private facility where we moved him after we realized what had happened. It's far more secure than the public hospitals."

Clay looked at the card, recognizing the area. "Any idea who attacked him?"

"We're assuming it was the same person or persons who vandalized Talin's home—Max wasn't able to tell us anything." He folded his arms in front of him and smiled. It was a shark's smile, full of teeth. "He got one of them, though. The others took the body, but from the blood splatter and tissue left behind, it was a head shot."

Clay was surprised to find he liked Max, was furious the cop had been targeted. "Let me guess—DNA came back 'record unknown'?"

"Of course. But we were able to determine the race as

human." The hand he'd placed on the table clenched. "Casualty or not, the attack succeeded in taking Max, and therefore Enforcement, out of the equation. We believe he'll recover fully but until then, you appear to have become our best source."

Talin took a shaky breath but her next question held an edge. "Dev, you keep talking about 'we' and 'our.' Who are the others?"

"Shine's backers. They control the board."

Clay heard a sound coming from inside the walls and identified it as a dumbwaiter, likely part of the "olde-worlde" charm advertised on the restaurant's menus. "Tally, would you do the honors?" He had no intention of turning his back on Devraj Santos.

A quick, adrenaline-inducing brush of her hand on his thigh and she rose. "Just don't start expecting this every day."

Santos remained in place while she went to retrieve the dishes. "Thank you," he said when Talin put them on the table. He didn't attempt to reach for his plate until she'd retaken her seat. Trying to appear friendly. Harmless. Yeah, right.

"Why come to us instead of going to another cop?" Clay asked, ignoring his coffee. "Our chances of having anything are close to nil."

"We've had an interest in DarkRiver for some time." Santos took a bite of his pasta. "You're surprised by my candor."

"Yeah." What surprised Clay more was that though he'd forced Santos to take the less secure seat, the other man had subtly angled his chair so he could keep the exits in sight. Interesting. He'd expected a desk jockey and gotten a soldier.

"I don't understand." Talin pushed aside the cake she clearly no longer had an appetite for. "I thought this meeting had to do with the missing children, not DarkRiver."

Santos's face became a cool, dangerous mask. "It does. But the abductions are part of a larger issue."

"Is Shine behind them?" Talin asked point-blank.

"We aren't taking them off the street, but we are responsible."

CHAPTER 24

"Why?" Talin whispered. "Why would you hurt them like that?"

"We aren't killing the children." The other man put down his fork, having finished his meal despite the distasteful topic. Another betraying act. Soldiers ate when they could. "We're responsible because we're too good at identifying them. At which point, somebody is betraying that information to the others."

Clay couldn't figure out one thing. "From what I know, Shine has a lot of political power—why didn't you push harder with Enforcement?"

"It's not a secure system—leaks happen on an hourly basis." Santos took a long drink of water. "We chose Max because he has a natural shield against Psy interference and integrity. There aren't many like him. To pressure Enforcement would've done more harm than good in this case."

"Why?" Talin insisted. "No one else is doing anything to find these kids."

"On the contrary, we've been trying from the start." His skin pulled taut over his cheekbones. "But our enemy is too good at hiding. That's why we've stopped recruiting."

"I wondered about that," Talin murmured. "You haven't sent out street teams for months."

"We can't risk fingering any more children." He shook his head. "We're also trying to protect the ones already in our system, but you know these kids. Most of them move to their own rhythms."

Talin didn't argue. "What can you tell us?"

"They're being taken because of their abilities."

"We already knew that," Talin responded.

"We think the Psy are taking them."

Clay kept his face expressionless in spite of that unexpected bit of news. "Why?"

"These children represent the best humanity has to offer. They are the brightest stars in our arsenal—a potential threat to Psy power." He nodded at Talin. "Your ability to remember everything you ever see is almost a Psy ability in itself."

True enough as far as that went, but Clay didn't buy it. Neither, it seemed, did Talin. "There are gifted kids around the world. Heck, a lot of them are in special schools, ripe for the picking. Why take only Shine children?"

"Because"—Santos's tone turned bitter—"we've painted bull's-eyes on their backs."

An answer that told them exactly nothing, Clay thought. "Why the interest in DarkRiver?"

"You have Psy connections." The other man leaned back in his chair but continued to keep both hands in view. "Your alpha is mated to a cardinal. Sascha Duncan's mother, Nikita, is a Councilor."

"That relationship has been terminated," Clay said, knowing he was betraying no secrets. Nikita had made it publicly clear that she no longer considered Sascha her daughter.

"You also have Faith NightStar, the strongest F-Psy in the world. She has ongoing links with the PsyNet."

"She subcontracts her services." Clay shrugged. "She's not in the Net." The biggest information archive in the world, it could only be accessed by those Psy uplinked to it. Sascha and Faith had both cut that link on their defection to DarkRiver.

"That doesn't mean she's not in touch with others who are uplinked." He paused but Clay remained silent. "The deciding factor is that DarkRiver has shown itself both capable of, and willing to, go up against the Psy. The foundation's backers believe you may prove amenable to helping us mount a search and rescue operation for the children."

"You had to have followed me to get to Clay, so you know the pack's already agreed to help," Talin said, cutting through the bullshit in her direct way. "You could've told us your theories in a simple call."

Santos's lips curved at her arch reference to the fact that he hadn't given them anything worth shit. "I wanted to express the foundation's support of DarkRiver's actions. You will have our total cooperation."

"We want to put people inside Shine to weed out the spy," Clay said.

"We can't allow that, but we're taking all possible measures to corner the culprit."

"Nice definition of total cooperation," Talin muttered.

"So, in a nutshell—you have nothing we don't already know and you came to give us permission?" Clay let the leopard's arrogance out to play. "Is that right?"

Santos's hand fisted against the tablecloth. "There are things we're not ready to share."

"How about the complete files on the missing kids?" Talin's tone was harsh. "The ones you gave Max are doctored."

Santos couldn't hide his surprise this time. "You don't simply remember everything, do you, Talin? You rearrange the pieces until you find a pattern. I forgot that aspect of your abilities."

"Answer the question. Can you get her the files or are you even more useless than you appear?"

The other man's eyes turned assassin cold. "Careful, Mr. Bennett. I'm not the easy prey you think I am."

"I think you're a wolf in corporate clothing but as far as the search goes, you haven't given us shit. Either front up or get out of it."

"These are our kids." Santos's voice held a raw protectiveness Clay hadn't expected. "Everything we do is to keep them safe."

"Then give me the files," Talin pleaded. "You said it yourself—I see patterns. Maybe I'll see something that'll help us find the children."

The Shine director didn't say anything for several minutes. "I'll have hard copies couriered to DarkRiver's Chinatown

HQ by tomorrow morning. Destroy them after you memorize them." He pushed back his chair. "I have a flight to catch."

Clay rose. "We'll call you if we find anything."

"I'll give you what I can." His sophisticated mask slipped to display the ruthless interior. "There are those who want to go softly, but I'm not having any more children die on my watch." He seemed about to say something else but then glanced at Talin. "Read the files without the blinders of knowledge. Let's see what patterns you find."

Dev waited until he was in his soundproofed rental car before making the call. "You underestimated them."

"We can't risk—"

"Yes, we can." His hand threatened to crush the phone. "Children are dying."

"We need to know if DarkRiver is secure enough to entrust with this information."

"Who are you afraid will find out?" He was an inch away from throwing the phone through the windshield. "*They already know.* That's why they're taking our children!"

Talin was irritated and tired by the time they parked the Tank in its hiding place next to the lair. She had wanted to visit Max, but Clay had nixed that idea on the grounds that they could lead danger to Max and vice versa. Instead, he'd made a call on a secure line and been told that Max was unconscious but stable.

Frustrated by her own inability to protect those she cared for, she struck out. "I can't believe Dev's hiding things that might help us find Jon!"

"He did give us one crucial piece of information," Clay said, his hand on her lower back as they walked toward the lair. "The Psy."

She shook off his hold. Her skin reacted to his touch in ways she found disturbing—because, her bold statement to Faith aside, she wasn't sure what the hell she wanted. Only that she couldn't lose Clay. "We have no proof of a Psy link. Max is a good cop—he'd have found it if it existed."

Clay pulled open the door and used the newly installed voice activation system to turn on the lights. "What the hell is it with you and Max? He's fine—I've been injured worse and survived," he muttered after she entered. "What, you have the hots for the guy?"

Her heart stuttered at hearing he'd been that badly hurt, but she hid it. "You're making me crazy!" Swiveling, she headed toward the ladder. "I just happen to think he's a nice, trustworthy, considerate guy. You know, I could do a lot worse!"

Clay snorted and followed her up the ladder. "Nice. Trustworthy. Considerate," he mimicked. "Makes him sound about as exciting as shoe leather."

"Maybe I don't want exciting," she said through gritted teeth, wondering how they had ended up in this conversation. Turning, she faced him. "Maybe I want normal."

"Normal?" His tone was edgy, dangerous.

For the first time in days, she felt a hint of wariness. Clay was tired and annoyed, too. She probably shouldn't push him. The woman who had flinched at his first touches wouldn't have. Somewhat to her surprise, Talin found she was no longer that woman. "Normal," she repeated. "I want a nice, human boyfriend who doesn't have any kinky hang-ups like licking."

Clay took a step toward her. "Kinky?"

She took a step back. "Uh-huh."

"Human?"

"Definitely human. No claws. No growling. No sharp teeth." She made her tone so firm, she almost believed herself. "Normal. Ordinary." Things she had never been. "White picket fence."

Clay's eyes darkened to near black and he stopped his stalking advance. "Really?"

"Really." She forced it out. "I'm tired of being on the outside."

Clay's instincts flared awake. "What aren't you telling me, baby?"

"Nothing." She looked up, then back. "I need to get to bed."

"Where you can dream about your ordinary human boyfriend?" He advanced toward her once more, his shock that she might actually prefer a human male disappearing under the naked intensity of the emotions swirling in her eyes.

"Maybe you'll imagine yourself into a safe little fantasy world where bad things never happen?"

She held up her hands as he reached her. They hit his chest, palms flat. "What's wrong with that? At least humans don't go mad-protective and tell me I'm not—" She snapped her mouth shut, but he'd heard enough.

He lifted one of those slender feminine hands and pressed his lips to each fingertip in turn, aware of her racing heartbeat, her breakable bones, her trust in him. It was the last that ripped him to pieces. "Human families can be as territorial."

She shook her head. "You predatory changelings take it to the next level. I feel as if I'm running a gauntlet."

It was an unexpected confession. The Tally he'd come to know didn't spend much time feeling sorry for herself. But, he realized with a deep wave of excruciating tenderness, she'd had a lot of shocks in a single day. "You're mine. Therefore you're perfect."

Her lips twitched. "Idiot."

"Maybe." He nibbled at her fingers. "Once accepted, you'll have the pack's strength at your back. We never leave one of ours to drown. *Never.*"

"I won't be accepted, Clay," she whispered, shifting to lay her head against his chest, one hand still in his. "I feel like a dirty street urchin around the other women, my nose pressed to the window with you on the other side. I can't shift, I don't have Psy powers."

The image broke his heart. "Did the women say something to you?"

"Forget it." She drew back. "I was having a 'woe is me' moment. I'm over it."

He knew better. *"Tally."*

She pressed her lips together. He waited. She blew out a breath. "Fine! I got interrogated about my intentions toward you."

He pulled her closer, holding her with his arms around her waist. "And what are your intentions?" he murmured, leaning down to brush his lips over hers. "Are you planning to divest me of my virtue? I'll even ask nice."

Her breasts rose against him as she drew in a deep breath. "Be serious. They'll never accept me." She put her hands back on his chest, spreading out her fingers as if testing the strength of him. He liked it.

"Some of us wanted to torture Sascha at the start."

Her fingers dug into him. He liked that even better. "What? Why?" she asked.

"A Psy serial killer had murdered Dorian's sister. We thought Sascha might have information. The pack was enraged and she became the target—Dorian almost ripped out her throat. As for Faith, the first time we met, I accused her of being part of a psychopathic race."

"I never would've guessed." Her fingers straightened, petted absently—he wanted to purr. "How did Sascha and Faith become so much part of DarkRiver?"

"They've proven their loyalty."

"I have to do the same before they'll accept me." Sighing, she braced her forehead against his chest. "Is it okay for a human to bite people, too?"

He grinned, wondering if she even realized how easily she was cuddling into him. "Go to bed, Tally. You're tired and grumpy." He kissed the tip of her ear. The beast's hunger was a razor-sharp blade, but it had been soothed by this contact. Not that it mattered. Clay would not take Tally until she was ready to come to him. He never again wanted to see fear of him in her eyes. It had damn near killed him the first time around.

She rubbed her face against him. "I might be, but you don't have to point it out." But she took his advice and broke away. "See you tomorrow morning?"

"Bright and early." He waited until she was safely in her room before going downstairs and using the main communications panel to put through a call.

Vaughn's face wore a scowl when he answered, his hair sleep-tangled. "What? Something wrong?"

"I need to talk to Faith."

The other sentinel's scowl deepened. "You got me out of bed because you want to talk to my *mate*? There are laws against that sort of thing." A slender hand touched his bare shoulder and then Faith's face appeared on-screen beside Vaughn.

"Clay? What's the matter?"

"The matter is that I want you to leave Talin be." Tally could look after herself but that didn't mean she should have to. She'd spent too long doing exactly that. It was time for someone else to look after her.

Concern instead of insult dawned in Faith's eyes. "I'm your friend." She seemed to wrestle with her thoughts before adding, "I care."

"Vaughn," Clay growled.

Vaughn pressed a kiss to his mate's temple. "Come on, Red. I'll explain the facts of life to you."

"Wait—Faith, you talked to the NetMind recently?" The NetMind was a neosentience that lived in the PsyNet—it *was* the Net, to some extent—and it liked Faith. It might prove the perfect source of information about any Psy involvement in the kidnappings.

Faith shook her head. "I get the feeling it's being careful not to contact me. It may be because Councilor Krychek is too good at tracking its movements and it doesn't want to give away the fact that it can talk to Psy outside the Net."

Clay shrugged off the loss. Even if Faith had been able to contact it, communication with the neosentience was difficult. "Thanks."

"Clay," Faith said, her face tormented, "I want you to be happy."

"Tally makes me happy." He turned off the screen, a feeling of rightness in his gut. It was true—Tally might infuriate, anger, and frustrate him, but she also made him happy in a way no one else ever had. He wanted to do the same for her.

That thought in mind, he decided to bed down on the second level in case she needed him. They hadn't spoken much about her episode from the previous night—she seemed to be trying to ignore it—but the fact was, whatever it was that was wrong with her, it was getting worse. And unlike when he'd been fourteen, Clay couldn't slay the monster for her.

His claws sprang out. To hell with that! He'd kidnap an M-Psy if that was what it took to help Tally. He had no limits when it came to her. *None.*

The dream was one Talin had been having for years. Unlike the other things that haunted her, this one wasn't a nightmare. It was almost peaceful.

She floated in a field of black, her body insubstantial. Occasional stars flickered in greeting, but it was the strands of living rainbow weaving through the darkness that truly captured her attention. They seemed almost alive, full of sparkling mischief.

As always, she halted, reached out, touched a strand. And as always, that was the moment when the peace disappeared. Need raced through her body, such deep, aching, incomprehensible need that it rocked her to the core of her soul, had her jerking awake, grasping the night air for . . . something, something important.

But there was nothing but emptiness there, nothing but stillness.

Heart thudding, she glanced at the small bedside clock. Four a.m. Her personal witching hour. She should stay here, she told herself. If she went downstairs, she'd disturb Clay—his hearing was too keen to allow her to move about undetected. A branch shifted against the window, throwing shadows into the room.

They didn't frighten her. The forest was Clay's home. It spoke of safety and strength. Just like him. Admitting that she didn't want to stay up here, much less alone, she got out of bed and pulled on a pair of sweatpants to go with her tank top and panties. Usually, she slept in clothes she'd be ready to run in, but two nights with Clay nearby and she felt secure enough to indulge. Ready, she opened the trapdoor and began to head down.

"Tally?"

Startled by the sleepy murmur, she squinted into the darkness. Night-glow eyes looked at her from below the window, distracting her enough that she forgot to be afraid of the dark. "Clay?"

"Hmm." Those eyes closed, but their position told her he'd made up a bed on the floor.

Totally unprepared for his presence, she hesitated midway down the ladder.

"Can't sleep?" His eyes opened again.

She shook her head, realizing he could see her perfectly well.

"Come here." It was a lazy masculine invitation.

CHAPTER 25

***That voice.* Deep.** Husky with sleep . . . and an oh-so-seductive hint of bad.

She shivered, her nipples tightening against the soft cotton of the tank top. She'd asked him to be her friend but at that moment, friendship wasn't what her body wanted. Panicking, she gripped the ladder with desperate hands. "I shouldn't."

"Come on, Tally."

He sounded so drowsy, so persuasive, that she hesitated. What harm would it do to sit with him for a while? And he had promised to behave. She told herself that that wasn't disappointment biting into the most sensitive parts of her body. "I can hardly see." With small, careful steps, she made her way to the foot of his mattress.

"Very little ambient light," he murmured. "Lights on, night setting."

A soft glow lit up the kitchen area. She adored him for the thought but decided she could handle this. "Lights off. I'm okay. Just don't close your eyes."

The tempting sound of sheets sliding over skin. "Made you a space by the wall."

She hadn't expected anything else—Clay would never allow

her to be on the vulnerable open side of the mattress. Dropping down to her knees, she felt her way around and on to what seemed to be a very well made futon. "It's so comfortable," she said, fitting herself between the wall and Clay. The bottom part of the mattress was firm, but he'd thrown some kind of thick feather duvet over the sheet. "Like being on a cloud."

"Mmm." His hand touched her hip and he moved her until her back spooned against the delicious heat of his chest.

She let herself be pulled, let him cover her with a soft blanket and push one muscular thigh between hers, let him wrap his strength around her. Not only that, she made herself quite comfortable on the arm he slipped under her head. "Are you awake?" He was so hot and he smelled male in the best sense of the word. She blushed at the realization that she was tempted to lick his skin to see if he tasted as good as he smelled. "Clay?"

The arm around her waist squeezed. "I'm sleeping."

She smiled at the bad-tempered response and snuggled even tighter against him. He dropped a kiss in the curve of her neck, pretended to snore. Her smile turned into a grin. "I want to talk." About Max, about the children, about nothing and everything. Sensing his indulgent mood, she dared play her fingers over his arm, trying to quiet the hunger inside of her, to assuage this need she had for him. "Wake up."

He growled low in his throat and bodily shifted her until she faced him, or more accurately, the hard wall of his chest. Then one of his hands stroked up to her nape, pressing her cheek against his heated skin. "Sleep."

Putting her hands against the resilient strength of his pectorals, she opened her mouth to argue when a yawn overtook her. "I don't wanna," she murmured, conscious of him rubbing her lower back with his other hand. The slow circles were nice . . . they made her limbs feel heavy, relaxed. Safe.

Clay felt Tally surrender to sleep minutes after she'd refused. It would've made him smile had he not been fighting the urge to wake her right back up and ease the pain in his cock. The leopard was drunk on the scent of her. It urged him to taste her in every way a man could taste a woman. He wanted to lick, to bite, to drive into her with raw animal heat.

Patience, he told himself. She'd been scared of him only days ago and now she slept in his arms. Tally was remembering what she was to him. Soon, her childhood memories of absolute trust would merge into the liquid heat of adult desire. God, the scent of her arousal was a drug he could lap up for hours. One of these days, she was going to get curious enough to taste him, too. Then they'd play his kind of games.

Tonight he'd hold her, and when she woke, he'd tease her just enough to make her wonder about what came next. Smile slow and satisfied despite the heavy ache in his body, he closed his own eyes, settled her firmly against him, and let sleep take him under.

But things didn't go according to plan. The leopard clawed to life at the first sign of her distress. Birdcall filled the air, the room lit by stray beams of dawnlight, but all he could see was Talin on her back, eyes closed, breath coming in tortured gasps.

"Talin, wake up," he ordered in his most steely voice.

Her eyes snapped open, the cloud gray washed to black in violent panic. Her breathing got worse, a gulping scrape that was almost metallic in its harshness.

"Stop it." He cupped her face with one hand. "You're hyperventilating. Calm down."

After three more dangerously shallow breaths, she seemed to focus on him and nodded. He watched as she tried to bring herself under control, felt her fear when air continued to elude her. Her hand raised to her neck and her eyes pleaded with him. "C-c-can't," she somehow managed to say and he realized this wasn't a psychological issue.

"Is something blocking your airway?" he asked, terrified but knowing he had to keep his reactions under control. Tally needed him to think.

She shook her head, then lifted both her hands and closed them together, palm to palm, those remarkable eyes of hers furiously focused. The thin ring of amber seemed to glow molten gold in the morning light.

"It feels like your airway's closing up?"

At her nod, he lifted his hand from her cheek and rose to a sitting position. Then, putting his hands under her shoulders, he helped her up, too. She sat leaning against the wall below the window, eyes locked to his, one hand fluttering at her throat.

"Is that better?"

She shook her head, reaching for him with her other hand. He held it, his mind racing. He had emergency medical supplies in a first aid kit Tamsyn kept updated. He also had some medical training—enough to patch up himself or another packmate until they could get to their healer. But what Talin was now experiencing was nothing close to a bleeding gash or broken arm.

"I'll be back, baby." Breaking her hold with that promise, he ran to grab the medical kit from under the sink, then snatched up his cell phone from where he'd dumped it on the breakfast table. Punching in Tamsyn's number as he arrived back at Tally's side, he saw that her breathing had worsened. Her skin was starting to lose color.

"Hold on, Tally." He stroked his fingers down her throat. "You hold on for me." An order, not a request.

Fighting to keep her eyes open, she closed her hand over his wrist as he waited for someone to answer the call. He knew it would be answered—as their healer, Tamsyn was never out of contact.

"Clay, what is it?" Her voice came on the line, all business.

"Something's wrong with Talin. She can't breathe. It's like her throat's closed up."

"Any blockages?"

"She says no."

"Has she got any major allergies?"

"No, nothing," he said on the heels of her question, knowing that from childhood.

"Ask her—it's something she could have developed."

"Baby, major allergies?"

Another shake of her head, this one slow, heavy. Faint traces of blue edged her lips.

"Nothing," he repeated, before a memory flickered awake. "But she used to have a small pollen allergy. Used to make her sneeze."

"How's her heartbeat?"

He pressed his fingers to the pulse in her neck, his control growing ragged with each erratic beat. "Too damn slow."

"Turn the phone toward her so I can see her face."

Clay did as ordered, then brought the phone back to his ear. "Tammy?"

"Do you have the kit?" Her tone was calm, assured.

"Yes." He opened it.

"There's a small preloaded pressure injector on the top left-hand side of the lid."

He saw it at once. Sliding it out of the built-in slot, he flicked off the cap. "Where?" He didn't ask what it was, what it might do. There wasn't time.

"Wait. Make sure it's the right one. Has it got 'epinephrine' on the side?"

He saw Talin's eyelids flutter down. Her hand dropped off his wrist. The leopard scrabbled inside his mind, trying to get out, get to her. "Yes!"

"Do it. On her thigh. Clay—I have to warn you, this is a wild guess. It could be the absolute wrong thing, could hurt her."

"There's no choice. We don't do anything, she'll die." Using his claws to tear a hole in her sweatpants, he pressed the injector to her skin and pressed the button. The transparent tube cleared of the medicine in a flash. For three of the longest seconds of his life, nothing happened. Then Talin jerked and her eyes flashed open. Another second and her hand reached blindly in his direction.

He gripped it, held on tight. "Breathe, baby. Please, Tally, breathe. *Breathe.*"

Fingers clenching around his, she sucked in a deep breath. Then another.

"Is it working?" Tamsyn asked.

"Yeah," he whispered, a fucking fist around his heart. "Yeah."

"I'm coming over to check on her. Keep her warm, give her fluids."

Clay was barely conscious of closing the phone and putting it on the floor, his gaze locked with Talin's. It ripped him apart to see the single tear that leaked out of her eye. When he broke his hold on her, she made a small vulnerable sound. "Shh. I need to hold you." Settling himself with his back against the wall beside her, he pulled her into his lap.

She didn't complain when he crushed her to him, her head tucked under his chin, his embrace this side of bruising. Neither of them spoke. She breathed, slow and deep, and he just held her, making wordless sounds of comfort. Finally, one of her fists spread on his chest. It burned, as if she'd branded him. "I can breathe."

"Good." It was hard to talk with the leopard fighting to get out.

"What did you give me?"

He wrenched back control as his claws threatened to erupt. "A shot of epi."

"I've become that badly allergic to something?"

He wanted to kiss her, take her, convince himself he hadn't lost her. "This the first time you've had this kind of a reaction?"

She nodded. "It doesn't make sense. It has to be connected to—"

"Tammy's coming to check you out," he interrupted, not ready to talk about that fucking disease after the terror of the past minutes. "We'll see after that."

Talin shifted until she could look up at him. "I'm okay."

"You almost died."

Her fingers trailed over his unshaven jaw. "I knew you'd pull me out."

"You *can't* die." It was an order.

She blinked those big gray eyes, the ring of fire sparking. "I'll try my best."

He knew he was being unreasonable, but the leopard had taken charge and it didn't care about logic or reason. All the animal wanted was to know that she was alive, on a level that nothing could erase. "I'm going to break my promise."

Her eyes widened, but she didn't ask which one. Instead, she tilted her face for him and when he flicked his tongue across the seam of her lips, she opened, warm and giving and his. Undeniably, irrevocably his. No matter what she thought or how she'd run from him, Talin had always been, and always would be, his. He let her feel his certainty in the sweep of his tongue against hers, in the way he held her anchored to him, in the confidence with which he took everything she had and demanded more.

Talin felt a new kind of breathlessness crash into her as Clay claimed her mouth in what she recognized as a blatant stamp of ownership. It was a kiss she would have never allowed any other man. This kiss wasn't about the body. It was about the soul. He was stripping her bare, shattering her defenses, breaking her heart. "Clay." A plea, a reminder that she couldn't keep the promises he was asking her to make. The insidious disease eating away at her brain was beyond her ability to control.

He bit at her lower lip in response, and when she made a complaining sound, he did it again. Hungry feminine arrogance shot through her, wiping away all thoughts of the uncertain future. She bit back. He seemed startled, his reaction—a watchful stillness—very feline. Smiling into the kiss, she nibbled on him before opening her mouth and tangling her tongue with his in a duel she intended to win.

That was before Clay moved those big, warm hands up over her body, spreading one on her lower back while the other curved around her nape. The hold was so proprietary, so aggressive, it should've scared her into running in the other direction. Instead it sparked a darkly sexual heat in her, stoking her need past blazing. She melted into him, pressing her aching breasts against the solid wall of his chest.

He purred into her mouth.

Nipples shocked into sudden pleasure by the vibration, she pulled back. "You purr?"

His smile was pure cat. "Only for you."

Any resistance she might've harbored to this dangerous, inevitable escalation in their relationship dissolved into a big fat pool at her feet. He was being charming. Clay did not do charm, not for anyone. Except, it seemed, her. She pressed a kiss to his jaw. "Stop being so sexy."

His smile widened and, sliding his hand from her nape to her hair, he tugged back her head so he could kiss her again. The embers in her stomach burst into flame as she realized she was rubbing her nipples against him. He didn't seem to mind—he was doing that purring thing again. His hand dropped down to cup her bottom and she was startled to find she'd shifted position so she straddled him. As he resettled her, she bit back a whimper. The hard ridge of his erection now pressed right into the wet heat between her thighs.

Breaking the kiss, lips wet, breath jagged, she lifted a hand and traced the shape of his mouth with a finger. "You're rushing me."

"I'm not a patient man," was his unrepentant answer as she trailed her finger down his jaw and along his throat. "You *feel* when we touch, baby," he said, wiping away one of her deepest fears. "This will be damn good. I can smell you, so hot and wet, so ready." He bit her ear. "Let me make you come. I'll be good—I won't lick . . . much."

The playful request made her thighs clench, her breasts swell. *"Clay."* She nuzzled at his throat, tasted the exquisitely male scent of him. "What if we do this and then . . . then things don't work out?"

"They will."

"But what if they don't?" she asked, refusing to let his stubbornness dictate this. He hadn't brought up her promiscuous past since that explosive argument in the Tank, but that didn't mean he'd forgotten it. Clay was simply too possessive to accept what he viewed as a betrayal. She saw that knowledge in his eyes every time he looked at her. "I can't lose your friendship." It was the only thing standing between her and a desolation so great, she knew she wouldn't survive. Not this time.

"Tally, you tried to run from me and look where you ended up." He bit down on her lip again, released it, licked at the sensual hurt. "I'll always be there if you need me."

That didn't answer her question, but before she could say anything, he closed his hand over her breast. "Clay!" It was a half-shocked, half-exhilarated shout.

He held her in place with the arm he had around her waist as he bent to watch his fingers move on her thinly covered flesh. "Take off your top."

She was having real trouble thinking. "No. Slow down."

His answer was to press a kiss to the hollow at the bottom of her neck. Then he licked at that spot, shooting arrows of sensation straight through to the need between her thighs. As if that wasn't enough, he kept massaging her breast with firm, masculine approval. She didn't need his rough, "Mine," to understand the possession in his touch.

Her body shuddered under the impact of what he was making her feel, the sensations crashing endlessly in her mind. Driven to the edge, she put her hand over his. "I'm not ready." Pleasure wasn't enough, not when he kept a part of himself shut off from her. "I'm sorry." For the past she'd put between them. For the future she couldn't promise

He kissed his way up her neck. "Don't be." He took her lips again before she could be certain what he was referring to. "I'm only playing. Tamsyn's on her way over."

She was too delighted by the boyish mischief in those green eyes to get mad at the way he'd been leading her on. "Kiss me one more time, then." *Make me forget the disease killing me from the inside out. But most of all, make me forget that you don't trust me anymore.*

CHAPTER 26

The first day Ashaya came up from the underground lab and into the light, she was stopped as she exited the elevator hidden within the old farmhouse.

"Ma'am, you don't have the authorization to be outside." The security officer wore the standard black uniform of Security but with Ming's emblem on one shoulder—two snakes locked in combat.

"No," she agreed. "But, on the other hand, unless I attempt an escape, you have no authority to take any action against my person. I need to think and I do it better outside."

"Surveillance—"

"—has been blocked from the sky, all but our own satellites nudged in other directions. And there is no one out here to see me." Just corn, endless rows of spring-green corn. "You can accompany me."

A military nod. "After you."

She was under no illusion that she'd won the battle. He was simply buying time while telepathing Ming for further instructions. The expected mental touch came mere seconds after she stepped onto the deceptively decrepit-looking porch.

Councilor, she said.

Ashaya, you're disobeying a direct order. Ming's mental voice came through with crystal clarity. Either he was still in the country or his telepathic powers were stronger than she'd previously believed.

You should have known the rules would never hold. She walked down the steps and into the rows of corn, conscious of the guard shadowing her every move. *I have a psychological flaw that has never been subject to rehabilitation.* Because she was too valuable an asset to chance to the sometimes fatal side effects. However, that shield wouldn't last forever.

Your tendency toward claustrophobia was taken into account when designing the lab. It's wide open.

And underground. She had been buried underground once. It had left a permanent mark. *The flaw is not debilitating in any sense,* she said, knowing she had to be careful, *but it does make clear thinking difficult after an extended period of time below.*

Then it's our design that is flawed, he accepted with cool Psy logic. *The psych consult was of the opinion that your abilities would remain unaffected by the location given the layout and your mental strength.*

The consult was correct—my abilities have not been adversely affected. Conceding weakness would get her killed. *It's more a case of efficiency. All I need is an hour or two upside on a regular basis to maintain peak productivity.*

Ming paused as if thinking. *There's no security risk. I'll allow it.*

Thank you. I would also prefer that the guard not follow me. His presence is distracting. I do a considerable amount of my work in my head. That much was true and would be borne out by the records Ming was undoubtedly accessing as they talked.

Another small pause. *Agreed. We have the whole area secured.*

The most subtle of threats. *Excellent.*

Be careful, Ashaya. So much hinges on your work.

It was a hidden reference to Keenan. But it wasn't an emotional threat—nothing so easy as that. Maternal love was for humans and changelings. Other things drove Ashaya. Ming knew that far too well.

But she was outside now. One minute step at a time. She was an M-Psy with the capacity to sequence DNA inside her mind. Patience was her strong suit.

Deep in the PsyNet, the psychic network that connected millions of Psy across the globe, the Ghost came across a piece of information that made little sense—whispers about the kidnapping of human children. Nothing said in the PsyNet ever left it, but the fact that this whisper hadn't yet fragmented and begun to be absorbed into the fabric of the Net meant it was recent. That knowledge gave him pause.

He was a renegade, determined to oust the Psy Council from power and free his people from a Silence that was false. He had killed in the name of that freedom, would do so many more times before this was all over. But he was still Psy. He felt nothing, not love, not care, not hate. Nothing.

So when he considered this unexpected speck of data, it was with the ice-cold mind of a man reared on logic and reason alone. Touch was something he barely understood, affection nothing he had ever known. In the end, it was the very lack of reason in what he'd found that decided him.

He filed away the discovery, to be passed on to the sole human he trusted. Father Xavier Perez might be a man of God, but he was also a soldier. And for reasons of his own, he was the Ghost's ally in the fight to stop Ashaya Aleine and the Council from bringing Protocol I into force.

Decision made, the Ghost banished the kidnappings from his mind, his focus on something far bigger, something that had the potential to disrupt the entire PsyNet—the assassination of a Councilor.

CHAPTER 27

Tamsyn put away the last of her instruments and leaned back in the chair beside Talin. Both Clay and Nate—talking quietly out of earshot—moved closer.

"I can't find anything wrong with you." Tamsyn thrust a hand through her hair. "The allergy tests are all negative and I have the best damn equipment on the market."

"You can tell immediately?"

"Yes. Which leaves two possibilities. One, whatever you're allergic to is so rare as to not be in the computer's analysis program—"

Talin shook her head, sighing in relief when Clay's hand landed on her shoulder. It felt so right, so what she needed. "I can't think of anything—"

"What about a forest organism?" Clay interrupted. "It's a new environment as far as Tally's body is concerned."

Tamsyn was the one who shook her head this time. "It should've still come up as an unknown. That's the problem—I'm picking up *nothing*."

"What's the second possibility?" Talin asked.

"That it wasn't an allergic reaction at all. We just got lucky with the epi." Tamsyn frowned. "How are you feeling now?"

"Fine."

"No heart palpitations, nausea, anything out of the ordinary?"

Talin's heart was certainly racing, but it had nothing to do with the medication and everything to do with the man who was playing his fingertips along her collarbone. She wondered if the cat considered that as behaving. "No. No side effects."

The healer blew out a frustrated breath. "I can't make heads or tails of your condition. I agree with Clay—you need to go to an M-Psy for a scan. Problem is, we don't have one we trust yet, though we've been putting out feelers ever since Sascha and Faith joined the pack."

"I'm okay for now." Talin didn't want to die. But neither could she live with herself if she put her life before Jon's. That didn't mean she wasn't scared, wasn't angry. "We'll deal with my problems after we've found Jon."

Clay didn't say anything, but she could feel the wild energy of his leopard racing over her skin. He was furious with her.

Two hours later, Talin walked into a small meeting room located in DarkRiver's business HQ, viscerally aware of the storm building inside Clay. He set her up in the room with the files Dev had had delivered and said, "I have to go check on some things. If you need anything, ask Ria. She's Lucas's assistant." He showed her the key to press on the comm panel. "You oriented?"

She nodded. "I remember everything. Did you forget?"

Instead of laughing at the small joke, he turned to leave the room. Disappointment bloomed on her tongue and she decided if he could brood, she could pout. "Hey!"

He turned in a smooth, sensually feline move and bent down to press a hard, possessive kiss on her lips. "Don't be a brat while I'm gone."

She raised her fingers to her lips as he left, wanting to smile—he might have gone dark and silent on her but he hadn't left without a kiss. Hope struggled to defiant life in her heart. Yes, the possessive leopard in Clay remained wary of her. And yes, she admitted with brutal honesty, part of her kept waiting for him to leave her again.

That distance, those hidden fears, they hurt.

But even so, they were coming back together step by slow step, their bond stronger and far more intimate than it had been during childhood. It was a wonderful surprise—after all these years apart, she'd been scared to come to him, afraid that the truth of the man she discovered would forever taint the happiest memories of her life.

It had never occurred to her that she might adore the adult Clay even more than she had the youth, but there it was. The man her friend had grown into—well, he enchanted her, brooding temper, dark kisses, animal protectiveness, and all. To her delight, the feeling seemed to be mutual. But the separation had scarred them both. What would it do to Clay if this disease succeeded in killing her?

. . . The future hasn't yet changed.

It terrified her that Clay could lose his humanity because of their growing relationship. Her hand clenched. No, she thought, *no*. The future wasn't fixed. She would not let him fall— A knock on the door had her swiveling.

It opened to reveal a pretty brunette with laugh lines around her mouth and a tea tray in her hands. "I'm Ria and I'm nosy as hell."

The introduction disarmed Talin, cutting through her churning emotions with laughing efficiency. "I'm Talin."

Ria put the tray on the table. "So, you're Clay's?"

"He's mine anyway."

The other woman grinned. "Oooh, I like you. Must admit you're not what I expected, though."

"Oh?"

"You're human. He's . . . intense, even for a cat." Her eyes widened before Talin could reply. "No offense! I'm human, too."

Talin jumped at the chance. "What's it like being human in a pack of leopards?"

"They tend to have to be more careful with us—we break easier," Ria said with candid warmth.

Talin didn't like the idea of Clay holding back with her. "Yeah."

"But you know, human men have to watch themselves around women, too. They're bigger, stronger, regardless of race." She shrugged. "These guys just have claws and teeth to worry about, too."

"Huh." The practical explanation made complete sense.

"And," Ria added, "we have to be careful with them, too."

Talin felt her eyebrows rise. "What could I possibly do to Clay, to any changeling?"

"Think about it—their hearing is so sensitive, we scream loud enough, we blow out their eardrums." She winced. "I learned that the hard way."

"Is he—"

"Healed. Thank God. And he mated me, so he wasn't too mad." A rueful smile. "Though he pulls it out now and then to tease me about being gentle with him."

Talin had never considered the downside to Clay's incredible senses. "I guess perfume's out then?" She thought of the way he liked to lick, to taste, and felt her body heat up from the inside out.

Ria screwed up her nose. "You have to buy the changeling stuff. Get Clay to pick it 'cause you sure as heck won't be able to smell anything."

Talin released a slow breath. "Give and take from both sides." Exactly as in any other relationship.

"Yep. Oh, yeah," Ria added, "be careful about claiming skin privileges." When Talin gave the other woman a blank look, she rolled her eyes. "I bet Clay just touched you like it was his right? Figures." She didn't wait for an answer. "It might look as if the pack's easy as far as touching goes, but they're actually very, very choosy. Wait for an indication it's okay, especially with the dominant males and females." She glanced at her watch. "Damn, gotta go. We should do lunch one of these days."

"I'd like that," Talin said as Ria waved good-bye.

It was tempting to ponder the mass of information Ria had shot at her, but she knew she had to focus. It was far harder to banish the tantalizing image of Clay nuzzling the scent of perfume from her neck, so she took it with her as she set up a small writing pad, grabbed a plain old pen, and reached for the first of the files Dev had sent. It was Jonquil's.

CHAPTER 28

Jonquil looked at the fine needle marks on his arms and knew he'd gotten off easy. The wolf-eyed woman, the one he'd named Blue, had done nothing to make him scream, hadn't hurt him at all. In fact, *all* the screaming had stopped since the day of her visit.

He was too terrified to wonder what that meant.

She'd taken blood, skin, and hair samples, made him answer what felt like a thousand questions. Today he was supposed to go in for a brain scan. He had a feeling that that was what Blue was really interested in, though you wouldn't be able to tell from her or the Blonde's expressions. They were the coldest, most icy people he had ever met. He knew what they were, of course. What he didn't know was what they wanted from him.

But no way in hell was he going to let his uncertainty show. Talin had taught him better. That thought in mind, he was waiting tall and proud when they came to the door—the Blonde and an unfamiliar male. No woman with wolf blue eyes and smooth chocolate skin.

Jonquil figured he could flatten the man in a physical fight, no problem. But these people didn't fight with their bodies.

They fought with their minds. He'd been on the streets long enough to have witnessed the end results for those who got on their wrong side. Like when Sal had tried to pull one over on that group that had wanted to buy him out. He'd been found with his brains leaking out his ears.

"I'm ready." He didn't bother trying to see if they'd fall for his voice. When he spoke in a certain way, all slow and easy, people seemed to get real caught up in it, but Blue had known about it, had warned him not to try it on the others. She'd said not only would it not work, it would sign his death certificate. He had decided to believe her . . . for now.

The Blonde nodded. "Your cooperation has been noted."

He wondered if that meant they would give him anesthetic when they tortured him. He opened his mouth to ask about Blue, then snapped it shut, remembering what she'd said after returning him to the cell.

I was never here. You will keep your silence on that point.

Why? Who are you to me?

The woman who caused you no pain.

True enough, he thought, very aware of the reptilian light in the male's eyes. Cold or not, that one liked hurting people. Jon's senses were screaming at him to run, *run*, RUN! But there was nowhere to run—not yet—so he followed them down the corridor.

As he walked, he decided to call the man Lizard. He had secret names for everyone, even Talin. She'd think her name was hysterical, he thought, fighting to keep up his courage in the face of the threat emanating from Lizard.

"Please enter." The Blonde pushed open a door.

Halting a few steps inside, he frowned. "What the hell is that?" He was facing a chair but one hooked up to devices that, even to his inexperienced eyes, promised pain.

"A machine that will allow us to better understand your brain." The door shut behind him as Lizard spoke for the first time, his voice cool . . . dead.

Jonquil got a queasy feeling in the pit of his stomach. He *knew* Blue hadn't authorized this. He stared at the Blonde, a silent question in his eyes.

Her expression didn't change. "Take a seat in the chair."

"No." A sharp pain stabbed into his skull, making him stagger. But he didn't scream.

The Blonde glanced at Lizard. "Perhaps we should use one of the others?"

"There's only one other left. Open the screen."

Jon clenched his head in his hands as the wall behind the chair suddenly silvered from opaque to clear. There was a little girl on the other side. She was sitting hunched into the far corner, her knees drawn up to her chest. Her eyes met his. Big, brown, filled with excruciating fear and—at seeing him—a desperate flash of hope.

"If you don't cooperate, we'll use her," Lizard told him.

Jon decided he'd have to kill the bastard before he escaped. "Why do you think I care?"

"You're human."

And Jon knew that this time, there would be screaming.

CHAPTER 29

Teijan was waiting for Clay above ground, looking sleek and well-groomed, a small man with a solid aura of power. "Hello, Clay."

"Teijan." He could still taste Talin on his lips, tart and familiar. It calmed his possessive instincts, but didn't make him any less pissed with her for refusing to get medical attention until they found the boy. "Wanted to ask—you know anything about a man being jumped around here last night?"

"The cop?" A spark of pure surprise lit Teijan's inky black eyes. "A group of my people took exception to the event." His mouth firmed into an unforgiving line. "Most of them know about bullies. They scared off the perpetrators, called the paramedics."

"Anyone see anything?" He knew the Rats would've disappeared Down Below before Enforcement arrived, wary of a law that often treated them like trash. Yet they had saved a cop's life, with no hope of gain for themselves. He'd make sure Max knew that.

"No." He spread out his hands. "It was dark and they are human, with human eyes. Suyi did mention the thugs looked like hired muscle."

Clay had expected as much. If it was a Psy behind the kidnappings, he or she wasn't anyone with access to the kind of power the Council wielded—otherwise Max would've been dead by now, his brains turned to jelly. But the fact that this was happening in Nikita Duncan's city, without her apparent involvement—Nikita didn't need to hire ineffectual human thugs—made him wonder exactly how bad things had gotten in the PsyNet. "So," he looked to Teijan, "why the call?"

"The boy," Teijan said, "one of the children is adamant she saw him disappear off the street."

His leopard sat up in interest. "She saw him get snatched?"

"No, she saw him disappear." Teijan made a flicking notion with his fine-boned hand. "Poof. Like magic. Her words."

Everything in Clay stilled. It didn't make sense—if the kidnapper was a teleportation-capable telekinetic, he or she would have had no need to hire humans to do the dirty work. Tk-Psy that strong could crush a human body with little effort.

"We didn't believe her at first." Teijan frowned. "But then I realized why the picture of the boy disturbs me and mine so much."

"Why?"

"He's not human. He's not changeling. He's not Psy. He's more *other* than anyone I've ever before met."

Talin could barely grasp the enormity of what she was reading. Dev might not have told her the truth, but he'd given her what she needed to find that truth herself.

She was standing there stunned when the door opened and Clay walked in. "You're not going to believe this," she said, tugging him to the table.

"Try me." The edge in his tone scraped over her spine like a fine nail.

She glanced up, belatedly noticing the furious expression on his face. It was obvious it wasn't directed at her. "What's the matter?"

"You first." His hand closed around her ponytail and he stroked the length through his fist. Then he did it again, top to bottom.

To her surprise, she could feel him relaxing. And that

relaxed her. *Skin privileges,* she thought with an inward smile. "Alright. Here, look." Bending over the table, very aware of him playing with her hair, she showed him the crucial pages.

"Family trees," he murmured. "Detailed."

She nodded. Her hair slipped out of his grasp but a second later, she felt a tug as he recaptured it. The caress was strangely soothing. "Looks like Shine went way beyond the most recent generations."

Clay was caught by the fierce light in Talin's eyes. Her intelligence blazed hot and damned sexy. "For all of them?"

"Yes." She grinned. "It's as if they were tracing the families, not the individual children."

"Shine doesn't take on whole families."

"I'm not so sure. Look." She tapped a particular record. "One kid in this three-sibling family has Shine support, but *all three* are being monitored. The only reason the other two were left alone is because they have other scholarships."

"That can't be the case with all of them."

"No. But if you look carefully at the charts, you'll see that a lot of the unfunded or untraced ones are actually stepsiblings. They're following bloodlines."

Clay stopped sliding Talin's hair through his fist, though he kept the smooth, silky stuff in his grip. "That explains a lot."

Lines formed on her forehead. "Why do I get the feeling you already know what I'm leading up to?"

He tugged at her hair, tipping up her head. Then he kissed her. A short, fleeting brush of lips on lips that tantalized the cat, teased and tempted in a way that would eventually become dangerous. But not yet. He still had enough control to pull back. "I have suspicions, no proof."

Her eyes were catlike in their smugness. "Look at the heads of the family trees."

He finally released her hair so he could spread out the charts. "I'm not seeing anything obvious."

"That's because it's not." She picked up one particular sheet. "This is Jon's record. I was staring at it this morning when it struck me that I'd heard—read—the name Duchslaya Yurev before. He's at the top of this tree. I did a search." She pointed to the computer built into the side of the desk. "Yurev was one of his generation's greatest minds. He's half the reason we know as much as we do about genetics."

"Kid's full name is Jonquil Alexi Duchslaya," Clay said, looking at the chart. "Okay, it's an ancestral name. Not unusual."

"No, but guess what." She traced a line on the chart. "Jonquil is Yurev's only remaining *direct* descendant."

Excitement gripped his gut. "Was Yurev human?"

"No." Her next words were a whisper. "He was a cardinal telepath."

"Damn."

"Yeah."

For a minute, they just stared at each other. "What about the other names?"

Her face fell. "Nothing. It's like they've been erased from the system—I only realized about Yurev because he was mentioned in an out-of-print textbook I read when I was fifteen. I was bored and it was the last physical book in the library I hadn't read."

"Geek."

She stuck out her tongue at him. "I guess Yurev was too famous to wipe out completely—though you know, he's not in any of the electronic textbooks, hasn't been for over half a century. Even the Internet databases have very little on him. If he was that hard to trace, I have no clue how Shine did the others."

"Maybe," he murmured, "they had a head start, a list to a certain point."

"Hold on." Tally liberated a small notebook from the confusion of paper on the table. "See on the family trees, they also have locations listed next to the names. Around two generations back, sometimes three, they start to scatter."

"A diaspora." Clay blew out a breath. "Yurev wasn't the only Psy."

"No," she said. "I can't prove it but it fits. The murdered kids were all gifted in a way that was *almost* Psy." Her mouth fell open at the echo of Dev's words. "Dev was telling us without telling us."

"Someone's trying to gag him, but I don't think he's happy about it."

"You don't think we could be jumping to conclusions?"

He shoved a hand through his hair. "My instincts say we're right, but one name isn't enough to go on."

"And," Talin pointed out, "once, the Psy were like us. I mean they intermarried with humans and changelings. It wasn't anything weird." Her tone became less certain. "A lot of us probably have Psy blood in our past."

"I know for certain that Lucas does." Turning, he leaned back against the table and wrapped an arm around her waist, delighted when she automatically put her hands on his shoulders. "We need a Psy perspective."

He felt her body go stiff, but her response was a nod. "You're right. Here or—"

"Sascha's likely to be around." He was male, but he wasn't stupid—no sense in aggravating Tally with Faith. The cat preened in the heat of her possessiveness. "We've got a new development deal going with a Psy corporation."

"Psy?" Curiosity had her leaning into him. "I thought they liked to keep to their own businesses. I've heard rumors saying, you compete with the Psy, you die."

He couldn't resist reaching out to trace the curve of her lip. She pretended to snap her teeth at him. His cock was suddenly taut with need but he resisted the urge to lay her on the table and satisfy his hunger. "DarkRiver ran a project for Nikita's mother. The profits were huge."

"It's a big shift," Talin murmured, her heartbeat steady under his stroking fingertips but her scent edged with the exquisite bite of arousal. Her mind might not have made the decision yet, but her body craved his. "I wonder if you guys even realize it."

"Oh, we realize it." Clay relaxed at the clear signs that she wasn't suffering any ill effects from that morning. "But no sense tipping off the enemy."

"You make it sound like a war."

"It damn well is. And these children"—he pointed to the files—"are some of the casualities."

That shook her. "I have the feeling there's more going on here than I know." But she wouldn't ask. He either trusted her or he didn't.

He drew her between the vee of his thighs, one hand sliding down to press over her lower back. "Are you trying to pretend to be stoic?" he asked. "It doesn't work if you tap your toe in temper."

She glanced down and blushed. "That wasn't nice."

A warning graze along her neck with sharp leopard teeth. "I'll tell you anything you want to know." His unshaven jaw rasped over the skin exposed by her V-necked sweater. "But right now we have to focus on this. We'll talk about the other stuff later." He pressed a row of kisses along that same triangle of flesh. "Freckles. I want to count them."

"You'll lose count after the first million." Her heart felt like it would burst from inside her chest. Did he have any idea what he meant to her? She didn't think so.

"Go get the others." It would give her time to compose herself, to put her heart back together. "Call Faith, too." She made a face and pulled the short hairs at his nape. "I'm not a baby. I can handle her."

He shot her an amused look. "Very mature."

"Shuddup. Go."

"I can call them from here." He proceeded to do exactly that. "Sascha will be here in about an hour. Faith's tied up with something, so you don't have to be mature."

"Really not nice." She began to sit back down at the table.

Clay grabbed her hand and pulled her toward the door. "First, we eat."

"But—"

"Did you have lunch?"

She considered lying but knew he'd catch her out. "No."

"It's three o'clock."

"Did you eat?" she countered.

His response was a grunt.

Scowling at his back, she let him tug her down the corridor and past several startled people she assumed were his packmates. "Answer my question."

"I'm a man. You're small and weak. Different rules apply."

"Of all the—!" she yelled. "That's it. I'm going to kill you this time."

The woman in front of them pressed her body to the side of the corridor, computer tablet held up like a shield, eyes in danger of popping out of her head.

"Clay, I swear to God, if you don't—"

He stopped so suddenly, she almost careened into his back. Turning, he fixed her with an intimidating look. "Behave." Cool, calm, a voice that dared her to disobey.

Her mouth fell open. "Take that back or I'm not going anywhere with you."

"How are you going to stop me?" His smile was pure, conceited cat.

Her temper, hard to arouse, quick to blow over, but steaming hot while it was up, flared into full life. She smiled, patted his arm. "Oh, Clay darling, if you had *told* me you were feeling irritated because of your . . . problems, I wouldn't have made a fuss." She knew very well the changelings around her could hear every whispered word.

"Tally." It was a warning growl.

"I mean it must be embarrassing for you . . . being that you're such a big man." Her tone implied all sorts of things. "Last night was an aberration, I'm sure. And if not, there are always the pills."

Gasps sounded up and down the corridor.

Clay's eyes blazed hot. "I'm going to show you aberration, you brat." He turned and glared at their audience, as if memorizing every single face.

Suddenly, everyone had somewhere else to be. Only when he'd intimidated the corridor clear did he turn back to her. "I bet you think you're funny."

She grinned. "Yep."

"I hope you still think that when I'm proving to you just how *big* I am."

Her eyes dropped involuntarily to his pants and she realized she might have pushed him a tad too far. "Now, Clay . . ."

Pressing his body against hers, he hugged her to him with one arm and bent to speak with his lips against her ear. "Now, Tally," he mimicked.

"Bully."

"Brat."

At the familiar exchange, Talin felt something else "click" into place between them. Clay's expression told her he felt it, too. Giddy, she pressed a kiss to his throat, the affectionate act completely spontaneous. "I'm hungry."

"So am I." His tone was a lazy invitation. "When are you going to feed me?"

A rush of damp heat between her legs. Lord have mercy but she couldn't remember any of her rational reasons for not having a sexual relationship with Clay.

CHAPTER 30

By the time they returned from lunch, Sascha and Lucas were already in the meeting room. "There you are. We were waiting for you."

It was impossible to do anything but smile in response to the incredible warmth in Sascha's voice. "Clay decided to eat the place down."

"Yes," Sascha said, a frown forming between her eyes, "I heard that you've been having some problems." The last word was a sympathetic whisper.

Talin felt Clay stiffen behind her and was about to set Sascha straight when she noticed the glint of humor in the cardinal's eyes.

"Better watch out, Clay," Lucas drawled from where he sat on the side nearest the door, feet on the table and chair tipped back. "You'll be getting helpful advice from the juveniles before you know it."

Clay clasped Talin's nape with one hand. "You are in so much trouble."

Her laugh made the others grin. "It was your own fault."

"We'll discuss that later." He pushed her toward a chair—

beside the one Sascha had just taken, on the other side of the table.

She sat, while Clay chose to lounge against the wall to their left. The mischief leached out of her as soon as she focused on the papers. It had been over a week since Jon's abduction. That in mind, she raced through the information as she bought Sascha up-to-date. "I was hoping you could pick out other Psy names."

"It's a long shot." Sascha made a sound of utter frustration. "If I was uplinked to the PsyNet—"

"Which you never again will be." Lucas's tone was flint hard.

Sascha shot her mate a scowl. "As I was saying before I was so rudely interrupted"—another scowl, which Lucas responded to with a grin—"if I was uplinked to the Net, I could run a specific search, but now that I'm out, my data is based on what I knew before I dropped out."

"What about the library stuff?" Lucas asked.

Sascha nodded. "I've been doing research in human libraries," she explained to Talin. "Lucas is right, I might know some names from there . . ." Her voice trailed off, her eyes on a particular chart.

Lucas tipped his chair to the ground. "What is it?"

"Nothing," she murmured, but her tone said otherwise.

Getting up, Lucas walked around the table to lean over Sascha's other side, even as Clay did the same with Talin. It would've been very easy to be overwhelmed by the size and presence of the two men. Both were big. Both were undeniably dangerous. But Talin felt incredibly safe. *Because these were men who cared for their women.*

The revelation shocked her. So simple and yet so powerful, disproving as it did the conclusion that violence in one situation inevitably led to violence in another. Talin felt one of her strongest barriers fall—there was no longer any worry in her that Clay would one day lose his control and hurt her. Even now, he was doing that thing he seemed to like doing with her ponytail.

A possessive act. But also an act of deep tenderness.

Emotions a wet knot in her throat, she tried to focus on Sascha. "What do you see?"

The cardinal's night-sky eyes clashed with Talin's and for the first time, Talin saw not peace but confusion. "Can you show me the other family trees first?"

"Here's the one they had for Mickey." She forced herself to say his name. He deserved to be remembered, to be mourned. "Jon's was one of the most intricate, but they're all pretty in-depth."

"You're right," Lucas murmured, fingering one of the printouts. "How the hell did they manage to trace this many relatives and descendants?"

"Easiest explanation is that someone was keeping records from the start," Clay said. "Like changelings do."

"You do?" Talin and Sascha asked at the same time.

Clay released her ponytail, only to stroke it again from the top. Her heart hitched. "Sure," he said, his voice quiet, full of power. "The pack historian always does it."

"It's the best way we had in the past of tracking genetics, including any possible inherited diseases," Lucas added.

"Like isolated farming communities," Talin said, her mind flying back through the years. "The Larkspurs had their genealogy written down in the front of the family Bible."

Lucas picked up the file Sascha had been staring at earlier. "Sascha?"

"Yes."

"What are the odds?"

"Precisely."

Talin looked up at Clay. "Do you know what they're muttering about?"

He shook his head. "They're mated."

Oddly enough, Talin understood. Different rules applied to couples, especially couples as profoundly in sync as Lucas and Sascha. Their connection was a near visible line of pure emotion, one that made her hurt with envy.

"Tally." Clay tugged at her ponytail.

She glanced up, knowing that unlike the alpha pair, she and Clay remained divided. In her mind, she saw them on opposite ends of a glass bridge. Able to see the abyss that awaited if they didn't make it to each other, but unable to take the steps that would close the gap forever. "Sit down," she said, angry at him for being so possessive, at herself for being too scared to trust in his promise to never leave her again. "You're giving me a crick in my neck."

He raised an eyebrow at her sharpness but grabbed a seat, angling it so he could keep an eye on the door. Even in this safe place, Clay was on guard. She wasn't surprised—he was too protective to be any other way. And her flash of frustrated anger aside, she adored him exactly as he was. She didn't want to change Clay. God, no. She just wanted to reach the secret heart of him, the part he kept hidden . . . because she had once torn it right out of him.

"Talin." Sascha's tone was solemn enough to have them both paying complete attention. "If we can trust these records, then you're correct, there appears to be a Psy link. It's not the names—though a few of them set off alarm bells—it's something you might not have realized the significance of." Her hand clenched on the sheets she held. "All these trees start between a hundred to a hundred and five years ago."

"God damn," Clay whispered, dropping his foot from the rung of her chair and shifting to sit with his arm around the back. He explained before Talin could ask. "That was around the time that Psy began to condition their kids not to feel."

"You think some of them got out?" she asked, then noticed Sascha fingering the edge of one particular tree. "Sascha?"

"I really can't be sure about this." Her voice was hesitant. "Please understand that."

"I do. We're just throwing out ideas here." But she could *feel* the answers so close.

Nodding, the cardinal pointed to one particular name. "Mika Kumamoto was the name of my great-great-grandmother. Her daughter Ai was six years old when Silence went into effect. She became one of the transitional children." Her voice held a wealth of pain.

Talin put her hand over Sascha's in silent comfort. The other woman curled her fingers around Talin's and continued to speak. "I stole my family history before I left the Net. The file on Mika stops eighteen years after Ai's birth. I thought that that meant she had died, and for some reason, the death hadn't been noted. That time was chaotic," she told them. "It was more than a decade after the implementation of Silence, but there were still problems, because of the elderly who couldn't be fully conditioned."

Lucas was stroking Sascha's cheek with his knuckles now and she seemed to gain strength from her mate's touch. Taking a shuddering breath, she continued, "But if Mika disappeared because she dropped out of the Net, that means she did it after Ai turned eighteen, well after Silence was first put into place."

"Is that important?" Talin released the other woman's hand, tangled her own with one of Clay's. Her heart was in her throat—if they were right, then Jon was in even more danger than she'd believed.

"I don't know. What I do know is that Psy can't survive outside the Net. We need the biofeedback provided by a neural net of some kind. Our brains are different. *This* Mika Kumamoto not only survived, it says here that she went on to have another child."

Talin didn't ask how Sascha was still alive. She didn't need to know to make the connection. "So if she was your ancestor, she had to have had a net in place to link to?"

Sascha's eyes were bright with hope. "Exactly. And unless humans have some unknown way of providing such a net, that means there are more Psy out there, Psy who have never been part of the PsyNet."

Talin shook her head, her mind immediately seeing the patterns Sascha couldn't. "Not quite—they would be mixed race, all of them." She stared at family tree after family tree. "There might have been Psy-Psy marriages at the start, but after Silence went into effect, the conditioned Psy wouldn't have wanted to drop out, right?"

"Not unless they were renegades," Sascha said, her excitement dimming. "I didn't hear of any others before my defection, but that doesn't mean there weren't any."

"True. But most likely," Clay picked up, "the children and grandchildren of the Psy who left the Net would have mated with changelings or humans."

"Yes." Sascha's renewed sadness was so heavy, Talin felt it in her bones. "I just wanted to believe that more people had escaped Silence. If this is my Mika, then she left her own child because she couldn't stand what her child had become. Can you imagine how much that must've hurt?"

"Come on, kitten," Lucas muttered, a tenderness to his tone that made Talin turn away, it was such a private thing.

As she did, her eyes met Clay's and she saw something dark in them, something so passionate it was beyond intense. It shook her. "Clay?" she mouthed more than said.

His response was to brush the thumb of his free hand over her lower lip. "Later."

Feeling herself teetering on the jagged edge of that glass bridge, she nodded and returned her gaze to her notes. An instant later, Sascha turned back to the table, too.

"So," Lucas began, "let's think this through. One thing's clear—some Psy were already married to, or had mated with, non-Psy, when Silence began."

Sascha nodded. "There was no way the Council could have torn mates apart."

"They might have tried," Lucas said with a careless shrug that did nothing to hide the steel in his tone. "Wouldn't have got them very far."

Sascha's lips curved. "So, the mated pairs would've stayed outside but they—at least the ones with predatory changeling mates—probably wouldn't have needed a separate net."

Her words confirmed Talin's guess that DarkRiver was somehow able to give Sascha and Faith the biofeedback they needed. "But the ones who loved humans," she said, "or even other Psy, would have needed a net, right? Unless two Psy can provide it for each other?"

"No, it doesn't reach the critical threshold for the multiplication effect."

"English, Sascha," Clay drawled.

"Sorry. With the millions of minds in the Net, the biofeedback actually multiplies, so that it becomes more than what was put out. The same principle holds true for a smaller net. But two isn't enough. The one—" Sascha broke off so quickly, Talin knew she had been about to betray confidential information.

Her hands tightened on the chair arms. "Would you like me to leave the room?" She wasn't going to let pride get in the way of finding Jon, no matter how angry it made her to come face-to-face with the truth that she remained on the outside—because Clay hadn't brought her in. *That* was what hurt the most.

Clay touched the stiffness of her shoulder. "Stay."

"She can't," Lucas said. "This isn't about us."

"It's all right, Clay," she began, mollified by his support.

His hand closed around her nape, hard and inflexible. "She stays. Talk around it."

There was a taut moment when the two men stared at each other, then Sascha whispered something very low to Lucas and the alpha seemed to relax his stance. "Fine."

Clay gave a short nod, glad that Lucas had understood. If he hadn't, they would've had a serious problem. Clay wasn't a sentinel because he bowed down to his alpha's every word. He was a sentinel because he could fight back and draw blood. And for Tally, he'd do a lot worse. "Sascha?"

"We know of a small net," Sascha said, referring, Clay knew, to the Laurens, the family of defectors who had found unlikely sanctuary with the SnowDancers. "That net is strained. I'd say their number is at the outer limit of what's safe. And it's more than two."

Talin's hand clenched on his thigh. He wondered if she realized she'd put it there when the first signs of aggression had entered the room. The desire it sparked aggravated the hell out of him but the leopard was pleased she saw him as a point of safety. He eased his hold on her nape, though she didn't seem to mind the possessive gesture.

She gave him a small smile before returning her attention to the others. The utter rightness of it cut him off at the knees, made him want to wipe away the past and make her his. *Only* his. It was what she should have always been. "If we carry our theory through," she said, "it means that Shine is tracking down children with a Psy bloodline, more specifically descendants of those Psy who defected from the Net because of Silence."

Her eyes widened. Letting go of him, she scrabbled through the files. "These numbers—I couldn't figure out what they meant. But if you look at Jon as a descendant with a lot of Psy blood, it makes sense. He's labeled as .45."

"Forty-five percent Psy?" Sascha nodded. "What about—"

Talin had already found the numbers for the other abducted kids. "Forty, thirty-six, thirty-nine—nothing lower than thirty-five percent." Her fingers touched the edge of the extra file Dev had sent through. She'd figured it to be a mistake. "And here's mine."

"You Psy, Tally?" Clay lips lifted up in amusement.

"Hardly. Look." She showed him the percentage marker next to her name, her sudden fear shifting into scowling outrage. "Point zero three! *Three* percent! It's a joke!" Though her minuscule Psy blood might explain her "feelings." More likely, she snorted inwardly, they were the result of plain old human intuition. "Makes me wonder why Shine took me on in the first place."

Clay's amusement turned into disbelief. "That low? What about your memory?"

"According to this, my maternal grandfather had an eidetic memory. And he was a hundred percent human." Her heart quieted. "We humans aren't without our gifts."

"I know that." Clay slid her hair through his fist. "Maybe we're not giving Shine enough credit. Could be they take on mostly human children, too. After all, a lot of the renegade Psy had to have married humans, so they can't think of themselves as Psy."

"I think you might be right. There's another consideration." She stared at the documents in front of her. "Some of the Shine kids are too gifted to worry about mundane things like files and organization. We worker-bee types pick up the slack—could be one more reason for seeking out the mostly human descendants."

Sascha gave her an odd look. "You know, I've heard other humans refer to themselves as the worker bees of the world. But I don't—" She shook her head. "We'll discuss that later."

Talin nodded. "We need to talk to Dev now."

"Probably go better if you do it alone. We'll wait in my office," Lucas said.

Talin waited until the mated pair had left before getting up and walking to the computer screen. Touching a key, she activated the comm function.

Clay went to stand behind her and when she leaned back into him, he felt something tight in him ease. "Call him."

Putting one hand over the arm he'd wrapped around her middle, she entered the private code Dev had sent with the files. "Clay, if we're right, it means I'm part Psy."

"You smell human. You taste human." He nipped at her ear. "And you have the heart of a human. Don't worry—hell,

I'm pretty sure even Luc has more than three percent Psy blood."

"How did you know I was worrying?"

Because he understood her with a part of him he couldn't explain. "You're transparent." Putting his hands on her hips, he nudged her attention forward as the screen cleared to show Devraj Santos.

Deep grooves bracketed the other man's mouth. "You've read the files."

"Yes," Talin replied. "Is Shine collecting descendants of the Psy?"

Santos didn't bother to pretend surprise. "Not collecting but reconnecting with. The history of the Forgotten—the Psy who left the Net after Silence was voted in—is convoluted, but basically, we had to scatter and hide our identities about three generations back when the Council started hunting us."

Clay's leopard didn't trust the Shine director's sudden bluntness. "You're very cooperative today."

"You could say there's been a coup in management." His jaw firmed to granite. "I showed the old ones pictures of what they're doing to the kids—kids we promised to protect. Two of them had heart attacks. The rest handed over control to me." Santos's tone was cool, but his eyes betrayed the cost of the choice he'd had to make. "I'll cooperate with the devil if it means stopping the murders."

"Do you know where Jon is?" Talin asked.

"No," Santos grit out. "We're almost certain the Psy Council is behind the kidnappings, but we don't know why they're taking the children after so long. We're all of mixed blood now, hardly a threat to their power. Our organs are as mixed as the rest of us—of no use to pure-bred Psy."

"Focus on locating the mole in Shine," Clay said. "We'll find Jon."

The other man's eyes met his. "He's not your child." Unasked was the question—will you fight as hard for him?

"He's Talin's." That meant the boy was his, too, was DarkRiver's.

"I'll find the son of a bitch, don't worry about that. Every Shine kid—official and unofficial—has now been warned and offered protection. Those who won't cooperate are being detained until things clear up."

"You're keeping them prisoner?" Talin asked, then added, "Good."

Ending the call on Dev's surprised face, Talin relaxed into Clay, finding her strength from his. He pressed a kiss into the curve of her neck and her body hummed, remembering the hard promise of the kiss he'd given her earlier.

"Home?"

"Yes," she said, *home*.

"Where I can teach you not to mess with me," he growled. "My reputation is in shreds."

She wondered if he'd brought up their earlier play on purpose, her leopard's way of giving her a moment's respite from the agony of knowing Jon was out there, being hurt, being brutalized. "I'm not scared of you."

"You should be. I bite."

The warning tore a smile from her. "You'd never hurt me." He'd killed for her, let himself be imprisoned for her, taken her back despite her betrayal in running from him, and, even now, when she might leave him again in the most final way, he stood with her.

Her world rocked on its axis, a hidden door in her mind slamming wide open. All these years she'd told herself she was staying away from him because of the scars of violence, because she didn't want to hurt him, because of so many things. But in this one moment, this instant of absolute clarity, she knew the truth.

She hadn't run because she'd been afraid of Clay.

She'd run because she'd been afraid of being loved that much, terrified that she would lose the precious gift of it when Clay finally saw the reality of who she was—a used-up, discarded bit of trash, what Orrin had made her, good for only one thing.

So she had left him first.

CHAPTER 31

Ashaya checked through the records and found well over a hundred names. It was far more than she had expected, far more than could be explained by even the most convoluted idea of research. Why had Ming let this continue? Larsen's research theories made no rational sense, and, its murderous tendencies aside, the Council did not waste time on useless endeavors.

She began to examine the list with a closer eye. It was the first time she had seen it.

Just like the meeting with Jonquil Duchslaya had been the first time she had spoken to one of the children. Larsen had been very, very careful—at least at the start. As far as she could figure, the majority of the children had been experimented on at one of the Council's covert northern labs.

However, the base of operations had been moved to this lab after it went fully functional—without her agreement or knowledge. Not only had the parties responsible shown a flagrant disregard for her status as the lab's head scientist, once here, they had made less than a token effort to hide their actions. They must have thought her oblivious to what was going on because she spent so much time in her private research areas.

They hadn't been far off the mark, but for the wrong reasons. It didn't matter. Because of her delay in realizing the truth, several children had died, in *her* lab. Two more remained—the boy, Jonquil Duchslaya, and the girl, Noor Hassan. Ashaya stared at the files and knew that they would meet the same fate if she didn't prevent it.

She didn't feel pity for them. She was Psy. She didn't feel anything. However, the fact that one of her putative research assistants was doing this without her authorization made this about who held the reins of power. Which was why she wasn't going to go to Ming and complain. Nor was she going to take Larsen to task.

This was the opportunity she'd been waiting for. If her strategy worked, then not only would these children survive, the Psy Council would no longer have anything with which to coerce her cooperation.

That thought in mind, she began the journey that would lead her upstairs and to the cornfields outside. The guards were becoming accustomed to her daily walks, exactly as she'd planned. Of course, her plan of misdirection was hampered by the fact that she had a very short period in which to lay the groundwork. But the haste couldn't be helped, not if Jonquil and Noor were to walk out alive.

Some might have said she didn't want the children to die because she'd somehow retained a conscience, even in the depths of Silence. Ashaya would have disagreed. She had no conscience, no heart—like her own son, Jonquil and Noor were nothing more than bargaining chips.

All she had to do now was find a party willing to negotiate their release.

CHAPTER 32

Night had fallen in a soft whisper, but Talin hardly noticed. She sat at the small breakfast table on the second floor of the lair, her mind still spinning with the realization she'd had mere hours ago. She wanted to deny it but it rang with the clarity of absolute truth, a truth she had to understand. Yes, her fear of watching Clay turn from her in disgust had been at the root of her actions, but that fear had been tangled up with so many other threads.

She had been on the cusp of womanhood when she'd run from Clay with that most brutal of lies—young, confused, lost. Now that she was willing to *see*, it was stark that in her confusion, she had mixed up the protective fury of Clay's love with the jealous rage she'd seen in Orrin. That twelve-year-old girl who had missed Clay so desperately had also been terrified that he would destroy her trust if she let him back into her life. The memories of Clay protecting her, keeping her safe, laughing with her, had been the only treasures she'd had left.

Even that wasn't the whole story. It was too simple, and she was through with hiding. The unforgiving reality was that in spite of her youth, she must have subconsciously known that he wouldn't be an easy man to love. No, Clay was hard through and through. But he had loved her enough to put everything on the line—his sanity, his freedom, his pride. All so important to a dominant predatory changeling. She didn't know what he felt for her now, but she knew it was time to hold up her end of the bargain. *To love him enough.* Enough to not let fear stop her, whatever guise it took.

A slight noise cut into her thoughts as Clay pulled himself up to the second level. "Damn, I just got a sharp reminder from Tammy about a pack thing. You've got fifteen minutes to get ready or we'll be late. It's close to six already."

"I can't," Talin said, gesturing at the papers spread out on the table, papers she'd barely looked at since coming home. Guilt stabbed. "I have to see if I missed anyth—"

"I told you," Clay interrupted. "We're taking care of that. We've got people out there right now. I've tapped a Psy connection who might get us something very useful. But this dance, tonight, is important to the pack."

"I'm not part of DarkRiver." And she needed time to consider her next step. She didn't know how to be in a relationship, didn't know how to open herself up that much. "I'll be a stranger."

"No, you won't. You'll be with me." He stroked his fisted hand along her ponytail. "Please, Tally."

Her heart clenched. He called her Tally, but he didn't trust her with his soul, the leopard's wariness hidden behind a near-impenetrable shield—yet she knew. Did he think she didn't? Silly, arrogant leopard. She knew him too well, loved him too much, to not see. "You said 'please,' " she teased, fighting past the painful insight that no matter what happened, he might never again love her as he once had.

"Very funny."

"I want to. But I'd feel so guilty having fun while—"

"A few hours, that's all. It'll help you get your head back on straight."

She had to agree with that. Her focus was shot, which reminded her—"Did you get an update on Max?"

"He's fine, conscious. I had a packmate swing by and do a physical check."

Some of the weight crushing her lightened. "Tell me, why the dance?"

"It's to celebrate the formal blessing of a mating."

"Like a wedding?"

"Mating is nothing like marriage. It's forever. Mated pairs never choose to leave each other," he said. "Complete loyalty till death."

Her soul ached at the thought of the beauty, and the terror, in such a commitment. "Why the blessing if it's already decided?"

"To show the pack's acceptance, welcome Zach's mate into DarkRiver." His eyes grew intent, penetrating. "You okay, Tally?"

He knew her far too well, too, but she couldn't let him sense this hurt, didn't want her new knowledge—of the love she might've lost forever—to come between them. "I'm fine. Just a little tired."

His expression gentled. "I need to be there, baby. I'm a sentinel."

"Your presence matters to them," she said, so proud of what he'd become. "I understand. Let me freshen up."

Once in the bedroom, she quickly washed her face and hands, then pulled on the newest and nicest shirt she had packed. It was white and long-sleeved, the severe lines broken up by slender panels of fine lace down both sides. She left on the jeans she was wearing, but let down and brushed her hair. Then, on a whim, she dug around in her bag until she found a little zippered pocket. She thought she'd forgotten to take out something from there the last time she'd— Her hand touched metal.

"Bingo!" She lifted out the faux-silver earrings. A Celtic design, they would swing gently from her ears, dressing up her simple outfit. Her smile dimmed as she stood in front of the mirror slipping them into her ears.

Jon had given her these a few months ago. They were cheap—he'd found them at some flea market—but they meant everything, because he had bought the gift with honest, hard-earned money. "I haven't forgotten you," she promised with fierce dedication. "*We* haven't forgotten you." Because finally, after much too long, she had realized her leopard would stand by her through every darkness.

* * *

Clay was leaning against a tree at the edge of the Pack Circle, watching Nico swing Talin around, when he felt a familiar presence. Sascha came to stand beside him, keeping a small distance between them. Though most changelings craved touch, she knew he wasn't one for casual contact.

"She looks like she's having fun."

Clay nodded. "Yeah."

"So why are you standing here?"

"I'm not a big dancer."

Sascha shifted and he knew she'd folded her arms. "That's your excuse for tonight. What about all those other times you choose the shadows?"

"What's this—free psychoanalysis?" He had made it very clear that he didn't want anyone, even Sascha, peering into his emotions. "Been peeping, Sascha?"

"I don't actively have to look, you know that. I pick up emotional echoes like you pick up scents." She leaned back against his tree. "Things have improved a considerable amount since Talin came into your life, but you're not happy."

"You're a genius."

"Stop being flippant," she said, quiet power in her voice. "This is important. You aren't helping Talin by being this way."

He glanced at her. "Tally is my business."

"She might have been once," she replied. "But you brought her into the pack and now she's ours, too."

Clay felt the leopard uncurl into a crouch inside of him. "What are you saying?"

"We like her. We'll look out for her. Even against you."

He tempered his response with cold steel. "I will look out for Talin."

"I don't know." She shrugged. "All I see is this wall you've got around yourself, so hard, so thick. She's your way out, Clay, but only if you let her be."

Nico jerked Talin in a particularly energetic whirl and Clay scowled. She was human, not changeling. He hoped the boy remembered she could be more easily hurt. Then she laughed and he relaxed. "Stop talking in riddles and give it to me straight."

A frustrated sound. "Fine. Whatever it is that you're letting poison your relationship, you need to get over it. You're not good for *her* like this."

The blunt comment stunned him. Sascha was intensely loyal to DarkRiver. The fact that she'd put Talin's well-being above his gained her another slice of his respect, even as the implications of her statement angered him. "I'm giving her everything I can. More than I've ever given anyone."

"Not enough, Clay. And she knows it."

Claws raked his gut. "She's not like you. She can't feel what I feel."

"You tell yourself that if it makes you feel better." She moved into his line of sight, tall enough that he only had to lower his head a few inches to meet her gaze. "Your Tally is one of the most sensitive human beings I've ever met. Some abused children become that way—alert to the slightest changes in the emotional temperature of a room or a relationship. She knows exactly what you feel."

"Sascha!" Lucas called out from the Circle. "Stop flirting with Clay and come dance with your mate." His grin was a bright slash.

Sascha turned, her face softening even in profile. "I've said what I had to say. The rest is up to you." Then she walked toward the Circle and into Lucas's arms. Talin was dancing with Nico right next to the alpha pair and Clay saw her look up at Lucas as he said something and smiled down at his mate.

Even from this distance, he could read the look on her face: *hunger.*

Not sexual. Deeper, needier—as if she was witnessing something she thought she would never have. It cut him far deeper than anything Sascha had said.

Pushing off the tree, he strode toward her. Nico saw him over Talin's head and his eyes widened. Clay never danced. The juvenile said something to Talin and released her, backing off to find another partner. She turned, her own eyes huge. "Clay?" He wrapped his arms around her waist.

She seemed not to know where to put her hands. After a few hesitant seconds, she slid them around his waist but kept enough distance between them that she could look up into his face. "What's the matter?"

"Nothing." He tried to pull her closer, but she resisted.

"Nothing wouldn't make you look like you want to bite someone's head off."

"Dance with me."

"Clay—"

"I'll tell you after the dance." He'd *show* her. She damn well wasn't going to keep hurting the way she was right now.

"Promise?"

His low growl made one of the nearby juveniles give him a wary look. Talin smiled and snuggled close enough to press her cheek against his heartbeat.

He looked down, bemused. He figured a hundred years later, he still wouldn't understand her completely. The cat in him was pleased by the thought of such an intriguing mate.

Mate.

Of course she was meant to be his mate. Something settled in him at the conscious recognition of a truth he had always known. The second she accepted the mating bond, she was going to belong to him in the most indisputable of ways. Mates were forever. No leopard mated twice.

Even if their mate died.

His arms tightened reflexively around her.

"Hey," she complained.

"Sorry."

"It's okay." She squeezed her own arms around him as they swayed in opposition to the lively music. "I like dancing with you."

"Yeah."

Talin didn't know what was wrong with Clay, but the emotion in that single word was so raw, so powerful, her heart about stopped. She wanted to ask him so many questions, but for now, she held on to him and they danced. It was a perfect moment, a dance with this man she adored beyond all others.

The clock had barely ticked past ten when they returned home. "I had fun. And now I feel bad." Taking off her earrings, she put them carefully by the comm panel, then collapsed onto one of those huge cushions Clay used as sofas. "It seems so wrong to have gone dancing while I could have been doing something."

"What?" Closing the door, he came to loom over her. "What could you have been doing?"

"Well, I could've looked at the files again."

"And seen nothing you haven't seen ten times already." Shaking his head, he sat down in a quintessentially masculine sprawl opposite her. "We've set things in motion. Now we wait—sometimes the best way to hunt is to let the prey think you've given way."

She gave a reluctant nod, knowing he was right. There was nothing else she personally could do. It was time to have faith in Clay and his pack. "Thank you for helping me. For asking your pack to help me."

She could almost see it, almost touch it—the slow rising of the same heat that had been in his eyes most of the night. And she was its sole focus. Her body tightened.

"I would've done it for their women."

Implication wasn't enough, not with this heavy warmth threatening to hijack her body. "Am I your woman, Clay?"

It seemed as if even the forest hushed as she waited to hear his answer. Those green eyes, so bright, so beautiful, skated over her face, down her throat, over the rise and fall of her breasts, the curve of her waist, and the legs she had curled under herself. She sucked in an unsteady breath and his body went predator-still.

"Come here, Tally." It was a command, sensual, rich, erotic.

Heartbeat in her throat, she uncurled her legs, a visceral awareness sweeping across every inch of her skin. What he'd said, the way he'd said it. He wanted her to accept this thing between them, accept it in a way that left no room for argument, a way that reversed her girlhood decision to cut him out of her life.

She was moving before she knew it—she had already made her decision. *To love him enough.* When she stopped, it was to find herself kneeling on his cushion, trapped by the muscular strength of his legs on either side. Placing her hands on his raised knees, she said, "I'm here."

He ran a finger down the row of buttons that closed her shirt. "I want to peel apart this shirt and see your breasts."

It was getting difficult to breathe. "O-okay." Her hands clenched on him.

"This isn't friendship." A blunt statement, underscoring the dividing line they were about to cross.

"No. It's okay," she repeated when he just watched her.

"Is it?" A finger nudging aside cloth to stroke the dip of her breastbone.

"What do you want?" she asked, desperate to give it to him.

"Is this punishment, Tally?" Cat-green eyes clashing with her own. "Are you giving in to me because you want to hurt yourself? Am I another faceless fuck you plan to forget?"

"What?" Her hands fisted against the roughness of denim. "No!" She couldn't believe she had ever worried about not feeling with Clay during sex. It was impossible to be anything but fully engaged—his leopard demanded it and so did her own fierce hunger. "I'm not giving in. I'm *choosing* this because you make me crazy with need, you arrogant cat. I want to mark you, make sure the world knows you belong to me."

Those male lips seemed to soften. "Then tell me what you want."

If her heart hadn't already been his, he would've captured it then and there. He might be in a dangerous mood, but he was hers—maybe she didn't have all of him but what she had, she would cherish with every breath in her. "I want to see you," she whispered.

His eyes snapped up to meet her gaze. "I was thinking more along the lines of what would pleasure you. I don't have much patience left."

"You never had much patience," she teased, though her stomach was tight with such frantic sensual craving, it hurt. "Seeing your body gives me pleasure."

Eyes holding a surprised, strangely vulnerable look, he reached down, undid a few buttons on his dress shirt, then pulled it off and threw it to the side. All at once, his beautiful, naked chest was there for her to taste, kiss, enjoy. This very dominant male had just given her total skin privileges. Delighted, she flattened her hands on him, luxuriating in the tensile strength of pure muscle covered by hot, dark, beautiful skin. The crispness of the hair that curled under her palms was yet another seductive sensation.

She felt him place his hands on her hips but was too focused on his beauty to pay attention. Never, before Clay, had the mere sight of a man been enough for her body to ready itself for penetration. But today she was melting from the inside out and oh, how she liked it. Trailing her fingers down his chest, she found herself wondering what it would feel like to strip off her clothing and rub her nipples against the rough heat of him. Something tightened between her thighs, a hungry, aching need that begged to be satisfied.

There was a vibration against her palms. She bit her lower lip, fought the wave of sheer pleasure . . . and the piercing realization that that vibration would serve to intensify the sensations she craved. "You're purring again."

His lips curved. "I can scent your arousal."

It should've made her blush. But it only made her hotter. "I can see yours." He was hard under the straining zipper of his jeans. And big. Very big. Her body clenched and unclenched, urging her to unzip him, let him fill her up. It would hurt so-damn-good.

"Drop your arms."

Face hot with the erotic images dancing through her head, she raised it to discover he'd unbuttoned her shirt. "No." Wrapping her arms around his neck, she leaned in. "Kiss me first."

"Going to be a brat in bed, too?" His hands slipped under her open shirt to hold on to her waist as he took her mouth in hot, languorous kiss that made her feel so sexy she thought she might just be able to conquer the world.

"I get to give a few orders, too," she murmured.

His hands slipped down, closed over her bottom. Squeezed. She was still gasping over that when one of those deliciously callused hands slid up over her back and around to her front. She held her breath.

CHAPTER 33

He didn't just touch her breast. He held with bold possessiveness. Squeezed there, too. And she decided to obey his order. Dropping her arms, she tugged off her shirt. It stuck at her elbows. Clay took full advantage, wrapping the material in his free hand and using it as a binding to keep her hands behind her back.

"I don't like being restrained," she complained.

He squeezed her breast again, then cut through the straps and the middle section of her bra with a single sharp claw, retracted a second later. "Can't I even pet you in peace?"

Then her bra was gone and Clay was looking at her, his hand spread big and confident below her breasts. Her heart galloped. With each indrawn breath, it was as if she was pushing up her breasts for his enjoyment. They weren't huge. Not even close. But right now, they seemed to have taken over her body.

"Apples," Clay said, his eyes cat-bright.

She had no idea what he was talking about. "Apples?"

"I love apples." He bent that dark head and closed his teeth around one nipple.

She couldn't breathe.

Then he flicked his tongue over the flesh and the air rushed out of her in a burst of hunger and need and pleasure. Releasing the nipple, he took her breast in a scorching hot kiss that reduced her to whimpers. Somewhere along the line, she got rid of the shirt and thrust her hands in his hair, wordlessly urging him to give her more.

God, she was being greedy. But he didn't seem to mind. She promised her half-dazed mind that she'd make it up to him. Right now, she wanted to indulge herself, to let him indulge her.

He pressed a kiss to the heated valley between her breasts and nuzzled his way up her neck. "We should go up to bed."

She kissed him, unable to resist the temptation of his sensual lips. "Later."

"Later," he agreed and pushed her backward.

When her back touched a soft surface, she realized he'd used his foot to drag the other cushion closer. She raised her arms and he came down on top of her, the cushions forming the perfect bed. His hand stroked her from neck down to waist as he claimed her mouth in another ravaging kiss. She had never felt more taken, more possessed. But for the first time, the possession held tenderness. And she knew that what was happening in this makeshift bed with Clay was something new, something indefinably precious.

Under her roaming palms, his muscles moved in a slow symphony that was as seductive as his kiss. Clay was all big shoulders, heavy muscle, and tremendous power. She dug her fingers into him and was fairly sure he barely noticed. "Clay," she murmured against his mouth, "tell me what you like."

"Harder," he said, nibbling at her lower lip. "I'm not soft like you."

She caressed him with firmer strokes and was gratified to hear his breath catch. But he didn't give her long to enjoy that, dipping his head and suckling at her neck in a way that she knew was going to leave a mark. "So good." She shuddered.

His response was to bring up one of his hands and stroke her breasts with heavy boldness. No flirtatious passes for Clay. He petted and teased with the confidence of a man who knew what he wanted, what his woman wanted.

"Mine," he said, pressing a kiss to the skin he'd sucked.

And she knew she'd been marked. "Ditto. I don't share."

She had always been unreasonably possessive of him. If he had so much as smiled at another girl, she'd sulked for days.

He raised his head. "Neither do I." Their eyes met in a collision of pure fire.

This, she realized, was it. Either she kept protecting herself or she upheld her vow to love him without fear. Put that way, it wasn't a choice at all. So she gathered up her courage and did something agonizingly, blindingly hard for a woman who had learned to distrust early and never quite forgotten the lesson. She ripped open her heart and took the final step across that glass bridge. "It was you. *Always*. Only ever you." At that instant, she felt something wrench and re-form deep inside of her, almost as if her soul itself changed shape, then the odd feeling passed and she found herself face-to-face with the predator that lived inside Clay.

His intent expression hadn't changed, but his eyes were those of the leopard who was as much a part of him as his human skin. "This, too?" He growled and she felt the roughness of it scrape over her skin in a caress that was at once frightening and mind-blowingly erotic.

Blood flowed to low, heated places. "I'm not afraid of you." Never again would she fear him. "Sometimes, I'm afraid of what I feel for you"—and the cost the emotional connection would demand from him if this damn disease took her—"but I'm not afraid of you hurting me."

He kissed her again, an unflinching male brand that left her gasping. "Took you long enough."

She bit him for that remark, a sharp closing of teeth on one shoulder. It was over before she'd stopped to think about it. When he growled this time, she felt the rumble of it vibrate against her breasts. Then he bit *her*. The second his teeth closed over the peak of her breast, she felt her thighs attempt to clench. If he hadn't been between them, she would've been squeezing them tight in an effort to quench the liquid fire threatening to burn her up.

Teasing her by rocking his erection against her, he bit her again. Mercy! When he did it to her other breast, she decided she'd have to provoke him more often. Pushing her hands into his hair, she tugged. "Too much." Too much pleasure, too much exquisite sexual heat.

He said something against her breast and the sensation made her skin feel as if it was stretching ever tauter, as if her breasts were swelling to please this sexy changeling who seemed determined to enslave her. His hair was heavy silk under her hand, his jaw rough with stubble. She wanted to stroke every inch of him.

When he shifted his lower body, she locked her legs around him, holding his strength to her, luxuriating in the knowledge that while she might not control it, or him—nor would she want to—it was completely at her disposal.

Finally releasing her needy flesh, he kissed his way freckle by freckle down to the curved plane of her abdomen. When he looked up, the erotic beauty of him stole her breath. "You taste good. Pretty freckles." He flicked out his tongue as if tasting one. "Mmm."

"You're making me crazy." He was so honest in his blunt male appreciation of her body. "I thought you said you had no patience."

"I don't. You're just hot for me."

She grinned through the crimson veil of desire. "Yeah?"

"Yeah." Smug, very male, very Clay. But only for her.

Pursing her lips, she blew him a kiss. "Yeah."

Her agreement had him prowling up her body to give her a slow, sensual kiss that made her moan into his mouth. The feel of his chest hair against the damp tips of her breasts simply added to the overload. She rubbed against him as she'd imagined, inciting him, pleasing them both. His hands slipped under her bottom. "Off."

She was too busy kissing him to listen. He used his teeth on her lower lip. She used hers on his. It was a very sensual fight but he won—because she wanted to be skin to skin, too. All over. Unlocking her legs from his back, she lifted up her bottom and let him undo and peel off her jeans. He threw them aside and ran his finger along the lace edges of her panties.

"Pink?" A row of kisses along the waistband.

She swallowed at the image of those wicked male lips so close to the most private, most delicate part of her body. "I like pink."

Spreading her legs, he licked along the inner-thigh edges.

Her hands gripped at the cushion as her body bucked with a twisting pleasure she'd never before felt. Then he licked the other side. And that pleasure roared through her like a fever. But through it all, she was aware of him, holding her, touching her, caressing her.

When the room stopped spinning, she lifted up her head then dropped it back down. "Oh, man." She had known that being with Clay would be good, that it would eclipse the other times into nothingness, but this was beyond good, beyond anything. All she could think was—no wonder women liked sex. But of course, this was nothing so simple as sex. This was . . . "Oh, man."

Clay chuckled. "Is that all you're going to say?"

"Uh-huh." Her brain was mush.

"In that case, I'll talk." He placed a kiss on her inner thighs, one for each side, then ran his claws very carefully along her hip. "Snap." The right side of her panties fell away. "Snap." So did the left.

That quickly, she was naked and he was between her thighs, so close his breath whispered over her intimate flesh. Her body was suddenly a tight fist, expectant, waiting. It scared her a little, how deeply he touched her, how easily he'd stripped her of her barriers, but she had made a promise and she would keep it. Talin McKade was no coward—she was strong enough to dance with a leopard. "Clay?" she said when he didn't make a sound.

"I like pink, too," he said, his expression wholly masculine.

"You're making me blush." It felt as if he was touching her with his eyes.

"Mmm." An utterly sexual, utterly content sound.

She felt every sense in her bow in surrender. Sure the wetness between her thighs must be embarrassing by now, she clenched her body in a futile effort to control her need. Clay's fingers spread her open again and she felt the impact of that touch to her toes. She dug them into the cushions, but Clay had other ideas. Lifting one leg at a time, he put both over his shoulders—after pressing nibbling kisses along the inner thighs.

"You," she managed to say hoarsely, "are a very bad kitty

cat." That made him laugh, his breath stroking her exposed folds. She moaned, anticipation racing along her skin, burning with hot, sweet hunger.

"Meow." His tongue flicked over her parted flesh. "I love cream, too."

Anticipation turned into the most extreme pleasure. Again, she dug her fingers into the fabric of the cushion, but it was no use. There was no way she could control this. Not when he was licking at her with those quick, catlike flicks that were driving her certifiably insane. "Harder," she found herself whispering, shocked at her own daring.

"Not yet." Another flick. Another moan. "I want to make you a little crazier first."

"Bully." It was a gasp.

"Brat."

That clever, clever tongue was doing things to her she had never believed possible. She found herself pressing closer, begging him with her body, her thighs tight around him, her heels digging into his back. Then he bit her.

She made a sharp, shocked sound before the world exploded around her. The pleasure was so raw, so rich, so acute, it blasted through her body with the strength of a supernova, leaving her quivering in its wake. If she could've found the willpower to speak, the brain cells to construct thought, she would've told Clay he was a god. It was a good thing she was too wiped out or he would have never let her forget it.

His hands slid under her bottom, fondling and squeezing as he continued to lap at her. She was fairly certain that that last incredible orgasm had wiped her out, but it felt so nice she didn't ask him to stop. A minute later, it felt better than nice. It felt exquisite. She heard a low, husky moan and it took her several seconds to realize the unashamedly sensual sound had come from her own throat. "I am so greedy."

He looked up, eyes glittering with arousal. "Don't worry, I'm keeping score."

The eye contact was exhilarating, rocking her to the soul. "Do I get to lick you?"

His hands tightened convulsively on her flesh, his expression promising retaliation. "Do you want to?"

It was an act she'd never willingly performed. But there

was a deep curiosity in her about the taste of this man who made her feel like the sexiest thing on this planet. "Maybe." She stretched, ran her tongue along her upper lip. "Depends how far in debt I am."

Her provocation had the desired effect. His head dipped and he wasn't lapping now. He was kissing her in earnest, destroying any puny defenses she might've had.

She got into a lot more debt before he was finished.

"Embarrassing and undignified?" he asked as he kissed his way up her trembling body.

Her face flushed at the reminder of how she'd once described the luscious thing he had just done to her. "I think it's growing on me."

"Good. Because I like the taste of you." His voice was rough.

She glanced down his body, saw the arousal shoving at his jeans. "Take them off." Her hands went to the waistband and she found the first button already undone.

"Careful," he whispered in her ear as she began to lower the zipper. It caught on something. "Jesus, Tally."

She kissed his chest. "It's only your underwear. Don't be a baby." A second later, the zipper was undone and she was sliding her hand into that underwear and finding him, hot, hard, and oh-so-aroused.

He seemed to stop breathing as she closed her hand into a small fist. "You're so big." He would fill her up, take her over.

"Remember that," he groaned. "And tell everyone you know."

It made her want to laugh, except that her body was starving of this hunger that had been a lifetime in the making and all she wanted was to see him. She released him, to the accompaniment of his complaining groan. "Take off your clothes." She began to push at his jeans, exposing the erotic line of his hip bones.

He kissed her before rising in a smooth catlike move and disposing of his clothing in what amounted to seconds. Then he was coming down on her again and in the light, his body was pure male animal, his skin molding to muscle, his body heavy with arousal.

He settled between her thighs, making room for himself by

spreading her legs wider. She cooperated. But she wasn't ready to surrender yet. Not giving him warning, she slid her hand between their bodies and gripped him once more. He groaned, his back arching, the tendons on his neck standing out in vivid relief.

Raising her head, she kissed him at the base of his neck before lying back down, her hand fisted around him. He shuddered, dropped his head. "You can play later."

She ran her fisted hand up and down the straining length of him, pushing her own arousal to the limit even as she pushed him. To her delight, he didn't rush her, though his eyes warned that she was about to push him too far. It only made her hotter. To be in bed with a man she trusted this much was a revelation. "I adore you."

He groaned. *"Tally."*

Her hunger spiked and when he tugged off her hand, she didn't fight him. He was nudging at her a second later. She gripped his shoulders, drew the scent of him into her lungs, and waited. He nudged the tip of his erection into her and every nerve in her body went haywire. He was so hard, she was buttery soft. It was perfect—if he'd move. She tried to rock forward but he held her in place.

She was about to tell him this was no time to tease when she realized he was trying to find control. He was much bigger, far stronger than her. But she didn't want him in control. And she trusted him with every cell in her body, her surrender to him absolute.

"Clay, I swear to God, if you don't bury yourself in me right now, I'm going to reach down and bring myself to—" Her throat froze up as he pushed himself into her in a single thrust. He was stretching her apart, killing her with pleasure. Parts of her body that had never before been touched were being touched and she wanted to beg for more. Because this was Clay, she did. "Move," she said, voice husky. "Please move."

He nuzzled at her throat, caught her lips in a kiss. "Ready?"

She looked into his eyes and nodded. "Ready."

The last thing she remembered thinking was that she had never seen a more beautiful man in her life. A moment later, pleasure crashed through her like thunder and Clay became her world, her universe, her reason for being.

* * *

Sometime during the night, Clay had carried her upstairs and to bed. Talin wasn't sure how—she had vague memories of being tossed over his shoulder, his hand on her upturned bottom. But really, she didn't care. Because when she woke, it was to find her face snuggled against Clay's chest, his thigh between hers.

Smile wide, she pressed a kiss to the skin below her lips. He did that purring thing again. "My kitty," she teased, stroking her fingers over the silky heat of him.

Grumbling, he squeezed the thigh he'd pulled over his hip. "Go to sleep."

"It's daytime," she pointed out, able to tell from the light seeping in through the windows.

"Too early." Then he pretended to snore.

She kissed him again and laid her head against his chest. His heart beat strong and steady, anchoring her. "What will we do today?" Her laughter faded.

"Get one step closer to finding your Jon." He pushed his hand into her hair, cupped the back of her head. "Have faith."

"I do. I just . . . I wish I could swoop in and save him like a hero out of some comic book."

"You are his hero, Tally. You made sure he wasn't forgotten."

"You know, when I thought I might have a lot of Psy blood, I was angry. I like being human." The genetic link had threatened her identity, the one thing no one had ever been able to steal from her. "But at the same time, I can't help but wonder if I could've done more to save the children if I had had Psy gifts or changeling strength." Surrounded by the extraordinary power of both races, it was difficult not to feel weak.

"Don't." Clay's voice was firm. "You're you because you're human. I like you."

She rolled her eyes even as her lips threatened to curve. "I like you, too, even if you're only half human," she teased. "But sometimes, being only human—"

"Be quiet and listen," he ordered in that dominant tone that intrigued her even as it infuriated. "Do you know about the eighteenth century's Territorial Wars?"

CHAPTER 34

"Sure, we learned about it in school." Thousands of changelings had died in the bloodshed, taking the other races with them.

"Do you know the name of the man who helped draft the laws that ended the war?"

"Adrian Kenner," she said, flipping through her memory files to retrieve the name. "He was a side note in a history textbook."

"A side note to the other races, maybe," Clay said. "He's considered a critical figure in changeling history. All our children know his name. What most people forget, though"—he brushed his lips over hers—"is that Adrian Kenner was only human, too."

She wiggled up the bed until they were face-to-face. "Really? But how? Why?"

"The predators would've torn each other's throats out. A nonpredatory negotiator would've been ignored by the predators." Matter-of-fact words. "As for the Psy—they tried but the changelings wouldn't trust anyone who had the ability to mess with their minds. Plus, they had a nasty way of looking down on us for being animals."

"The Psy were like that before Silence?"

"Why do you think Silence took so well? The seeds were there."

Talin mulled his words over. "You're saying we're neutral territory."

"No, you're the bridge. Changelings trust only Pack. Psy stay in the PsyNet. But humans move freely between all three—or did, before Silence."

She bit her lip. "The Forgotten—more of them married humans than changelings."

"Yes. It's almost impossible to breach the walls of a changeling pack. We're as unwelcoming to outsiders as the Psy."

"You're not so bad," she murmured. "I like how you care for each other." The depth of that loyalty was an almost visible force.

"But we need the occasional human to come in and shake us up. All the humans who've mated into DarkRiver have made us stronger, given us bonds outside the pack. You're not *only* human, Talin. You're beautifully, powerfully human."

She nodded, but her mind was less on his words than why he'd said them. For her. To bolster her confidence. Was it any wonder she loved him? "I'm so glad I came to you," she said, just as a low beep cut through the air.

"That's my cell phone," Clay told her. "It's on the bed stand—can you grab it?"

Knowing it had to be important if he was willing to cut short their conversation, she turned, grabbed it, and gave it to him. She stayed with her head on his arm but put enough distance between them that she could see his face as he flipped open the phone. "Thanks for getting back to me," were his first words.

"Yes."

"When?"

"I'll see you then." He closed the phone.

She figured it had to be pack business and was practical enough to know it would most likely not include her. It was, she thought, one thing to become his lover, quite another to be welcomed into DarkRiver. "You have a meeting?" She tried to keep her voice bright, unwilling to spoil the morning by asking for something he didn't want to give her.

"*We* have a meeting." There was a satisfied glint in his eye.

Her determination not to ruin things gave way to interest. "With whom?"

"A SnowDancer. I gave him a call last night before the dance. I had a feeling Judd still had some very interesting contacts inside the PsyNet."

"But, the SnowDancers are wolves." She frowned. "How could he have contacts?"

"He's Psy. Mated to a SnowDancer wolf."

Excitement tore through her with the force of lightning unleashed. "Would he be able to find out if they're taking the children, confirm if it *is* the Psy?"

"Damn Psy walks like an assassin—who knows what info he can get his hands on." He kissed her without warning, derailing her thoughts with the dark heat of it. "But I know what I want to get my hands on."

Half an hour later, she glanced at her neck in the bathroom mirror and scowled. "Why didn't you just bite me?" she asked, rubbing at the mark he'd left.

"I did." Patting her on the bottom as he passed, half-dressed in jeans, his hair wet, he gave her an unrepentant grin. "Want me to do it again?" His gaze angled downward.

Blushing, she pushed him out of the bathroom and continued brushing her own wet hair. "Make me tea!" she called out after him, knowing they had time since this Judd person was coming down from the Sierra Nevada.

"How the hell do you make tea?" he muttered. "I don't have tea."

"Yes, you do. It's on the top shelf—I got some from Tamsyn." She really had to go grocery shopping if she was going to be living with Clay. That thought froze her. "Clay?"

He heard her, though her voice had been a whisper. "I'm making the damn tea."

"I had a question."

"What?"

"Are we living together?"

A few seconds of silence and then he was in the doorway,

his eyes cat-green. Walking over, he kissed the mark on her neck. "You try to leave and I will hunt you down."

Relief poured through her, but she smacked at his thigh with the back of her brush. "Like a rabid dog? Very romantic."

"I'm serious. This is it. Forever."

She met his gaze in the mirror and wondered how long forever would be. As yesterday's inexplicable allergic reaction had proved, the disease in her blood was getting stronger day by day. But, she thought with a fresh wave of fury, damn if she was giving in. "Forever." She'd fight hell itself to stay with him this time.

He rested his hands on her hips and bent down until their faces reflected side by side. He was so beautiful—all masculine arrogance and possessiveness—that she knew she'd have to be on her guard constantly. Otherwise, she'd give him everything he wanted.

His fingers pushed up, touched skin. "You want me."

"We'll be late." But she leaned into him, luxuriating in the strength contained within that muscular body, needing him enough to indulge this small selfishness.

"Judd hasn't been mated long," he murmured, hands slipping up to curve over her unbound breasts.

Her breath caught at the bold move, at the sultry image of his hands moving under her T-shirt. "What's that got to do with anything?" The last word was a moan as he began playing with her breasts, sure of his right to touch her as he pleased.

"It was early when he called." He flicked out his tongue in a quick catlike caress she was already addicted to. "He'll be delayed."

It took her desire-fuzzy brain several seconds to get his meaning. "Oh. *Oh!*" The last was a cry as he did something with those big hands that was surely illegal. But even as she surrendered to him, part of her knew that this was an illusory happiness. The ache in her belly, the endless need, it was a silent cry for something Clay could no longer give her.

Now that she'd met some of the couples in the pack, learned more about the leopard side of Clay's soul, she understood the depth of her mistake. These predators loved with wild fury, but they were also darkly possessive, crossing the boundary into what humans might term obsession. But for a leopard male, it was simply part of his nature. Clay would never forget what she'd done, the way she'd given her body to others.

With a human man, she might have continued to argue that he had no right to judge her. But the truth was, it wasn't about judgment. And Clay wasn't human, his changeling blood was too strong. For him, it was about fidelity, about loyalty. It didn't matter that they had been children when he killed Orrin to keep her safe—they had already belonged to each other. Until she had cut their link. Now the past was an unacknowledged third between them, pouring a corrosive acid on the love they had managed to salvage.

He kissed her. *Enough,* she thought, banishing the ugly thoughts to a far corner of her mind. She was with Clay; that was what mattered. Finally, for the first time in two decades, she was almost whole.

She and Clay arrived at the meeting point—a small cabin on DarkRiver land—at almost exactly the same time as the SnowDancer. Judd Lauren was the coldest man she had ever seen. Dressed in a black T-shirt and black jeans, his eyes measured her with icy precision. She'd have run very fast in the opposite direction had Clay not been beside her. And had Judd not been holding the hand of a small blonde with amazing eyes of brown shot with blue, and the brightest smile Talin had ever seen.

"Judd's mate, Brenna," Clay said, lips brushing her ear.

Brenna's expression shifted to pure astonishment. "Good Lord, the rumors are true—Clay actually talks to you."

Talin couldn't help it, she burst out laughing despite the painful thoughts swirling in her head. "Does he?" She gestured at Judd.

"If I'm *very* good, he sometimes says two whole sentences in a row."

Talin was about to reply when Clay clamped a hand over her mouth from behind—at the same time that Judd wrapped an arm around Brenna's neck. "Before they start comparing other things," he said to Clay, "let's talk." Taking Brenna with him, he walked up the steps and grabbed a chair, while Brenna curled up on the swing.

Following the other couple onto the porch, Clay chose to lean against the railing. Talin stayed attached to his side, all amusement gone. Judd wouldn't have asked them to sit unless he had something to tell them, which meant Dev was probably right—the Psy were kidnapping the children . . . doing things to Jon she might not be able to erase.

"You trust her?" Judd asked, cold gaze fixed on Talin.

The blunt question froze her in place. She told herself not to hope, not to wish for the impossible. Yet, when Clay replied, she felt as if he'd flayed the skin off her flesh. "Tally's mine." Possession, not an affirmation of trust.

But it seemed to satisfy Judd. "Are you aware that Silence functions by conditioning young Psy not to feel?" he asked her.

She scrambled to regather her shattered resources. "Yes. Clay explained."

"The process no longer works well enough for the Psy Council," he responded.

Sliding a hand behind Clay's back, Talin held on to him as Judd continued speaking. Clay's arm—already around her shoulders—tightened.

"Because of the number of people who aren't taking to, or who are breaking, Silence," Judd continued, his voice getting ever more arctic, his eyes shifting to killing black, "the Council has initiated the beginnings of an Implant Protocol."

As Talin watched, Brenna reached out to curl her hand around Judd's upper arm. Though he didn't seem to notice the touch, when he next spoke, his voice was less inhuman. "They want to put implants in children's brains to ensure full implementation of Silence. The chips will turn the PsyNet—currently composed of individuals—into a hive mind, with the Councilors as the controlling entities."

"Don't they see that it'll kill the Psy?" Talin asked, horrified at the idea of cutting into developing brains. "It'll destroy innovation, bury brilliance for the sake of conformity."

Judd's classically handsome face burned with deep anger. "The Council sees power. That's the only thing that matters to them."

"What's the connection to the kidnappings?" Clay asked.

"Until a few months ago, the Implant lab was located in this state. But after it was sabotaged and the research destroyed, the Council moved its activities to a hidden location."

Talin felt her hand turn into a claw against Clay's chest. "You're saying the kids are being taken to this hidden lab?"

"I'm guessing," Judd corrected. "They could have other facilities. But this one is isolated enough to provide the perfect base of operations."

Clay put his hand over hers. "Any way to find out for sure?"

"My contact was able to confirm Psy involvement, but nothing further."

"Do you believe him?"

Judd shrugged. "He's loyal to the Psy race, so he won't betray them. But he considers the Implant Protocol the worse evil. I pointed out that there is a possibility the kidnapped children are being used as test subjects."

Talin choked back her rising terror. "Do you really believe that?"

"I can't see the worth of using non-Psy organs to test such a sensitive implant." He paused. "However, things are chaotic in the Net at present. The Council's attention is scattered. It may be losing control over some of those it previously contained."

Brenna's expression grew solemn. "The monsters are starting to escape."

"That could explain why we're finding bodies at all—if the Council was running this, they wouldn't have left a trail," Clay said, as Judd picked up his mate's hand and pressed a kiss to her palm. "Is there any way to infiltrate this lab and verify whether or not it is the base of operations?"

"That," Judd said, continuing to keep Brenna's hand in his, "is the issue. If I give you the location of the lab and you go in openly, it may blow my contact's cover. Only a select few have access to that data."

"But if we could save Jon—and others they haven't yet taken—wouldn't it be worth it?" Talin asked, angry at the SnowDancer male for being so damn uninvolved.

Then she saw the quiet fury in his gaze and realized her mistake. "If my contact is unmasked and the Council shifts the lab again, we might not be able to stop the Implant Protocol. It'll affect hundreds of thousands. I'm not asking you to make a choice between this boy and the Psy children who will be implanted. I'm telling you there is no easy answer."

With those words, he turned black and white into gray, left her grappling with a moral dilemma that appeared to have no solution. "I don't suppose we could sneak in?"

"It's located in the middle of cornfields deep in Nebraska, open visibility in every direction."

Clay found himself thinking of the story Tally had told him about her secret caves. "What about underground? There has to be some system to bring in supplies—even if it's just replacement medical equipment. It can't be a hermetically sealed environment." He also knew that if the children *were* being taken to this facility, the Psy would need to have a system in place to transport the bodies out. But he kept his silence. Tally's heart was already breaking—she didn't need to hear that.

Judd's expression shifted, became thoughtful. "They could be teleporting in everything, but I'd say that's unlikely. Teleporters are thin on the ground—the Council would never waste them on such menial tasks."

"And," Brenna murmured, "they can't be trucking or flying things in. The traffic would give away the location."

"There has to be a hidden access point." Animal instinct told Clay he was right.

"Pity we don't have a teleporter ourselves," Talin muttered.

"Wouldn't help," Judd told her. "They need an image of where they're going, particularly when buildings are involved. Otherwise, they could end up inside a wall or stuck halfway through a ceiling. Organs sliced in half, instant death."

Talin shivered.

"There's one other thing," Clay said. "A witness saw Jon disappear off the street. Any way to explain that if we work on the theory that this isn't a teleporter?"

"They probably threw out a wave of telepathic interference. It would've blocked any humans from 'seeing' the snatch. Sloppy work if your wit was aware Jon had disappeared—either that or the wit was changeling."

Clay made a note to check up on that. If one of the Rats

had fathered a child, he could understand their protectiveness in hiding the kid, but DarkRiver needed to know. "What's the closest safe insertion point to the lab?"

"Cinnamon Springs—only town within any reasonable distance."

"We'll fly there tomorrow, check it out," Clay said.

Judd reached into his pants pocket and pulled out a data crystal. "The exact location. Keep it on an absolute need-to-know basis. One slip and they'll move the lab. If you want me to go in with you, call. Otherwise, everything I know is on that crystal."

"There has to be a way in," Brenna murmured. "Sorry, darling, but Psy often don't think about us animals."

"Even Psy learn," her mate responded with an amused smile that was so unexpected, Talin's mouth fell open. "They're wary of cats and wolves now. There's a high probability the area's been seeded with sensors calibrated to pick them up."

Clay stirred. "Yeah, but what about snakes? Snakes can hide in corn and, in animal form, they're unique enough that the sensors shouldn't go off."

"You know a snake? Oh!" She suddenly remembered his story about a changeling with shimmering black scales. "Do you think your friend will help us?"

"I'll ask." Clay nodded at Judd. "Best-case scenario—we go in without setting off alarms, kids are there, we get them out." A pause. "High-tech security like that—I'm not sure we can maintain your secret."

"If you think it's going to turn to shit, warn me. I need to alert my contact."

Talin met the Psy man's cold gaze. "Why?" They could be undoing everything he had worked to achieve, but he hadn't flinched.

"Sometimes," he said, "you have to save the innocents you see in front of you and worry about the ones to come later."

At that instant, Talin realized that who Judd seemed was not who he was. She was about to thank him when her brain suddenly presented her with the answer to a question she hadn't been conscious of considering. "You know, I was always good at puzzles."

Everyone looked at her.

"How do we get information from inside a locked room without opening the door? We have someone send it to us, of course."

Judd shook his head. "The lab is under a blackout. No PsyNet access."

"What about the Internet? Telepaths tend to ignore it, but it works just fine." Brenna sat up straighter. "Judd, baby, do you have a link on the inside?"

"We have suspicions that a certain scientist may be open to being turned but no proof."

"You able to put out some feelers?" Clay asked.

A sharp nod. "I don't know how much good it'll do. My contact is . . . not *good* as you would think of it. He's not evil, either, but he won't do anything unless it complies with his personal code. That code involves a deep loyalty to his race. However, since he passed on the information about the kidnappings, he may be willing."

Talin hoped with all her heart that the humanity within this unknown Psy was stronger than the Silence.

CHAPTER 35

Jonquil opened his eyes and for a horrifying second, thought he was blind. His lungs grew tight as he fought the screaming urge to panic.

Then cool fingers touched his forehead. "Lie still."

"You." Relief turned his limbs to water. "What's wrong with me?"

"Your eyelids are grossly swollen." She touched them and even that feather-light brush caused excruciating pain. "I apologize. I was applying a salve—give it a few minutes and the swelling will reduce to a negligible level."

He trusted her. She was the only adult in this place who hadn't tortured him. "What did they do to me?"

"I'm not certain, but I believe they were testing a new compound that's purportedly meant to help with the integration of an implant."

He didn't understand most of that, but he caught the idea. "They poisoned me?"

"That wasn't the point, but let's say it's a good thing for you that their science was flawed. Had it not been, you'd be dead now."

He was used to listening for nuances in people's voices.

However, Blue . . . she was beautiful, with her smooth skin and wolf eyes, but her voice was utterly toneless. So he made a guess. "Did you help that flaw along?"

A small silence. "You're highly intelligent. Yes. It was to my advantage that their experiment failed."

"Why?"

"I need you alive." She touched his face, then his neck. "Why do you have so much bruising? It should have been a simple injection."

He could make out some light now. Relieved that she'd been telling the truth about his eyes, he answered almost absentmindedly. "I think I might've tried to hit them while I was out of it."

"That explains Larsen's black eye."

Fear clawed through him. "The little girl—did that guy hurt her? He said they wouldn't if I cooperated."

"He lied," she responded, cold as the chill of these antiseptic walls. "Nothing you can do will stop him. But the girl is safe for now. He's having some trouble getting new subjects so he's taking care with the single undamaged one he already has."

"Trouble?" He began to smile. "Talin. Talin did something." He'd nicknamed her the Lioness after seeing her hair. It had been meant to be a joke because she was so little, but it had turned out to be perfect—she never gave up. "She told me she'd fight for me."

Blue's face was now a fuzzy shape above him. "Who is Talin?"

He realized he'd been led into a trap. "No one."

"It's in your best interest to tell me. You're a bargaining chip. I need to know with whom to negotiate."

He refused to open his mouth. He had already been enough of an idiot. If Talin was trying to help him, he wouldn't give her away to the enemies. He'd seen enough of life to know that, sometimes, evil wore a sweet face. "Thank you for the eye balm." Everything hurt, but he forced himself into a sitting position against the wall.

She was dressed like before, but she had pulled down her mask to uncover her lips. No laugh lines marked the corners. "Swallow this." She gave him a pill. "It'll capture the last of the poison and you'll expel it during normal bodily processes."

He took it. He didn't trust her, but she'd been up front about calling him a bargaining chip. That, he believed. So she'd keep him alive until it suited her to do otherwise. "Thank you."

A knock came on the door. It was Ashaya's cue to leave while the corridors were clear and the cameras had been looped to cover her retreat. Ming LeBon might have tried to seize control of her lab, but she commanded the loyalty of most of her staff. It helped that the Council had forced them all under a psychic blackout, in effect amputating a limb. A Psy was a psychic being by definition—to cut off their access to the PsyNet was a punishment. An undeserved one.

Standing, she pulled up the mask and looked down at the stubborn countenance of the boy. His recalcitrance didn't matter. Talin was an unusual name and she had Jonquil's entire file.

She went straight to that file upon reaching her private quarters. She wasn't stupid enough to assume they weren't keeping tabs on her even in there, but she did know they couldn't access the organizer she carried twenty-four/seven. The size of a small notebook, it had the capacity to store large amounts of data as well as act as a mobile comm device. It was where she kept files that could compromise her.

Files such as the heavily encrypted e-mail she had received an hour ago.

If you plan to act, do it now.

The e-mail had been unsigned, could well be a setup. However, it might also be an attempt to initiate contact by the underground rebels who were currently making the Councilors' lives very difficult. She had ways of getting news despite the psychic blackout and she knew these rebels were doing more damage than most people knew. She also knew that the Ghost, the most lethal rebel of them all, was an expert at finding classified information—such as Ashaya's very well hidden covert e-mail address.

Setup or not, she'd already made her decision. Things were getting problematic with Ming. Either she acted now, or she could find herself permanently compromised. The Councilor was a master of mental combat—should he decide that the deterioration in her productivity would be balanced out by her guaranteed allegiance, he wouldn't hesitate to imprison her mind. The humans called it mind control. It was exactly that.

Ashaya had no intention of becoming one of Ming's puppets. She also had no intention of allowing him to take control of her son.

So she would take this calculated chance and trust the probability matrix to hold true. If she had made an error in her calculations, both she and Keenan were dead. But if she did nothing, the outcome was *certain* death. Of course, there was one other person she could go to for help, but the price Amara would demand was not one Ashaya was willing to pay. This was the only viable option.

Taking a seat in the corner she had arranged to shield her from surveillance equipment while appearing natural, she brought up the file on Jonquil Duchslaya. She didn't need to look very far before finding his Talin.

Talin McKade was listed both as Jonquil's point of contact at the Shine Foundation and as his next of kin. According to the file, the woman was part of Shine's street team, holding the official title of Senior Guardian.

It wasn't what Ashaya had wanted to find. This Talin was not going to have the kind of influence or contacts Ashaya needed. She'd have to take the chance that, as a Senior Guardian, the woman could somehow attract the attention of the Shine board. Ashaya did not like to take chances without statistical support, especially not now, with so much at stake.

But the young girl—Noor—was even more of a loss in terms of a powerful network. Excepting a few recent mistakes that appeared to have sprung from Larsen's increasing lack of discipline, the scouts for this genocide labeled an experiment had been careful to choose isolated children. They were all linked to Shine, but as the humans had proven over and over, it was the emotional connection that drove the greatest efforts.

A single committed parent or family member could achieve more than an entire organization—especially an organization such as Shine, which, according to her data, was hamstrung by a board full of old men and women who didn't want to accept the fact that the Forgotten were still being hunted . . . still being exterminated.

If they wanted proof, she would give it to them.

But first, she had to strike a bargain.

CHAPTER 36

Talin threw a small bag containing water and food into the plane. If all went according to plan, they would be in and out overnight. "How come you have a pilot's license? Is that what you do for a living?" she asked the tall, blond, and stupidly good-looking pilot. The last time she'd met him had been outside of Joe's Bar. Her gut twisted at the memory of what she'd revealed to Clay that day, the truth that sat a sullen intruder between them. "Dorian?"

Dorian scowled. "How come you're such a smart-ass?"

She winced, realizing he hadn't forgotten their meeting either. "Um, genetic flaw?"

To her surprise, his cool expression segued into a smile so charming, she felt sucker-punched. "You're sort of little. I like little."

Talin looked around. Where was Clay? He'd gone to grab something from the Tank, which was parked a short distance away. She wished he'd hurry the hell up. It looked like his "friend" was hitting on her. "I'm taken."

"I know. I can smell Clay on you." He pushed up the brim of his baseball cap. "And I'm an architect—flying's a hobby."

"Oh." She shifted her feet, wondering if she'd ever get

used to changeling sensory abilities. It was unsettling to realize his pack would know beyond a doubt that she and Clay had been intimate. But . . . it was also kind of nice. Because if she carried his scent, that meant he had to carry hers, too, didn't it? "Why are you staring?" she asked when Dorian didn't look away, his blue eyes bright in the midmorning light.

"Curiosity." His tone betrayed the fact that, charming or not, he suffered from the same arrogant masculine streak as Clay. "Wanted to know what you had that was strong enough to bring Clay down."

She bristled. "I don't think he thinks he's been brought down."

A grunt. "I figure if I know in advance, it'll be harder for a pretty woman to sideswipe me."

"How about an ugly one?" she snapped, irritated by the way he was making it sound as though she'd trapped Clay.

"No such thing," he responded, and there was an honesty beneath the charm that got to her. "I like women."

She had a feeling women liked him right back—when he could be bothered to lay on the charm as he was doing now. That time she'd seen him hauling the teenagers out of the bar, he'd been pure, lethal predator. "If you like women," she said, wondering why she merited the charm, "why are you so scared of committing to one?"

Those surfer-blue eyes were suddenly chrome—cold, flat, dangerous. "It's more a case of having things to do, people to kill, before I set up house."

"I don't want to know."

"No, you don't."

Talin froze, able to sense his deep-seated anger. She felt tension begin to knot up her spine. Male anger was not something she did well with. That level of trust—for them to not turn on her even when angry—she had only with Clay. And the depth of that trust was a revelation, one that awoke wonder in her.

Dorian's eyes narrowed. "I'm not going to hurt you."

She answered his bluntness with the same. "I don't know you well enough to trust you."

He nodded. "Fair enough."

She could've left it at that, but . . . "Being that angry, holding it so close, it's not good for you." She could almost touch the vicious rage hidden beneath his handsome facade.

"I get enough of that from Sascha," he said with a scowl. "Why don't you stick to babying Clay?"

"How do you think he'd react?"

Dorian's smile returned, slow and more than a little satisfied. "I think you're the one person who could get away with it."

She hunched her shoulders, uncomfortable. "I don't have that much power." Wouldn't know what to do with it if she had. All she wanted was the chance to love Clay, to wipe away the past with the beauty of the present. Before this fucking disease ended everything. Her own ever-present anger grew a dull flame in her gut.

"You got him blind drunk. Clay doesn't drink."

Her head snapped up. "What?"

"He went on a bender the day you came back into his life." He raised an eyebrow. "I'm guessing you two have a history."

"Something like that," she muttered, sick at the thought of what Dorian had described, but trying not to betray what the knowledge had done to her.

Somehow, he knew. Taking off his cap, he put it on her head. "Suits you."

It was a gesture of affection, pure and simple. Her heart melted a tiny bit. "Thanks."

"And don't worry about Clay—he needed to cut loose." He grinned. "Man has a right to get drunk over a woman who matters. I'd have been more worried if he hadn't started acting crazy."

The words were light, but she got the picture. It seemed she hadn't been alone in putting her emotions in deep freeze. "If I wasn't already taken," she said, liking him for telling her what she needed to know, "I would kiss you."

"You're welcome to." He tapped his cheek. "Or how about one with tongue?"

She'd just begun to frown when she felt Clay's hand land on her hip. The growl that came from his throat vibrated into her bones. "Find your own damn woman."

Dorian shoved a hand through his hair, an unabashed grin on his face. "I kind of like yours, smart mouth and all."

"Clay, he said he's an architect—is that true?" she teased, easy now that Clay was back, but also because Dorian had grown on her. She was under no illusion as to how dangerous he was—his charm was a cover for an incredible amount of anger, but it was also a part of him. When he wasn't filled up with that deep-seated rage, she had a feeling he could charm the birds out of the trees.

"That's what it says on the degree on his wall."

Talin smirked, pretending amusement, though her stomach was a pit of nausea as she tried not to think about what Jon might be suffering at that very moment. "So, Boy Genius, what did you do—take an online course and get your degree in ninety days?"

"Clay, can I bite her?"

"No." Clay scowled at her. "I'll do it for you. We ready to go?"

"Yeah. You organized the other end?"

Clay nodded, reaching up to rub absently at his temple. "A guy I know will drop off a truck near the landing zone. It'll look beat up but it's been retrofitted for speed and defense."

"What about your snake friend? Any luck tracking her down?" Talin asked.

"No, so let's hope we don't need her. You're the easiest to disguise," he said, "so you'll drive into Cinnamon Springs, with—"

Her phone beeped. "Sorry," she said, scrambling to pull it out of her pocket. "Probably one of Rangi's kids." She flipped it open. "Hello."

Clay and Dorian were already turning to finish loading up the plane with what looked like surveillance gear.

"Talin. It's Dev." The Shine director's tone was edgy.

Very aware of both men returning to her side, she slid her arm around Clay and spread her hand against the stiff line of his spine. "Dev?"

"You with the cat?"

"Yes."

"He can probably hear this conversation then."

She looked up. Clay and Dorian both nodded. "Yes."

"Good," came the surprising response. "Someone's been trying to contact you through your Shine e-mail account."

Her hand clenched on the phone. "And you know this because you've been spying on me?"

"No." His voice turned cutting, then he sighed, as if in frustration. "Because of the kidnappings, I recently put in place a secret macro program. It scans *everything* going through our servers, red-flags and sends me a copy of anything that sets off certain triggers."

Her outrage disappeared. "You were trying to catch the mole."

"Yeah." Ice came through the lines. "I know it's a breach of privacy, but I don't give a shit. Shine is meant to be a safe place and I'll make it safe again even if I have to rip open every fuc—"

Suddenly, the phone was no longer in her hand. Startled, she found Clay had taken it. "Stop yelling at Talin," he ordered.

Scowling, she held out her hand. He returned the phone, but only after another comment. "Yes."

"Yes, what?" she asked him as he handed it back.

"Nothing."

Muttering about chauvinist pigs, she put the phone to her ear. "Dev, I want to find these bastards, too. This e-mail—when did it come in?"

"Four minutes ago. I could send it to your phone but I'd rather do it through a more secure channel. Any options?"

"Wait." Reaching into the plane, Dorian pulled out a sleek silver something from his knapsack before motioning for the phone. She handed it over and he said some technobabble on it before handing it back and flipping open the device, placing it on the floor of the plane.

She put the phone to her ear. "Did you get that?"

"Yes. Give me a second."

She nodded at the device Dorian was messing with. "Very tiny laptop?"

He shot her a distracted grin. "You could say that. This sweet thing is our attempt at creating a Psy organizer. The versions they allow on the market are nothing compared to the goods they keep for themsel— Tell Dev I've got it."

Moving around Clay to stand between the two men, she bit off her impatience as Dorian opened up a miniature e-mail screen. Clay's hand rested on her back, but then Dorian put one of his on her shoulder as he straightened and moved to let her take the central position.

The contact startled her, but it was okay. Dorian was . . . Pack. Shaking her head at that odd thought, she focused on the message.

> Jonquil Duchslaya is alive, but he won't remain that way if you don't fight for him within the next twelve hours. I'm willing to help you with that task, but you must do something for me—something of equal value—in return. The risk-benefit ratio is too unbalanced otherwise.

"That's it?" she said, trembling.

"Yes." She jerked at Dev's response, having forgotten she still held the phone to her ear. "Any way it could be legit?" Dev asked.

She was too shaken up to answer.

"Why use 'fight for him'? It's an odd choice." Clay began doing that thing with her ponytail again and maybe it was that that calmed her down enough to think.

"Oh, God," she whispered. "When we had that bust-up, I told him I'd fight for him if he fought for himself."

"Give me that." Dorian slipped the phone out of her lifeless fingers. "Did you trace the e-mail?" A pause. "You're sure?"

As she waited, Talin's earlier anger grew into an inferno, but this time, it was directed not at a disease she couldn't name, but at this faceless stranger. "Who is this person to demand something for Jon's life? What right do they have?"

Clay's body grew very still. "The language—it's Psy. A life reduced to a risk-benefit ratio." He paused. "Judd's contact must've come through, set things in motion. I owe him."

Glancing up at him, Talin noticed he was rubbing at his temple again. She was about to reach up with her own hand when Dorian spoke.

"Fine," he said, ending the call. "Dev got another hit—the possible mole this time—but he told me that he had someone trace the e-mail. It was easy, because whoever sent it didn't know how to hide their tracks."

Talin didn't dare breathe. "Nebraska?"

"Not only that. They tracked it down all the way to Cinnamon Springs."

Her hand crushed the back of Clay's shirt. "Jon's in that lab." It was a storm inside of her, this need to reclaim what was hers to protect. But no, she had to think. Her brain wasn't fuzzy now—in fact, it was almost dizzying how clearly she could think. Strange, given that the disease had to be escalating. "We can't just barge in. The lab is too huge."

Clay tugged at her ponytail, raising her face to him. "We bring in the pack and the wolves, we can do it."

Talin had never had that much strength behind her. Her mind filled with a split-second montage of the people she had met—Nico, Tamsyn, Nate, Lucas, Sascha, Faith, and Vaughn. That kind of backup, she realized, was both a privilege and a responsibility. "No." It was a painful decision. "We'll lose too many people."

"Pack is One, Tally. We bleed for one another."

"I know." She hugged him, strong enough now to accept the protective violence that was a part of him. "But it doesn't matter. Twelve hours is too short a time frame to mount an organized attack. They might kill Jon before we ever got close enough."

"Or," Dorian said, picking up and unrolling a printout of the lab schematics taken from Judd's data crystal, "they could have a built-in self-destruct mechanism." He tapped several spots on the plan. "The lab is designed to collapse if you apply pressure at specific points—all those spots are internal. I'd guess they have the whole place wired. Input a specific code and boom."

The coldness of such a plan shook Talin to the core. "They'd kill their own?"

"Without a pause," Clay and Dorian said in concert.

People like that, she thought, wouldn't hesitate to destroy a teenage boy if they didn't get what they wanted. "Will they be able to track it back to us if I reply to this e-mail?" She copied the address, opened a new window.

"No," Dorian reassured her. "I've set it up to encrypt all outgoing messages." He tapped in a quick code. "This will feed an encryption worm into their system, too."

Nodding, she typed in a single line:

What do you want?

Neither of the men said anything as she pushed Send.

They waited in silence. Dorian shoved a hand through his hair and began stalking up and down the makeshift runway. Clay, though he remained unmoving, was a vibrating column of rage.

She reached up to massage his temples with gentle strokes. "Maybe this person isn't evil. He's prepared to help Jon."

"Why now? Why not the other children?" His arms held her firm against him, though he bent his head so she didn't have to stand on tiptoe. "Whatever it is he wants, we'll give it to him. DarkRiver has more than enough funds."

"Thank you."

He growled at her. "Thank me again for taking care of my mate and I'll have to get mean."

Mate.

There was that word again, that incredible, impossible word. She knew it had been nothing more than a slip of the tongue on his part, but she hugged the mistake to her heart.

A second later, something flashed in the corner of her eye and she twisted to look at the screen. Striding back to them, Dorian opened the e-mail.

One day, I'm going need help to retrieve someone else. When I ask, will you answer?

"Hell," Clay muttered.

"Yeah," she said. "Not the mercenary demand we expected." Reaching forward, she sent back a reply.

Will you trust my word?

The response was close to instantaneous.

Humans have an odd thing called honor. Jonquil seems to believe in yours and he is an intelligent boy. I will hold you to your honor.

There was something deeply poignant in those words. Whoever this Psy was, whatever he wanted, he wasn't evil.

"Say yes," Clay told her. "I'll answer the damn IOU."

She angled her body so he couldn't see her next message until it was too late.

How do I know your request won't lead to more deaths?

"Damn it, Tally!" Clay gripped her upper arms. "Why the hell did you do that?"

"Because you're mine to protect, too," she snapped. She wouldn't barter Clay's life for Jon's. Losing Jon would break her, but, Lord help her, she couldn't give up Clay. Not even if it meant betraying her deepest principles. Not even if it meant killing. The realization should have nauseated her. It didn't. Truth never did. "I'm not having you sacrifice yourself again!"

"God damn it." He gripped her nape, spun her around to face him. Then he kissed her. Hard. "After this is over, I'm giving you a spanking."

She felt her face go bright red, though she knew he was simply blowing off steam. "Men," she muttered, then glanced at Dorian. He was attempting to look uninterested but she saw the grin in those bright blue eyes. "Dorian, I swear to God, if you laugh, I'm going to peel your flesh from your bones."

He picked up her hand and kissed the underside of one wrist. "I like you, too."

"Stop flirting with Tally." Clay wrapped an arm around her waist. "Okay, this falls through, we still have the original plan—we go in through that supply chute. Let's start double-checking our calculations on its probable location."

And that was how they passed the minutes as they waited for the answer to a question that might cost a child his life and shatter something deep inside Talin. When it came, it was so unexpected, it stunned all three of them.

It was illogical of me to ask you—you have neither the manpower nor the connections to assist me. But I will help Jonquil escape. Can you come to these coordinates at exactly 9 p.m.?

Detailed instructions followed.

Talin didn't hesitate, knowing Clay would get her there in time.

Yes!

The reply was immediate.

According to my information, you will have a 15-minute window to the second, after I give the signal. The satellites will be looking in another direction. Stay out of the coverage zone until then.

If you fail to get here in time, I may no longer be able to protect him. He is a boy with the capacity to achieve much. His life is worth more than this senseless death.

Don't be late.

With those last three words, this unknown Psy won Talin's loyalty.

CHAPTER 37

The Ghost walked into an upscale bar in downtown New York and was immediately shown to the table where his acquaintance awaited. She was a minor official, this meeting a front. But the public location would serve as the perfect alibi.

The bomb exploded to life exactly sixty-five minutes later.

The majority of the Psy Council convened in an emergency session eleven minutes after that. Two Councilors were nominated to do a physical investigation, while another took on the task of analyzing the bomb debris. The remaining members focused on damage control.

For a crucial window of time, the Implant lab was no longer under a Councilor's direct supervision. During that same window, its security forces fell to below fifty percent of capacity, the majority of Ming LeBon's army being pulled up into the PsyNet to strangle the spread of information. Their bodies remained in the lab, in a form of natural suspended animation, but their minds were working with furious speed.

In the chaos, no one noticed the surveillance satellites blink.

CHAPTER 38

At three minutes past nine, in the black of true night, Talin maneuvered a seemingly ancient truck over a deserted piece of land several miles from where the lab was supposed to be. The Psy's terse message had come precisely one hundred and eighty seconds earlier: *Now.*

Another minute of dangerously fast driving later, she brought the truck to a stop near a small ramshackle cottage. Hidden as it was by the slope of the land and the overgrown vegetation, it was no wonder it had remained undisturbed. Or maybe it was the deadly laser fence a ways back, a fence that had been disabled at nine p.m. on the dot.

Leaving the engine running, she got out of the truck alone. The plan had been for the others to hide in the truck bed, in case their uncertain ally had failed to turn the satellites. The Psy already knew about Talin's involvement in the investigation, so her being seen was no tactical disadvantage. The opposite applied to Clay and Dorian.

However, to their surprise, they had discovered the area to be heavy with concealing vegetation, including huge trees that had to have been transplanted here. It was as though someone had *wanted* to hide something.

After a hasty conference, both changelings had jumped out of the moving vehicle. Clay had gone cat. Meanwhile, Dorian had taken to the trees, rifle in hand. Right now, she knew his sniper's eye was located on the door to the cabin. The predators were ready to pull her out if this proved to be a trap.

Half-sick with hope and fear, she stood in place, in spite of her need to get inside, waiting for the signal that would tell her no danger had been scented or sighted. When she glanced to the side, it was to glimpse a pair of night-glow eyes hidden in the forest. They blinked once. *Go.*

Vividly conscious of time ticking down, she ran to the door and pushed it open. She was prepared to find anything . . . except what she did find.

Jon and a little girl lay on their backs on the dirt floor.

With a soft cry, she dropped to her knees and checked their pulses. Both beat strong. It calmed her as she waited for Clay to come. But the seconds ticked past without any sign of him. Something had to have gone wrong. Her instinctive urge was to run out to help.

Clay watched Talin walk in, his senses on high alert. A shift in the wind brought him Dorian's scent . . . and that of another. The leopard listened to what the wind told it and knew he could leave that scent to Dorian. The other sentinel was already moving.

He kept his eyes on the cottage into which Talin had disappeared only a second ago. But he wasn't blinded by focus—he heard the crack of a twig several meters away as someone stalked toward his mate. Fighting the protective urge shoving at him to move and get Tally out of there, he stayed in place, listening, watching.

The ugly metallic/dead/cold scent of Psy mingled with the more astringent odor of gun-cleaning fluid. His predator's mind immediately understood that they had either missed a sentry or triggered sensors their ally had not known to disable. He lowered himself into a crouch, hidden in the vegetation. He'd told Tally to stay inside the cottage until he or Dorian came for her. Trusting her to stick to the plan, he turned his attention to the intruder.

The man came into sight seconds later. Dressed in black, he moved with the careful gait of a trained soldier. But that wasn't what interested Clay. It was the emblem on his shoulder. Two snakes locked in combat. The leopard bit back a growl. That was the same uniform as those that had been worn by the men who had butchered the DawnSky deer clan in an unprovoked attack.

The Psy male's eyes glinted pure black, no whites, no stars. He could be telepathing.

Clay had to make a split-second decision. If this was their contact, killing him would gain them nothing. But if it wasn't, he had to take the man out. An instant later, the male made up his mind for him by going down into a shooting stance and taking aim at the door of the cottage.

Clay didn't bother with finesse. If the Psy felt him coming, he was dead. So he attacked in a heavy, silent rage. The Psy managed to turn slightly before Clay's claws hit his chest, smashing him to the forest floor. A burst of pain slammed into his brain but he was already ripping out the other man's throat.

However, even with that thousandth-of-a-second warning, the Psy had managed to get in enough of a psychic blow that Clay's nose bled as he shifted into human form and picked up the body, wiping away the blood with his hand. The body had to be disposed of and in a way that didn't give away changeling involvement.

He spent precious seconds wrapping the body up in a tarp from the back of the truck and dumping it in the bed. It was a good thing Tally and Jon weren't changeling; otherwise, they would have detected the scent of death. Aware of time counting down, he nonetheless returned to the site of the kill and covered his tracks. The Psy soldier would appear to have vanished into thin air.

"Oh, God," Talin whispered, gritting her teeth and staying in place as the clock ticked over to ten minutes past nine. Clay was a sentinel, she told herself. He would defeat whatever enemy roamed the woods. Trying to distract herself, she brushed the hair off Jon's and the little girl's faces. The little one was clearly of Persian origin, her skin a dusky brown, her bone structure fine enough for a princess.

Her hand moved to settle the little girl's shirt and that was when she found it. The note was short and to the point.

The drugs will wear off in a few hours. I couldn't have them attempting an escape before the correct time. After they leave here, both these children need to vanish—if they turn up alive, my life is forfeit. So, I hold you to your human honor after all.

Clay ran in as her watch clicked over another minute. "We only have four minutes to get out of the surveillance zone." She stuffed the note into her pocket, picked up the girl.

Clay was already out the door, Jon thrown over one shoulder. "It'll be enough." He dumped Jon onto the truck's single benchseat and pulled on his clothes at lightning speed. Going around to the passenger side door, she was inside with her own precious cargo by the time he turned the wheel. "Go!" Strapping in Jon beside Clay, she held the girl tight and pulled the remaining strap over them both as Clay started driving at a breakneck pace no human could have managed, his reaction time close to zero.

He didn't slow when Dorian wasn't waiting for them at the arranged spot. "He'll be fine."

Talin said a quick prayer for the other sentinel. With Clay's insane driving, they were on the road away from the cottage in the nick of time, just another outwardly beat-up farm truck among others. "How are the kids doing?" he asked once they were clear.

"Good," she whispered. She sat with one arm around Jon's shoulders, the other crushing the girl to her. Releasing her white-knuckled grip, she flexed her fingers, touched their cheeks to reassure herself they were okay. "Good." Jon was bruised and both children had dark circles under their eyes, but they were alive. "We'll talk to him after . . . about what happened."

"He'll be okay, Tally." His tone was rough, tender. "We made it, didn't we?"

She gave him a startled glance. "Yeah, we did, didn't we?" But she wasn't quite sure they had.

"I had to eliminate a threat," he said a few minutes later. "We'll be taking a short detour to dispose of it."

Her throat dried up. "In the truck bed?"

"Yeah."

He had killed for her. Again. The hairs on the back of her neck rose at the thought of her proximity to the result. But she was no hypocrite. Neither was she a child any longer. "It had to be done." Her arms tightened on the children's bodies. "Let's clean it up before they wake."

Clay's gaze met hers again and those forest-in-shadow eyes were incandescent with a fierce kind of joy. It shook her.

Had he expected her to run from him again?

The kids were awake by the time Dorian made it back. Dawn was edging the horizon and Talin was so happy to see him unhurt, she gave him a huge hug.

His smile was startled, less charming and more open. "Hey, hey, I'm good. No one saw anything but a pissed-off student hitching a ride after his girlfriend dumped him in the middle of nowhere."

She drew back and looked him up and down. "Where did you get those clothes?" He was wearing a T-shirt bearing the logo of a death metal band over his own black jeans. He'd also found a disreputable headscarf, which effectively hid his distinctive hair. She looked closer. "Did you put mud in your hair?"

"All part of being resourceful." Draping an arm around her neck, he walked them back to the plane. Clay was standing outside with little Noor in his arms. The girl had wrapped herself around him upon waking and hadn't let go since. Talin hadn't been the least surprised when Clay handled the attachment without a blink.

"Ready?" Dorian asked.

Clay nodded. "Later."

For once, Talin understood perfectly. Dorian had stayed behind for a reason and it had to have been something important. Giving him another hug, she climbed into the plane to settle in beside Jon. The boy was no longer drugged but there were emotional bruises in those striking eyes of his.

"Hey." She put her hand on his. He wouldn't look at her. Reaching over, she cupped his cheek. "What's the matter, Johnny D?"

This time, he did glance up and his gaze was wet with tears he refused to shed. "They fucking made me scream."

Male pride, such a fragile, precious thing. She nodded at Noor, now entering the cockpit with Clay. "She hasn't got a mark on her. Did you protect her?"

He shrugged. "They said if I cooperated, they'd lay off her for a bit, but that was a lie." His eyes went to Dorian as the sentinel slid into the pilot's seat. "Who's that?"

"Dorian," she told him. "He's Clay's packmate."

"Like a gang, huh?"

She didn't quite know how to answer that but Clay turned around and did it for her. "The ultimate gang," he said, his hand rubbing gently over Noor's back as she lay curled up against his chest. "We mean it when we say Pack is One. And you did good, kid. Screaming is a fact of life—hell, Dorian here would never shut up when he was your age."

Dorian threw Clay an unfriendly look, then glanced at Jon. "Don't listen to a word he says. He's scared of needles." He turned back to the gauges. "Ready for lift off, boys and girls?"

Jon relaxed, apparently happier now that he'd had some male feedback. Fighting the urge to roll her eyes, she dared put an arm around him. To her surprise, he let her hold him. When she pressed a kiss to his brow, he didn't even fidget.

Smiling, she met Clay's eyes. Her kids were home.

Turning back to face the windshield, Clay caught Dorian's tense expression. The other man was worried for the same reason as him, a reason Tally had forgotten in her happiness. This wasn't over. And the next target was most likely going to be Talin herself. Not that the fuckers would get anywhere near her.

Mind on their next move, he leaned back and closed his eyes against the glare. This was one mean bitch of a headache. It felt like red-hot pokers driving into his brain. He'd have worried the Psy soldier had caused permanent damage if he hadn't been in pain since waking up that morning. Reassuring

Noor when she shifted restlessly, he decided he'd have to talk Tally into petting him tonight.

They all ended up crashing at Nate and Tamsyn's upon their return late in the afternoon. Not only did she have a big house, the kids needed to be looked at, and together, Tammy and Sascha made a pretty good medical/healing team. By the time everyone had bathed, eaten, and been checked out, it was too late to talk, so they scheduled a meeting for midmorning the next day.

Noor fell asleep without trouble, but Talin had to coax Jon into a herbal sleeping remedy that Tamsyn had made up.

"I don't want any more drugs in my fuck—" He bit off the curse. "No drugs."

"It's natural, won't mess up your body or cause addiction." When he remained stubborn, she dared touch him, stroking her fingers over his face. "They hurt you, Jon. Your body needs to rest so it can heal. This'll help. Please."

It took ten more minutes, but she finally won. With both children asleep, she was free to tackle Clay. "Lie down," she ordered, careful to keep her voice lower than a whisper. "Do you want me to ask Tamsyn for headache meds?"

His answer was predictable and, unlike with Jon, she knew she wouldn't be able to wear him down. "Hate drugs." But he did stretch out on his back on the bed.

Having already spoken to Tamsyn about what worked best on changeling physiology, she poured out drops of an unscented natural oil onto her fingers and began to rub them in slow, gentle circles around the general region of his temples.

Groaning, he closed his eyes. It made her throat lock, he looked so vulnerable. It wasn't a word she associated with Clay, wasn't a face he often showed. But tonight, he had trusted her with it. Swallowing her tears, she continued the gentle massage. Some time later, she realized he'd fallen asleep. She sat there and watched him for the longest time.

He was her everything.

But the original reason for their coming together was now complete. Jon was safe. So was another child. What if Clay decided he couldn't forgive her enough to continue this relationship, his leopard's territorial nature too strong? She bit down hard on her lower lip when her fearful pain threatened to shift into sound. If Clay rejected her—now or later, for any reason—she would break once and for all.

So she watched him, drank in his image. By the time she forced herself to get up, strip off her clothing, and crawl into bed beside him, her skin was cold and she was aching with the hunger to belong to him, to prove to herself that he wouldn't leave her. But he slept. And after long, tortured minutes, so did she.

She woke to strong, sure fingers between her thighs, luscious wet kisses along her jaw, an aroused male body spooned around her. "Feeling better?" she managed to gasp out as he dipped his fingers inside her welcoming heat. She was wet, embarrassingly so.

"You feel like warm, lickable cream."

All embarrassment fled, to be replaced by sheer need. "Come inside me. I need you." To hold on, to never let go. *Please don't leave me alone again. Please, Clay.*

He spread her open with his fingers and began to slide in, so big from this angle, so hot. Then he murmured in her ear—earthy words of passion, quiet, sexy endearments that made her feel like the most beautiful of women. She pushed back into him, undone. When he lifted her thigh to deepen the penetration, she had to clench her jaw to hold off a cry.

He paused. "Did that hurt?"

"You feel too good."

A masculine chuckle. "I love the way you smell." He nuzzled at her neck, flicked out his tongue to taste her. "I love the way you feel. So soft, so hot." When he finally rocked her to climax, that hungry place inside her soul was almost filled up. Almost.

Even as Clay's heartbeat continued to race from having loved Tally, he could feel her hurting. It confused the hell out of his leopard. She was his mate. He should have been able to ease her pain. That he couldn't, struck a blow to his pride. "Tally, baby, what's wrong?"

"Don't let me go, Clay."

His heart broke a little at the unguarded statement, at the glimpse she'd given him into her deepest fear. "Never again, I promise you." Even if he had to fight the gods themselves to claim her, he would not let anyone—or anything—take her from him.

She didn't answer. He whispered more petting words in her ear. After a while, he could feel her hurt retreating, as if she had decided to trust his promise. His heart relaxed.

Tally's pain was the one thing he couldn't handle.

CHAPTER 39

Nine thirty the next morning, Talin stood with Clay's packmates in Tamsyn's kitchen, feeling deliciously sore and an idiot over her recent self-pity attack—Clay would never just decide to abandon her. He was far too loyal.

Her mood dimmed again. What if that was all that was tying him to her? Loyalty and friendship, the kind of friendship that wouldn't allow him to rest until they had beaten the unknown *thing* killing her from the inside out? Her illness hadn't struck since the day she had woken unable to gasp in air, but it would, and then Clay would have to look after her again, would feel obligated to do so.

Her mind filled with images of how she'd massaged him yesterday. That, done in love, had been no hardship. She wouldn't cheapen Clay's commitment to their relationship by imagining he felt any differently. But that's not what she *wanted* to be to him, someone to be looked after, a friend in need. She wanted so much more—she wanted all of him.

Clutching at her coffee cup, she looked out the window to find Jon talking to one of the teenagers she'd first seen at the bar—a tall, auburn-haired boy who was starting to grow into his long legs and powerful shoulders.

"That's Kit," Tammy said, coming to stand beside her. "Old enough to know better and young enough to get Jon. Your boy, he's strong. He's going to be okay."

"Yes," Talin agreed. "He'll become somebody if he's given the chance." But first, they had to make him disappear. Since neither of the children had family, Clay had told her the disappearing wouldn't be a problem. DarkRiver was happy to accept them.

"Tally." Clay held out his hand from where he was standing by the table.

She put down her coffee and went to him. His hand closed warm and safe around hers. "Where's Dorian?"

"Missing me already?" The blond sentinel walked through from the living room. With him were Lucas, Sascha, Nathan, and a redheaded female Talin hadn't yet met.

"I'm Mercy," the woman said, before Dorian took the floor to relate yesterday's events, with Clay and Talin filling in the gaps on their end.

"Judd coming?" Clay asked before Dorian could begin. "He deserves to know what happened. Man didn't have to help us, but he did."

Lucas nodded. "SnowDancers are turning out to be better allies than we thought."

"For feral rabies-infected wolves," Mercy muttered.

Dorian snickered. "Still mad over being the liaison?"

Mercy gave Dorian the finger, then twisted her head toward the front of the house. "He's here," she said, though Talin hadn't heard anything.

Judd walked through a minute later. "I have a certain antipathy toward this place."

Tamsyn scowled, hands on a muffin tin. "Why?"

"Because the last time I was here, I was bleeding half to death and you were torturing me with a stitch gun."

"See the thanks I get?" the healer muttered.

"If you ever need anyone killed, just let me know," Judd said with a straight face as he pulled out a chair and spun it around so the chair back was against his chest. His attention switched to Clay. "You said you got the boy and another child out?"

"Yes. Went like clockwork. Your contact have anything to do with that?"

Judd nodded. "But you got lucky with the timing, too. Something big went down in the PsyNet last night. Your op was hidden in the shadow of it."

Sascha leaned forward. "I talked with Faith this morning. She said she'd spoken with the NetMind, but that it was too agitated to make much sense."

"Damn," Clay muttered. "An assassination?"

Judd's eyes flickered in surprise. "Yes. A Council member."

Silence gripped the table. Talin saw open distress on Sascha's face. "My mother?" The cardinal clasped Lucas's hand in a tight grip.

"She wasn't the target," Judd said, and Talin was startled to hear a hint of gentleness in his voice. "Oddly enough, Nikita is one of the more moderate Councilors—as long as her business interests aren't compromised, she doesn't support the idea of wholesale genocide."

Talin shuddered at what that faint praise said about the Council as a whole.

"You can't confirm?" Lucas asked, his facial markings stark against skin pulled taut.

"No. My contact's gone silent and I have no way of knowing who was hit. I'm getting data through other sources. What I can tell you is that the Net is in chaos."

Talin wanted to hug Sascha. She knew too well the confused feelings of an abandoned child. Part of her would always miss the stranger who had left her at the clinic door. Then Sascha lifted her head and her eyes told Talin the sentiment had been felt and appreciated.

It disconcerted her to be in a room with someone who could sense her emotions, but she figured she'd get used to it, as she had to the changelings' ability to scent her moods.

"Dorian," Clay said into the silence, "do the report."

"Right." He glanced at Judd. "This is in relation to the classified data you gave us."

Judd's expression iced over. "That wasn't for public use."

"The location is still airtight," Clay said, meeting Judd's eyes, two predators weighing each other up. "But we've got another problem."

After a tense moment, Judd nodded. "Go."

Dorian ran through the events that had led to the rescue of the children with military efficiency. Then he told them about the woman he'd followed from the point where they'd picked up the children. "Our contact."

"She stuck around to make sure they were okay," Talin said, unsurprised.

Dorian nodded. "That's my take—she was heading to a hidden access point." He smiled at Judd's sudden alertness. "She said she doesn't support the Implant Protocol, but that she's being forced to work on it because she's the best."

Judd's eyes turned assessing. "What did she look like?"

"Skin like hot chocolate, dark hair, tall, built like a woman should be, pale eyes—couldn't catch the color with the distance. Sound familiar?"

Talin wondered at Dorian's sensuous description, but no one else seemed to notice. More to the point, Judd's response to the oral sketch was immediate. "Yes. What else did she say?"

"That in return for saving Jon and Noor, what she wants us to do is kidnap *her* kid. The boy—Keenan—is being held hostage by the Council as a way to ensure her good behavior."

Growls sounded around the table. Talin might've been startled had she not already known what these people were like, the lengths they would go to to protect children.

Sascha, one hand still clasped in Lucas's, sat forward. "Why? Why does her behavior rely on the child?"

Mercy choked on the muffin she'd grabbed. "He's her baby. Reason enough."

"No." Sascha shook her head. "Not for the Psy."

"Psy don't feel," Tamsyn agreed, "so the connection can't be emotional."

"Or maybe it is," Sascha said, tone thoughtful. "We know nothing about this woman—it may be that she's close to breaching Silence."

"I got frostbite just talking to her," Dorian muttered. "Trust me, she's a fucking emotional refrigerator. But she's right about the kid. He's four years old and in the hands of the Council."

"We have to help him." Talin spoke up. She might be sitting in the midst of some of the most powerful people in San

Francisco, but she was no coward. And she had the strength of a leopard at her side. "No matter why she did it, she got Jon and Noor out."

Clay hugged her back against him, a tenseness to his muscles she couldn't quite understand. "There's going to be a problem," he said quietly.

"The PsyNet," Judd murmured. "Boy will need another neural net to hook into."

"I don't know how to connect someone to our Net or if it's even possible," Sascha said with a frown. "And yours isn't stable enough to open up."

Judd looked thoughtful. "With my mating Brenna, it's gained some strength. Sienna continues to be erratic, but her control is better than it was when we considered the question of letting you in. It may work. We'll have to enter his mind and cut his connection to the PsyNet."

"That sounds like it would hurt him," Talin said.

Judd's eyes met hers. "Yes, it feels like dying. But if we don't do it, they'll track him down in seconds. And if the Council thinks his pain will sway his mother, they will hurt him again and again." His voice wasn't aggressive, but so icy cold that Talin shivered. When she felt Clay stiffen to attacking readiness, she put a hand on his arm and lifted up her head. *Let it go,* she mouthed. Judd hadn't exactly been politic about telling her she was wrong, but she was sure he hadn't meant to offend.

Clay held her gaze for a long moment, then gave a small nod. But as she turned back to the others, she knew he planned to have words with Judd later. She would just have to make sure she caught him before then. Startling as it was, Clay—big, intense, dangerous Clay—seemed to listen to her. "Who is she that the Council wants her that bad?"

"Her name," Judd said, a deep satisfaction in his tone, "is Ashaya Aleine. She's the M-Psy in charge of Protocol I. We had a suspicion that she might be on our side, but so long as the Council had her cooperation, we couldn't trust her. I don't think we can now, either—we have no idea why she wants the child removed from the equation."

"She give you a time frame?" Clay asked Dorian.

"Within the next two months."

"Then we can discuss the details later," Clay said. "Noor will be up soon and we need to decide what to do to make her and Jon disappear."

"Not a problem," Lucas said, and for the first time, Talin heard the alpha in his tone. "Noor's looks will change soon enough. Until then we use cosmetic methods to keep her hidden. We're going to have to get her used to a new name, too. Maybe a nickname."

"It'll take time," Sascha said, "but she's young enough for it to be natural. With Jon, he has to make the choice."

"I think he'll be okay with that," Talin said, a lump in her throat as she thought of the future now within Jon's reach. "And he hasn't hit his growth spurt. Another year and he'll be taller, his body different. He'll start shaving."

"Tell him he's getting that tattoo lasered off." Tamsyn made a face. "It's hideous."

Talin had to agree. "And distinctive. His hair—it's distinctive, too."

Clay grunted. "He'll cut it, no problem."

Talin went to argue with him, then stopped. Jon probably would cut his shoulder-length hair without a peep—the boy was already showing the first signs of hero worship, and it was Clay he'd fixated on. Just like Noor. Talin could guess why. There was a deep protectiveness in Clay, a sense that once he made you his own, he'd do anything to keep you safe. Like he had for her.

She turned into his embrace. He dropped an absentminded kiss on her hair and at that moment, everything was right in her world. The Psy weren't out there looking for more innocent children, she wasn't slowly dying from a disease that was stealing into her very cells, and Clay trusted her without exception.

A few hours later, Clay found himself standing in a corner of the yard, watching Talin talk with the kids. When Dorian walked up to him, he didn't waste time. "What didn't you say in front of the others?"

The blond sentinel folded his arms. "How did you know?"

"I'm older and wiser, Boy Genius."

"Knock it off." Dorian scowled in Talin's direction. "I swear if that nickname takes off, I'm going to take your Tally and dump her in the nearest body of ice-cold water."

"Then I'd have to beat you up."

"Hey, I spar with a Psy assassin on a regular basis and I'm not dead." He began to play his pocketknife over his fingers in a familiar fashion. "Ashaya gave me some information I didn't think you'd want Talin to hear."

Clay kept his eyes on the tableau in front of him as Sascha came out of the house and headed toward Talin. For the first time, Clay realized how glad he was for Sascha's presence in the pack. Without her, they might have lost Dorian forever after his sister's murder. The sentinel Talin teased—it wasn't the same Dorian as the one who had once wanted to tear open Sascha's throat.

He hoped his alpha's mate could help Jon and Noor, too, but knew that even the most gifted empath couldn't fix everything. Until Tally had come back to him, Clay had been in danger of hurtling into such deep violence that nothing could've brought him back. And if she dared die on him, he'd hunt her into the afterlife.

"So," he said, calming the leopard's possessive violence by focusing on Tally. She made his heart so fucking tight, it hurt. "What did Aleine tell you?"

"That these two"—Dorian nodded toward the children—"might be safe, but the people running these experiments aren't going to stop. Head guy's name is Larsen. Ashaya thinks the man will come after Talin, too."

His leopard roared to angry wakefulness. "We knew that. With Max down, she's become their most visible adversary."

Clay reached up and caught a football that seemed to come out of nowhere, then threw it across to the other side of the yard—in the direction of the woods that backed onto Tamsyn's home. Nico and Jase were just walking out. The teenagers grabbed it, waved, then jogged over to join Talin and Sascha.

Nico was clearly taken with Tally. Clay didn't interrupt the kid's flirting. The boys knew what lines they could and couldn't cross, and the fact that Nico was secure enough to seek affection from Tally meant he saw her as part of DarkRiver.

"We've got to clean up the loose ends." His blood simmered at the hint of danger to his mate, but that wasn't his top concern. Anyone who dared threaten her would die, end of story. He had seen her broken once. Never again.

Tally, eyes glazed, face splattered with blood, huddling in the corner. Quiet. So quiet. Even then, even after he'd terrified her with his violence, even after he'd left her alone with strangers, she had protected him with her silence.

Zeke got desperate when I still wouldn't talk . . .

His Tally had gone mute rather than betray him. She had continued to love him though he'd broken every damn promise he'd ever made to her. It enraged the leopard that he couldn't keep her safe now, reminded him of those years when Orrin had been hurting her and he hadn't known. *She was his life.* He'd destroy the world for her. Yet this disease left him helpless.

"I had a call from Dev Santos earlier." He forced himself to think past the blood fury. "He's disposed of the mole."

Dorian gave him a curious look. "Disposed?"

"I'm guessing in very small pieces."

"I like this guy already." Leaning back against the wall of the house, Dorian frowned. "You know, if these kidnappers have lost that source of information, they're going to need a new one." He swore. "They won't kill Talin. They'll try to take her alive."

"No, they won't." Clay felt the claws of the animal unfurl within his skin, felt the power of it rip through his flesh. "It's hard for dead men to do anything."

CHAPTER 40

Ming LeBon sat in Ashaya's office once more. She hadn't expected to see him for days, given the situation in the PsyNet.

"Larsen seems convinced you had something to do with the disappearance of the two remaining test subjects."

"I did," she said, wondering if she'd made a fatal mistake. Had Larsen had Ming's active support? Her findings had led her to conclude that the other scientist had gone far beyond the limits of anything Ming had authorized.

Ming didn't even blink at her confession. "What did you do to them?"

"I terminated them."

"Where are the bodies?"

"Gone." She met his expressionless face with a blank look of her own. "It would've been stupid to kill them as a message and then leave their remains to be found so Larsen could utilize the brain tissue."

"And my man?"

Ashaya had no need to lie. "I'm afraid you have me at a disadvantage. I did this on my own."

"I don't take well to losing one of mine."

"Ming, while I'm happy to take on Larsen," she said with

absolute truthfulness, "I have no desire to make an enemy out of you. We both know who would walk out alive. If one of your men has disappeared, I would look elsewhere for the culprit."

A pause that lasted sixty seconds. The chill of the lab worked its way into Ashaya's bones but she remained unmoving. She was glad for her control when Ming said, "A traitorous e-mail has been traced to this facility."

An inexcusable error. She had acted on the assumption—always dangerous—that the outmoded Internet pathways out of Cinnamon Springs were not being monitored. "I'm sure you've taken care of the culprit."

"I will—as soon as I break the encryption on the remaining e-mails."

She thanked Talin McKade for whatever it was she had done to hide their tracks. "Would you like to scan my organizer?" she offered, having prepared a duplicate for this very purpose. It would pass most checks. The critical word was "most."

Ming watched her. "Not at present. If you were to prove the traitor, I would have to kill you. That would be inconvenient."

Ashaya held his gaze, very aware her death would be nothing easy. "Indeed."

"Tell me, why did you sabotage Larsen's work?"

"Because this is *my* lab." Her tone was ice. "You assured me I was the head M-Psy on the project."

"Larsen was taking a parallel but different approach to the implant issue."

"Nonsense." She handed him a slim electronic data file. "Look at the results."

"Where did these scans come from?"

"From the experimental subjects."

"These don't correlate to the ones I've seen."

"Then I suggest you ask Larsen to explain." She kept her tone unflinching. "He must have been doctoring data in order to gain support for his unauthorized experiments." Anything that went on in her lab was supposed to go through her, and, when new lines of research were involved, through Ming.

"According to these readings, the brain patterns of the Forgotten are nothing like ours."

"Yes." Not quite the complete truth. If Larsen—now on his way to San Francisco—survived the next twenty-four hours, she would have to ensure she had enough "data" to refute his conclusions. Ashaya didn't think she'd need her backup plan, not if Talin McKade's friends were as lethal as they appeared.

The only problem was that Larsen had taken Ekaterina with him and Ashaya had no way to share that information with Ms. McKade—Security had cut off all access to the Internet. "Any experiments run on the Forgotten are worthless in terms of Protocol I, even had Larsen followed proper research methods."

Ming put down the file. "Be that as it may, these experiments allowed Larsen to exterminate those Forgotten who might one day have posed a threat."

"And who would these mythical creatures be?" She gave him another file, wondering what the line was between pragmatic unemotionalism and sociopathy. As far as she was concerned, genocide could not be justified, not by any logical reason. "None of Larsen's test subjects had anything comparable to our abilities. They've interbred with the humans and changelings for too long." Not a lie, as such. But there were things she was withholding, unexpected, powerful mutations caused by generations of intermingling.

Ming put down the file. "I could make it a condition of your . . . situation that you cooperate with Larsen's research."

The threat, to her son, caused an unknown cluster of neurons to spark to life in her brain. She was a researcher, but she didn't know what those awakening sparks implied. Her conditioning was flawless, her shields airtight. "You could," she responded. "But the time I spend on Larsen's useless endeavors will slow down my own progress."

"Is that a threat?"

"No, simple fact. I'll accede to whatever you decide, but I don't share power well." She had no doubt it was a trait Ming understood.

"We can run these experiments at another lab."

"Of course." She could not risk disagreeing with him. "However, I would suggest you not dispose of the subjects in so public a fashion."

Ming stilled. "Explain."

It had been a stab in the dark, but it seemed she'd hit on something Larsen had neglected to mention. "Larsen's method of disposal involves removing the organs, delivering a beating postmortem, and dumping the body in a major metropolitan location."

"I believe I need to have a discussion with Larsen."

Ashaya pushed her advantage. "I was under the impression that he had your support," she said. "According to the security logs, he's been using several of your officers to run interference with Enforcement. Their notes state he had authorization documents from you."

Ming's liquid black eyes swam. "Send a copy of those reports through to me. I don't have time to talk to him today." He rose. "Ashaya, it would be in your best interest to never forget that there is a difference between you and Larsen."

She waited.

"He is nothing, a pawn. You are necessary. I would never simply kill you."

No, she thought, he would rip open her mind, dig into her inner core . . . and turn her into the most compliant of puppets.

On the PsyNet, a Council session was taking place, the second emergency session in a row. Kaleb Krychek, the newest member of the Psy Council and possibly its most dangerous, noted that Ming's mind was the last one to appear.

"Marshall is dead." Nikita's pronouncement met with chill silence.

"Are you certain?" Tatiana asked.

"His remains have been formally identified. DNA cross-matched. I saw the process take place, with Shoshanna as witness."

"Confirmed," Shoshanna said.

No one argued after that. Shoshanna and Nikita were sworn enemies. Neither would cover for the other.

Henry Scott stirred. "Was it a changeling attack as we thought?"

"No," Shoshanna informed her husband. "That would have been preferable."

"It was one of us," Nikita added. "A precision hit."

"Any similarities to the bombing of the original Implant lab?" Tatiana asked. "It could be the same saboteur."

"That was my first thought, too," Nikita said. "Ming, you examined the weapon fragments."

"The signatures are different," Ming told them. "However, the skill and speed of the offensive makes me conclude we're dealing with the same perpetrator. It may be that he's working with accomplices."

"The Ghost," Tatiana said. "He's fast becoming a real threat. He's scattering our resources to the point where several of those we would rather keep chained have escaped their bonds."

Kaleb knew she was referring to the anchors. The PsyNet needed them, but unfortunately, they had a tendency to fall victim to one of the lesser-known side effects of Silence—homicidal insanity.

"Yes," Ming agreed. "I've recently come into possession of facts that suggest non-anchors, too, are now beginning to feel the effects of the disturbances in the Net. It's feeding into weak minds, disrupting their conditioning."

"It's imperative we stop the Ghost before he does more damage. How did he get the bomb into Marshall's home in the first place?" Tatiana asked.

"Unknown." Shoshanna's cool mental tone. "We're tracing all visitors but no one sends up a red flag. Ming may be correct—the Ghost may be the moniker for a group, rather than an individual. Regardless, the Ghost is too good at this."

"But," Kaleb said, having kept his silence to that point, "he is not Council. He doesn't have our resources. We need to start hunting in earnest."

"Agreed." Five voices in unison. "The Ghost must be eliminated."

Kaleb wondered if any of the five realized they had just responded to him as if he were their leader.

CHAPTER 41

Talin had known something was up the entire day. Clay had gone ever more silent as the hours passed, his eyes so darkly possessive she'd felt their touch to the core of her soul. God, the man made her shiver with need, all with a single hot look.

"Are you going tell me what you've been brooding about?" she asked the second they reached home that night.

"No."

Sometimes, the bond they'd formed in childhood was a problem. They had none of the walls that other couples did, had been friends far too long before becoming lovers. It was a brilliant, powerful feeling she'd never give up, but honestly—"You drive me crazy sometimes!"

He took off his jacket and leaned down to kiss her. She tried to dodge it, but Clay was in the mood to show off. He held her easily in place as he melted her bones from the inside out. When she could breathe again, she scowled. "I mean it. Tell me what's up."

"What did you say to get Jon and Noor to stay on at Tammy's?"

She bit her lip. "That we needed to make some additions to this place so that there would be enough room. Are you mad? I mean, I just assumed—"

He put a finger against her lips. "Jon can plug his ears when we make out. Noor's a baby. What the hell's she going to do—eat your chocolate?"

She wanted to be mad at him, but he made it so hard. "Jon's not exactly . . . good."

He laughed, a jaw-cracking laugh full of true humor. "Baby, I have bad covered. Leave the kid to me." He kissed her again. "This place is a bit far out. We might have to consider moving closer to the other families."

"Maybe later," she said. "Right now, they need the security of knowing no one can get to them and it's not going to get much more secure than the middle of DarkRiver land. They can study at home for a while. We'll get a computer tutor set up."

"Whatever you want." He pulled her hair out of its ponytail and thrust a hand through it. "Soon as we decide what we want where, construction can begin. Two, three days and we'll have new rooms."

"So soon?"

"DarkRiver's in construction and I'm the boss as far as building goes." He grinned. "They'll haul ass. Dorian's already drawing up some plans."

"Is he really an architect?"

He tapped her lightly on the bottom. "Yes, and don't sass him. He's threatening to throw you into the nearest body of ice-cold water."

She stood on tiptoe, arms around his neck. "Nah. You wouldn't let him."

His smile turned violent in its tenderness. "No. You're mine to protect."

"Tell me," she whispered, her own smile dying. "Tell me what it is you're going to do."

"Why do you think I'm going to do anything?"

"Because," she swallowed, "you had that same look in your eyes the day you killed Orrin."

Green filled her vision as those magnificent eyes grew flame-hot. "And does it terrify you now, too?"

"Yes," she admitted. "It terrifies me to know I could lose you again because you care too much for me." A tear streaked down her face. "I'm not worth your life."

Clay hated seeing Tally cry, *hated* it. It wasn't the usual male thing with female emotion. It was this deep, eviscerating pain. Reaching up, he wiped away the tears with rough strokes of his thumb. "You are worth everything!" He was angry at her for thinking so little of herself. "Baby, you need to let me do this."

"What?"

"Keep you safe."

"I am safe. With you."

He shook his head. "The Psy need to understand that you're protected. Anybody who comes after you takes their life into their hands."

"There's more than one," she pleaded with him. "If you go after them, they'll—"

"I'm not alone either." He nuzzled at her, wanting to reassure her, to soothe her, but unable to accept her plea to let it be. He couldn't claw out the disease inside her but he could get rid of this threat. "You're part of a pack now. Accept what they need to give you." What he needed to give her.

"I *adore* you," she whispered. "If you die, I'm not going to make it." The words were stark, her heart laid open on her sleeve.

"Then don't ask me to sit on my hands while you stand in harm's way," he demanded. "I need to protect you."

"I'm already si—"

He kissed her before she could say anything. She wasn't sick, wasn't dying. He refused to let her go. "We'll talk about that later," he told her. "Tonight, just . . . tell me you'll be here when I return." Ready to touch him no matter that he came to her with violence painted across his body.

Her face set in stubborn lines and he felt his predator's heart stop. "You get one scratch," she said, "*one single scratch*, on your body and you'll be sleeping in the living room for the next month." Her lips trembled. "Do I make myself clear?"

He smiled at the threat neither of them believed she'd carry through. "Yes, ma'am."

* * *

Talin walked back into Tamsyn's by now familiar home late that night. "I'm going to head to the lair with Clay when he returns," she told the healer, already worrying for him.

"I know." Tamsyn smiled. "Want a glass of wine?"

"It's late." She unclenched her fingers, told herself he'd be fine. He would come back to her, he'd promised. He wouldn't leave her alone again.

"I don't think you'll be sleeping. Neither will Sascha."

"Sascha's here, too?" Having come straight into the kitchen after Clay dropped her off, she hadn't seen the other woman. She swallowed her fear, not wanting the cardinal to sense the depth of her scars. She *knew* Clay wouldn't leave her by choice. He never had. But in some hidden part of her, she was still a shocked and bloodied eight-year-old, and that child knew that, sometimes, you weren't given a choice. "Where is she?"

"Upstairs. Julian woke up and demanded she come cuddle him—I swear the twins can scent her a mile away." She shook her head. "They have the most enormous crushes on her. I think they'd fight Lucas for her if he wasn't so much bigger."

Talin forced her mind to the present. "I can guess why." The two women might not see it but they were very similar, both of them with the warm hearts of healers. And yet there was a strength in them that promised protection. "Jon and Noor?"

"Noor's asleep and Jon's keeping Kit company while he studies." She pointed upstairs. "Second door on the left."

Talin shook her head. "I think I've used up all my fuss points for the next month."

Tammy grinned. "He'll be okay with Kit."

"You always seem to have people around," Talin began, eager to know more about Clay's world. She never wanted to hurt him as Isla had done by not acknowledging his beast, by not accepting that he was different—in a beautiful, unique way. "Do you mind?"

"Lord, no. It makes me content to care for the pack. Part of the healing gift, I suppose." The other woman pushed a flute of pale gold wine across the counter. "That's why the pack healer always has a big house. Somehow, their home inevitably becomes the social center of the pack." She picked up a bag of coffee beans.

"Are you making coffee, too?"

"Faith and Sascha don't drink wine—Psy have an odd reaction to alcohol."

Right then, someone knocked on the front door. "I'll get it," Talin offered.

When she opened it, it was to find Faith on the other side. "Oh, hi."

"Hi." The F-Psy smiled before turning to wave at the seemingly empty space behind her. "Vaughn," she said in response to Talin's bemused expression. "He and Mercy are running outside border watch tonight. Nate's doing the inner region."

Something clicked in Talin's brain. "Is that why we're all here?" She stepped aside to let Faith walk in. Everyone knew that Psy didn't like to be touched and Faith wasn't exactly her best friend.

"Yes." The F-Psy put a large shopping bag on the floor beside the hall closet. "It's easier for them to cover us this way, since they're three short." She hung up her coat and, leaving the bag on the floor, began to head toward the kitchen. Talin fell in beside her. It took incredible force of will not to ask the question she so desperately wanted to ask—had Faith had another vision of Clay's future? What had she seen?

Faith stopped halfway down the hall and turned. "I owe you an apology."

"Why?"

"Emotion is still new to me." She shoved her hands into the pockets of her black slacks. "Sometimes I find it hard to handle."

"Everyone gets that way." Talin wondered what it was like to grow up without emotion. She couldn't imagine ever not loving Clay.

Faith's night-sky eyes seemed to turn darker. "Clay scared me when I first came into DarkRiver, but then he became my friend. So when you—"

"It's okay," Talin interrupted. "You were worried I was bad for him, so you went overprotective. The truth is," she admitted, "now that I'm not blinded by stupid jealousy, I'm glad for the tenderness you tried to give him. That's nothing to apologize for."

"Yes, there is." Faith's expression was resolute. "Sascha and Tammy were so nice to me when I entered DarkRiver. I should've remembered their example and treated you with the same warmth and respect."

"I figure we're even." Talin filled her voice with sincerity—so that Faith didn't have to guess at nuances of emotion. "I called you all sorts of names in my head."

Faith gave a small smile. "We're okay?"

And the words came out. "You tell me."

"Sometimes," Faith said, her voice holding a crystal clarity that was almost painful in its beauty, "it's better not to know what the future brings. If I had known about Vaughn, I might've run and missed out on the best thing in my life."

"I doubt you would've gotten very far." DarkRiver men were nothing if not determined.

"Some things are set in stone." Faith's smile grew. "Like you and Clay."

Talin felt her stomach fill with butterflies. "You sound very certain of that."

"We, all of us who are mated, we're learning and growing into our bond, but you and Clay—it's like the bond's been there forever, it's so solid, so true." The foreseer shook her head and pushed through into the kitchen. "You have the bond of a couple that's already been together for decades."

A pungent mix of shock and panic dried out Talin's mouth. The way Faith was speaking, it was as if she could see the bond—if true, that meant Talin and Clay had truly mated. But that was a question she would ask only Clay. "So," she said, forcing down her disquiet, "what are we going to do tonight?" She had to do something or she'd go insane.

Tammy shot her a mischievous look. "Well, we know you had to clear out of your apartment in a hurry and that you probably didn't take much time to pack, so we did some shopping for you."

"Except," Faith added with a smile, "Sascha got lost in the lingerie department."

Tammy laughed. "Don't worry. We got you at least two non-X-rated pieces. Including this." She held up a beautiful green sweater, the one she'd begun knitting the night Talin had first traded barbed remarks with Faith. "It was always for you."

Talin felt off center, lost. "Why?" She didn't have friends, didn't know how to give that much of herself to anyone but Clay.

"Because," Sascha said from behind her, "you're one of us. And DarkRiver looks after its own."

Clay figured that if this Larsen bastard planned to hit Talin, he'd start off at either the last spot where she'd been seen or Max's hospital room. He and Dorian eliminated the latter option by getting Max discharged.

The cop thanked them for it. "I thought I'd never get out," he said as they helped him to the car. He wasn't so pleased when they took him to a small and very private changeling hospital, used only by wolves and, now, the cats. "What the fuck?"

"Tally likes you," Clay told him. "Shut the hell up and get better so she doesn't worry."

Max grimaced. "How long am I going to be stuck here?"

"Doc said you'll be out end of the week if you do what you're supposed to."

That made Max happier. "I'll be a boy scout. Happy hunting."

Clay didn't ask how the man knew they were hunting. "Thanks. We'll give you an update afterward."

"At least I got one of the fuckers." Yawning, Max dropped off.

That done, they got into the car and checked in with Lucas, who was keeping an eye on Talin's apartment.

"No movement," Lucas told them. "Rina's come and gone. Did a pretty good impression of Talin. Went in, turned the lights on and off, opened and closed the closets, played the recording you made of Talin muttering, then snuck out the back. Oh, yeah, she took the initiative and faked having a shower, too."

Clay hoped that that would be enough to draw out the kidnappers—earlier today, while Tally had been busy with Jon and Noor, he'd come in and confirmed that the apartment was being monitored. There were at least ten bugs inside.

He and Dorian arrived at the meeting spot across from the apartment building as the clock was ticking one in the morning. They weren't the only ones. "You really think this'll work?"

Judd asked from the shadows. "Correct me if I'm wrong, but you're just hoping the person behind this will turn up here once his surveillance tells him Talin has surfaced."

"We're going on instinct," Clay said, unsurprised the SnowDancer lieutenant had accepted his invitation. Judd was proving a good man to have at his back, though Clay had had to threaten to kick his ass after the way he'd spoken to Tally. "The bastard has to start somewhere and this is Tally's last known location. Thanks to Rina, we might even have fooled Larsen into thinking she's moved back in."

They all went silent. Minutes turned into tens of minutes. Nothing stirred.

"If it was me," Judd said, "I'd go for Max—far easier to get Talin's location by breaking him."

"Max is no longer accessible," Dorian muttered, smug.

Judd didn't say anything for another ten minutes. "It would still be inexcusably stupid to come here. He should go to Shine and torture Devraj Santos."

"Jesus." Lucas's scowl was in his tone.

"Logic says," Judd continued, unperturbed, "he'll go to those likely to know Talin's location, not run to this place she hasn't been to in days. He won't fall for the Rina gambit."

"You're thinking with the trained mind of a soldier," Dorian said. "Larsen isn't a soldier, he's a scientist playing at murder. He was smart at the start, I'll give you that, but the recent slipups all smack of an amateur overreaching himself—the failed attack on Max, the way the bodies were dumped, even the mess he or his goons made of Talin's apartment."

"Psychological warfare."

"No." Clay shook his head. "I had a look today. What they did was savage, like bullies trying to scare a child." Losing those pictures had to have hurt Tally. Clay intended to replace each and every one. "There was a senselessness to the whole thing."

Lucas's anger was a naked blade when he spoke. "You're thinking we have ourselves a sociopath using experiments as cover to prey on children?"

"Yeah." That was what he had never been able to understand—and what had probably confused Tamsyn—about the photos of those fragile, broken bodies. There had been too much glee in the way the victims had been brutalized. Someone had hurt those children simply because he could. "Worse, I think he's slipped the leash—no one in the Council superstructure would've okayed anything but the total disappearance of the victims. Larsen wanted them found because he wanted the attention."

"If that's true," Dorian added, "it means things are seriously shaky in the PsyNet."

"Because they've had too many mistakes escape lately?" Lucas asked.

"Think about it. Before Enrique"—Dorian's tone was a chilling frost as he named his sister's killer—"we hadn't heard of any violence in the Psy. But after him, we had that serial who was hunting Faith and now this."

At the time that Faith was being stalked, Clay had been so close to going rogue, he'd suggested leaving the Psy to clean up their own mistakes. He hadn't cared about anything. Now, God, how he cared about Tally. She could drive him crazier faster than any other person, he thought with a smile, but when she melted, she was pure honey.

"There have been other incidents." Judd's comment cut into his thoughts. "Killers they've managed to hush up, others who have become more active."

"Why the sudden signs of disintegration?" Lucas asked. "The assassination can't be the cause—it only just happened."

"Dissent is building up, starting to have a flow-on effect—the PsyNet is a psychic construct. Anything that happens in it has an impact on the minds of those linked to it."

"You saying the more the PsyNet destabilizes, the more vermin we're going to see?" Dorian blew out a disgusted breath.

"Yes. Notwithstanding its own murderous tendencies, the Council's iron fist—in conjunction with Silence—kept the majority of the viciously insane contained." He paused. "There's always a price for freedom."

Lucas swore. "If the Council falls, the backlash will hit humans and changelings as well as the Psy."

"The greatest danger lies in the uncontrolled dismantling of Silence. In the chaos, we could lose millions from all three races."

"You're defending Silence?" Dorian's asked in open surprise.

CHAPTER 42

"Silence was set up for a reason. I'd be dead now if not for it." Judd's tone was matter-of-fact. "It's ultimately proven false, but we can't go back to how things were before conditioning began—the killing, the insanity." His fists clenched.

"How bad will it get?" Clay asked.

"Measures are being put in place," Judd said, "but the fallout will be . . . substantial. Not only deaths from the psychic shock, but from the awakening of a thousand monstrous desires, things that were suppressed by Silence. Like this scientist—before the cracks in the Net, he would have never acted on his instincts."

Clay bared his teeth. "Means the sociopathic bastard's not thinking clearly anymore." Psy made excellent serial killers because they rarely made mistakes. But if this one was fragmenting . . . "He'll come here, he'll want to hurt the woman who stopped his fun."

"What if he and his associates don't turn up tonight?" Judd asked. "Do we return tomorrow? And the day after?"

"Yes." Clay looked at the Psy. "You have a problem with that?"

Judd smiled and it was the ice-cold smile of the assassin he undoubtedly was. "No. I like kids."

"How do we do this?" Dorian asked. "Get Judd to tear into the head guy's mind?"

"No," Clay said at once. *He* was going to do this, make sure Talin was safe. "Judd can't risk being made."

"I can hide very well," Judd responded. "But we also have to consider the fact that if I go into Larsen's mind, there's a high probability I'll destroy everything he knows. I won't have time to fine-tune the intrusion."

Clay's beast growled inwardly at Judd's reference to the Psy ability to kill with a single focused mental strike. "Psy can't strike at us if they're unconscious, correct?"

"Yes. That is," he amended, "if they're strong enough to take you out in the first place. Not every Psy is. Anything below a Gradient 5, you'd survive."

"Same problem," Lucas pointed out. "He loses consciousness, we lose the chance to extract information."

"I put some of our own bugs in the apartment when I checked it out earlier," Clay told them. "Switch your earpieces to frequency two."

"And here I thought you didn't listen when I talked about the tech stuff." Despite the lighthearted words, Dorian's amazement was evident. "So, we listen, let Larsen and his buddies tell us what we need to know. Might work unless they choose to telepath. Telepaths, hell—Judd, they going to be able to pick us up?"

"I don't think this Larsen is smart enough to run a telepathic scan. But if he does, we'll be fine as long as we're not too close. Most Psy only have the ability to scan a few meters in any direction."

"We need to be close enough to intercept when necessary." Clay scanned the area with a predator's cool mind. "One covering the back of the building, one the front, two on either side."

"Dorian—you're the sniper," Lucas said. "Get up high, set up your rifle, and aim it at the window of Talin's apartment. If we need a shot, we'll let you know."

Dorian was already moving.

Lucas touched his earpiece a few minutes later. "He has a sightline into the window."

The three of them moved out toward the building, one Psy

assassin and two leopards who knew how to turn to shadows in the dark.

"I'm in position." Lucas's calm voice.

"So am I." Judd.

"Copy." Clay's mind was working with near-Psy efficiency by then, his emotions contained until he needed their violent force. He was certain he would tonight.

Because he had no doubts whatsoever that the monster would come.

The animal had scented something in the wind, tasted something in the bruises Jon bore. The man who had preyed on the boy wouldn't be thinking straight right now. He'd want his plaything back. And the easiest way to get to Jon was through the only person he trusted.

Tally.

Larsen probably planned to torture her, break her. But evil, he thought with a fierce stab of pride, didn't understand good. Tally would rather die than betray those under her care. Just like twenty years ago, she had gone mute rather than betray him.

Don't kill me! I promise I won't touch her again!

Orrin had begged for his life, promised to turn himself in after the first slash of Clay's leopard claws. Clay had executed him anyway. For the pain he had put in Tally's eyes, for the childhood he had stolen, Orrin Henderson had deserved to die. But to the authorities, Orrin's words would have changed Clay's act from manslaughter in defense of a child, to cold-blooded retaliation.

They would have been wrong.

Clay had stopped thinking straight the second he'd heard that first, faint cry, the utter despair in it a violation. As Orrin broke Tally, something in Clay had broken, too. He could have no more stopped himself from killing Orrin than he could have left Tally to take the hurt. Part of him wondered if, deep down, she still blamed him. His leopard's heart remained deeply scarred by the failure.

Without warning, warmth soothed into his bones, a silent whisper telling him the past was over and done. What they were now was the truth. He accepted that whisper, accepted it was Tally speaking to him, though she might not know it yet. He understood full well that she thought they weren't truly mated. He hadn't done anything to correct her misapprehension—with the shadow of disease hovering over her, she didn't want to bond him to her in such an inescapable fashion, didn't want to handicap him.

Sometimes, Tally could be very stupid for a smart woman.

She was his life, his soul. Without her, he would have gone rogue sooner rather than later. Faith had said that to him, once. That he was on the thinnest of edges and that his time would come. Now, Clay felt blood fury roar through him, inciting the urge to maim, to tear, to annihilate this creature who had dared threaten Tally . . . and knew that what Faith had foretold had come to pass. Today would decide his future, tell him whether he could be the mate Tally deserved.

"They're coming." Dorian's voice. "Unable to confirm if male is the one described by Jon. Female is blonde, possible match to description of Ashaya's assistant."

Clay buried his emotions, knowing he had to act as a man tonight, not a ravaging beast. A second later, he felt his nostrils flare as the night air brought him the sharp metallic stink of Psy. Not all of the race had that scent—Vaughn's theory was that it only marked those who had accepted Silence on the most fundamental level. The ones who retained some spark of humanity, they smelled human, normal.

Clay could smell the female, too, but couldn't tell if the sharp metallic scent was her own or an overwhelming echo of the male's. The leopard didn't particularly like hurting women, but he had been in this cold war with the Psy long enough to know that female hearts and minds could carry as much evil as male—Nikita Duncan, Sascha's mother, would've had no compunction in ordering the extermination of her own daughter if she'd thought she could get away with it. But knowing that didn't make him any less uncomfortable with the idea.

"I can see them in Tally's room. No lights." Dorian again.

Clay frowned. "That's Talin to you, Boy Genius."

Dorian's growl was low. "Ice-fucking-cold water."

They went silent as their earpieces picked up the sound of floorboards squeaking. Neither intruder had spoken yet. If they remained silent, interrogation might have to give way to a simple execution, Clay thought with cold logic. Once his identity was confirmed, Larsen had to die, no ifs, no buts.

"Should I pull the curtains over this window?" a female voice asked.

Damn! Clay could've kicked himself for leaving those curtains up there. One pull and Dorian's line of sight was gone.

"Leave it," the male said. "We can't risk some nosy neighbor catching the movement and becoming suspicious."

"As you say. What should I look for?"

"Do you have no initiative?" The man's voice was pure Psy, but there was an ugly undertone to it the animal in Clay understood all too well. Safe behind the shield of Silence, this monster enjoyed abusing and bullying those weaker than himself. "Look for any signs of where Talin McKade might have gone after she left this apartment. She was here a few hours ago—there should be some evidence of her presence."

"This seems an illogical endeavor," the woman persisted. "Have you checked the detective's records?"

"Why do you think we wasted our time going to that motel in Sacramento? He had it listed as her place of residence."

Good on Max, Clay thought with a savage grin.

Something crunched and he realized one of the two Psy had stepped on the broken holo-frames scattered in Tally's living room.

"Careful," the male hissed. "We don't want someone calling Enforcement."

"I thought you had Councilor LeBon's support. Surely he can stifle any Enforcement action."

A pause. "It seems Ashaya has used my absence to convince him that my results are worthless. I need Jonquil Duchslaya to prove her wrong—and Talin McKade is certain to know his present whereabouts. The human will serve the dual purpose of providing me with a new access point into Shine's databases."

"You think Councilor LeBon will allow you to continue your experiments?"

"Yes, of course, once I'm able to return and show him the real results."

"Why continue?"

"Are you questioning my judgment?"

"Your findings indicate beyond any doubt that the brains of

the Forgotten are different from ours. They can't be utilized as test subjects."

"It's not about using them as test subjects." The man's voice held a superior tone, as if he was deigning to share a secret. "It's about finding out what they've become, eliminating the possible threat to the Psy."

"That's an illogical presumption," the female said. "They are no threat, their powers have mutated, weakened—"

"Mutated but not necessarily weakened." Shuffling, rustling sounds that Clay identified as that of paper. "Where is she hiding? According to our research, she hasn't returned to her adopted family and she has no close friends."

"Your approach makes little sense." The woman stood her ground, a point in her favor—if she really was loyal to Ashaya, she'd walk out of this alive. "Talin McKade isn't high enough up in Shine to give us the information we need."

"She has access to their computers. That's all we need. Once we break open her natural shields and implant a control link, we can direct her to search for what we want. The situation will be more draining on your powers than if she was a cooperative subject, but it'll work."

"My powers?"

"I need to be fully functional for the experiments."

Silence and then the sounds of the female finally moving about. Ten minutes later, the pair left the apartment.

"Dorian?"

"I've got them," Dorian said, tone cool and focused. "They just passed the seventh-floor window, took the stairs."

"Figures," Lucas murmured. "They wouldn't want to be captured on the elevator surveillance."

They were all moving into intercept positions as they spoke.

"Luc," Clay said, "can you get the girl away from the male?"

"Dorian, split them up," Lucas ordered.

"They're at the exit," Dorian noted. "Shot coming up. Silenced."

A short feminine scream followed soon afterward and then the sound of someone running away from Clay's location, heavier male steps in pursuit. Lucas had taken the girl.

"Judd—we need to find out what she knows," Clay said as Larsen ran past the alley where he stood cloaked in shadow.

"I'm on it."

Satisfied the two men would control the female, Clay went after the monster who had killed so many children. In a test of physical strength and speed, a changeling would always win over a Psy. He caught up within seconds, close enough to verify that the Psy fit the description Jon had given them.

"Judd—chances he's sending telepathically?" he asked as he tracked the man out of the residential streets and toward a quieter area full of warehouses closed up for the night. Fog curled up around his feet, muddied the air, but the leopard had excellent vision and a nose trained to track prey.

"If we're lucky, he might be too agitated to send. That won't last."

"Did he see Lucas?"

"No." Judd sounded as if he was running. "I'm blocking the girl, but she's too exhausted to try to send anyway. We're about to run her to ground."

The link went silent.

Clay waited. If Larsen hadn't seen Lucas, that meant he remained unaware of any changeling connection. Even if he did send a telepathic message, he could report nothing but an attack. His superior—Ming LeBon—would likely assume Shine involvement. Clay's blood boiled at the thought of Ming, but he knew the Councilor wouldn't pursue this particular evil if he destroyed the man who was driving it.

The Psy male began to slow down. As he bent over in a dark alleyway, breathing hard, Clay's earpiece activated. It was Lucas. "We've got her—blindfolded. She can't ID us and doesn't want to. Says she's one of Ashaya Aleine's people, and she fits Jon's description of the blonde he saw with Ashaya. She confirms the Psy you're chasing is Larsen Brandell, the man behind the experiments. Gradient 7."

A Psy that strong could shove enough power through a changeling's mind to cause instantaneous death. So Clay gave Larsen no warning. Slicing out with his claws, he cut through the man's jugular in a clean sweep.

Blood spurted in a dark splash, coloring the ground and the

wall beside the Psy. A gurgling sound followed. Larsen was dead before he hit the asphalt.

It was an execution. And that he felt no pity or guilt should have made Clay a monster. Perhaps it did. But as blood scented the air, sharp and metallic, he wondered if it took a monster to kill a monster.

CHAPTER 43

Dressed only in a pair of loose black pants, his body covered with sweat, Councilor Kaleb Krychek walked to the edge of his balcony and looked down into the gorge that fell away an inch from his feet. But he didn't notice the dangerous view, his mind on the problem of Shoshanna and Henry Scott. While Nikita, Tatiana, and Ming were all dangerous adversaries, the Scotts were particularly problematic because they worked as a unit. Neither of the two was cardinal strength, but together, they were a lethal combination.

With Marshall gone, Shoshanna had begun jockeying for control of the Council. Kaleb had won the first skirmish, but he was under no illusion the battle would be easy. He glanced down at the mark branded onto his forearm, a deceptively clean-appearing shape that had shifted the course of his life beyond redemption. It was a reminder of what he was, what he was willing to do.

Something brushed his mind then, an oily darkness that looked to him for comfort. It was the voiceless twin of the NetMind, the neosentient entity that kept order in the PsyNet. The DarkMind, by comparison, was pure chaos. Very, very few people knew about the DarkMind. And only one could assert any control over it.

As a cardinal telekinetic, Kaleb had a natural affinity with both the NetMind and the DarkMind. Now he reached out a psychic hand and touched the DarkMind.

Sleep, he said. *Sleep.*

The DarkMind was tired today. So it slept. Kaleb knew the respite was temporary at best. The DarkMind carried within it all the violence and pain, the rage and the insanity that the Psy refused to feel. It had no voice but spoke through the acts of violence it perpetrated via the weak minds of compromised Psy. It was, in a sense, a lost child. It was also pure evil.

Kaleb had first spoken to it at seven years of age.

Satisfied the DarkMind would cause no more chaos for the next few hours, he returned his attention to the problem at hand. If either of the Scotts discovered the truth behind the mark that branded him, it would give them the weapon they needed to challenge his meticulously planned takeover of the Council. That could not be allowed to happen.

He glanced at his watch. While the sun shone in Moscow, it was now three a.m. in San Francisco. But this conversation could not be delayed. Retrieving a secure phone from inside the house, he punched in a code. "Put me through to Anthony Kyriakus. PsyClan NightStar."

CHAPTER 44

"Tell me," Talin said to Clay hours later.

He'd come to her an hour before dawn, after he and the others had cleaned up the evidence and buried the body so far in the forest that no one would ever find it. Larsen Brandell had, for all intents and purposes, disappeared without a trace.

Judd had left the woman's mind unharmed. There was nothing anyone could learn from her other than that she'd been interrogated by two unknown men, men who had taken her organizer before setting her free.

DarkRiver and SnowDancer didn't mind going up against the Psy, but sometimes it was better to work in the shadows, to become stronger than your enemy could imagine. They now had further evidence of the failure of Silence, evidence Clay had a feeling would end up being used as a weapon in the building revolution in the Net.

"Clay," Talin prompted, as they lay face-to-face in bed. "Talk to me, darling. Tell me what's put that look in your eyes."

And because this was Tally, the one person to whom he'd never been able to lie, he told her everything. "I'm happy he's dead," he said, drinking her in as she leaned on her elbow and looked down at him, that glorious mane tumbling over one shoulder. "It had to be done."

"Was it like before?"

"No." He surprised himself with that answer. "That was rage. Rage and protectiveness and helplessness. But it wasn't like the soldier when we rescued Jon and Noor, either—that was in the heat of battle. This was a cold-blooded execution." He refused to dress up the truth. Tally had to accept him, animal brutality and all. If she couldn't . . . It would claw into his predator's heart, but it wouldn't make him set her free. He wasn't ever letting her go. "I cut his throat."

Instead of exhibiting disgust, she spread one hand over his heartbeat. "Why did you execute him?"

"If I hadn't, he would have found a way to go on killing children." Larsen's own plans—stored in the organizer they had found in his pocket—had provided ample proof of his murderous tendencies.

Talin bent her head until their foreheads touched, her hair a shimmering curtain around them. "If that bastard was standing here right this second, I'd drive a knife into his black heart without hesitation."

He put his hands on her hips. "Would you?"

"Yes." Her lips brushed his. "He hurt my children. Ask any other woman in your pack and they'll give you the same answer. Do you think I'm a monster for admitting that?"

"No."

"Then how can you possibly be?"

Something tight unfurled inside him and he lay quiescent as she kissed him with delicate feminine sweetness, as if savoring the taste of him. "Still adore me?" he said into that kiss, his tone husky. A tone between lovers, between mates, between a man and the only woman he had ever wanted.

"Too much," was her response. "I only feel whole when I'm with you. Does that make me weak?"

The cat stretched out inside him as she pressed kisses along his jawline, down his neck. "If you're weak, then so am I." He could function without her but in the way a machine functions. His heart, his soul, he had given to her a long time ago. Her hair stroked over him as she began to kiss her way downward. "Tally—"

"Shh." She put her hand over his heart again and looked up, such tenderness in her gaze that he felt captured, contained, caged. But his jailer was soft and so sweet, he was completely in her thrall. "Let me love you tonight."

"Just tonight?" he teased, pushing one of his hands in her hair.

Her smile lit up the whole room. "Maybe I'll do it again . . . if you behave." Dipping her head, she pressed more of those delicate kisses to his skin. "Are you sensitive here?" She flicked her tongue across one flat nipple.

Clay sucked in a breath, felt more than heard her laugh. Then she blew a breath across the damp flesh and he groaned. That was when she used her teeth on him. The cat growled but Tally didn't stop what she was doing. He hadn't wanted her to. The cat liked her teeth, her claws, her scent, everything about her.

Her scent? For a second, he thought he should remember something, but Tally was moving to the other side of his chest and he was having trouble thinking about anything but the soft curves of her body. Under his hands, he felt satin and lace. "What's this?"

"The women gave it to me. Hmm." The sound vibrated through him as she reached the waistband of the sweatpants he'd worn to bed. "Why did you get dressed?"

His abdomen grew rock hard as he tensed his muscles in an attempt to keep his dominant instincts in check. "I thought you were tired."

She ran her tongue along the waistband, excruciatingly close to his cock. "You're not tired." Raising her head, she brought up her hand to clasp him through the material.

His back arched. "Tally." It was both warning and plea.

She snapped her teeth at him. "Should I bite?"

His cock jumped. "I thought you liked me."

Her laugh was husky. Releasing him, she sat up on her knees and hooked her hands into the sides of his sweatpants. He let her draw them down, fascinated by the vision of her in that pink satin and white lace thing she was wearing. It was strappy and about as substantial as cotton candy. "You look like strawberry ice cream," he managed to say as she got rid of his clothing and retook her kneeling position between his thighs.

"Do you like strawberry ice cream?" She shrugged and one strap slid down, exposing the upper curve of her breast.

He dug his hands into the bed, cursing the freckles that laid a teasing path across her creamy flesh. "Oh, yeah. I like to lap it straight up." His mouth watered.

"Nuh-uh." She waved a finger in warning. "I get to do the lapping—and licking—today." The other strap went down, lace catching on the peak of her nipple.

"Jesus, Tally." His gaze was fixated in the shadowed valley between her breasts. "When did you get this mean?"

She ran her finger down that valley, teasing him. "You ain't seen nothing yet." Talin was . . . having fun. It was the oddest thing for her. Sex wasn't about fun. With Clay, it was wonderful and hot and pleasurable beyond her understanding, but she'd never expected this. It made her want to laugh and pepper his face with kisses.

"Drop the slip," he said, voice raw. "Please."

She fisted him instead, delighting in his bitten-off curse, in the way he lay there and let her play. Loving this man was so easy, it almost terrified her. Almost. "What do I get in return?"

"My damn cock thrusting you into orgasm."

Her hand tightened. He hissed out a breath but seemed to like it. So she kept it that way. "Well, that is very tempting." She stroked up, then down. "But I have a feeling I'll get that anyway."

His eyes became slits, cat-bright in the muted light of the room. And that was another thing—Clay never forced her into the dark, never belittled her for her childish fear. He just fixed the lights so no room was ever wholly without illumination. How could she possibly not be crazy for him?

"You want something," he accused.

She smiled and bent down to flick her tongue across the head of his erection. He almost came off the bed and the swear word he used this time was considerably bluer. "Nice," she murmured, licking her lips, hovering inches from his aroused length.

"What do you want?" He was breathing hard. She thought she heard something rip, wondered if he'd torn into the bedsheets with his claws. She waited for the spike of fear. What came was another rush of damp need. Her body had learned that for her, his strength meant only pleasure. She loved the way he could pick her up and do all sorts of wicked things . . . when she wasn't in control, that is.

"I want you," she said. "Naked."

His nostrils flared as if he was soaking in the scent of her arousal. "Tally, honey, I can't get any more naked. That's my cock you're playing with."

She grazed him lightly, very lightly, with her teeth for that remark. He swore again but didn't make any attempt to take control. "I want you," she said, "naked and on your front."

"Why?" A suspicious growl.

"So I can stroke you. Pet you. Love you." She ran her nails along the inside of one thigh, felt him shudder. "At least half an hour." Bending again, she closed her mouth over the top of his erection without warning.

Something definitely tore this time. "Fuck!"

She released him. "Yes?"

"Yes! Damn it, yes! Now suck me or I'm going to have you on your back so fast, you'll—" His threat ended in a roar as she took as much of him in her mouth as she could fit.

Clay, she decided, tasted good. Very good. She liked giving him this pleasure. But more, she liked that he allowed her to see the extremity of his reaction, no holds barred. So she loved him, learned him, tasted him. And when he tugged at her hair to pull her off him, she resisted. But Clay had reached the end of his patience.

Reaching down, he pulled her up by her shoulders and flipped her onto her back. His hand was tearing away her panties a second later and then he thrust into her in one solid stroke. It made her scream.

He froze. "Tally?"

She gripped his shoulders. "Move!" And that was all she had breath to say because he did exactly that. Wrapping her legs around him, she urged him on, vaguely aware that he'd snapped the straps of her flimsy little slip and that the material lay crushed between them, an erotic sensation. But nothing was as erotic as his hand on her breast, his hardness moving inside of her.

Then he licked a line across the freckles decorating her breasts. "I want to eat you up." His teeth closed over her nipple.

Her mind went blank.

"So this stroking thing," Clay asked some time later, his chest against her back. "When were you thinking of doing it?"

She snuggled into his embrace. "Whenever I want. So be ready to drop 'em and spread 'em."

He stroked his hand into the curls at the apex of her thighs, tugged. "Brat."

"Bully." With that familiar exchange, she suddenly knew the answer to the question she hadn't yet asked. "We're mated, aren't we?"

His hand rose up to lie flat on her abdomen. "Yes."

"How long?"

"Always."

She couldn't argue with that, because the truth was, she had been born for Clay. "I'm sick—"

"It doesn't matter."

"It matters," she whispered. "Leopards only bond once."

"Would you leave me if I was sick?"

"That's not fair."

"Hell it isn't." He enclosed her in the circle of his arms. "We're stuck, me and you. It was never going to be anyone else for either of us." Clay waited for her to argue but she didn't. The leopard inside him stopped pacing, hackles smoothing down. Satisfied that she'd accepted the truth, he pulled at the material still bunched around her waist. "Want me to tear this off?"

She slapped at his hand. "Don't you dare. I'll have to sew the straps back on as it is."

"Sorry." He nuzzled at her neck.

"No, you're not."

No, he wasn't. Hiding his smile against her, he bit back a groan as she wiggled and did little female movements that succeeded in getting the slip to the bottom of her legs, where she kicked it off. Now she was fully naked, all glorious golden skin and pretty freckles for him to stroke. "Skin privileges," he murmured, his hand on her hip.

Talin smiled. Part of her—the part that had never quite believed Clay wouldn't one day leave her again—was now at peace. Mating was forever. But a far bigger part of her was distraught. What would happen to him if she died? She had to make sure he didn't fall back into the darkness. "Promise me something."

"No." His tone said he knew what she was going to ask. "Don't you dare ask that of me, Tally."

She ignored the growled order. "I need to know you'll be there for Noor and Jon." It was manipulative to bring up the children, but she'd do anything to keep Clay safe, give up her pride, her soul.

"No."

"Promise me."

He released her, rolled off the bed, and stood. "You aren't going to die, so this conversation doesn't need to happen."

She sat up, tears in her throat. "Ignoring the truth won't make it any less true, you damn arrogant leopard!"

He shifted in a shower of brilliant multicolored sparks.

She was so startled, she couldn't speak. And then the most beautiful leopard was in the room with her, a glorious creature with defiance in its eyes. "Not fair," she whispered, throwing off the sheet to crawl over the side of the bed and slide onto the floor.

He came to her, laying his head on her thigh. She should have berated him for choosing to end the argument this way but what she did was stroke him. "Beautiful," she whispered, sinking her hand into the black and gold fir. "Magnificent." Petting words, because while he was big and tough, he was also hers to love, hers to adore.

Green eyes caught hers, a gleam of smug pride in their depths.

"Vain," she added.

He growled, bared his teeth. And still she stroked him. Her mate. Her everything.

CHAPTER 45

Talin was still drowning in a confusion of happiness and fear late the next morning as she sat on Tammy and Nate's back steps. The only reason she hadn't come earlier was that she'd spent the morning catching up with Rangi. The other Guardian had returned at last. He hadn't blinked an eye when she'd informed him that Iain's murderer was dead.

"Good," had been his response. "Thanks for looking after my kids."

She'd passed on the details he needed, then headed back, clear of all Shine responsibilities. Her resignation was already typed up, ready to be e-mailed. She no longer dared take responsibility for the welfare of innocents, not when her mind could go haywire at any second. Her eyes fell on Noor and Jon.

They were playing in the yard with the twins, with Dorian riding herd. Thank God she had Clay to make sure she didn't cause any harm to these precious children. He was on the phone inside the house right now, organizing a construction team for the lair.

"Morning."

She looked up. "Sascha? What are you doing here?"

"I came to check up on Jon and Noor." The empath's eyes were without stars, but her face wore a smile. "Can I join you? I have coffee."

Thankfully accepting the cup Sascha held out, she shifted over so the other woman could sit beside her. "Where's Lucas?"

"Talking with Nate about changes to the protective grid we run on our territory. We've had some problems with Psy incursions so we're increasing security. But from the sound of things, the Council's going to be too busy with internal problems to bother us for the next little while."

Talin slipped at the coffee. "Things are changing, aren't they?"

"Yes." Sascha held her cup with both hands, forearms braced on her thighs. "Far faster than I would've believed. Judd thinks my defection acted as a catalyst."

Talin heard the skeptical note in the cardinal's voice. "You don't think that?"

"I was considered a weak Psy, a useless appendage to Councilor Nikita Duncan." There was pain in that statement but there was also anger. "I hardly think my defection capable of causing that big a ripple."

Talin thought about that as they watched Tammy's little boys tackle a tolerant Jon to the ground while Noor grabbed the ball and ran. "Maybe it was your apparent weakness that had the catalytic affect."

Sascha tilted her head slightly to the side. "In what way?"

"You were seen as weak, but you got out. Maybe now, others who never imagined they might beat the Psy Council . . . maybe now, they think that they can, too."

"I never thought of my perceived 'flaw' as a positive."

Talin shrugged. "I'm no expert—"

"But you are very good at picking up and reading nuances of emotion," Sascha interrupted. "Who knows, perhaps you had an empath in your family tree."

Talin shook her head. "I'm human and I'm happy with that."

"You should be," Sascha said, eyes beginning to refill with stars. "Without humans, the Psy and changelings would have destroyed each other eons ago, Silence or not."

"That's what Clay said." She smiled at the memory of his tenderness, even as fear twisted up her gut. A sharp whistle made her look up. Dorian blew her a kiss. She scowled, but she was charmed. "That man is too gorgeous for his own good."

"He's different when you're around, you know."

"I don't understand."

"He flirts with you."

Talin colored. "He flirts with you, too."

"I'm his alpha's mate. I'm still not quite sure what that means to the unmated males, but it gives me a unique status in terms of what they expect and what *they'll* accept from me, affectionwise."

"He doesn't seem hesitant about touching," Talin ventured, having learned how important tactile contact was to changelings. As it was to her. To her surprise, she craved touch, could laze there like a cat herself and let Clay stroke her all day long. The image made her body melt.

"No, but this is the first time I've seen him act the way he does with you—he treats Brenna like a sister, Rina, too."

"What about Mercy and Tammy?"

"Mercy's not a woman," Sascha said, then laughed at Talin's look. "Not to Lucas and the others. She's a sentinel before anything else, and she'd be the first one to remind you of that. As for Tammy, Dorian's known her since childhood, but you, he treats like a woman. All that charm . . ." She shook her head. "I had no idea he could be like that."

"He knows I'm with Clay," Talin felt compelled to point out. "It's not anything—"

"Oh, no, that's not what I meant," Sascha interrupted. "Dorian would never poach, and if anyone else tried, he'd shred them on Clay's behalf, no thanks required."

Talin grinned at the cardinal's arch tone. "That's what I thought. Maybe you're just seeing a new side of him?"

"I think you're right." Sascha put down her mug. "I came into his life at a time when he was pure anger—after he lost his sister. I never knew him as he was before. Maybe part of that Dorian is coming back."

"He hasn't stopped being angry." Talin watched that golden head as he bent to pick up one of the twins and throw him over his shoulder.

"No." There was profound sadness in Sascha's voice, until

Talin could almost feel the pain of it in her own heart. Then the cardinal shook her head. "But enough about Dorian. He'll probably snarl at us both for daring to care." A small smile. "How about you tell me what's bothering you?"

Talin wasn't surprised at the other woman's perceptiveness. "I'm mated to Clay."

"I know."

"How can that have happened?" she asked, frantic. "I'm sick and—" And she'd been selfish. "I wanted him to love me, but I never intended to kill him."

"When I was going through the mating dance with Lucas," Sascha said, sympathy in every syllable, "Tammy told me the process is different for every couple. What does seem consistent though is that the female has to accept the bond in some way for it to come into being."

"But I didn't! I would have never willingly put him in that kind of danger!"

"Um, Talin, this is kind of personal, but Lucas says you smell of Clay."

Talin blushed, put down her coffee. "So? We're intimate, but obviously sex isn't all it takes."

"Well . . ."

"Tell me the truth. I promise I won't jump down your throat again and accuse you of invading my privacy." She was starting to understand that Sascha couldn't block everything—because her gift was in her skin, in her blood, in her every breath.

"Sex isn't everything, but in your case, sex is intertwined with the core of who you are. I'm guessing you were hurt with it—it was a damaging thread, but a thread that ran through your life."

"You're saying having sex with Clay was an acceptance on my part?"

"It wasn't just sex, was it? I don't know what happened but whatever it was, the mating bond took it as a resounding 'yes.' "

Talin thought back to the first time she and Clay had made love—yes, made love, not had sex—to that moment when she'd felt the inexplicable vibration in her soul. That night, she had surrendered to Clay with every part of her. She had trusted him with her soul. But she had never meant to steal his. "Oh, God," she whispered. "It'll destroy him if I die."

"So fight to live."

Talin had already made that choice. "We've scheduled appointments with medical people Tammy recommended." She would try, would fight, but she also knew that a dying brain was not an easy thing to fix. The best the doctors might be able to do was give her a little more time. "Is there anything you can do? I'll let you into my mind if you want." Her pride was nothing compared to missing out on a lifetime with Clay.

Sascha shook her head, her concern unhidden. "Your shields are impenetrable and so instinctive, they're nothing you can manipulate. I think it's going to take years for you to let them down with anyone but Clay."

"It was worth a try." She stared out at the children, fighting back tears. She wondered what Clay and her babies would have looked like. Her throat threatened to close up and this time, it wasn't anything deadly, but a painful knot of emotion.

"That doesn't mean I won't keep trying to find ways to help," Sascha said, jaw a determined line. "You're Pack and DarkRiver never abandons its own."

Talin had once envied Clay that sense of ultimate acceptance but now found herself unsure. "I'm not exactly good at the family stuff."

Sascha laughed and it was a joyous, infectious sound. "Welcome to the club."

"I'm an idiot." She felt her lips curve, despite the fear inside her soul. If she died, Clay wouldn't make it. She knew he wouldn't. It wasn't anything either of them could change and it had nothing to do with courage. They were simply too deeply linked. If one fell, so would the other.

The unfairness of it made her want to scream bloody murder—she and her beautiful leopard had paid their dues a hundred times over. "How did you do it?" she asked Sascha. "How did you learn to be in a family?" She had to learn, too. Pack was important to Clay, and whatever time they had left, she wanted him happy.

"There's not much choice with these cats," Sascha responded. "They have a way of accepting you that's pretty hard to resist."

Something bit Talin's bare toe. Yelping, she looked down. "Good Lord, how adorable are you?" Reaching down, she picked up the leopard cub.

Sascha leaned over and kissed his nose. "Hello, Roman."

The cub butted his head against Sascha, but seemed content to remain in Talin's arms. Stroking her hand down the cub's fur, she felt him purr as he lay there. Her and Clay's child would have been able to shift, she thought, would have had fur as soft. Such intense emotion seared through her that it hurt. "Did you get tired, baby?"

A nod of his head.

Amazed at the beauty of this creature she held, she looked up and met Sascha's eyes. "Like I said," the cardinal murmured, "they make it very hard not to be family."

CHAPTER 46

An hour later, having talked it over with Clay, Talin made sure Jonquil was included in the conference call they placed to Dev. Noor was engrossed in a board game upstairs, having become fast friends with Julian and Roman. Dorian had volunteered to continue babysitting. He seemed to have developed a soft spot for the shy little girl.

Good, she thought, with painful practicality. That meant Noor would be loved no matter what. As for Jon . . . he'd be okay. He wasn't as trusting as Noor, but his spirit was full of a warrior bravery she knew he didn't see. But she did—because Clay had been the same at that age. That thought in mind, she reached out and rubbed Jon's hair. It was now military short, the stunning white-gold dyed black.

He'd taken a seat on the floor, his back to the armchair where she sat. Clay was standing behind her, arms braced on the same armchair. She smiled. She was happy at this moment and she gloried in the sensation. Everyone she cared for—even Max—was safe. "You have any questions?" she asked Jon.

He leaned against her leg. "It's weird to think we have Psy blood. It makes us mutts, I guess."

She laughed. "Hey, watch who you call a mutt."

Smiling, he wrapped one arm around her leg. Clay tugged at her ponytail and when she looked up, he bent down to kiss her. One touch and he was in her soul, in her deepest, most secret heart. *I love you,* she mouthed.

His response was a nip to her lower lip that promised all sorts of things once they were alone. Another burst of happiness taking root in her heart, she looked back down—to find Jon watching her and Clay, those amazing violet eyes carefully neutral. "You'll need contact lenses," she said. "At least for a while." His eyes were too unique.

His expression didn't change. "Sure."

Recognizing that his protective walls had gone up, and able to guess why—he was afraid of losing her to Clay, to DarkRiver—she gentled her voice. Jon hadn't ever had anyone stick by him, didn't quite understand that he, too, was now part of the pack. "About being mutts," she said, "the truth is, I never knew who my parents were. At least now, I know something of my genetic history."

The Shine records had listed the name of her mother, though they had been unable to trace her father. Talin had no intention of making contact with the woman. She had no need to chase love, not when she was adored by a predator who would take on the world for her. But . . . "I think knowing is better than not knowing, don't you?"

"Even if what we learn isn't something we want to know?"

"Haven't you ever wondered why you can do the things you can do?"

He shrugged. "I can't do shit."

"Watch your language." Clay kept his tone quiet but infused it with steel. He knew teenage boys. They needed Talin's kind of softness, but they also needed discipline.

Jon's spine straightened. "Or you'll throw me out?"

Clay saw echoes of himself in that angry pride. "No, we're like the mob. Once you're in, you can't get out. Try it and see."

The boy's eyes widened, then shifted to Talin. "Is he joking?"

"I don't think so," she whispered. "They're a bit possessive." Her words were for Jon but Clay knew her mischievous tone was for him. "Would you really leave Noor?"

The boy shook his head. "How come you want me?" he asked Clay point-blank. "I'm a piece of sh—" He paused at Clay's growl. "I mean I'm a troublemaker."

"So was I," Clay said. "I came into the pack when I was eighteen."

"But you're a sentinel."

"Being a sentinel isn't hereditary. Earn your place and no one will deny you." It had been eight months into his stay with DarkRiver that he'd truly accepted his new way of life. That was the day he had walked out with Luc, Nate, Vaughn, and several others and destroyed a bloodthirsty pack called the ShadowWalkers. No one had made his acceptance hinge on blood. It was the leopard who had decided—this was his new family and he'd do whatever it took to keep them safe.

"What if—" Jon paused. "Kit told me about pack hierarchy. I can't shift into animal form. Guess that means I'll never get a high rank, huh?"

Clay raised an eyebrow. "Ask Dorian."

"He can't shift?"

"No."

"But he's a sentinel, too!"

"Exactly." He left the kid that information to chew on.

Talin had remained silent throughout the conversation, knowing the importance of what was going on. When Jon nodded and returned to his previous position, his head against her knee, she relaxed.

That was when Sascha and Lucas walked into the room. It had been decided the alpha pair needed to hear this, since by accepting Jon and Noor, they were allying themselves to Shine by default.

Clay stirred behind her, his hand sliding down to cup the side of her neck in a hold as protective as it was possessive. She swallowed, reached up to close her hand over his wrist. His fingers played over her skin. "I already input the code," he told Lucas.

Nodding, Lucas pressed the Enter key and sat down in the other armchair. Sascha perched on the arm, leaning into her mate, who slipped an arm around her waist, his hand lying loosely on her hip. It was an easy pose, the pose of a couple that had been together long enough to have created their own patterns, their own secret language.

She wanted that with Clay, she thought, would do everything in her power to gain it. Pulling his hand away from her neck, she pressed a kiss to his palm. He leaned down until his lips were against her ear. "Behave, Tally. Or are you calling in your winnings?"

The husky reminder made her grin. Releasing his hand, she sighed in pleasure when he pushed aside the neckline of her V-necked sweater to close it over her bare shoulder. That was when the comm screen cleared to reveal Dev's face.

"Sorry for the delay. Had a last-minute situation spring up in Kansas."

Anger rolled through her like fire. "Not another abduction?"

"No." His eyes looked over her head. "I think that problem has been permanently resolved."

"No," Clay disagreed. "We need to cut this off at the root—the Council. Long as they hold power, civilians will keep dying."

Talin felt Sascha jerk, but the cardinal nodded. "Yes, they have to be stopped."

"You won't get any argument from me." Dev shoved a hand through his hair and glanced at Jon. "I've organized a place for you at one of our prep schools. You've got more Psy blood than most—you need to learn about the Psy side of your lineage."

Talin took the lead when Jon maintained an obstinate silence. "Send me the information and we'll look it over." At Dev's nod, she took a deep breath, drawing the scent of Clay into her lungs. "Now, tell us everything we don't know about the Forgotten."

Dev's handsome face shadowed over. "That's a big ask."

"But necessary," Clay said from behind her.

"Yes." He paused as if gathering his thoughts. "In short, a hundred or so years ago, when Silence was voted into being, people who disagreed began to search for a way out. It had to be done in secret because dissidents had already begun to disappear."

When no one interrupted, he continued, "In the end, the only solution the rebels could come up with was to drop out en masse and attempt to link to each other in the seconds before psychic death. They hoped their gamble would lead to the spontaneous creation of a new psychic network. If it didn't, the defectors were prepared to die." The ruthless lines of Dev's face lit from within. "But they didn't. And the Shadow-Net was born."

"This is extraordinary," Sascha said. "I was a Councilor's daughter and I knew nothing of the Forgotten or their Shadow-Net."

"Not surprising. The Council would like to wipe us from the face of the planet."

"Can you still accept renegades?" Sascha asked and Talin realized how important the answer was for those who remained imprisoned by Silence.

Dev shook his head. "We could for the first generation after defection. Some people dropped out later. Most had children they couldn't bear to leave earlier."

Sascha gave a slow nod, her hand gripping Lucas's so tight that her dark gold skin had turned white over bone. "And now?"

"Everyone in the ShadowNet is of heavily mixed blood. Over time, the psychic pathways have shifted, become unique in a way that probably rules out the successful integration of a more 'pure' Psy and vice versa."

"Did the Council realize what had happened to the defectors?" Talin asked, trying to wrap her head around the implications of Dev's revelations.

"Yes. But since the ShadowNet was so small, and they were busy dealing with the aftermath of Silence, they didn't pay much attention. They figured the defectors would intermarry with the other races and their Psy blood would eventually diminish."

"That didn't happen?"

"It did and it didn't." He leaned back in his chair, his skin gilded a rich bronze by the sun lancing in through the window behind him. "Every so often, the result of a pregnancy between two descendants of the Forgotten is a child with remarkable Psy powers. These powerful births are exceptionally rare, but like Jon, many children of the Forgotten carry some functional or latent power. And the Council doesn't like anyone on the outside who might be able to challenge them on the psychic plane."

Talin thought back to one of their earlier conversations. "You said the Council started hunting you a few generations back. Is that why?"

A sharp nod. "The murders began as soon as Silence took a solid hold. Those descendants who didn't need the link to the ShadowNet—not all the kids did—were ordered to scatter and stay scattered."

"But the Net was too small to allow those who needed the biofeedback to go far?" Sascha asked.

"Yes. It might have led to psychic starvation. Shine was formed by those who remained in the ShadowNet. It's only in recent years that we've become powerful enough to chance tracing the others. We've focused our efforts on the marginalized children, those who need us most."

"Why?" Jon's tone was on the wrong side of insolent. "You might as well have pinned a target on our backs."

Dev's lips thinned. "We search because some of you need our help. Not all are 'gifted.' Some are cursed—we found one child dying because she needed the link to the ShadowNet, but her brain had lost the ability to search for it instinctively." His jaw tensed, eyes dark with fury.

"Another, a teenage boy, is a midrange telepath, but he was diagnosed as schizophrenic because he kept hearing voices and, according to his family tree, he's one hundred percent human. Those who scattered wiped their pasts so effectively that sometimes their own descendants don't know who they are."

It was too much information to process, but Talin had one further question. "What about changeling-Psy children? Why doesn't Shine help them?"

Dev shot a wry look at Lucas. "The packs closed ranks and disappeared the known Psy families so well, we don't have a hope in hell of tracing them. That secrecy probably saved their lives—then and now." Pure anger threaded through his voice. "What we are, what we've become, it's nothing like the Psy. We don't want to grab their power, but the Psy Council sees only evil because it is only evil."

CHAPTER 47

Hours later, Clay held Tally as they lay spooned on the futon they had made up on the first floor. The bed was taken—they'd brought Jon and Noor home with them. The boy hadn't said anything, but it had been obvious he wanted to be near Talin. And Noor went where Jon did. "They're asleep," he said.

Tally put her arm over his. "You can hear them from down here?"

"Uh-huh." Little Noor was snuggled up on a mattress on the second floor, while Jon had been given the bedroom, over his protests.

"Noor seemed happy with sleeping alone." She ran her foot over his calf, the affectionate act making him purr. "I figured she'd be scared—that's why I didn't want her at the top of the aerie."

"I think it's because she's in the middle. Hard for anyone to get to her."

"You're probably right. Jon's already so protective of her."

"Hmm." He kissed the curve of her neck. "We keep an eye on them they'll be okay. Look at us," he teased, "we tried damn hard to mess up something wonderful, but we made it."

She made a noise of assent, but said nothing else.

His leopard scented her quiet distress. "Baby, I can't read your mind. But I know you're sad."

"I wish . . . I wish I'd waited for you," she said without warning, her anguish so raw it crashed into him with the force of a tidal wave. "I know we're okay now, but I wish I could wipe out the past. I wish Orrin hadn't tainted me before we ever met."

"Don't." His voice came out harsh when he wanted to be tender for her. "Don't hurt that way. And don't you dare consider yourself anything less than perfect." God, she was sunshine and heart, light and beauty. How could she imagine he thought anything else? "You are the most beautiful thing I've ever dared to touch."

Her hand fisted against his. "But what about what *I* did? You must think about it," she insisted, voice thick with tears she refused to shed. "You must get angry sometimes."

"I did. Before." He'd been a fool, unable to see the truth. "Before I realized that you're mine and you always will be. No one, nothing, can come between us." Not even death. If she went, he would follow.

"How can you forget?" she asked in her stubborn, determined way, the same way she loved him. "You were so mad—"

"It wasn't easy," he admitted. "But I'm not stupid. I finally realized that what you did, the life you led, was what brought you back to me. If you'd become a good little Larkspur, you'd probably have married a farmer by now."

She gasped, obviously horrified. "I would not."

"No." His tone turned serious. "Because you were mine. You always have been."

"You're not angry anymore?" It came out hesitant, searching.

"How can I be angry with the other half of my soul?" he asked, his tone so tender it tore little pieces out of her heart. "I have a temper, baby, and I know I fucking brood. But even if I act pissed, even if I snarl, it doesn't mean I love you any less. Your soul shines, Tally, and I'm so damn glad it shines for me."

She felt a tear slide down her cheek at the unforgiving honesty of his statement. Somehow, he had achieved the impossible, made her feel young, innocent to the depths of her soul.

"You sure can talk pretty when you put your mind to it." Her voice came out husky. "I am so glad you're mine—I know you'll always be there for me, that if I call, you'll come."

His arms grew tight and she knew he'd understood. Never again would she wonder if he would one day leave her. His devotion humbled her, made her determined to love him until his own scars were nothing but forgotten memories. Then he said, "Forever, Tally," and her heart broke.

"Clay, what if—"

"Don't say it." He squeezed her hard. "We'll talk about it after we see the specialists. The first appointment is tomorrow."

She bit his arm in a light reprimand, hearing his unspoken pain in the way he refused to discuss the subject. "Don't you dare shift again," she ordered, wondering if one lifetime, no matter how long, would ever be enough to love Clay all the ways she wanted to love him. "We can't ignore the fact that I'm sick."

"You don't smell sick to me," he snapped.

Neither of them spoke for a second, then they both spoke at once.

"I don't?"

"What the fuck?"

She wiggled in his arms. "Lemme turn."

He loosened his hold enough that she could turn around and shimmy up to take a face-to-face position with him. "You said I smelled wrong before."

"Yeah, you did." He frowned and nuzzled at her, this time to confirm his finding. His tongue flicked out to taste her pulse. "It's gone. Nothing, not even under the surface."

Talin's eyes were huge as he met her gaze again. "Remission?"

"No, this is deeper." His beast was convinced of it, took another sip of her scent to confirm. "The decay is gone."

"Like I'm getting better?" Her hands clenched on his shoulders. "No, this kind of disease doesn't disappear on its own. It's a degenerative condition."

Clay's beast was roaring at him in agonized frustration, telling him to *remember*. "Remember what?" he muttered.

"Clay?"

He was concentrating too hard to reply. It was something

he'd heard, something important, something the cat had understood, though the man— "Hell!" He jerked upright without warning.

Talin bit off a cry of surprise as she sprawled off him and onto her back.

"Sorry," he muttered, reaching for and pulling on his jeans.

She got up behind him, dressed in that strawberry ice cream slip that drove him half-crazy. "Are you going somewhere?"

"Here." He threw her the lacy robe thing that came with the outfit.

She shrugged into it, eyes wary. "You okay, darling? Have too many beers with the boys maybe?"

He smacked her lightly on the bottom. "Smart-ass."

"Don't you forget it." Her smile had the power to knock his heart right out of him. "Why are we getting decent?"

He found himself petting the curve he'd smacked, pulling up the slip so he could touch bare skin. Smooth. Hot. *His.* "I don't want Luc to see you naked."

"Stop that," she breathed out as his fingers ventured south, dipped. "Or don't, I'm easy."

He kissed her hard on the lips before pulling down her slip and closing the robe tight. "Be good." God, he wanted to play with her like this for decades to come. She'd drive him crazy and he'd enjoy every minute of it.

"Why?" Her eyes narrowed in puzzlement until he stopped in front of the communications panel. "We're making a call?" At the same time, she grabbed the shirt he'd flung off earlier that night. "Put it on."

"Trust me, I'm not that pretty." But he shrugged into it before pushing in the code for the call.

"If no one's bleeding, I don't want to know," Lucas growled, audio only.

"Sascha there?" Clay asked, wrapping both arms around Talin and pulling her back against his chest. "Or did she finally come to her senses and dump your ass?"

"Clay, have you lost your mind?" Talin glared at him, voice whisper-soft.

But Lucas turned on the visual feed. His hair was rumpled, his shirt on as haphazardly as Clay's, and it was obvious he hadn't been sleeping. "I swear this had better be good. Do you know what I was about to tas—"

A feminine hand clamped over his mouth, then dropped away as Sascha looked over his shoulder, hair curling wildly around her face. "Clay?"

"Dev Santos said something tonight about a girl dying because she wasn't getting the feedback her part-Psy brain needed." Hope weaved through Clay's voice with tensile strength. "Something about not knowing how to link to a psychic network."

Sascha was nodding before he finished, her eyes going from night-sky to obsidian in a single blink. "You think—"

"Yeah," he finished for her. "She doesn't smell sick. Luc?"

Lucas's facial markings became more defined as he frowned in thought. "You're right. I smelled it that first night we met, but nothing set off my beast today."

Talin stood frozen in the circle of Clay's arms, trying not to hope. If she didn't hope, the disappointment wouldn't tear her to pieces. But she failed. "Can you check that?"

"I don't know," Sascha said. "I can't get into your mind, but I'll try on the Web of Stars—that's the network that connects all the sentinels and their mates to Lucas. I'm contacting Faith, too. She's not as good with the Web yet, but she's had a lot of experience looking for hidden patterns." Closing her eyes, she seemed to melt into Lucas, her bare arms wrapping around the alpha from behind.

Talin turned and half buried her face in Clay's chest. "It can't be true. My Psy DNA is a joke. Three percent, remember?"

"Shine was unable to track down your father," he said, confusing her for a second, "but what if *both* your parents were long-removed descendants of the Forgotten? What if they each carried a single dormant gene that came together in you? Maybe that gene *is* the three percent."

"A million-to-one chance."

"Not necessarily," he said. "Silence has been around for just over a hundred years. Before that, anything went. A lot of humans and changelings had Psy relatives pre-Silence—the pool for dormant genes is wider than the descendants of the Forgotten."

"But the specialists," she said, playing devil's advocate

because she wanted this too much, "they did genetic tests, found no markers."

"Because they weren't looking for the right thing," he said, not budging. "Remember what Santos said about a kid's family thinking he was full human, so no one looked for a Psy cause?"

He was fighting for her, fighting so damn hard. "I love you," she whispered.

He stroked his hand down her back. "Yep, you do."

"You're supposed to say it back," she said, pretending to be offended because the silliness kept the fear/hope at bay.

"Why?" He scowled down at her. "You know you're my heartbeat."

The blunt words cut her off at the knees. Reaching up, she kissed him, uncaring that the other couple might be watching. But when they parted, she glanced at the screen to find Sascha's eyes still closed and Lucas focusing on her. "I wonder what she sees."

"Faith told me once—our minds are like stars, each one connected ultimately to Lucas. That's why Sascha calls it a web."

"And I'm in there because of my bond with you." It gave her a sense of peace to say that. "I'm glad we're mated," she said, speaking the truth for the first time. "I know that's selfish, but I'm glad."

"Good, because there's no getting out."

It was at that moment that Sascha's eyes flicked open. Talin was startled to see the blackness cascading with color. The wonder of it astonished her, made her want to reach out and touch the screen in delight.

But what Sascha had to say eclipsed even those magnificent eyes. "Clay was right."

Her knees would have collapsed had Clay not been holding her upright. "What?" she croaked out. "Did you see something?"

"It was hard," Sascha said, her smile growing so wide it was in danger of cracking her face. "Your mind is different—we thought it was because you were human, and we were mostly right, but our preconception kept us from seeing the whole truth. You don't suck in the biofeedback the same way a

Psy does. The flows aren't obvious. It's like"—she paused her rapid-fire explanation—"like you need a misty rain, while we need a downpour. Do you see?"

Talin was so dazed, she had trouble formulating speech. "Not enough to die immediately without, but not quite right unless I have it?"

"Yes!" Sascha's expression glowed with excitement. "What we saw around you is a slight, very slight, draw on the biofeedback. Your brain is taking in what it needs through your link to Clay and therefore to the Web." Her eyes sharpened. "Are you feeling much better?"

She didn't have to consider the question. "Yes. I can think so clearly. Ever since—" Blood rushed out of her face. "Clay's headache."

"That explains it," Sascha said, smile not dimming. "There had to be a strong draw at some point, because, if we go by your symptoms, your brain was well into starvation mode. I didn't notice a shift in the Web that would have alerted me to the truth, but that's because you took it directly from Clay."

Terror spread through Talin's veins. "Did I hurt him?"

"No, no, it's like a blood donation," Sascha assured her. "If you'd been taking in that much constantly, it *would* have hurt him."

"Can it kill?" Talin asked, mouth full of cotton wool.

Sascha's eyes grew poignant. "Yes. For the PsyNet born, yes. But you don't need as much. You would have simply made Clay very tired. As it is, you only took a big bite"—she smiled—"from him once, and he's had time to regenerate. With the bond settled in the Web, you're soaking it in from the general extraneous buildup, like me and Faith. It harms no one."

"Okay." Now that she knew Clay was fine, it was all she could say, her mind numb.

"Clay," Lucas said, "how about we pick this up tomorrow?" His eyes were intent on Talin. "I think your Tally needs time to recover, and my Sascha darling needs to work off some of her excitement."

There was a gasp and a chuckle from someone, but Talin was barely aware of it. As she was barely aware of Clay ending the call, peeling off her robe, and dropping it to the floor along with his own clothes. But when he kissed her, it was as if a switch had been thrown inside her. She came to life and what exuberant life it was. She laughed and they played and when it was over, she lay with her head on his heart, and thought about forever.

CHAPTER 48

In the PsyNet, the third emergency session of the Psy Council was taking place.

"We can't have a repeat of the situation we had last year with Enrique," Shoshanna said, referring to the Councilor whose death had led to Kaleb's ascension. "We need to swear in a new Councilor before anyone starts questioning the true circumstances of Marshall's death."

"Yes," Tatiana agreed. "Though the populace does seem to be accepting the explanation of accidental death very well."

"There's one more thing we need to discuss," Ming interrupted. "We may have a situation with Ashaya Aleine."

"She's controlled," Kaleb said, brushing the issue aside. "We have her son, correct?"

"Yes. However, I'm not sure how long that's going to hold her."

"But it does for now," Nikita responded. "Shoshanna's right—we need a new Councilor fast."

"Agreed," Ming replied. "But unlike with Kaleb, there's no one ready to step into the role. We considered Gia Khan in the last round, but she's since proven weak, unable to stop unrest in her local region."

A taut silence.

"I have a suggestion," Kaleb said. "He was once a Council candidate, is now powerful enough that he defies us, and he's strong enough to take on Marshall's responsibilities."

"You're talking about Anthony Kyriakus," Shoshanna said. "The man is a thorn in our side, but you could be right. Make him Council and we gain access to his considerable resources and business network."

"He turned down a Council seat once before," Nikita reminded them. "He may not accept now."

Kaleb considered his next words with care. "After the confirmation of Marshall's death, I had a discussion with Anthony."

"Without Council authorization?"

"Give me credit, Ming," Kaleb responded. "There are ways to gauge interest without saying anything of the least note."

"Your conclusion?" Tatiana asked.

"He may be willing."

Shoshanna's mental star swirled in thought. "He has considerable contact with changelings—he's still subcontracting work to his daughter, Faith."

"That," Nikita said, "could be another advantage. He has to have gained a lot of knowledge about the cats."

"A good point," Ming acceded. "I have no reservations against him as a candidate."

"I have one," Henry said. "Like Nikita, he also has a daughter who has dropped out of the Net. Will that weaken the Council's image?"

"In my opinion, no," Kaleb responded. "He's already proven he can hold us at bay. He has more businesses backing him than any of us."

"I agree," Shoshanna said. "I vote yes."

One by one, the others all agreed.

A day later, Anthony Kyriakus, leader of the influential NightStar Group and father of the most powerful F-Psy in the world, accepted their offer.

At the same time, Ashaya Aleine unfolded a plain pen and paper note hidden inside the latest batch of equipment she had requested. Keenan would be flown in for his next scheduled visit, but the one after that would be by car.

She hoped the man who had held a gun on her the night she'd set Jonquil Duchslaya and Noor Hassan free had told the truth. Because they would have only one chance. Ming was watching her. She had overplayed her hand, and now the Councilor was inches away from enforcing her obedience through the most vicious of mental violations.

EPILOGUE

Two days after the night that had given her forever, Talin met with the specialists at Shine and they put her through a rigorous series of tests that confirmed Clay's hunch and Sascha's diagnosis.

"Your need for the feedback is so small," Dr. Herriford exclaimed, "it wasn't picked up on the initial tests we run on every Shine child." He shoved a hand through his hair, making the bright orange stuff stick up in untidy tufts. "We're going to have to redo that testing. If you slipped through, so will others." His distress was open. "We'll need to start doing periodic checks as students age, too, rather than just the intake scans."

Talin had every intention of helping reboot the system, but first she wanted solid answers. "So I don't have to worry about any of the symptoms?" No more fugues, no more having her sense of choice taken from her. Her hand curled around Clay's, held on tight.

"Everything you've told me," the doc said, glancing at his small electronic notepad, "the fugues, the lost memories, even the mysterious allergic reaction, they're all symptoms of Process Degeneration."

"Doc," Clay said, cutting to the heart of the matter, "is she going to be okay?"

Herriford beamed. "Whatever you've done to address the feedback issue—and if you changelings ever decide to share, please let me know—"

Clay growled.

"Right." The doctor smiled on, undaunted. "I'm happy to say that Ms. McKade is in perfect health. No Forgotten weirdness—you wouldn't believe the things I see."

She jumped off the examining table. "Thanks, Dr. Herriford."

The doctor's handshake was warm, solid. "By the way, did Dev have a chance to catch you up on everything?"

Talin shook her head. "We got the CliffNotes version. Why?"

"Well, this isn't common knowledge," Herriford said, "but Dev told me to be honest with you. You know about the power discrepancy?"

She nodded. "A rare few descendants have a massive amount."

"Yeah, but that's not the interesting thing." The doctor's eyes were sparkling. "These kids, they're not being born with a lesser version of Psy abilities, they're being born with completely *new* abilities."

"How is that possible?" She glanced at Clay and suddenly had her answer. "Mixed blood. The genetics are intermingling and creating something new." Something beautiful.

The doctor nodded. "There were instances of such spontaneous abilities appearing in the PsyNet pre-Silence—our theory is that these changes stopped because the Council has a firm line on eliminating any mutations from the gene pool."

"But that's not happening with the Forgotten."

"No." The doctor's smile grew. "What we're now seeing are the results of a long-term genetic shift. In some cases, it's as if the Psy genes express themselves by intensifying the bearers' *human* strengths." He gave Clay a pleading look. "Are you sure you can't find me some changeling—"

"No."

The doctor sighed. "As I was saying—these new abilities

aren't Psy or human but a mesh of both, perhaps even all three where the individual has changeling blood as well." Another hopeful—but futile—glance at Clay. "Very, very exciting."

Talin scowled. "And all I got is this stupid need for feedback."

The doctor winced. "I sympathize. Technically, I'm twenty percent Psy. But in terms of my physical and mental abilities, I'm one hundred percent human. That's the good thing about Shine—we don't discriminate between descendants. Lots of mostly human kids pass through these doors."

At least that definitively answered Talin's question of why she'd been chosen. "Good. But I still think I should have superpowers to compensate." When she'd finally calmed down enough to process everything, her need for biofeedback had made her feel like a vampire or succubus.

She'd gotten all teary about it to Clay . . . until the idiot male had started laughing so hard he couldn't talk. He'd bought her a pair of "genuine vampire fangs" that day. She was smiling at the memory when Clay wrapped an arm around her neck. "What are you talking about, Tally? You have special powers."

"I do?"

"Yeah, you have the power to bring me to my knees."

That made her blush. Then it made her kiss him.

"Isla," she said that night.

"What?"

"That's what I want to name our child if it's a girl."

A heartbeat of silence. "How about Pinocchio for a boy?"

"No," she said, scowling but aware the comment was his version of "thank you." Isla had been broken, but she had loved her son and Clay had loved her back. Talin would honor that. "You don't get to pick if you're going to sentence our poor child to a life of humiliation."

"Brat."

"Bully," she said, smiling lips grazing his as he lifted himself over her, his body a protective wall. "How about Fabien?"

"Sissy name. Even I can do better."

"So?"

"Joshua."

She smiled. "I like it. Joshua and Isla."

"How many kids are we having again?"

"Lots."

"I guess I can always add more rooms to the lair." He ran his lips over hers in a quick caress. "Anything you want."

"In that case, I want you." She melted into the possessive heat of his kiss, the magic of his love. It was nice belonging to a leopard who would never let you go, she thought as logic surrendered to emotion. It was perfection.

A few hours later, Sascha woke to the awareness that something was happening in the Web of Stars. Snuggling into Lucas's warmth, she opened her mind's eye and looked at the strands of light that made up the Web. It took her several minutes to realize that the bonds had become exponentially stronger, the resulting feedback well above any projected rate. Startled, she checked and rechecked for the reason why, but the only difference was Talin's vibrant, and very much human, presence.

And she understood.

The Web of Stars was now fed by the thoughts and dreams of all three races. Their world was a triumvirate, and for the first time in a hundred years that triumvirate was complete on the psychic level. Sascha didn't know what that meant, but she knew it was a good thing.

She slipped back into sleep with a smile.

Turn the page for a preview of
the next paranormal romance
by Nalini Singh
Hostage to
Pleasure
Coming soon from
Berkley Sensation!

In the end, the retraction was deadly simple. The sniper had been given the precise coordinates the car would travel along the sleepy rural road, knew exactly how many people were in the vehicle, where the child was sitting. According to his information, the child was blindfolded, but the sniper still didn't like doing this with an innocent in the vehicle.

However, if left in the hands of his captors, the child would become the unwitting instrument of the worst kind of evil. And then he would die. The sniper didn't kill lightly, but to keep a child safe, he would do much worse.

"Go," the sniper said into the air, his earpiece picking up and transmitting the sound to those below.

A slow-moving truck veered out of the opposite lane without warning, crashing into the side of the target car with a smooth expertise that forced the vehicle off the road but did little damage to the people inside—the sniper and his team couldn't afford to harm the child. More than that, they *refused* to harm the child. But it wasn't the child the sniper found in his sights as soon as the car came to a halt.

A single precise shot and the windshield shattered.

The driver and his adult passenger were dead within the

next two seconds, a clean bullet hole in the center of their foreheads. The bullets were designed not to exit, thereby minimizing danger to the backseat passengers.

An instant later, the rear doors slid back and two men jumped out, one of whom stared straight up at the sniper's location high in the spreading branches of an ancient pine. The sniper felt a blunt force graze his mind, but the guard had sent his telepathic strike too late. A bullet lodged in the Psy male's throat with fatal accuracy even as he focused his power. The fourth man went down with a silent bullet through his chest, having failed to locate the sniper's partner.

The sniper was already moving by the time the last body hit the ground, his rifle in hand. He left behind no trace of who he was, and when he reached the car, he touched nothing. "Did they get out a psychic alert?" he asked the unseen watcher.

"Likely. Road's still clear, but we need to move fast—reinforcements will be here in minutes if the Council has teleport-capable Tks on hand."

The sniper looked through the open doors and saw the final remaining passenger. A tiny boy, barely four and a half years old. He wasn't only blindfolded. His ears had been plugged and his hands tied behind his back. Near-total sensory deprivation.

The sniper growled and became a man named Dorian again, his cold control falling away to expose the deeply protective nature of his beast. He might have been born lacking the changeling ability to shift into animal form, but he carried the leopard within. And that leopard was enraged by the callous treatment meted out to this defenseless child. Reaching in, he gathered the stiff, scared boy in his arms, his hold far gentler than anyone would've believed. "I have him."

Another vehicle appeared out of nowhere. This one was sleek, silver, nothing like the now-abandoned truck, though the driver was the same man. "Let's go," Clay said, his eyes a flat green.

Getting into the back seat, Dorian ripped off his face mask and put away the gun before cutting through the boy's bindings with the pocketknife he carried everywhere. Blood slicked his fingers and he drew back so fast, he sliced open a thin line on his own palm. But when he looked closer, he realized he hadn't accidentally cut the child—the boy had been struggling against his bonds for what must've been hours. His wrists were raw.

Biting off a brutal oath, he slid the knife back into his jeans and took out the plugs from the boy's ears, removing his blindfold a second later. Unexpected blue gray eyes looked into his, startling in a face with skin the color of aged gold, a dusty brown that almost glowed. "Keenan."

The boy didn't say anything, his face preternaturally calm. So young and he'd already begun the road to Silence, begun to learn to suppress his emotions and become a good, robotic Psy. But his calm facade aside, he was too young to hide his blinding fear from the changeling who watched him; the sharp bite of it was insulting to Dorian's senses. Children were not meant to be bound and used as pawns. It was not a fair fight.

The car came to a stop. The opposite passenger-side door opened and then Judd was sliding inside, his gun strapped to his back. "We have to do it now or they'll track him through the PsyNet." The other man's eyes were a cold brown when he stripped off his own mask, but his hands were careful as he touched the boy's face. "Keenan, we have to cut the Net link."

The boy stiffened, leaned into Dorian. "No."

Dorian put an arm around his fragile, breakable body. "Be brave. Your mom wants you safe."

Those astonishing eyes looked up at him. "Will you kill me?"

Dorian looked to Judd. "It gonna hurt?"

A slight nod.

Dorian held Keenan's hand, the boy's blood mixing with his own where he'd sliced open his palm. "It'll hurt like a bitch, but then you'll be okay."

Keenan's eyes widened at the vulgarity, exactly as Dorian had wanted. In that moment of distraction, Judd closed his eyes. Dorian knew the Psy male was working furiously to unlock the child's shields and get inside his mind—so he could cut Keenan's link to the PsyNet, the psychic network that connected every Psy on the planet, except for the renegades. Bare seconds later, the boy screamed and it was a sound of such brutal suffering that Dorian almost killed Judd for it. The sound cut off as abruptly as it had begun and Keenan slumped into Dorian's arms, unconscious.

"Jesus," Clay said from the front, merging onto a busy highway even as he spoke. "The kid okay? Tally will kill me if we get a scratch on him."

Dorian brushed back the boy's hair. It was straight, unlike his mother's curls. She'd had it tamed into a braid the one and only time he'd seen her—through the scope of his rifle—but he'd been able to tell. "He's breathing."

"Well"—Judd paused, white lines bracketing his mouth—"that was unexpected."

"What?" Dorian took off his jacket and covered Keenan in its warmth.

"I was supposed to pull him into our familial net." The other man rubbed absently at his temple, eyes on Keenan. "But he went . . . elsewhere. Since he's not dead, I'm guessing he's linked into DarkRiver's secret network—the one I'm not supposed to know about."

Dorian shook his head. "Impossible." They all knew that Psy brains were different from changeling or human ones—Psy needed the biofeedback provided by a psychic network. Cut that off and death was close to instantaneous; that was the reason why defectors from the PsyNet were few and far between. Judd's family had only just made it out by linking together to form the tiny LaurenNet. Their psychic gifts meant they could manipulate that net and accept new members. But DarkRiver's net, the Web of Stars, was different.

"There is no way he could've entered our web." Dorian scowled. "It's a changeling construct." Created by loyalty, not need, it welcomed only a select few—leopard sentinels who had sworn an oath to the DarkRiver alpha, Lucas, and their mates.

Judd shrugged and leaned back against the seat. "Maybe the boy has some changeling blood."

"He'd be a shapeshifter if he had that much of it," Clay pointed out. "Plus, my beast doesn't sense an animal in him. He's Psy."

"All I know is that as soon as the PsyNet was closed to him, his consciousness arrowed away from me and toward Dorian. I can't see your web, but my guess is that he's linked to you"—he nodded at Dorian—"and through you, to the Web. I could try to cut that bond," he continued, his reluctance open, "and force him into our familial net, but it'd only traumatize him again."

Dorian looked down at the boy and felt the trapped leopard inside him rise in a protective crouch. "Then I guess he stays with us. Welcome to DarkRiver, Keenan Aleine."

Miles away, in a lab located in the bowels of the earth, Ashaya Aleine staggered under the backwash of a devastating mental blow. A sudden cut and he was gone, her son, the link she'd had without knowing she had it.

Either Keenan was dead or . . .

She remembered the first of the two notes she'd gotten out through the lab's garbage chute the previous week, a note that would have been transmitted to a human named Talin McKade by those who were loyal to Ashaya rather than the tyrannical ruling Council.

I'm calling in my IOU.

The best case scenario was that Talin McKade and her friends had come through. Ashaya's thoughts traveled back to that night two months ago when she'd put her life on the line to free a teenager and a young girl from the lethal danger of the lab—before they became the latest casualties in a series of genocidal experiments run by another scientist.

It was as she was returning to the lab that he, the unnamed sniper with a voice as cool as any Psy assassin's, had found her.

"I have a gun pointed at your temple. I don't miss."

"I saved two innocent lives. You won't kill me."

A hint of a laugh, but she couldn't be sure. "What did you want the IOU for?"

"You're male. Therefore you aren't Talin McKade."

"I'm a friend. She has others. And we pay our debts."

"If you want to repay your debt," she said, "kidnap my son."

With her note, she'd set that very event in motion. Then she had cashed in every favor owed to her and put psychic safeguards in place to protect Keenan against recapture through the PsyNet. But now Keenan was gone—she knew that beyond any shadow of a doubt. And no Psy could survive outside the Net.

Yet, another part of her reminded her that the DarkRiver leopard pack had two Psy members who had survived very well. Could it be that Talin McKade's friends were cats? That supposition was pure guesswork on her part as she had nothing on which to base her theory or check her conclusions. She was under a psychic and electronic blackout, her Internet access cut off, her entry to the vast resources of the PsyNet policed by telepaths under Councilor Ming LeBon's command. So she, a woman who trusted no one, would have to trust that the sniper had spoken true and that Keenan was safe.

Head still ringing from the shearing off of that inexplicable bond, she sat absolutely still for ten long minutes, getting her body back under control. No one could be allowed to learn that she'd felt the backlash, that she knew her son was no longer in the PsyNet. *She shouldn't have known.* Every individual Psy was an autonomous unit. Even in the fluid darkness of the Net, where each mind existed as a burning psychic star stripped of physical limitations, they encased themselves in multiple shields, remaining separate.

There were no blurred boundaries, no threads tying one consciousness to another. It hadn't always been that way—according to the hidden records she'd unearthed in her student days, the PsyNet had once reflected the emotional entanglements of the people involved. Silence had severed those bonds—of affection, of blood—until isolation was all they were . . . or that was the accepted view. Ashaya had always known it for a lie.

Because of Amara.

And now, because of Keenan.

Keenan and Amara. Her twin flaws, the double-edged sword that hung over her every second of every day. One mistake, just one, was all it would take to bring that sword crashing down.

A door opened at her back. "Yes?" she said calmly, though her mind was overflowing with memories usually contained behind impenetrable walls.

"Councilor LeBon has called through."

Ashaya glanced at the slender blonde who had spoken. "Thank you."

With a nod, Ekaterina left. They knew not to speak treasonous words within these walls. Too many eyes. Too many ears. Switching the clear screen of her computer to communication mode, she accepted the call. She no longer had the ability to call out. The lockdown of the lab had been ordered after the childrens' escape, though officially, Jonquil Duchslaya and Noor Hassan were listed as deceased—by Ashaya's hand.

However, she knew Ming was suspicious. In lieu of torture, he'd shut her inside this plascrete tomb, tons of earth above her head, knowing that she had a psychological defect, that she reacted negatively to the thought of being buried. "Councilor," she said as Ming's face appeared onscreen, his eyes the night-sky of a cardinal, "what can I do for you?"

"You're meant to be having a visitation with your son this week."

She focused on regulating her pulse—an aftereffect of the sudden disconnection from Keenan. To carry this plan through to its completion, she had to remain cold as ice, more Silent than the Council itself. "It's part of the agreement."

"That visitation will be delayed."

"Why?" She had very little power here, but she wasn't completely under Ming's thumb—they both knew she was the only M-Psy capable of completing the work on Protocol I.

"The child's biological father has asked to offer him specialized training. The request has been granted."

Ashaya knew with absolute certainty that Zie Zen would never have taken that step without consulting her. But knowing that didn't tell her whether Keenan was dead or alive. "The delay will complicate the training I'm giving him."

"The decision has been made." Ming's eyes turned obsidian, the few white stars drowning in black. "You should focus on your research. You've made no significant progress in the past two months."

Two months. Eight weeks. Fifty-six days. The period of time since the children's escape . . . and her effective burial in the Implant Lab.

"I've conclusively solved the problem of Static," she reminded him, dangerously aware of the growing tightness around her rib cage—a stress reaction, another indication of the chinks Keenan's sudden disappearance had made in her psychological armor. "No implant would work if we were constantly bombarded with the thoughts of others." That was what the Council intended for the PsyNet—that it become a huge hive mind, interconnected and seamless. No renegades, nothing but conformity.

However, *pure* conformity was a nonviable goal. In simple terms, a hive could not survive without a queen. Which was why Ashaya had been instructed to devise several different grades of implants. Those implanted with the highest grade would possess the ability to exercise total control over every other individual in the hive, to the point of being able to enter their minds at will, direct them with the ease of puppet masters. No thought would be private, no disagreement possible.

Ming gave a slight nod. "Your breakthrough with Static was impressive, but it doesn't compensate for your lack of progress since."

"With respect," Ashaya said, "I disagree. No one else even came close to eliminating Static. The theorists all stated it to be an impossible task." She thought fast and took another precarious step along the tightrope. Too far and Ming wouldn't hesitate to kill her. Too little and it would paint her as weak, open to exploitation. "If you want me to rush the process, I'll do so. But if the implants then malfunction, do not look to place the blame on me. I want that in writing."

"Are you sure you want to make an enemy out of me, Ashaya?" A quiet question devoid of any emphasis and yet the threat was a sinister shadow pressing at her mind. Ming flexing his telepathic muscles? Probable, given that he was a cardinal telepath with a facility for mental combat. He could turn her brain into mush with a glancing thought.

Ashaya supposed that if she had been human or changeling, she'd have felt fear. But she was Psy, conditioned since birth to feel nothing. Hard and inflexible, that conditioning not only allowed her to play politics with Ming, it acted as a shield, hiding the secrets she could never reveal. "It is not a case of enemies, sir," she said, and—making another rapid decision—let her shoulders slump a fraction. When she next spoke, it was in a rapid-fire stream. "I'm trying my hardest, but I've hit what appears to be a major obstacle, and I'm the only one with the skill to solve it so I've been working round the clock and I've been buried underground for two months with no access to the PsyNet and—"

"You need to have a medical checkup." Ming's stance had changed, become hyperalert. "When was the last time you slept?"

Ashaya pressed the pads of her fingers over her eyelids. "I don't recall. Being underground makes it difficult for me to keep track." A debilitating condition such as claustrophobia would have gotten most Psy "rehabilitated," their memories wiped, their personalities destroyed. Ashaya had been left alone only because her brain was more valuable undamaged. For now.

"I think I had a full night's sleep approximately one week ago." Her logs would verify that. She had deliberately interfered with her own sleeping patterns, building her story for this very day . . . on the faith of a human's honor.

. . . we pay our debts . . .

But even if the sniper had kept his word, it was clear that *something* had gone wrong. All her theories to the contrary notwithstanding, it was highly probable that Keenan was dead. She dropped her hand and stared Ming in the face, letting her own go slack as if with fatigue. If Keenan was dead, then she no longer had anything to lose by putting this plan in motion.

"I'm sending a pickup team," Ming said. "You'll be taken to a specialist facility."

"Not necessary." Ashaya closed her hand over her organizer, the small computer device that held all her experimental and personal data. "One of my team can check me out—we're all medically trained."

"I want you fully evaluated by the clinicians at the Center."

She wondered if he was threatening her even now. The Center was where defective Psy were sent to be rehabilitated. "Ming, if you believe me to be compromised, please have the courtesy to say so to my face. I'm not a child to run screaming." Except of course, Psy children didn't scream much beyond the first year of life. She wondered if Keenan had screamed at the end. Her hand tightened, the cool hardness of the organizer anchoring her to reality. *Silence*, she reminded herself, *you are a being of perfect Silence*. An ice-cold automaton without emotion or heart. It was the only thing she could be.

Ming's expression didn't change. "I'll talk to you after the evaluation." The screen went off.

She knew she had less than five minutes, if that. Ming had access to airjets and teleportation-capable telekinetics. If he wanted her whisked out of here, she would be. She flipped over her organizer, slid down the cover and pulled out the one-centimeter-square chip that held every piece of data in the device. Not allowing herself second thoughts, she swallowed the chip, her movements calculated to appear innocuous to the watching cameras.

Next, she reached into her pocket, found a replacement chip with enough duplicate data to allay suspicion—at least for a few days—and slotted it in. Just in time. There was a flicker at the corner of her eye. She swiveled to find a male standing there. He was dressed in pure unrelieved black, but for the golden insignia on his left shoulder—two snakes locked in combat. Ming's personal symbol.

"Ma'am, I'm to escort you to the Center."

She nodded, rose. His eyes betrayed no movement as she slipped her organizer into the pocket of her lab coat, but she knew he'd noted its placement. Ming would have plenty of time to go through it while she was being analyzed. "I didn't expect pickup by Tk."

It wasn't a question, so the other Psy didn't answer.

"Do you require touch?" she asked, coming to stand beside him. Psy did not touch as a rule, but some powers were strengthened by contact.

"No," he said, proving her deduction that Ming had sent one of his strongest men. It mattered little that his eyes were gray rather than cardinal night-sky—exceptions such as Ming aside, cardinals were often too cerebral to be much good at the practical side of things. Like killing.

The male met her eyes. "If you would please lower your basic shields."

She did so and a second later, her bones seemed to melt from the inside out. Part of her, the scientist, wondered if

Tk-Psy felt the same loss of self, the same sense of their body liquefying into nothing. Then the sensation ended and she found herself facing a door that existed nowhere in her lab. "Thank you," she said, reengaging her shields.

He nodded at the door. "Please go through."

She knew he would stand guard, make sure she didn't attempt an escape. It made her wonder why he'd teleported her outside, rather than inside, the room. Since, no matter what happened, this was her last day as the head M-Psy on the Implant Team, she asked him.

His answer was unexpected. "I am not a team player."

She understood but pretended not to. Was Ming testing her allegiance, trying to tempt her with the kinds of statements used by the rebels to communicate with one another? "I'm afraid I don't follow. Perhaps you can explain it to me later." Without waiting for an answer, she pushed through the door, already able to feel the tingling in the tips of her fingers and toes.

The chip she'd swallowed contained close to a terabyte of data, the result of years of research. But it also contained something else—a coating of pure, undiluted poison. She had spent hours that she should have been working on the implant, perfecting the unique properties of the poison for this one attempt.

The calculation was simple: Ashaya intended to escape the Implant Lab.

With the heightened security, the only way to escape was to die.

So Ashaya would die.